"Ramsey Campbell is the best of us all."

—Poppy Z. Brite

"Campbell has solidly established himself to be the best writer working in this field today."

—Karl Edward Wagner, *The Year's Best Horror Stories*

"Ramsey Campbell is the best horror writer alive, period."

—Thomas Tessier

"Britain's leading horror novelist."

—*New Statesman*

"A horror writer in the classic mould . . . Britain's premier contemporary exponent of the art of scaring you out of your skin."

—*Q Magazine*

"The greatest living writer of horror fiction."

—*Vector*

"Ramsey Campbell is better than all the rest of us put together."

—Dennis Etchison

"The most sophisticated and highly regarded of British horror writers."

—*Financial Times*

"Britain's greatest horror writer . . . Realistic, subtle and arcane."

—*Waterstone's Guide to Books*

RAMSEY CAMPBELL

CREATURES OF THE POOL

LEISURE BOOKS   NEW YORK CITY

for Jenny, with all my love—
my dream come true

A LEISURE BOOK®

April 2010

Published by

Dorchester Publishing Co., Inc.
200 Madison Avenue
New York, NY 10016

Copyright © 2009 by Ramsey Campbell

ISBN 10: 0-8439-6384-0
ISBN 13: 978-0-8439-6384-7
E-ISBN: 978-1-4285-0841-5

The name "Leisure Books" and the stylized "L" with design are trademarks of Dorchester Publishing Co., Inc.

Printed in the United States of America.

10 9 8 7 6 5 4 3 2 1

Visit us online at www.dorchesterpub.com.

ACKNOWLEDGMENTS

As ever, Jenny was the only other reader of the first draft, which is considerably unlike this one. John Reppion and Niki Flynn sent me along branches of the labyrinth I would otherwise not have explored, and in a talk at the World Horror Convention in Toronto, David Morrell gave me a solution to a problem of depiction. Sections of the book were written at Tammy's and Sam's house in Brockley, in Saratoga Springs (during the World Fantasy Convention), York (a British Fantasy Society open night), Manchester (the Festival of Fantastic Films), Nottingham (the British Fantasy Convention), and at the Mercure Napoli Angioino hotel in Naples and the Deep Blue Sea apartments in Georgioupolis, Crete. At about 7.30 on the morning of 11 August 2008, an unseasonable shower of rain in Georgioupolis set about corrupting the topmost page of the text. No frogs were spotted.

The helpful staff of the Local History Library (where I'm especially grateful to David Stoker for all his support) and of the Williamson Tunnels and Merseyside Constabulary have been replaced by characters quite unlike them for the purposes of the tale. The affidavit cited in chapter two is reprinted in *Jack the Ripper: the 21st Century Investigation* by Trevor Marriott (John Blake, 2005), and can also be found online.

Since I've had fun once again with inventing local restaurants, let me list a few real ones we recommend. In Liverpool our favourites include the Valparaiso (Chilean), the Maharajah (South Indian), the Sultan's Palace and the Mayur (Indian), the Akshaya (Sri Lankan), the Yuet Ben (Beijing Chinese), the Mei Mei, Jumbo City and City Rendevous (Cantonese) and La Viña (Spanish). On the Wirral peninsula, we're fond of the Sawasdee and the Siam (Thai), the Capitol (Chinese), the Kerala Kitchen (South Indian), the Saffron Delight and the Jalali (Indian), Lazaros (Greek) and the Mezze (Turkish). Bon appetit (and my curse on the spellchecker that insists I meant to type appetite)!

The lines from *Europa 51 / Liverpool—London 85* are quoted from *The Gates of Even* (Ekstasis Editions, 2002) by permission of the author, John O. Thompson.

CREATURES
OF THE POOL

"Behold the Pool, where Neptune's kin doth dream
Of antic life in marsh and secret stream . . ."
—William Colquitt, *Description of Liverpool* (1802)

"Long too has Mersey rolled her golden tide,
And seen proud vessels in her harbour ride;
Oft on her banks the Muse's sons would roam,
And wish to settle there a certain home . . ."
—George Colman the Elder, *Prologue for the Opening
of the Theatre Royal, Liverpool* (1772)

"The great damp cut between Lime Street
and Edge Hill stations: lime-enough green
the moss on the rock. Edging
out beyond Edge Hill the tracks angle
across the rows of houses, raised above them
like a writer vis-à-vis
his material? . . .

When am I out of it?

Turner: 'When the "threshold"
is protracted
and becomes a "tunnel",
when the "liminal"
becomes the "cunicular" . . .' "
—John O. Thompson, *Europa 51 / Liverpool—London 85*

"In this delightful place
We gain a special treat—
We see reflected woman's face,
And little fishes eat."
—Anonymous verse on the Ranelagh Gardens in
Liverpool, c. 1750

Chapter One

LITHERPOOL IS LYTHERPOL IS LIUERPUL

We've rowed out of the Mersey and under the first bridge across the Pool that gives the town its name. Against a sky that would be as black as the water except for countless stars, a figure wobbles over the unenclosed bridge from the Heath into Litherpool. Perhaps he's returning from the deer park north of Lytherpol. He may have gone in search of country air, away from the outbreak of plague in Chapel-street, unless he wanted to escape the presence of so many animals, most of them alive, in the seven narrow thoroughfares of Liuerpul. Now he's heading towards the Castle, where a sentry transforms the end of a yawn into a challenge all the sterner for its unauthoritative genesis. Beyond the Castle the streets are unlit except for a lantern at the stone cross beside the stocks on the ridge where Castle-street meets Juggler-street, and a second lantern in front of the cross at the far end of the latter. The villagers who attended church beside the upper reaches of the Pool have gone home to Everton, and the winding line of fitful lights has vanished from the slope, although others flicker above the marsh around the Pool. He may be able to keep his bearings by the squeals of pigs in the churchyard at the foot of Chapel-street, or the challenge of the watch at the end of each street, if they aren't too busy fighting one another. Perhaps they'll behave themselves for the bellman when he calls ten o'clock. By then the wanderer should be in his house and cursing as he tries to wield a flint and steel. But we're in the Pool, where we ought to be careful not to snag the oars on fragments of the wrecked ship that lodged in its marshy bed.

We aren't, of course. The Pool was drained long before any of us was born. We're walking where it used to be, along Frog Lane or, if you feel more old-fashioned, Frog's-lane, alongside which the ribs of half-built ships would once have loomed over us. They weren't the only reminders of the Pool. Local people dread storms at high tide, because the cellars flood. Behind us in Paradise Street where the bridge was, the muddy road is often blocked by families driven out of their subterranean accommodations together with their beds and other furniture. The swamp alongside Frog Lane has been drained, and dark twisted streets lead to the Theatre Royal. Even if animals are no longer slaughtered in the streets, the ways to the theatre reek of refuse from the market that occupies the square in front of it. Perhaps we can hear ducks squabbling in the square, though at this time of night the uproar may belong to crowds of young delinquents. Even if they're penniless, they're eager to watch the show. Fights seem to have been taken for granted, since the newspapers seldom named—

"Why are you calling it Frog Lane? It's Whitechapel."

"Jack the Ripper did his women in Whitechapel."

"That's the one in London. I'm asking the feller what's this got to do with frogs."

"The atrocities," says someone else.

I've opened my mouth to answer the original question, which came from a large woman who looks as if she would be more at home with knitting and bingo, when I'm distracted by the comment. "Which atrocities are those?" I wonder aloud.

The tour party gaze at me, and I can't identify who made the reference. Was he behind one of the barriers surrounding roadworks in Whitechapel? As a puddle ripples in the cracked uneven pavement outside a pizza joint someone says "Don't you ever talk about anything nice?"

He's even more American than the pizza place, where a girl behind the counter is reading *The Drowned World*. His wide face topped by a bristling hint of reddish hair looks clenched with earnestness, which has reduced his nose to a disproportionate stub. Most of his mouth is playing straight to less than an inch of wry grin. Despite or because of the steely glare of the streetlamps, his pale eyes are muddily introverted. "Are you on the wrong walk, son?" says the talkative woman, who outdoes him for ruddiness and bulk of face and hair. "We signed up for murders. It's called the Liverghoul Tour."

"Don't you think there's more to your history than that?"

"Plenty. More than, no offence, you Yanks are ever going to catch up with."

"We don't like people putting Scousers down," says her companion, rubbing the small of her large back, though he seems too young by several decades to be her husband or anything along those lines. "Enough of your lot make a living out of murders," he tells the American.

"Jack came first," the woman insists. "He's a legend, and maybe he was a Scouser."

The rest of the party are staying clear of the argument. They're an average assortment—a couple who constantly lag behind, a handful who seem to think they need to impress me with their willingness to learn, a man who produces yet another vaguely relevant question whenever I pause for breath—but even he is resting his attention on the sluggish ripples in the puddle presumably left by this morning's summer downpour. "We'll come to the Ripper," I promise.

I lead everybody to the end of Whitechapel once buses of various competitive companies have finished swinging uphill on Roe Street across our path. St John's Lane climbs past gardens where a churchyard used to be and meets Roe Street once more at the site of the Fall-well, a name that acquired a different significance once the stone surround crumbled and children sent onto the Great Heath to fetch water fell in. Opposite the junction, behind the Royal Court Theatre, a Holiday Inn raises its brow signed in green handwriting. As I wait for the last of the party to catch up there's a thunder of luggage, and a trainload of commuters begin to descend the steps from Lime Street Station. Some can't elude the woman whose boyfriend has always left her short of money for the train home. The blurred hollow voice of a busker in the subway to the trains beneath St George's Hall is singing about the sea. The Hall was where Virginia Woolf's uncle went mad while trying Florence Maybrick for the poisoning of her husband. After the judge found her guilty, a mob a thousand strong chased his carriage up the hill to Everton. Presumably none of them could have known that a hundred years later James Maybrick would be identified as Jack the Ripper, and I'm about to tell my audience how this happened when the Beatles commence singing about the town where I was born.

At least, my mobile does, having made itself felt in my breast pocket. The caller isn't owning up to a number. "Gavin Meadows," I say. "Liverghoul Tours."

"I'm hoping you're somewhere close."

"Just the far side of the gardens, Lucinda. Why?"

She hasn't answered when a voice more distant than hers reveals the nature of the problem. "Don't tell me," I say and return the mobile to my pocket. "Next stop the library," I announce.

Neither the American nor the homicide enthusiast seems to care for the prospect. "We didn't join up to read books," she protests. "We like walking, us."

"Maybe he wants to check his facts," says the American.

I won't bother to respond to that. I lead the way behind St George's Hall, which towers above us like a white whale. In the middle of the broad path greenish dignitaries gesture from plinths higher than our heads. A breeze mounts the slope of the gardens, twitching raindrops out of shrubs and awakening a shoal of shadows to swarm over a drunk or an addict who's beached on a bench under a tree. Beyond the gardens William Brown Street is massively classical except for scraps of modern architecture patched in among the columned porticoes. Straight ahead, between the art gallery and the museum, a bicycle is chained like a suffragette to the railings outside the library. As we cross the street I read the slogan along the horizontal bar, LEAVE LIVERPOOL ALIVE! I'm all too aware that the legend on the other side is www.ruinedcity.com. "Someone's been getting some exercise," the loquacious woman remarks.

The door to the library slides aside to admit me and my unwelcome American sidekick. The others follow us into the lobby, and I indicate the fiction library with an upturned hand. "Seats for everyone, or if you want to browse while I leave you for just a few minutes . . ."

I might as well not have spoken. A voice can be heard down the main staircase from four floors up. As the murder fan makes for it the doors back away from her and stand wide enough to be inviting everyone else to join her at the foot of the stairs. By the time I do they're listening to the impassioned monologue with the kind of shocked amusement they might have expected my tour to provide. "What's up with him?" says the woman who led the detour. "Where'd they let him out of?"

"Nowhere," I say. "He's my father."

Chapter Two

A Ripper Legend

I should have asked the members of the tour to wait downstairs. Once the American starts after me and the others straggle in pursuit I'm wary of directing them in case I run out of politeness. We're still two floors short of the ranting when I feel driven to intervene. "What's the problem?" I shout.

My father leans over the banister. His face resembles a beginner's sketch of mine—large eyes set wide for surveying whatever's to be seen, flat blunt nose more equine than my own, not quite enough mouth to go with the other features, lower lip drooping as if to compensate. I've the edge in terms of hair, however unkempt his passion has rendered the remnants of his, bristling like a jagged black halo above his high forehead. "She's sent for the heavies," he declares, having adopted a Cockney accent. "You'll never take me alive, copper."

I've lost count of the voices he put on when he used to tell me about our local history, not that he has finished doing either. I can't allow myself to be amused even when he produces his apologetic grin. "What have you been making a fuss about?" I need to learn.

"Your girlfriend's saying they haven't got some papers. I know they have. I've seen them."

"Excuse me," the American says, "but maybe you should keep it down. Remember where you are."

My father peers at him, and I'm dismayed to be able to predict but not prevent the style of response. "Howdy, pardner. Where'd you mosey in from? Left your mule outside?"

As the American emits a sound too dry for a laugh I say "Wait there. I'm coming up."

That doesn't halt my party. As I reach my father and they troop after me, Lucinda emerges from Local History. She succeeds in looking professionally efficient despite having to backhand a lock of blonde hair out of her eyes, but her small almost elfin sharp-chinned face risks softening to greet me. "Here's more trouble," my father says in his ordinary voice. "All right, love, you've got me put in charge. I'll go quietly."

Lucinda seems to doubt this. "Mr Meadows—"

"If you and Gav are as close as I'm guessing you are you'd better call me Deryck."

"I was going to say we've checked the stacks, and there's no trace of the material you were asking about, not even a space on the shelf. You saw it wasn't in the catalogue."

His answer seems completely random. "Where do you live?"

He has always been eccentric—one of his charms, my mother thinks, and so does he. "You said you were leaving, dad," I remind him. "I'm in the middle of a tour."

As he tramps towards the stairs while the tour party eyes him with various degrees of interest or apprehension, I give Lucinda's hand a quick squeeze. "Sorry about whatever happened," I murmur. "See you later?"

"I'll tell you about it then."

I hurry after the tour, which is now led by my father, and catch up with him as he's unchaining his bicycle. "I'll call you, shall I? We need to talk."

"Can't I tag along? I've never been on any of your outings."

We've already delayed the tour long enough. "So long as you don't distract people," I murmur.

"I'll try not to show you up."

He's silent while he wheels the bicycle to the foot of William Brown Street, close to the edge of the original town. Ahead on Byrom Street cars race three abreast under concrete walkways and mostly vanish into the mouth of a road tunnel where the Haymarket used to be. Traffic lights dam the flood of vehicles barely long enough for all my customers to cross. A nondescript concrete lane smudged with shadows of foliage brings us to Great Crosshall Street, but there's no sign of a cross among the apartment buildings that box up students from one of the Liverpool universities. As I talk about the area—behind the apartments Addison Street used to be Deadman's Lane, under which plague victims were buried and still are, according to the tradition that some were sunk too deep in the mud to be moved elsewhere—my father paces me on the wrong side of the road. He pedals across Vauxhall Road and bumps his wheels over the kerb to wait outside the John Moores campus building for my next anecdote.

A university official frowns through a glass door as if she thinks I've brought a gang rather than the tale of one. She's standing where Lower Milk Street was in 1885—where Richard Morgan was kicked to death in front of his family for not giving a youth some money for a drink. One of the killers lived around the corner in Maiden's Green, once a fashionable perambulation but by then a narrow court with a filthy central gutter, and another inhabited a nearby cellar just off Leeds Street. The murder became known not just as the Tithebarn Street outrage but as the start of the High Rip gang violence. "I also do the High Rip Trip along the docks," I take the chance to add.

"They kicked him all the way across the street and back again," my father says, "and a mob cheered them on. You'd have thought they were playing a footy game."

This illuminates images in my mind—the family returning by the ferry from a seaside jaunt across the river, the lurid glare of the ale-house transforming this mean end of the dark street into a stage, the shadows of the gang converging on the supine victim, the crunching underfoot of ribs and eventually of a skull as all that Richard Morgan knew and had been and might have become was engulfed by the marsh of his crushed head. I refrain from conveying any of this, because my father's words have earned a disgusted scowl from the American. Instead I press the reassuringly modern button at a pedestrian crossing and move the tour onwards to Cheapside nearly opposite. "They used to call it Dig Street, Cheapside," my father says. "They're forever digging this town up. You'd think they'd have learned to leave some things alone."

He's thinking of the Big Dig, the redevelopment that has overtaken streets along and around the route of the Pool, narrowing them with roadworks so that they're no wider than they would have been in the Georgian era, and all this to leave the shopping centre indistinguishable from a dozen other towns—at least, that's one of the themes of his web site. Tithebarn Street has been spared, and patches of waste ground dating from the blitz isolate derelict buildings and a couple of small pubs that stand for the side streets—Highfield, Smithfield—that Lower Milk Street used to parallel. Cheapside retains a few small shops and a pub opposite the black stone Bridewell prison of a disused police station, where shrubbery sprouts behind a massive wall. Much of the narrow sloping street consists of a multi-storey car park facing unadorned offices twice the height of the houses they supplanted. In one of those houses Thomas Cosgrove murdered his wife and poisoned himself, less than a minute's walk from the High Rip killing but seventy years earlier. Black water streams beneath the Bridewell gate and down to Dale Street as if the well has spontaneously revived and overflowed. Tithebarn Street grows more whole and more Victorian as I lead my audience towards the river, having told the Cosgrove tale, and then my father says "Don't you take them on the Maybrick walk?"

"That's where we're going, where his office was."

"I'm talking about where he took his constitutional every day he was at work before he went home to his poor scared wife."

Even if I seem less informed than my customers deserve to expect, I have to admit "I don't know where that is."

"Along Dale Street and up Cheapside. He'd stop for a while outside the Cosgrove house and then he'd hang round where Richard Morgan died. Once his clerk saw Maybrick pacing up and down like he was marking territory or in a cell. Tom Lowry, the clerk's name was. He never dared tell while Maybrick was alive, and he didn't even when he was a witness at the widow's trial."

"He always liked murders, didn't he, Maybrick?" The loquacious woman has rediscovered her voice. "They say he bought the house he died in because there was supposed to have been one there. And that clerk was in his diary. Maybrick thought he'd found something out and it reads like he'd have killed the boy as well if it mightn't have given him away."

"I can't speak for anyone else," the American complains, "but I've no idea what all this is about."

"Gav will fill you in," my father says and rides ahead.

James Maybrick was a cotton broker who often stayed in London with one of his brothers. Six months after Jack the Ripper's last recorded crime, Maybrick died of arsenic poisoning in the riverside mansion into which he'd moved with his wife and children the previous year. Just over a century later, a Liverpool man produced a diary that was signed Jack the Ripper. Numerous references in the diary lead the reader to conclude that it was written by James Maybrick.

I've barely finished relating this when the woman and her companion start to disagree about the authenticity of the item. The man who took it to a London literary agent said he'd had it from a friend who wouldn't tell him where it came from and who'd died, you might think conveniently, the previous year. Yes, but experts have tested the paper and confirm that it's a real Victorian journal. Fair enough, but why are nearly fifty pages missing at the front? Maybe they contained things that someone didn't want the rest of us to read. Not so likely considering what was left in, and mightn't the writer have needed a Victorian journal to convince the experts and just cut out pages that were already used? He made it look as if they were written by the same person, because the diary starts in the middle of an entry, but it's pretty convenient to have Whitechapel on the first page to explain why he killed women there. The experts say the ink is the kind Maybrick might have used, and you can't buy it any more. Maybe, but they don't say the writer made a mistake about Michael Maybrick. It's full of verses like the ones the Ripper sent the police, and the writer says he's as good at poems as his brother Michael. Only Michael never wrote any. He was well known as a composer and set verses to music. For James Maybrick not to know this is as likely as that Sir Arthur Sullivan's brother would believe Sullivan wrote the words of *The Mikado* when Gilbert did.

By now we're abreast of the offices that have occupied Exchange Station since the railway went underground along a new route. My father is still playing outrider, as if he's looking for danger ahead, and the woman turns to me. "What do you think?"

I think the diary reads like the work of someone trying to sound like the Ripper of the letters that have been public for many years—the work of a writer dreaming of publication. The narrator keeps forgetting how sophisticated or otherwise his language is meant to be, and addressing not just himself but the reader. In the last entry he writes "I place this now in a place were it shall be found" but is compelled to add several sentences before signing himself "Yours truly Jack the Ripper." How artificial is all that? Later the man who made the diary public signed an affidavit that it was forged and then denied it was, supposedly because someone had scared him into keeping the legend alive. I don't want to undermine my tour, and so I say "I think there are arguments on both sides."

This satisfies neither the woman nor her companion. As

we overtake my father the man asks him "Do you think the diary's real?"

"We'll never know. That's how legends work. It's another tale like Liverpool's full of. You should wonder who dreams them all up."

A drain beside the kerb emits a gurgle that could be mistaken for mirth as I lead the way to Exchange Street East, which is almost opposite the station. Maybrick's office used to be in Knowsley Buildings, a gloomy Victorian hulk close to the far end, now the site of modern offices. A security man behind a desk in the lobby gives me a resigned look of recognition. As I direct the tour across the side street to a stubby alley between two Victorian office blocks, my father pedals ahead.

The alley opens into Exchange Flags, a wide square enclosed on three sides by offices and on the fourth by the back of the town hall. The square is dominated by a central group of black statues, spotlit from high on the white facades and radiating pale shadows like stains seeping up through the flagstones. In Maybrick's day the square was known as the Change. Cotton dealers conducted their trading on it, and I invite my audience to imagine Maybrick in the midst of a multitude of shouting men crowned with bowlers or, like him, top hats. What might he have been plotting while he fought to make a profit? Was he unsuccessful because his mind was deep in its own dark, making plans unsuspected by his rivals? Was the greatest clamour around him in the Change or inside his head?

Recounting all this feels like continuing someone else's dream. My father has cycled through the shadows around the statues before halting to listen to me. In a moment I'm aware of a surreptitious movement above and behind him. The nearest statue is betraying signs of life. Its blind eyes, so black they might never have seen the sun, have started to water.

As a trickle of liquid escapes from the side of its mouth I hear a whisper almost underfoot, and the flagstones break out in a black rash. I'm distracted by thoughts of the plague—of the fear the townsfolk had that it would rise out of the earth however deep its victims were buried—until two people jerk open their umbrellas and the rain begins to tap on my scalp as though it's impatient to waken my mind. My father is already cycling across the square, calling "Here's a bit of shelter."

It's a passage one storey high that leads through an office block to Chapel Street, the continuation of Tithebarn Street down towards the river. It only just shelters the tour as we huddle in the middle while the July downpour intensifies, veiling both ends of the passage with translucent bead curtains that swing inwards to find us. "Seems like you should provide umbrellas," the American says to me.

The leaping of rain in the square and in the equally deserted streets has begun to subside. Is it worth leading the way past the cellars where the Allies had their local headquarters, close to Maybrick's office? Apparently the pressure of monitoring Japanese and German communications made some of the personnel imagine they heard voices in the earth beyond the walls. As the shrill hiss that encloses the passage diminishes to a whisper, my father says "Hands up whoever's voting to go to a pub."

In one way I'm glad of the rain, because I've just realised that I omitted part of the tour. From St George's Hall we should have turned along Lime Street to the Royal Mail sorting offices, where builders digging the foundations unearthed coffins lined with lead. The detour to the library must have driven the route out of my mind, but I feel as if I've made almost mindlessly for the river. Before I can own up, the Ripper fan says "How about the Slaughterhouse?"

"I'm afraid I don't drink," says the American.

This earns him a chorus of sympathy, ironic or otherwise, and I see my father readying a remark. I'm not swift enough to head him off from drawling "Ain't a man ever laughed at the Milkshake Kid and lived."

The debunker of the diary peers out at the square, in which just the odd raindrop twitches on the flagstones, and tells his companion "Maybe we're best going for the train."

As they turn away I promise anyone who'd like to know "You can join another of my tours free when it's not raining."

"Tell us when that's going to be," says the woman.

True enough, the city seems to have acquired a monsoon season. "Remember I do the High Rip Trip as well," I say, "and during the day I'm Pool of Life Tours."

The party disperses into the square, past the statues that appear to be dreaming of flexing their watery muscles. I'm disconcerted to realise that although my head count outside the library and since then was correct, I've kept including my father. Presumably someone stayed in the library, and I wonder if it was the unidentifiable informant who knew more than me about Frog Lane. The American stays with me, and I'm afraid my father may find more opportunities for teasing. He cycles past the stealthily restless statues and the monumentally silent Town Hall, however, and I follow, alert for bits of yesteryear that may be to my companion's taste. I can't show him the sanctuary stone in Castle Street, where it indicates one limit of the oldest market, because it's hidden by a limousine double-parked alongside a cash dispenser in a classical facade. There's no trace of the enormous hand that used to be erected on market days, supposedly symbolising or appealing to some element of the Pool. I point out the stone figures nesting high on the Victorian frontages, mermaids and mermen and serpentine monsters that might almost be dreams that have risen from the banks and restaurants at street level. I summarise the history of Derby Square at the end of the street, where my father is riding around a giant statue of Victoria under a dome that drips like an umbrella. The monument is where the tour begins and ends. Part of the Castle of Lyverpull occupied the site of the square, and later St George's Church did, a reference my father elaborates upon. "There used to be graves under the church," he says, "only the coffins came up through the floor. Seems like the Pool got into them even though it was filled in. The town covered up the graves so fast hardly anyone saw what was in them."

"I should hope so." Having paused to emphasise his disapproval, the American says "May I ask who's supposed to be running this tour?"

"I'd tell you who's not," my father retorts, "if I knew your name."

The American gives him a long look and me a longer one. "I'll be calling you," he informs me and marches down James Street towards the giant birds perched on the Liver Building to survey the river.

My father widens his mouth in a grimace at the comment, though presumably the call will be about a free tour. Rain is pooling at the foot of the steps to the monument, and I wonder if that was how the church floor looked as the coffins prepared to appear. "Come back to my flat," I say, "and we'll have a talk."

"You want to think about selling while all the money's coming up from London. Make yourself a profit and buy somewhere bigger further out."

Is he regretting the deal he made on my behalf with a friend on the council when Liverpool offices converted into flats were both rare and cheap? "You haven't told me what was so important at the library," I point out.

"I'll show you." His eyes flicker as if the streetlamps are guttering with age. "Don't worry," he says. "Not here."

He's glancing about at the hotels and offices and sternly concrete law courts that surround the square. The streets are deserted except for a possibly homeless person in the shadow of a doorway opposite James Street Station. Though his shapeless clothes are so sodden they're glistening, he seems too drunk or too resigned to his lot to move out of the way of a persistent drip that runs under the lintel. Perhaps his battered umbrella isn't worth raising; half the crook of the handle is gone, and spokes protrude through the torn canvas. Even if he's watching us, that's no reason for my father to pedal skittishly forward. "When are you coming to see us?" he urges. "Gillian was asking. Everything I've got is at the house."

I should visit my parents more often, and I tell him so. "Maybe you can help me with something else now. Atrocities in Frog Lane, do they ring a bell?"

His head jerks as if he's heard one tolling through the oldest streets. Perhaps he's reacting to the first drops of an imminent downpour, but he looks anxious not to be overheard, which isn't remotely like him. "I'll show you everything I've found," he says, "when you come to us."

"Don't you want to shelter at the flat till this goes off?"

"Who says it will? I've got to get rid of this." I gather that he means his body when he calls out "Getting too bloated. I feel like the old frame's ready to let me down. The quack's got me on so many pills, if I threw up I could open a pharmacy." He leaves me with this flash of his usual humour, and I watch his admittedly plump form dwindle towards the sanctuary stone, which is hidden by water now. The figure in the doorway opposite the station lifts its wet blurred face to the drip. As I run homewards along Castle Street while my father vanishes across Exchange Flags, I feel as if I'm alone in needing protection from the renewed deluge.

Chapter Three

In Trident Street

The merman carved above the door to the apartments is spilling rain from his cornucopia. Whatever he originally bestowed must have been eroded long before the offices were transformed into homes. Despite his age he has retained his scales and most of his upraised tail, but his face is little more than a grey pockmarked hollow. Only the eyes remain, and they're large and blind, as if he's dreaming of a new face or something even less imaginable. Although it seems unlikely that I could be wetter, I dodge the jagged stream from the stone horn as I twist my key in the lock dwarfed by the imposing door.

The lobby sports a massive old black desk adorned with a pen in a well, together with an inkpot and a blotter and a wind-up telephone. Perhaps all this was left as a reminder of the building's origins. The desk faces the white discreetly arched corridor that divides the pair of ground-floor apartments, each of which boasts a door impressive enough for any breed of official. Behind the desk a door leads to the basement, where I hear a muffled throaty sound that must be the exhaust of a vehicle in the car park. As I make my soggy way up the marble stairs, which are a little wider than the thick carpet, I overhear activity on the middle floor. In one apartment rats clatter over bare boards, or rather someone is frenetically typing, while across the corridor there's the hollow downpour of a shower. In the rooms opposite mine on the top floor my bearded neighbour—a cellist with the Philharmonic—is saying "Don't be so wet" at such a volume that I could take it personally. I unlock my door, and then I hesitate, gripping the handful of brass doorknob. By the sound of it, a considerable amount of rain has found its way into my flat.

Somebody has. The corridor light is on, and all the doors I closed on my way out are wide open, displaying the no longer untidy bedroom, the bathroom where the mirror has grown opaque, the toilet keeping itself to itself, the spare room that's several kinds of a library besides a workroom, and ahead the largest room—a kitchen and dining area for half its space, leaving the rest for leisure. I ease the door shut behind me and pace towards the bathroom, where the sound of water is.

A figure is just distinguishable in the mirror. Beneath the patina of steam its nakedness seems mysterious, close to a dream. I don't need to dream about Lucinda, because another few paces bring me the sight of her and all the details the mirror omitted: her hair towelled wild as the sprite's her face resembles, her long slim limbs, the brown mole that barely flaws the underside of her left breast, her trim triangular blonde bush. Her pink lips grow full of a smile, and she says "I thought we might be glad of a bath."

"I didn't think you were that dirty."

"Later," she says, and more maternally "Let's get all those off before you have to take to your bed."

This can't help being erotic, but as she gives me a hand at undressing she rewards the effect with no more than a brief promissory squeeze. The result begins to subside as I realise she has erected a rack in the spare room with her clothes draped over it and space for mine. "We'd better move that," I say. "We don't want damp getting into the computer."

"Stupid girl," Lucinda says. "The blonder the dumber. I shouldn't have left this door open either."

"Never mind," I say, though the nearest of the framed photographs of old Liverpool along the corridor have acquired a mist that adds to their nostalgia. "Let's shift the rack."

She turns off the bath, which isolates a vigorous bubbling

of water in the kitchen—the percolator. Once we've frog-marched the rack into the toilet, I arrange my drenched garments while Lucinda carries mugs of coffee to the bathroom. We soap each other in the intimately cramped bath, but she's visibly preoccupied. As I sponge her shoulders she murmurs "Your father doesn't like me, does he?"

"I'm sure he does or he'd have said."

"Why did he want to know where I live?"

"Don't worry, he won't be planning to stalk you. He's been a bit odder than usual recently, but he's as harmless as I am."

"I hope that's entirely." The glint fades from her greenish eyes as she says "I still don't understand why he would ask."

"Maybe he was trying to find out if you're living here."

"You know I like having my own place now I've got one."

"I wasn't trying to move you in." Unless you want to, I refrain from adding, since I know she values her independence after having lived most of her life with her parents in Tuebrook, even her university years. Instead I say "So what happened before I arrived?"

"Just what I said. He wouldn't be told we didn't have something."

"Aren't you going to tell me what it was either? I thought you were all about providing information."

She lets go of my shoulders and hides her hands under the foam. "I'm sorry if you think that's all there is to me."

"You know I don't." I trace her delicate spine with a finger and then lift her face by its chin. "You're beautiful and funny and articulate and erudite and I can't count the other things I don't even know about yet. And I'm very lucky to have you in my bath." Having roused her smile, I risk adding "And you are a mine of information too, you know."

She releases a barely audible sigh, and I feel a hint of it on my face. "It wasn't even published. I did check. We used to have a book by the same author but it seems to have walked."

"Didn't you say there wasn't a space on the shelf? If it never existed, how could there have been?"

"Your father said we'd brought it for him from the manuscript archives. He kept insisting he'd copied some of it."

"Did he say who'd brought it?"

Lucinda stands up and takes hold of the showerhead. Foam streams between her breasts and glitters in her navel like a jewel from the sea and lends a lacy pattern to her bush. "Me," she says.

I have no answer to this, especially while she's fixing my gaze with hers as she stands above me like an apparition risen from the waves, brandishing the shower in lieu of a trident. "Maybe he dreamed it," she says.

"I'll see if he's written anything down. He wants to show me what he's been putting together."

Lucinda turns away to shower her back. "Can I come?"

"Any special reason?"

"Ready for your shower?" As I rise to my feet she sets about watering me. "I'd like to try and make my peace with him," she says. "I expect I'll be seeing him again."

Perhaps she feels that our visiting my parents ought to mean more to me, but I'm unsure how much it should. I do my best to compensate for my reserve by taking my time over towelling her, and then I say "I'm afraid all there is in the fridge is historical pizza."

"How historical?"

"Last night's."

"I hope it's seafood." When I confirm that it's her favourite she finishes towelling me and rewards me with a quick kiss. I'm dressing in the bedroom when she reappears. I thought she was consigning pizza to the microwave, but she's wearing the slightly schoolgirlish outfit she wore to work: white blouse, black dress with shoulder straps, flat shoes. "I won't be long," she says.

"Where are you going?" I demand, having almost snaggle-toothed my zip.

"Just to bring my car in if you'll give me the control."

She watches with unblinking patience in the dressing-table

mirror while I pull open several not too tidy drawers until I find the remote that opens the street door to the basement garage. As I hand her the control I wonder "Aren't you getting wet all over again?"

"The rain's taking a breather. I'll only be round the corner."

I meant her clothes, but before I can say so she's out of the apartment. I finish all the dressing I intend to do tonight and am padding barefoot to the kitchen when I notice that she has left her underwear on the rack. I can't help panicking as I run to open the window beyond the pine and steel and granite rectangles of the kitchen. It shows me the junction where a street slopes towards the river, but no sign of Lucinda, unless that's her shadow protruding around the corner. The pavement is still streaming with rain, so that I'm unable to put much of a shape to the hidden figure or even to be sure of the size of its fluid outline. In a moment Lucinda's green Spirita swings around the corner and, having hesitated outside the garage entrance, vanishes underground. When I glance back at the intersection the shadow has been washed away—has retreated out of sight, at any rate. I shut the window and lay slices of pizza on plates, and then I seem to wait an unnecessarily long time for the sound of a key in the lock. Eventually I open the door to the outer corridor and hold my breath until I hear soft footsteps on the stairs.

Chapter Four

A Springheel Legend

"Look at the masts," says Lucinda.

I'm put in mind of the skeletal towers the landscape is sprouting to unite us all through mobile phones, and then I realise she means the windmills bristling in the sea. We're on the ridge of Everton, which overlooks the mouth of the river. I should have thought of the past; that's my job. We would indeed have seen the masts of ships on the Mersey even before the first dock was built at the narrowed entrance to the drained Pool, and in time the riverbank would have been strewn with the rib cages of ships under construction. The slopes below us would be scattered with the towers of mills and the smoking stumpy conical chimneys of potteries and limekilns. They stood beside rudimentary roads up which horses and carts laboured, together with the occasional carriage and stagecoach to London. Most of the streets were still crammed between or around the first seven thoroughfares that grew up near the Castle, but as the town spread towards Everton and the neighbouring ridge of Edge Hill, the streets multiplied without growing much straighter or wider. The burgeoning streets were pinned by more than a dozen church spires. Towards the edge of the settlement we might see women trudging the ropewalks, which were longer than many of the streets, as they twined hemp to make ropes for ships. I have a sudden image of humanity breeding on the surface of the buried Pool and the drained marshes, increasing faster than the maze of cramped streets ought to be expected to contain—in the last three decades of the nineteenth century the population of Liverpool increased by two hundred thousand—until whole families were packed into each unsanitary house little better than a prison and eventually into the cellar too. Up here the gentry hunted along the ridge on horseback, which might suggest a more refined form of savagery that presumed to rise above the sort that infested the diseased streets. I'm reminded that the mysterious Joseph Williamson of Edge Hill turned up at his wedding in hunter's attire and rode off to the hunt as soon as the ceremony was over. I'm distracted, which must be why my brain is seething with the past when it doesn't need to be. We've just parked outside my parents' house, and I'm disconcerted to find it's for sale.

It belonged to my father's parents. It was where he spent his youth. When they died he persuaded my mother to move into it and sell the Kensington semi where they'd brought me up. They didn't need the space now that I was at university in Durham and wouldn't be moving back into our old home. He was able to cycle downtown to the art gallery where he worked until retiring last year, after which he seemed happy just to be close to the heart of the city. My mother found she liked this too, all of which is why I'm thrown by the sale board standing guard in the small neat garden. The house is the end of a terrace of six that survive from a longer Victorian stretch. Lucinda gazes past it at the latest threat of a storm, which darkens the bay as if it's muddying the water, and says "Aren't we going in?"

By now she may think she's the problem. "Of course we are," I say and climb out of the Spirita.

The small two-storey house is painted as red as a university. The front door and windows are bright yellow. Between the gathered orange curtains the windows display enough nets for a fishing expedition. When I open the gate the latch emits a clang that calls my mother to the front door as Lucinda follows me along the short path between rockeries. My mother's large reddish face framed by cropped greying hair seems to grow even rounder with a smile as she holds out her arms from the dress I always call her floral wallpaper outfit, if only to myself. Her arms are still plump and surely no more wrinkled than last time I saw them. She keeps up the smile and the gesture when she notices I'm not alone. "Who's this?" she cries.

"Who is it?" my father demands.

"It's us, Mr Meadows. Deryck," Lucinda responds, and slips past me on the stone border to take my mother's hand. "I'm Lucinda."

"Well, I'm sure I'm glad to meet you."

My mother gives me a blink that hints at reproof, but she's not the only one who has been kept uninformed. "Since when has the house been for sale?" I want to know.

My father hurries out of the front room with a haphazard armful of books and magazines and sheets of paper. "It's the damp. It gets to your throat," he croaks as if to demonstrate.

"That doesn't sound like much of a selling point."

"They can have a damp course put in if they want."

As I wonder why anybody wouldn't, my mother says "Come in, you two. It's still drier in than out. I'm Gillian."

A series of hollow boxy clatters fills the narrow hall as my father runs upstairs. I could almost fancy he's fleeing the intrusion, but he dumps his burden somewhere and is down just as fast. "I didn't get the chance to tell you, Deryck," Lucinda says. "I'm in a little place on top of Edge Hill."

"Sounds like you're near the tunnels."

"Nearer than I thought. They've found another one and they're clearing it now."

I feel as if she and my father are reminding me of my job. In the early 1800s Joseph Williamson employed dozens of workmen to excavate a labyrinth of tunnels under Edge Hill, and nobody's sure why. After his death the tunnels were found to extend for at least a mile, but the explorers retreated for fear of becoming hopelessly lost in the dark. Since then many of the tunnels have been blocked by debris. Recently the Friends of the Tunnels have devoted themselves to reopening the labyrinth. I've yet to work out how to include the tunnels in a tour. "About time they left well alone," says my father. "They want to remember how old Joe the Mole used to carry on. Half the time he'd no sooner have a tunnel dug than he got his men to brick it up."

"What are you saying that means?" Lucinda wonders.

"Think about it," he says, but to me, and tramps into the front room.

The pile he took upstairs was just a sample of the apparent chaos. Books and magazines and photocopies and printouts are strewn all over the already crowded room, on the tapestried fat suite of furniture and beside it, around the television and the player heaped with discs of Westerns, on the dresser wherever there's space between the best china, even on the mantelpiece, among the photographs documenting my progress from a round-faced baby to my present lanky popeyed big-nosed self. As he selects another armful by some principle I can't fathom, my mother says "Well, I'm glad you're clearing up after I've been asking you for weeks. Would everyone like a cup of tea?"

"I'll do it," he declares and hurries to the kitchen with his burden, which he dumps on the table. He's about to fill the kettle from a large plastic bottle out of the refrigerator when he turns on my mother. "You haven't been refilling this, have you?"

"I wouldn't dare. It isn't worth the trouble," she assures him before murmuring "He's got a thing about the tap water. It tastes like it always has to me."

"Nothing to boast about," my father mutters and, having spilled a few drops from the bottle into his hand to touch his tongue to them, sets about filling the kettle.

"This is just silly," my mother says and strides into the front room, where she transfers all the material that's occupying the sofa to my father's chair. "Now you can sit down," she says and asks Lucinda "Have you come to hear Deryck holding forth as well?"

"I'd be interested to hear what he has to say."

"I wouldn't take too much notice of some of it. I don't know where he's been dreaming up—"

My father appears in the doorway, and his frustration homes in on me. "You could help."

"Tell me how."

"Saints help us, Gill, what have we brought up? Grab all you can carry," he directs me, "and put it where you're told."

However rough his mockery is, it isn't far from welcome. I've been growing uneasy that since we arrived he hasn't adopted a single playful voice. As I pick up a pile of books I'm disconcerted to feel how damp the carpet is; even the cover of the volume on the bottom of the pile seems to be. "I could too," Lucinda says. "It's part of my job."

"He'll do," says my father.

"What job is that?" my mother asks Lucinda.

"I'm in the central library."

"I used to work with books when there were more bookshops. Philip Son and Nephew. I was there for—" My mother's wistfulness abruptly deserts her. "The library's the council, isn't it?" she realises aloud. "Careful what you say, Deryck."

"No need. I'm not a spy for them," Lucinda says.

My father's impatience appears to have left the conversation behind some time ago. As soon as I straighten up with all the items I can risk carrying, he heads for the stairs. At the top he veers into the back bedroom. Around a desk bearing a computer, shelves and much of the floor are loaded with research. Last time I saw the room I was glad he was keeping his mind alive since his retirement, but now I'm seeing evidence of an obsession. "Put them anywhere there's space," he says and demonstrates, then lowers his voice. "Why's she here?"

I wonder if he means to hide his research from her—from any stranger. "Because I am."

"You're stuck with her, you mean."

"I wouldn't put it like that, no. Would you say you're stuck with my mother?"

"We're both stuck with what we turn each other into," he says and grimaces for silence as we hear footsteps on the stairs. He scowls downhill at the Collegiate, a Victorian Gothic building patched at the back with aggressively anonymous concrete. "There's another place the city's taken care of," he complains. "Left it to rot till the arsonists got in. I've seen places on the stage look more real than that."

He pokes at the computer mouse with a plump stubby thumb, and his site fades into view on the monitor. It shows the oldest engraving of Liverpool, with a few dozen buildings clustered between the Castle and, closer to the river, St Nicholas's Church. Just a couple of streets are distinguishable, leading virtually from the water's edge to the wild slopes that rise to Everton and Edge Hill. The image dissolves into an engraving in which the streets have spread alongside the Mersey and the Castle has been ousted by a church above a dock that extends a pier into the river. The pier and most of the buildings apart from the church of St Nicholas fade away, erased by a photograph of the familiar waterfront around the Liver Building and its gigantic tethered birds, and then the skyline starts to crumble. In a few seconds only a wasteland remains, from which question marks rise like huge serpents slithering out of the earth.

I have to be impressed by my father's computer skills, which are certainly in advance of mine. We're still on the home page when my mother and Lucinda look into the room. "We thought we'd bring you boys your tea," my mother says, then notices the display on the screen. "If they're going to play with their toys we'll go down again, shall we? It's a long time since I've had a really good chat about books with someone who knows about them."

"Is that your site, Deryck?" Lucinda says, handing me one of the four Don't Knock the Dock mugs. "I've been wanting to see what was on it."

"Why?" says my father. "Watch where you're putting that, Gill." He moves his mug away from the keyboard and squints over his shoulder at Lucinda. "Where'd you hear about it?"

"Gavin told me."

"You've been advertising it wherever you ride," I point out to him.

"I've got to change it after the stuff I've been finding out lately," he says and presses his lips wide and almost grey as if he thinks he's said too much.

"Will it be a bit more balanced?" my mother hopes aloud.

Perhaps he thinks that she's suggesting he's the opposite. As he continues to mum, invisible fingertips try the window beyond the computer—rain does, at any rate. It lets Lucinda change the subject as she gazes downhill under the blackened sky. "Do you think they saw Springheel Jack from here?"

He's another urban legend I've yet to incorporate in a tour—the leaping figure that was said to have haunted Victorian Liverpool and London. Some reports even suggested he could be the Ripper. He was rumoured to have appeared in Aigburth, close to where the Maybricks lived, and was last seen about a hundred years ago, springing the length of High Park Street on the slope below my parents' house. "I know they did," says my father.

"Who?" my mother is anxious to learn.

"My mam and dad. They were at this window. Saw him jump from one end of the street to the other like a frog, and they couldn't even move when they saw him coming. My dad used to say he was glowing like the lights you see on marshes, and his eyes were too. He jumped over our roof and they never saw him again, but my mam screamed for an hour and couldn't sleep for weeks. She said she felt as if he was trailing a fog behind him and left some of it in the house. Sometimes I think that's what started me off."

As I conclude he means his interest in lost Liverpool history, my mother protests "Well, you've never said any of that before."

While he's feeling informative I take the chance to re-mind him "You said you'd show me everything you've found."

"I can't now," he says, scowling around the room without looking at anyone. "It's in a mess."

"I hope you aren't blaming me," my mother says. "I'm sure I haven't touched one single thing."

"Blame my head. There's too much sloshing round in here."

Has he lost confidence since he retired? I want to restore it if I can. "The Frog Lane atrocities," I say. "How about those?"

"You've got me there," he says and gazes at Lucinda. "Has he got you?"

"They don't ring any bell with me, Deryck."

Perhaps he has forgotten that he invited her to use his first name, because his stare doesn't waver. "Penalty to you, Gav. You've turned up something your friend doesn't know."

"If they're going to bring football into it I'm leaving them to it," my mother says, though surely she remembers I've no interest in the game. "Shall we go and sit down while there's space?"

Lucinda gives her a faint smile without otherwise moving as I say to my father "I'm sure you said last time we met you'd tell me about Frog Lane."

"When was that?" says my mother.

As Lucinda and I agree on silence my father says "I went on one of his walks."

"Well, you never told me you were meaning to. I would have liked to have gone."

"It wasn't planned," I say. "We just—"

I've blundered ahead of any useful words, and my nerves aren't helped by the sight of Lucinda opening her mouth until she says "I know what I'd be interested in seeing."

"Let me guess." Having closed his eyes so tight that they look capable of vanishing, my father says "The bottom of the pool."

His eyes seem to flinch as he blinks. My mother has switched on the overhead light, because the sky has grown so dark that it felt as if some chilly medium had begun to invade the room. "If you've got any pictures of that," Lucinda says, "I'm sure we'd like to see."

"Not even any of the things they dredged up and didn't tell the town about. Buried them instead, and quick." Before I can ask about this he says "Go on then, let's hear your request."

"Whatever you have from John Strong."

"Who's that?"

My mother might almost have glimpsed someone in the streets steeped in darkness, but she's sharing my bemusement. "He was a pathetic nasty character who convinced a few vulnerable people that he had some kind of power over them," says Lucinda. "I don't think it was even his real name."

"He knew things nobody else knew or didn't want to admit they did," says my father.

"We still aren't in on the secret," I say for my mother as well.

"He was an occultist of the worst kind," Lucinda says. "He was up to his tricks in Liverpool just after the last war, apparently. He ran some kind of cult and published a book about his beliefs. Published it himself, though you'd wonder who for when he had so much contempt for everyone."

"If that's all you think of him," my father says, "it's more of a wonder you're so interested in him."

"I'd just like to see what you say you copied in the library so I can—"

"It's not on the computer."

"You'll have it somewhere, won't you?" my mother says as if she's determined to participate. "Shall I help you look?"

"I'll tell you where I know it is, and that's the library."

"Look," I say, "Lucinda told you—"

"You can believe her or you can believe me."

"I'm really sorry if you thought I was unreasonable, Deryck."

Perhaps that's a little stiff, but as far as I'm concerned she has no need to apologise, any more than my father needs to retort "You mean I was."

"I wouldn't necessarily put it that way. I expect you were carried away by your enthusiasm."

As my mother readies a question my father demands "What are you trying to get at?"

"Simply what I said. You're so committed—"

"More like I should be, eh? I'll bet Gill thinks that sometimes too." As my mother wards off the idea with her hands he says "Tell us how I managed to copy all those pages out of something you're telling us never existed."

"I don't think I went quite that far."

"A damn sight more than far enough. Do you want them thinking I dreamed it there at your library table? You brought it me, so don't pretend you've forgotten. Don't bother trying to confuse me at all." As she parts her lips he says "I never invited you in."

Perhaps he only means the room, but even that's too much. "I'm afraid you get both of us," I say and would stop there if his gaze at Lucinda relented. "Or neither."

"Right now that's no choice."

"I could wait outside if you like," Lucinda says.

"I don't like at all." I'm infuriated to see him considering the offer. "I couldn't be sorrier," I tell my mother, "but you're going to have to excuse us."

"You haven't drunk your tea," she rebukes some or all of us.

Does she honestly think this can alter the situation? I'm dismayed by the notion that in her own way she's becoming as odd as my father has grown. As he turns back to the screen Lucinda tells her "I'm sure we'll be seeing each other again."

"Don't get your dreams up," my father says and gazes out at the premature darkness.

My mother shakes her head and leads the way downstairs. By the time she has opened the front door while Lucinda and I take token mouthfuls of tea, she seems to have shaken the last few minutes out of her mind. As she plants her mug on the doorstep and reclaims ours she says "Better get away before it teems."

I leave her with a hug that feels unexpectedly flabby and damp. I hope I react no more than Lucinda does to hers. My mother watches until we climb into the Spirita. "I'm sorry I spoiled whatever that might have been," Lucinda murmurs.

"You didn't, you know that. I can only apologise for him. Maybe it's retirement. We'll work it out," I say, but I don't know how much of this she hears as the car rattles and thunders like a set of percussion while the roadway roars at the top of its voice. The latest downpour is upon us, and as the front door slams the house turns wet and dark as mud at the bottom of a pool.

Chapter Five

THE DRAINED LAND

Frog's-lane took its name from the inhabitants of the marshes around it. The creatures used to croak so loudly at night that householders dreamed of them. Attempts to hunt the frogs down and wipe them out always failed, and one maddened hunter almost drowned in a marsh. Once the ground was drained the frogs went elsewhere, although several local people complained of still hearing them at night, no doubt another dream. Could this have driven one or more of them to commit some atrocity? None is mentioned on the web site. After the street was renamed Whitechapel it became known as a place of ill repute, which I take to mean the territory of prostitutes, like the London district with which it shares its name. Later the Ripper diary claimed that the author had seen his wife with her lover in the Liverpool location. By then it had developed side streets, some leading to Williamson Square, which wasn't named after the builder of the tunnels; indeed, the city seems to have tried to ignore his legacy for decades. The square was surrounded by concert rooms, and the York Hotel contained a mock courtroom that satirised contemporary scandals until the trial of Jack Myprick saw the players and the hotel manager prosecuted for obscenity. The web site has left Frog Lane behind, and it's the last of the very few references the search engine produced. My attention drifts until it snags on the address of the site. It's www.ruinedcity.com.

The search engine brought me straight to this inner page, and I scroll to the button that calls up the home page.

The visual history of the growth of Liverpool ends with the devastated landscape occupied by fat question marks, which remind me more of giant maggots than of serpents now. Topics in the sidebar include LIVERPOOL AS IT WAS and AS IT WASN'T, not to mention AS IT SHOULD BE and AS IT SHOULDN'T besides AS THEY DON'T WANT YOU THINKING IT IS and even AS IT'S DREAMED . . . I'm intrigued by the last one, but it shows me only my reflection on a page that has yet to be created. The underlying notion of the site appears to be that much of Liverpool has been destroyed or buried, so that the developers have no idea what they may unearth, although I'm not sure my father has; the site reads more like notes for one, and not very coherent notes either. Theatres and music halls and circuses sprang up where or close to where the Pool had been, and he wonders why, since one of the first historians of Liverpool called the area "building land of the worst description." Why were so many early streets built there? As I share my father's puzzlement, the Beatles announce that they'd like to be under the sea.

I've changed my ringtone, but it's still designed to sound Liverpudlian. The display withholds the caller's number. "Gavin Meadows," I tell whoever's there.

"Liverghoul Tours?"

"And High Rip Trips," I assure her. "Pool of Life Walks as well."

"It's the council, Mr Meadows. The Tourism Events Coordinator would like to see you."

"Is that what they're calling her now? I hope I can still call her Rhoda."

"When do you think you'll be able to come in?"

"How about now? As soon as I can walk there. Fifteen minutes."

"I'll pass that on."

I would ask to speak to Rhoda and confirm it if I didn't suspect she's attempting to cope with whatever changes her latest job description has loaded on her. She's enthusiastically disorganised but able to produce impressive paperwork. I shut down the computer and gulp the last of my lukewarm coffee. Having dumped the mug in the sink, I lock the apartment and tramp downstairs.

After this morning's rain the streets look immersed in a dream of reverting to streams and rivers. On Castle Street the remnant of the sanctuary stone—a roughly circular stub etched with four irregular parallel lines—glistens like a wet fossil embedded in the roadway. At the town hall I turn along Dale Street, another of the seven ancient thoroughfares. It's full of lunchtime crowds, not least of smokers cast out of the ornate Victorian office blocks. Wide-eyed faces implanted in the frontages watch the pedestrians unobserved or, higher up, gaze in stony reveries at sights beyond my imagining. Opposite Cheapside a tower and a spire poke at the blue sky. They belong not to a church but to the massive grey Municipal Buildings, outside which stopped buses throb and chug.

Wide steps lead to the pillared entrance. Beyond an enquiry desk, people are chattering in a selection of languages while they queue to pay bills in an expansive hall beneath lofty skylights. "Gavin Meadows for the Touristic Eventualities Coordinationist," I tell the woman behind the desk.

Her official expression doesn't relent as she wields a phone. "I have Mr Meadows for you," she says, and to me "If you could wait."

"I'll give it time," I say, which proves equally incapable of lending her a smile. Perhaps it was how my father used to say such things that made them work. I listen to the clamour of languages, and then I hear another one along a corridor. "I'll get back to you," an American is saying.

I seem to recognise the voice, and I do once he unlocks the door to the corridor. The corner of his mouth lets the hint of a grin subside, and the features of his wide face appear to clench even smaller. I'm able to believe he has been visiting some official until the receptionist indicates me with the phone. "Here's your one o'clock, Mr Waterworth."

His preoccupied eyes barely take me in as he says "We'll talk in my office, Gavin."

Chapter Six

WATERWORTH

The green paint of the high arched corridor has never seemed so institutional. Once the glass door shuts off the global hubbub in the payment hall there's silence except for the measured tread of my escort, which puts me in mind of a pulse in mud, and my own imitation. He pushes open a fire door and another, presumably expecting me to keep up, because he doesn't hold them. Beyond the second one he marches into Rhoda's office.

She's gone. So are the photographs of the river, ousted from their places on the walls by a map of Liverpool I hardly recognise and an artist's impressions of the future of the city, full of shopping malls and more of the skyscrapers that have invaded the famous skyline, towering above the tethered birds. Outside the window behind Rhoda's desk a bus trundles away from the stop, exposing a row of small discoloured shops and the lower end of Cheapside. "What happened to Rhoda?" I'm anxious to hear.

"Close the door, Gavin," Waterworth says, which I assume is a prelude to sharing a confidence until he adds "I can't discuss council personnel. We're here to explore what happened to you."

He sits in Rhoda's chair and permits himself an almost invisible grimace at the unstable jiggle it has acquired from her rocking and swivelling in it during discussions. As he more or less upturns a hand to indicate that I should take the chair opposite I say "She was good at your job."

I feel as if he's trying to write her out of her own history, erasing every trace of her that he can find. He treats me to a mute stare before saying "Did she observe any of your tours?"

"She mustn't have felt she needed to." His muteness provokes me to ask "Shouldn't you have told me what you were?"

"What difference would it have made to the tour?"

I'm tempted to point out that without him we might have taken refuge in a pub where I could have told Liverpool stories. Instead I say "Was there much on it you didn't know? I'm betting yes."

"My antecedents are here." Before I can take back any implication that he's an ignorant foreigner he says "The core issue isn't how much people knew."

When raising an eyebrow and then both doesn't prompt him to continue, I have to ask "What, then?"

"How reliable you are."

"I've had no complaints."

"You have now."

"From whom?" Having been subjected to his scrutiny again, I say "Sorry, you, yes? Fire away. I'm always trying to improve."

I haven't finished speaking when I realise that he may have a complaint about the encounter with my father. It's a surprise, if hardly pleasant, when he says "I felt as if you'd done the walk so many times you were sleepwalking through it. You never brought it alive for me. Too much of the time you seemed to be drifting off the point into some kind of dream of your own. I believe you left most of your customers as confused as I was."

"About what?"

"The Jack the Ripper business, for one thing. I don't think anyone was clear how much of it was made up."

"If you're asking for my opinion, I think the diary's fake."

"Then you shouldn't be including it in your tour."

"It's about legends as well as history. They're part of what we are."

"That's another issue. You're supposed to be promoting

Liverpool and yet you spent all that time on somebody who killed"—he wrinkles his nose as if the water in the glass he's raising to his lips is stagnant—"people in London."

"Prostitutes," I'm provoked to clarify. "Someone else brought him up before I did, if you recall."

"Sure enough, you did seem to keep needing to be prompted. You didn't always have the answers, though."

"If you mean the atrocities I'm working on them."

"Don't you ever think about anything else?"

"Somebody wanted to know," I say, only to remember it was me. "Anyway, when you made that kind of comment on the tour—"

"We need to move this forward. I'm interviewing a team with a proposal for some tours. They're actors and they'll play figures from Liverpool history. How do you think you'll compete?"

"We'll have to find out," I say, which his stare convicts of insufficiency. "I've got bookings for this week and next."

"I'd like to see the figures since you started, particularly for returns. You need to show me why we should continue to include you in our brochures."

"I'm offering a lot of knowledge about Liverpool and what it means to be a native."

As I realise he could take this as a gibe he says "Maybe once upon a time that could mean small-town and disorganised, but it doesn't hack it now."

"Sorry," I say, which I'm anything but. "Are you telling me that's me?"

"You must have known there was a strong possibility of rain on your tour, but you didn't have a contingency plan. All you could offer was hanging around in a passage and coming back for a rerun." Before I can remind him of the proposal to head for a pub he says "Did anybody take you up on that?"

"Not yet. I expect they're waiting for the weather to improve. I'll invest in some umbrellas if I have to. Bumbershoot Tours, that'll be me."

I thought the term was American—certainly my father would adopt that accent when he used the word—but Waterworth seems not to find it worth recognising. Having stared at it, he says "I'll hold off making a decision till all your tours have been looked at."

"You'll be tagging along, you mean."

"Somebody will." His gaze makes it clear that no further questions on the subject are invited. "May we assume your father doesn't usually accompany you?" he says.

"That was the first time."

"And the last, can we hope? Along with the last time you make a detour to visit your girlfriend."

"You know that was to sort my father out." My anger grows as I feel I've been forced to blame him. "I think most people quite liked having him along," I say. "You saw how much he knows. He used to work for the museums."

"But doesn't now."

"He did since before I was born. He only took early retirement to make way for someone younger."

A strip of seated figures glides into sight behind Waterworth as if a slide depicting an audience has been inserted in a viewer. It's the upper deck of a bus, which offers little distraction from his stare. Far too eventually he says "Who told you that?"

"Who would?"

"He did, I imagine. This is unfortunate." He takes a sip of water, apparently to help him say "I regret to have to be the one to tell you he was asked to leave."

All the visible passengers on the bus appear to be joining in his scrutiny, through so much glass that I have the wholly useless notion that they're gazing at me out of or into an aquarium. "Why?" I hear myself demand.

"I understand he was telling the public—"

The shrill bell makes my heart jerk. Waterworth lifts the receiver and listens and returns it to its plastic niche. "I've already told you I won't discuss council personnel," he says.

"You'll have to excuse me now. I'll be in touch in due course."

Some of the glassed-in heads rise to watch me stand up. I follow Waterworth along the corridor, where I feel like an afterthought to his progress. The doors he doesn't bother to hold open thump shut behind me like insubstantial yet painful blows to the back of my head. I shove the door to the lobby aside before he can, a triumph that seems worse than petty. As he blocks it with his foot a man booms "Mr Waterworth?"

He's expansive in every way, not least his enthusiastically ruddy face. The two young women who flank him are half his width and not quite so thoroughly bald. He heads straight for me, thrusting his brawny arms out of a T-shirt emblazoned HISTRIONIC HISTORY. It looks as if he's threatening to hug me, but I'm let off with a moist handshake while I say "He's Waterworth. I'm the competition."

Of course the actor wasn't trying to turn Waterworth even further against me. I've enough to worry about, and Waterworth reminds me of some. As a bus draws away, giving me a glimpse of a ragged pedestrian bearing an incongruously open dilapidated umbrella up sunlit Cheapside, he calls after me "I need those figures on my desk this week, and the names of your clients as well."

Chapter Seven

Old Words

As I phone my parents' house I seem to hear a hiss of waves, the sound of wheels beside me on Dale Street. Like the rest of the city, the street scarcely has time to dry between bouts of rain. I'm more concerned about hearing my mother. "Who's that?" she urges. "Is that you, Deryck?"

"It isn't. I was going to ask if he was there."

"Oh, Gavin," she says without betraying too much disappointment. "Did he call you?"

"Not unless he rang the flat while I was out just now."

"Oh, were you? Anywhere nice?"

"Not especially. Why would he have been calling me?"

"I don't really know. Why did you want him?"

The conversation has begun to feel like being trapped in a small but inescapable labyrinth. I'm not sure what this suggests about her mental state, but I don't want to upset her. "Just to see if I can sort things out," I confine myself to saying.

"I liked your girlfriend. We didn't cause any problems for you two, did we?"

"You certainly didn't," I say while managing not to emphasise the first word.

"They come from being close to someone," my mother says as if she didn't hear me. "Try not to be angry with him. He seems to have a lot on his mind."

Because I'm unsure how much she knows, I can risk saying only "That's why I wanted to talk."

"You used to like going out for a drink together, didn't you? I thought he might have more time for it since he stopped work."

"What did he say about that?"

"He's found more to do than he expected. Whether it's worth all his time, that's a different story. I suppose at least it keeps him active." As traffic lights release a flood of pedestrians across North John Street at me, my mother says "I'd love to see you getting him to relax a little. You could try calling his mobile if you like."

"I'll do that now."

"Yes, now." Her enthusiasm flags as she adds "You might have a bit of a job. I think he may still be at the new tunnel."

I phone as I head past the town hall and down Water Street, beyond which the perspective reduces the mile's width of river to a stream. A thin young but patchily empurpled businessman strides uphill towards me, haranguing his mobile as he mimes a crisis that I can't help hoping exceeds any of mine. I listen to the imprecisely distant bell that feels engulfed by the shapeless murmur of the crowd on the broad pavement, and then I hear my father. "I've got on my bike," he says, "or I'm otherwise engaged. State your name, rank and serial number. Make that just your name and number and I'll ring you back."

For the middle sentence he assumes the accent of an officer in an old British war film. I feel as humourless as Waterworth for not responding in kind, but I'm busy saying "It's me, dad. We should talk. Let's work out whatever needs it. Give me a call."

Wherever I've been speaking to, he isn't there. He hasn't replied by the time I arrive home. Above the entrance the blurred flood from the merman's cornucopia is growing green with lichen. Perhaps some of the moisture responsible has trickled down the door, wetting the brass handle. I rub my stained hand on my trousers as I shoulder the door shut with an imposing thud.

It sounds designed to daunt the lower orders—beggars, thieves, whoever might have roamed the streets after dark when the offices were built. It resounds through the building and, if I'm not mistaken, under it too. It dies away beneath me, and then the building is as silent as the old disconnected phone on the desk. So is my mobile, but suppose my father called the apartment instead?

I run up the padded marble stairs and let myself in. A photograph of the waterfront glints as if a ripple on the sepia Mersey has moved to catch the light. The red zero of the answering machine beside my desk has rearranged its segments into an angular three. I thumb the button and sit at my desk, and wonder why the hooded figure in the dim depths of the office across the street is so immobile as I wait for the tape to speak.

"Mr Meadows? Are you there, Mr Meadows? This is Moira Shea. Are you there? Me and the lad were on your tour when your da was talking about old Jack. We'd like to take you up on your offer, specially if he's with you again. Are you not there? I'll have to leave you our number, then, and you can let us know when you want us."

The next message is from my father, but at first I'm not sure if it is. It begins with a long loud breath that's the basis of an even more protracted sigh, apparently of resignation. "I'm sorry you're not there," he says, "but I'm ready to say this, so I will. If somebody's got to be worried I'd rather it wasn't your mother." Perhaps he plans to own up about his retirement, but his voice turns aside for an altercation, returning to say only "I don't think this is the place. Give us a ring, Gav, when you get this."

By us, like many Liverpudlians, he presumably means just himself. I'm distracted by attempting to make out a face within the green or greenish hood of the still figure beyond the office window rendered little better than opaque by sunlight. As I reject the notion that the hood contains a pallid flat featureless lump reminiscent of a jellyfish, the tape produces its third message.

At first this seems to consist entirely of the chatter of a drill in stone. The aggressive rattle lessens, though not a great deal, and I'm just able to hear my father remarking "This is a joke." Through a clangour of scaffolding he adds "Don't call me for a bit. Give it half an hour at least."

I mustn't waste any more time on the spectacle in the office, even if the featureless contents of the hood have begun to suggest some underground denizen that owes its pallor to never having seen the light. I crouch to replay my father's first message. He has just finished expressing his reluctance to worry my mother when the mobile strikes up the octopus song on my desk.

It's out of reach unless I'm on my feet, and I need to squat lower to hear what he was saying away from the phone. "I just want a look at your—" The song of the sea blots out the next muffled word and accompanies "I won't be riding anywhere near them. Look, I'm getting off." As the ringtone ceases I rewind the section of tape and play it yet again. Was my father viewing bones or stones? Several replays leave me unsure, and I lurch to my feet to see that my mobile has taken a call. Once I'm past the bright young female voice that Frugo uses on its network and online and at its automatic supermarket checkouts, I hear my father.

"This is fun, isn't it?" he says but doesn't mean. "I expect we'll meet up sooner or later. I really could do with a word before I'm much older." As his hollow voice is almost drowned by the thunder of a train I deduce that he's under a bridge. "Hang on a minute," he says, and I assume he's waiting for the train to pass until he adds through the uproar "Bloody hell, Gav, you won't believe—"

That's all, and it's lent a full stop by the single yip of a car alarm. Or is that a solitary clink of bricks? There's certainly plenty of rubble around town just now. As I poke the key to call him back I reflect that while I was listening to him I ought to have been listening to him. It's as if he's able to inhabit two places and a pair of times at once, though he didn't sound particularly happy with the trick. A bell signifies his ringtone, and then he says "I've got on my bike . . ."

"Get back off it, then. Why aren't you answering now?" I imagine him speeding away from whoever threw a brick at him. "It's me again," I say as soon as he gives me the chance. "You're right, this isn't much of a joke. I'm at home now, so ring either number. I promise I'll pick up."

I sit on the edge of my chair, ready to grab the mobile or the cordless phone, while the sun removes the patina of light from the window opposite. Are the offices disused? I can't recall seeing anyone at work in there or even entering them, though admittedly the entrance is out of sight from my apartment. The view into the room is still blurred by dust or grime, through which I see parts of two desks and the edge of a grey filing cabinet and a calendar beside it on the wall, but not the date. Behind and between the desks the greenish hooded shape isn't a figure after all. It's an old coat abandoned on a hook.

I need to produce the information for Waterworth, and I bring up my accounts on the computer. I've listed all the payments for my tours, though not the tips some customers added, but I've never bothered listing names. If Waterworth wants some, I'll provide them—he has no means of checking how genuine they are. I copy the amounts and dates into a new file. The amounts represent the takings for each date, and I have to divide them—twenty pounds for Liverghoul, twenty-five including train fare for the High Rip Trip, twenty for Pool of Life. There are years of them, and by the time I've finished making sense of them it feels like years since my father last rang. I gaze at the indirectly sunlit street while I think of calling him, and then I see there's no hooded shape in the room opposite.

So the offices are in use after all. Why am I wasting time over them? In a rage at my procrastination I grab the mobile. "Where are you?" I demand once my father has gone through his routine. "Are you down a tunnel? My mother said you might be. I really would appreciate it if you'd call as soon as you get this."

Will he think we've been discussing him behind his back? Anything I add may aggravate the impression, and I terminate the call. I put the names I can remember to the amounts on the screen, and then I set about inventing. Derby, Strange, Underhill, Colman, Aikin, Houlston, Farren, Roscoe, Lemon, Molyneaux, Pocock, Hime . . . I've no idea where I'm dredging up these names from; I feel as if I'm dreaming them into existence as the home-going murmur of pedestrians and traffic fades from the city and the sunlight starts to follow. I could imagine that I'm wakened by the Beatles singing where or what they'd like to be. I snatch up the mobile and see the number is unidentified. "Hello?" I urge.

"Gavin. Are you terribly busy?"

"Never too busy for you, Lucy. Why?"

"You aren't usually so abrupt."

"I'm just in the middle of some work. Nothing I can't get back to."

"I'll let you. I was just going to say you'll be on your own tonight."

"Oh. All right then." Audible disappointment might seem too possessive, but at least I can ask "Where will you be?"

"There are some things I ought to get on with at home."

"I'll see you soon though, I expect."

"Of course. I'd better go. I'm on the phone at work."

This explains why it kept its number to itself. Perhaps concentrating on my task will bring my father, however childishly magical the idea is. Tayleure, Ryley, Raymond, Thillon, Copeland, Levey, Loraine, Chute, Egerton, Tearle . . . When my ringtone dams the gradual but steady stream of names, I look up to see the summer dusk.

The call is from my parents' house. My father's mobile must have run out of power, and he's had to wait until he returned home. This time I'm simply glad to say "Hello?"

"Did you hear your father?"

All I can hear is a mocking chorus of seagulls down towards the river. "I'm not with you," I tell my mother.

"On the radio asking people to phone or get in touch."

"So that's where he's been. No wonder his mobile's switched off."

"Not now. At lunchtime."

"I didn't catch him. So where is he now?"

"I haven't seen him since breakfast. I haven't heard from him and I can't get through to him." As the gathering darkness appears to trigger the streetlamp at an intersection, erasing a dim shadow or a stain on the pavement, she says "I don't know where he's got to, and I'm worried sick."

Chapter Eight

RADIO DESPERATION

"Don't listen to anyone else. If anybody tells you not to tell, that's a reason to. Tell us things you thought were too strange to talk about and people would think you were mad if you did. Tell us before they're forgotten or somebody covers them up. We need to hear the things you won't see in the official books, things the people in charge wouldn't let in even if they knew about them, and I'm not saying they don't. Doesn't matter if you aren't sure if your story's true. We need to look at the legends as well and see how it all fits together."

"You sound like you're reading off a script, Deryck."

"Well, I'm not. It's all up here."

"All in your head, you mean. Where can listeners call you if they've got something for you?"

"Here. Phone you is what I'm saying. That way everyone can hear and nobody can pretend it wasn't said or didn't happen."

"Don't know about that," the presenter says, but he's an amateur, one of the winners of the competition to front the phone-in show for a day of Liverpool Diversity Week ("Including You" is the slogan). The radio station has also hired a blind man to review films and adults with learning difficulties to cover concerts. "We can give them your mobile, can't we, Deryck?" the temporary anchor says. "They'll find you wherever you are."

"That's second best," my father says, which is the last of him.

It has taken me nearly an hour to track him down. I've

heard callers insisting that the name of Liverpool's new French wine bar—the Legless Frog—is racist, or advertising the Learning Differents cinema matinees for the mentally impeded, or complaining that John Lennon Airport is named after a druggie, to which the next contributor retorts that Lennon's widow displayed a poster of her cunt in Church Street . . . The word has the caller removed from the air, but otherwise the presenter seems content to let monologues run uninterrupted. My father's sounded all too reminiscent of the kind a late-night phone-in show attracts.

I may as well carry on listening, since I have to stay home in case my father calls the landline. My mother is giving him until midnight to phone one of us before she contacts the police, a deadline that seems both magical and ominous. Next on the air is a woman from Garston who declares for several strident minutes that she wasn't involved in the slave trade and sees no reason why the city should apologise to the descendants of the victims for owing some of its wealth to the business. I'm tempted to retort that when the government proposed to abolish the trade, the city council objected at length. I'd be wasting my time, since her call is close to twelve hours old, and playing back on the station's web site. "Maybe some of our black listeners have an opinion," the presenter risks suggesting when she eventually departs. "Now I hope you're listening, Deryck."

For a moment I share the hope, but I'm not making sense. "Here's Frank from Old Swan," the presenter says. "What's your story, Frank?"

"They used to say the devil left his footprints in St Cuthbert's down near the docks."

"The devil they did. Did you see yourself?"

"Some of us thought we did. We were just kids. It was bombed in the blitz and we used to play there. We'd dare each other to stand in the footprints. Told the girls if you looked behind you while you were standing in them you'd see the devil creeping up."

"Used to make your own amusement in the good old days, eh? What did these footprints of yours look like?"

"Nothing much. They got bigger and smaller as they went along, and you wouldn't know what shape they were trying to be, except one looked like a man's foot with the toes gone wrong. They must have been worn away, all the footprints. My granddad said that part of the floor was made out of mud so old it'd turned to stone. One kid swore he went in there one night and saw the devil wriggling out of a hole in the floor. Said it didn't know what shape to be. He was always a bit peculiar, though. Got put away when he grew up. Is that the kind of thing you're after?"

"Deryck might be. Are you out there, Deryck?"

I don't know if my father heard. Did he follow up any leads the show provided? "Now here's Mildred from Great Homer Street," the presenter is saying. "Have you got a tale for us, Mil?"

"It's another one out of the blitz."

"Before my time, love. Part of our history, though. Were you there?"

"My dad was, and his mate Tommy Lawless. You'll have heard of Tommy, will you?"

"I'd call a lot of folk lawless these days, but I don't know about him."

"They were in the papers and a book as well, and it wasn't for doing anything bad. They found the man in the metal thingy, what do you call it, a cylinder. He must have crawled in and not been able to get out, that's what the book said. We used to wonder what he was trying to crawl away from. It was in the 1880s, and then he stayed hid till a bomb dug him up. Thomas Cregeen Williams, his name was, and he had his own business in Leeds Street. And the coroner that did the inquest was a Mr Mort."

"Mort the coroner, eh? Never heard that before. The old ones are the best. Next up is Beverley from Everton. Hiya, Bev from Ev. Is that what your friends call you?"

"Not to my face."

"We can't see that. We'll use our imagination. You're on about the blitz as well."

"We never liked going down in the shelter because one boy kept saying he could hear somebody on the other side of the wall where there was nothing but earth. Funny, his name was Deryck as well. It wasn't Deryck Meadows on before, was it? That was him."

"A friend of his, are you? We'd never have guessed. Have you told your tale or is there more you've thought of?"

"I think he thought the blitz was stirring things up that shouldn't be. If you call him back you could put him in touch. We've not spoken since he went off and got married."

"You're certainly full of—" The presenter coughs on the way to saying "You're certainly full of surprises, Bev. Bev?"

Perhaps she's tired of his increasingly blatant scepticism, but I wouldn't mind sharing it so late at night when I'm already nervous about my father. Across the street the deserted office lit by the lamp at the intersection seems unsettlingly reminiscent of my childhood bedroom—the dim discoloured oblique light from outside, the long misshapen shadows that resemble dream versions of the furniture. I could almost imagine that one rounded blotch is a face that's peering at me around the edge of the grubby window. I mustn't be distracted from listening to calls my father may have followed up.

They're all about tunnels. Someone whose grandfather was involved in digging Queensway, the first of the pair that take roads under the river, says attempts were made to block up the excavations. The bosses accused the workmen of trying to prolong the job, but some of her grandfather's colleagues insisted the tunnel had been blocked from within. While I reflect that the digging began at the Old Haymarket, a square built on the highest reach of the Pool, the wife of a worker at the sorting office on Copperas Hill reveals that the postmen are loath to use the tunnel that links the office to Lime Street Station. Perhaps it's a tale to frighten new recruits, since the veterans say the lights in the tunnel sometimes fail, unless they're switched off as a prank, at which point you may realise you have company that doesn't need to see you to find you, because you'll hear its whisper in your ear before you encounter its wet flabby touch. The construction of the offices unearthed coffins lined with lead, but the presenter is growing so openly cynical about the behaviour of workers that I wouldn't blame his listeners if they kept any more anecdotes to themselves. A ticket collector rings to talk about the underground railway, a loop of which passes beneath the centre of Liverpool, starting and returning at the bottom of the street the Castle used to dominate. All the tunnels leak, and the loop has to be closed every spring while rails corroded by salt water are replaced. The employee says he's been told by contractors that they've heard intruders running or rather sloshing ahead of them in the dark, even in sections of the tunnels where there's no water underfoot. It occurs to me that the loop crosses the route of the Pool. The presenter bemoans attitudes to work again before conceding the air to an amateur historian who points out that the city below the ridges of Everton and Edge Hill is riddled with passages—sewers, old hydraulic systems, abandoned railway tunnels and others still in use. As I wonder if my father might feel driven to explore any of them, whatever his reasons, my mobile sets about performing its underwater song.

The call is from my parents' house. As I pause the broadcast I think something like a prayer—an unspoken wish, at any rate. "Hello?" I say aloud.

"Have you heard?"

Both my mother's question and her dull voice make me afraid to ask "What?"

She almost laughs. "No, I mean have you heard from him."

"I haven't. You haven't either, obviously."

"I haven't." Her silence suggests that our words have been

engulfed by the mire of repetition until she says "I suppose it must be time, then."

She means for the police. "Would you like me to call them?"

"Oh, would you? Or do you think I better had? I was only thinking with him living here . . ." Perhaps she wants me to compete or at least to answer this, because some seconds take their time before she says "Maybe it would be best coming from you."

I feel childish for observing that it's ten minutes short of midnight. If her watch isn't fast, her anxiety must be. I let a last hope turn my gaze on the street, but it's deserted; even the shadow at the window of the office has vanished while I wasn't looking. "I'll phone them now then if you like."

Of course liking doesn't come into it, and I feel more childish still. "Go on, Gavin," she says. "Tell them what I told you and give them my number." This sounds like a pre-amble, and she adds "Tell them they can come and see me if they like. I won't be sleeping till I know what's happened. You have to stay there, promise me you will, but I wouldn't mind not being on my own."

Chapter Nine

What the Night Spawns

I wish I'd said it was an emergency, but I suspect the police wouldn't think it was much of one. Instead of 999 I called the number for Merseyside Constabulary, where the operator put me through to a policeman who seemed frustratingly remote. He made it clear that he found this an odd time to report a missing person and wondered why I hadn't waited until morning, so that I had to use my mother's concern as an excuse. He was surprised I wasn't with her, even once I'd explained about the landlines; if my father couldn't contact us on one, wouldn't he try the other? I described him and his bicycle and said he'd been researching local history for his web site. Since the policeman was as unfamiliar with its address as with mine and my mother's, I gathered that he and his whereabouts were far from local. When I mentioned that my mother would appreciate a visit, I wasn't sorry that it wouldn't be from him.

He won't be conducting the search. Having established that someone will contact me if there's any news, I'm left with an occurrence number so protracted that it feels as if my father's disappearance may be crushed into insignificance by the weight of the multitude of reports. I listen to the rest of the phone-in, which turns into an argument about workers' rights and responsibilities. There are no more calls in response to my father's, but should I have told the police about the earlier ones? I did say that when I last heard from him he was under a railway bridge, and that's really all I know. I shut the computer down and head for the bathroom.

I leave the mobile and the landline receiver in the corridor.

There's little space to keep them with me now that some of Lucinda's toiletries have moved in, and the phones might be affected by the damp that sometimes seems to linger in the bathroom. In the midst of the buzz of the electric tooth-brush I imagine that the mobile stirs on the floor, but it must be my nervous eagerness to hear, unless someone's in the corridor between the apartments. Having finished foaming at the mouth, I send some water on a journey to its source and fill a glass from the bedewed tap before retrieving the phones on my way to bed.

Although I've shared it with Lucinda just a few times, it feels deserted. I lay the phones next to the clock on the bed-side table, where the colon between digits almost an hour past midnight blinks insistently as I tug the cord above the pillows. Darkness swallows me, but it contains no sleep. I'm lying with my face towards the table and the window, and soon I hear a whisper that becomes a liquid chorus. The rain sounds torrential, almost blotting out the uneven sluggish tread of someone in the street. At last the presumably drunken wanderer grows inaudible, and at some point the rain does, because I'm asleep.

I would rather not be. I'm in utter darkness and wet with it too. Am I swimming blindly or groping my way along a tunnel? I'm being drawn towards a presence so unimagin-ably vast that I can sense its eager awareness of me. I've no idea how close it is or where. I'll find out by touching it, be-cause it apparently has no need to breathe, unless its breaths are too immense and slow for me to identify them as such. I would very much prefer not to encounter it—to learn any-thing about its shape or nature—and I struggle to cry out, to dredge myself up from the dream. While it seems to take not much less than forever, I succeed in projecting a feeble shriek into the darkness.

At once I'm afraid that it will attract some part of the presence to reach for me. Dreams have no logic, or perhaps panic doesn't, because the thought raises another cry. It manages to travel beyond the dark, and I flounder in pursuit until I see the darkness of my room. I would be reassured by its dim but familiar outlines and the amicable winking of the colon of the clock if the cries hadn't followed me out of the dream. They're no longer mine.

It's past three o'clock. No doubt everyone is asleep except me and whoever is uttering scream after scream, but how can anybody sleep through that? I kick off the quilt and lurch to the window, where I fumble at the lock. The sash slides up, spattering the sill with traces of rain. The cries sound as if they're streets away. I want to believe they're the natural call of some animal—an urban fox, perhaps—but they're all too recognisably human, even if I can't tell the gender. They seem close to exhaustion by terror or agony or both. If anyone besides me can hear, how can they bear not to find out what's wrong? Are they too afraid to see? That's how I'm behaving, which is almost as awful as the screams. I blunder away from the window to switch on both lights in the room.

They provide no relief. They simply make the screams more real. I'm dragging yesterday's clothes on when the cries falter, and I can't help hoping they've come to an end. Their source must have been drawing breath, because in a few seconds they recommence, sounding more outraged and agonised than ever. I shove my feet into socks and shoes and almost forget to lock the window before dashing out of the apartment and slamming the door.

If the slam awakens any of my neighbours, they aren't apparent as I run downstairs. Apart from my footfalls the building is silent, and I'm able to hope that someone more qualified than I feel has dealt with the problem outside. When I emerge into the temporarily rainless street, however, the cries are just as atrocious, and my whole being shrinks from imagining what they express.

They're behind the building, away from the river. They aren't in Castle Street, which is deserted except for a few empty cars. The street is staked out by pairs of traffic lights mindlessly juggling colours and staining the drowned sanctuary stone, which glows like luminous moss before it turns the colour of a false daylight and then flares a warning red. As I sprint down Cook Street I hear the baying of a police car. I'm willing it to head for the scene of the crime when the siren shrinks into the distance and is gone.

Why haven't I called the police? I might feel absurd for calling them twice in a night, especially if the same policeman answered, but the truth is that the screams haven't let me think. I even forgot that I was meant to be waiting at home in case my father rang the landline. The doormen who bar undesirables from the restaurants on Victoria Street have left their posts, and the deserted road stretches to the site of the Old Haymarket, where a car with its roof lights flashing swings around the roundabout at the tunnel entrance. "Police," I yell despite the distance, "police," and then I realise that the lights are reflections of streetlamps. As I leave Victoria Street for the narrow lane of Temple Court I hear the rattle of a window behind me. "Shut your row," a man bellows, and the window slams like a lid.

How can anyone respond that way? He sounded as if he thinks he owns the night as well as wherever he lives. He has left me feeling more alone than ever between the shuttered shops that occupy the lowest floor of the unlit buildings. I hurry into Matthew Street, the lane where a cellar produced the Beatles and other Mersey sounds. The cellar used to resound with screams, but the ones I'm hearing aren't down there. They're to my left, beyond a bend of the lane. They're in Whitechapel.

They sound raw and weary, yearning for an end. The lane seems to channel them towards me as I venture to the corner. Figures dressed in very little confront me across Whitechapel—women as still as the stone that frames them. They're dummies in the window of a sex shop. The screams are to their left, but my view is blocked by a cage around roadworks. I have to force myself to head that way, not least because the screams aren't the only sounds I can hear.

Beyond the roadworks Whitechapel leads to the Old Haymarket. Even the taxi rank outside a shopping mall is deserted. The only object anywhere on the pavements is lying at the intersection with Richmond Street, which leads to the theatre square. The object is a body, and it's naked.

If it's male, it's horribly incomplete. That would explain the screams, but not the chorus of croaking. The legs are splayed towards me, and a glistening shape lies between them, separate from the body. The abdomen is heaped with items, wet with them. The mouth is as wide as lockjaw, but the shrieks are growing feebler, and the victim appears incapable of any movement other than an uncontrollable twitching of the stomach. I stumble forward, groping for my mobile with a shaky hand.

I shouldn't have moved. The torso jerks, or the mass that's strewn over it does. Perhaps this was all I saw twitching. The creature between the legs hops towards me with a croak, and another springs over the victim's chest to land in the gaping mouth as if the cries have served their purpose. I'm hardly aware of lurching forward to determine whether the horde of creatures is on top of the body or inside it or both.

I'm so anxious to see and equally to avoid seeing that I barely hear a rush at my back. It sounds like water, and my assailant doesn't seem a great deal more solid. All the same, the pavement thumps my forehead before I've time to catch my balance. Is the stain that spreads around my vision more than a shadow? I've hardly glimpsed it when I'm engulfed by my personal dark.

Chapter Ten

REPRESENTING THE LAW

It hurts. It hurts. It hurts. That's the message my head is repeating, verbally and otherwise, while various parts of my body throb in agreement. The waves of light flicker so much that they could just be pain made visible. I can see little more when my eyes falter open, because my face is pressed against a dark unyielding blur. That's the pavement, but is it so dark at the edge of my vision because whoever attacked me is standing over me? Perhaps I'm next for the treatment that was dealt to the screaming victim. My body prickles, aggravating the roughness of the pavement and discovering a sweaty trace of rain on my back. The world rolls upside down, or at least I do, confronting the attacker.

There's nobody above me. When I plant my hands on the damp pavement and waver into a sitting position, the huge soft drum that's my head barely lets me determine that nobody is to be seen anywhere around me—nobody, not even the screaming victim. The city seems as quiet as stone, and straining my ears until my head redoubles its painful pulse only brings an undercurrent of sound, the omnipresent urban murmur. I rise or rather wobble to my feet and dodge unsteadily around the enclosed roadworks before stumbling to the lane I came along and then to the one that leads to Williamson Square. Neither of them shows me a corpse, and across the road Sir Thomas Street is just as innocent of any, like the entire length of Whitechapel with its patina of rain. Why am I wasting time? I drag out my mobile so hastily that it almost ends up in the gutter, a prospect that leaves me nearly blind with pain.

A few fumbles at the keys recall the police. "Just put me through," I snap at the operator, because the pulse in my skull won't let me describe the situation twice. Either she's spurred by my urgency or she wants the police to deal with me, because with almost no delay a man says "What's the problem, please?"

I should have rung 999. Surely this is still an emergency, and more to the point, I'm sure I recognise the voice. It's the policeman to whom I spoke at such length about my father. What would my father do in the circumstances? The pounding of my head drives me to adopt the thickest Scouse accent I can summon up. "Mergencee," I declare. "Youse need—"

"Who is this?"

"Youse don't need me name. Dere's no time, like. Dere's been—"

"Is this Mr Meadows?"

My skull seems to grow enormous, or the pain does. He must have recognised my number. "Mr—" I blurt, but that won't work. "It is, yes."

As if to compensate for my abandoning my Liverpool sound, his Lancashire accent becomes more pronounced, emphasising the distance between us. "What's this about, Mr Meadows?"

The best I can produce between jabs of pain is "I was trying not to confuse you."

"How were you going to do that?"

"I thought you might think I was calling about my father. Is there any news of him?"

"You just said you weren't calling about him." The policeman lets my head pound several times before he says "We told you we'd inform you if there was."

"Has anybody been to see my mother?"

"I couldn't tell you without checking. Is that why you rang?"

"No, it's because somebody, I think somebody's been murdered."

"That's why you put on a silly voice."

"No." I grope through the pain for an explanation. "I was confused," I try saying. "I was attacked. Knocked out. Knocked down."

"How long ago was this?"

You could use the pain in my head for a metronome, and it barely lets me read the time on my mobile. "Maybe quarter of an hour," I say. "There was a body but it's gone."

"Where are you calling from?"

"Frog Lane." My headache has befuddled me, or the atrocious memory has. "It isn't called that now," I say. "I run historical tours, that's why. It's Whitechapel."

"Which town?"

As long as he recognised me, how can't he know? "I haven't gone anywhere. Liverpool."

"Please stay where you are and don't touch anything."

He has nothing more to say to me. Presumably he's busy sending a car. I pocket the mobile and hold on to the barrier around the roadworks. I should like to close my eyes in the hope that it might ease my headache, but it would make me feel open to attack. The city murmurs all around me like a subterranean flood. I can't hear any vehicle, even one without the siren it surely ought to be sounding. I'm sure rain is imminent, unless the climate has grown so wet that there's always water in the air. The police need to examine the scene before the next downpour washes away any evidence. Just because I mustn't touch anything, that doesn't mean I can't look.

I stumble forward to squint at the pavement where the body was. The flagstones are cracked and tilted by years of parked cars and vans and trucks. They're moist with rain and stained with oil, but I'm able to distinguish faint tracks. A trail that I'm sure was left by the dragging of a body is flanked by prints that must have lost shape in the rain. They lead towards the tunnel at the Old Haymarket, but once they've crossed a deserted taxi rank beyond the last shops they veer away from Whitechapel, along the approach to an entrance that lets shoppers drive under the theatre square to collect goods from beneath the stores on Church Street. Has the corpse been abandoned in the underground area? I can't see any tracks to suggest whoever moved it has emerged. If they do before the police arrive, shouldn't I photograph them with my mobile? I'm venturing towards the entrance when my headache gives me a moment to reflect that I'm better staying out of sight. Before I can retreat, a police car screeches into the approach road and halts, blocking my way. "In there," I call, pointing past the car.

The front doors fly open, ejecting officers who resemble bouncers in a different uniform. The driver's broad nose is dented in the middle, and his colleague looks quite as ready for the fight the driver must have had. "In the car," he grunts.

Is that how he usually speaks to the driver? I share his urgency but am shy of aping his brusqueness. "I'm sure they've gone in there," I say under my breath. "Have they got a car, do you think? Maybe one of you should—"

"In the car."

This time it's the driver, and I grasp that he's addressing me. "Let me just show you—"

"Car."

It's the turn of the man whose nose has yet to be broken. "They've left tracks," I protest. "Hadn't you better, I mean, in case—"

"Car."

Both guardians of the law have said it now. Each repetition feels like a flare of pain in my head, and the latest goads me to say "You don't seem to understand. Suppose—"

There's only one way for them to use fewer words. The man with the unbroken nose steps around the car, and they close in on me. They've moved just two weighty paces in unison before their wide faces, which look flattened and blanched by the glare of the streetlamps, break out in drops that trickle over their skin, and their uniforms begin to glisten. As if they've brought it with them, the black sky is releasing a cloudburst. "This is what I was afraid of," the drumming of rain on my skull drives me to object. "Can't you see—"

"Car."

Do they mean to overcome me by speaking in chorus? I suspect it was inadvertent, and the scowls they're training on me are designed to pretend it didn't happen. My mouth struggles to contain a giggle that may border on hysteria. As my face works like a schoolboy's, the men stretch out large hands that drip luridly illuminated water. The hands look like a threat of bruising if not worse, and all at once I've had enough of the downpour and the men's monolithic refusal to listen. Before they can grab me I make for the vehicle. "Fair enough, car. As you say, car. Right you are, car. Where would you like me? Up front or behind?"

The dentless officer lunges at me—no, past me—and throws open the door behind the driver's. As I duck under the roof spiked with raindrops he finds it necessary to give me a hand, which revives the pounding of my head and presses me down into more of a crouch. He slams the door after me, and his unstable dim misshapen blur appears on the other side of the car. He and his colleague regain their bulky shapes as he climbs in beside me while the driver sits at the wheel, and then there's silence apart from the metallic thunder of rain overhead. "You're keeping watch," I say. "There isn't any other way out."

Perhaps this sounds insufficiently questioning to deserve an answer, and I raise my voice. "Shouldn't you put the wipers on?"

"We've been watching," says the driver.

"You'll have seen what happened, then." Apparently this too is unworthy of a response, and so I try "You'll have seen where they went."

My seatmate turns so that his knees crowd me against the locked door. "Anything you want to tell us?"

"I saw someone killed. Worse than killed." The policemen look as if they know this isn't true, and I say hastily "I don't mean I saw it happen. I saw them."

"Saw what?" the driver insists.

"They'd been cut open and things put in." The memory lights up in my head like a glaring slide projected on a screen, and I wish I could extinguish it. "Frogs," I say. "Live frogs."

The staccato metallic barrage above my head is slackening, but I'm reminded that the rain must have washed away the trail. The policemen are staring at my words with no expression I can read. "What did you see?" I demand.

The rain pats the roof a few times and streams soundlessly down the windows. The driver might have been waiting for quiet before he says "You."

"We've been watching you," his colleague finds it necessary to add.

"Did you see who attacked me? Why didn't you—" Perhaps it's inadvisable to accuse them, and I interrupt myself. "How long was I out?"

"Depends what you mean by out of it," says my bulky seatmate.

"You haven't told us what we want to hear yet."

"Been having yourself some fun, have you?"

My head throbs with mingled pain and anger as I blurt "Maybe violence is your idea of fun. It's certainly not mine."

Have I invited some? My seatmate hasn't finished watching me as though he's daring me to make a move when the driver says "Sounds like he still is."

"Had a bit to drink, have you?"

"I haven't even had dinner."

"Had a bit more than a drink?"

"Certainly not. Nothing of the kind. That's not my scene at all." Perhaps I should have appeared not to understand, and I fundamentally don't, which is why I protest "Just what are you accusing me of?"

The driver scowls at me out of his mirrored strip of face. "Wasting our time."

"If anybody's doing that, it's you. Why aren't you finding the body and the people who did it?"

The man beside me sits towards me, and I've nowhere to retreat. As my head throbs as if to warn me that I've gone too far he says "There's nobody. Just you."

My shoulders thump the window. The windscreen squirms with rain dislodged from the roof, and I feel as though the world has shifted too. "What are you trying to say? I—"

"The camera saw you fall down all by your own self," says the driver.

Another trickle traces a random path down the windscreen, but it seems more like a fissure in my reality. "Where did you come from?" the driver says. "Got anywhere to live?"

"I live right here in the city. I own my apartment. I'm Pool of Life Tours and a whole lot more. If you mean how I look, I was in bed when I heard what was happening. I put on the first things I could lay my hands on. Give me a breath test if you want. I'll take a drug test too."

"No need for that," my seatmate says, though ominously. "Where do you live?"

"Trident Street. It's off—"

"We know it," says the driver. "Long way to hear whatever you're saying you did."

"There wasn't anything else to hear, and for God's sake, they were screaming."

"Funny nobody else heard," says my seatmate.

"Someone did. I still can't believe he was shouting at them to be quiet."

"Maybe they meant you," the driver says.

"Maybe you were sleepwalking and making a row in your sleep."

"Looked like you were," the driver says and starts the engine. "We'll get you home."

"You're not just going to drive off without—"

His colleague plants a fist on the narrow gap between us on the seat, displaying scabbed knuckles. "Count yourself lucky as fuck that's all we're doing."

The car swerves up the sloping road, throwing me against the door as if I've flinched from him. We're speeding into Whitechapel when a small wet shape leaps into the headlamp beams. The driver yanks at the wheel, and I think he's avoiding the creature until his intentions become clear. Though I scarcely feel the impact, his eyes in the mirror express satisfaction. "What was that?" I almost shout.

"Bloody nothing," says the driver.

His stare and his colleague's could be applying the description to me or anticipating its appropriateness. I'm silent while the car veers uphill through a red light into Dale Street. As we race past Waterworth's office I'm able to reflect that I did at least email him the information, even if simultaneously listening to the phone-in made me add Lucinda Wade as a recipient by mistake. Cheapside and the neighbouring lanes appear to be reaching underwater for their inverted selves. A sweep of the windscreen wipers reveals a vista of the black river before the car plunges downhill and swings into Trident Street, pinning a shadow against the wall opposite the apartments. The shadow of the lamppost flees towards the entrance to the offices and vanishes as I say "Here. I'm here."

The car halts not quite violently enough to thump my head against the back of the driver's seat. As my skull celebrates the revival of pain, the driver says "That's where I'd stay if I was you."

When he releases the locks I clamber out of the vehicle and fumble for my keys while the policemen watch as if they suspect me of only pretending I'm home. For several seconds the key doesn't turn in the door, and I've begun to wonder if it's the wrong one by the time it works. I ease the door shut behind me and hear the car disappear none too swiftly into the distance.

The pen in its pot on the antique desk emits a faint rattle as I cross the lobby. Otherwise the building is quiet except for my padded footfalls. My head feels like a raw lump embedded with incomplete bewildered thoughts. Has my father phoned while I was out? I only just remember not to slam my door as I hurry to the answering machine, where the blind eye of a zero meets my gaze. I'm unzipping my jacket and trudging to the bathroom when, as though in response to my hopes or fears, the mobile wriggles against my hip. It's halfway through its undersea verse before I see that the caller's number is withheld. I'm dismayed to have to nerve myself to say "Hello?"

"Mr Meadows?"

"Gavin Meadows, yes." It's the Lancashire policeman, and I'm nervous of learning why. "What's . . ." I say, and eventually "What's the news?"

At first he doesn't answer, and I switch on the bathroom light in case that provides any reassurance. A large drop of water plummets from the tap into the sink as though the light has drawn it out of hiding. I'm reluctantly opening my mouth to urge him to tell me the worst when he says "Where were you?"

This is one more bewilderment to add to the mass in my aching skull. "Where—"

"You weren't where you called us to," he says, and with even less patience "I'd advise you to tell me where you were and why."

Chapter Eleven

Here we are Again

How long does it take to convince the police that I was with the police? It feels like the rest of the night as surreptitious hints of dawn creep into the street outside the windows, under cover of the light from the lamp at the intersection. No, I don't know the names of the policemen or their numbers or where they came from. All I know is that they said they saw me and nothing else. They didn't see a murder or any evidence of one, but they didn't arrest me for wasting police time because (I tell him, having discovered some craftiness in the midst of the pain in my head) they said they saw me sleepwalking. I must have tripped over a broken section of pavement and knocked myself unconscious, which surely gives me grounds to sue the council. My not entirely fake display of rage seems to impress him with my truthfulness, perhaps even when I suggest that, having regained some kind of consciousness, I mistook imagination for a memory and called him in a panic. My increasingly genuine anger, or the pain it exacerbates, almost goads me to point out that if whoever he sent had treated my call as more of an emergency, there wouldn't be all this confusion. Eventually he warns me that I may be hearing further from the police.

I hope so—about my father. I say as much before ending the call and stumbling to the bathroom for a drink of water and a handful splashed in my face. It's too soon to add to the pair of painkillers I swallowed while suffering the interrogation. I have to shut my eyes and plant a hand against the corridor wall in order to retrieve the mobile from the floor.

I grope my way into the bedroom and subside on the bed. My thoughts have already started to clamour. Do I really believe I could have imagined the murder? It wouldn't be the first or the hundredth time that a security camera missed an incident. Shouldn't I go back and look for any evidence I could photograph with my mobile? I need to rest my head first. It's not yet five o'clock, but it's more than twice that when the mobile brings me back into the world.

I feel as if I've hardly slept. Too often when I tried I was confronted by a supine body from which objects appeared to be hatching and swarming under a glare as white as moonlight but less natural. I force my eyes open a second time despite the painful glow through the curtains and read my parents' number. "Yes," I say far too sharply out of nervousness. "Sorry, I mean hello."

"It's only me," my mother says. "Am I interrupting? Isn't this a good time?"

I hope it is, especially for her. At least I seem to have left patches of my headache somewhere in my sleep. "I was just dozing," I say and shut my eyes.

"I wish I hadn't woken you. You've got enough to keep you busy without me bothering you."

"You know I'm always here if you need me. You call whenever you've a reason, and don't think twice."

"I haven't much."

"You haven't . . ."

"Heard from your father, no. You won't have either, will you?"

"I haven't." Part of my brain must still be asleep for me to add "Well, except—"

"What, Gavin? When did you speak to him? What did he say?"

"He didn't. That is, I didn't. He left messages before I got home." My head revives its ache as I concentrate on not betraying that he was loath to worry her, though now of course he has. "He wanted to talk and that's pretty well all I can tell you," I say. "He seemed to be ringing from different places but I don't know where."

"Do you think the police should have a listen?"

I'm dismayed to realise that I didn't store the messages, which could be erased by more recent ones. I open my eyes and dash into my workroom to find the zero glaring sightlessly at me. The quickest way to protect the messages is by turning off the machine, and I flick the switch at the foot of the wall. "I'll give them a ring," I say as I straighten up, none too steadily. "Did they contact you?"

"They did."

Her tone is so much more tentative than her words that I say "Was there a problem?"

"They came when I was asleep. I just hope I gave them everything they need. They took a photo, took one away, I mean. And one of them had a good look at the computer." As if she's anxious to prove she wasn't wholly passive she says "I told them to listen to the phone-in to see if that's any use."

This prompts me to ask "Did you ever meet Beverley from Everton?"

"I don't know the woman. Your father used to go on about her. She sounded like she made things up to get attention." With barely a pause my mother says "Had you better call, then?"

"The police."

"That's right, Gavin. Not that woman. I know your father loved the past, but there are limits."

We murmur reassurances and goodbyes, and eventually my mother brings the routine to an end. I give the occurrence number to a woman whose briskness sounds like a caution against wasting police time, and then I'm wary of hearing the familiar Lancashire voice. She connects me with another woman, however, who undertakes to send someone to listen to the messages. "I don't suppose you could say when," I wonder, and her silence makes me add "If you could call this mobile that would be a help."

At least I should have time to use the bathroom. Once
I've shaved, having been put in mind of an identikit sketch
of my father's face, I leave the mobile and the landline receiver outside the door. I've turned down the shower so that
its onslaught doesn't fall too vigorously on my tender head,
which is decorated with a large painterly bruise that I'm glad
my mother can't see, when a bell sounds in the corridor.

I quell the shower and run to thumb the intercom. I'm
only beginning to speak when a voice announces "Police."

"Well, that was quick. Pretty superheroic." I don't mean
him to hear this; it's more the kind of comment my father
would relish. I hold down the button to release the street
door and am blurring my wet footprints with another trail
when the bell peals again. I trudge back to the intercom.
"Hello?" I say. "Problem?"

"Something's blocking your door. You'll need to come
down."

I dash to the bathroom and grab my robe. Donning it and
stuffing phones into the pockets restart my headache. My
bare feet find a chill through the carpet as I run down the
marble stairs. Has someone moved the obstruction? There's
nothing in front of the door except a dark stain on the carpet. It's water—it must be from outside—and chills my feet
further as I open the door.

A police car is parked on the pavement less than two feet
beyond it. A voice is croaking inside the vehicle, and it takes
me a moment to identify it as a message on a radio, because
I'm distracted by the sight of the pair of policemen in front of
the car. Their closeness isn't the only reason why I retreat a
soggy inadvertent step. "Good God, it's you again," the man
with the dented nose says, or I would.

Chapter Twelve

GETTING THE MESSAGE

It must have been raining while I was in the bathroom. The roadway still glistens, and as he follows his broken-nosed colleague the other policeman shakes spray doglike from his hair. He shuts the door hard, and they stare at the carpet in front of it. "Looks like somebody wanted to get in our way," he says.

"Scared of us too by the looks."

Once they've surveyed the lobby with particular attention to the desk, the dented man remarks "Rickety old item."

"Wants getting rid of." They gaze at me, and the dented fellow enquires "Fond of museums?"

"I am, as a matter of fact. My father worked for them."

"Doesn't now."

"Who told you that?"

Perhaps I just did, in which case I must seem as paranoid as I feel, but the man with the uninjured nose says "His old girl when we went to see her."

I find the thought that my mother was alone with them in the house at night—presumably before they found me in Whitechapel—so unwelcome that it feels like having failed to protect her, and I don't need him to add "Must be lonely up there on her tod."

"Well, that's why you're here, isn't it? To help find my father."

"We know why we're here, Mr Meadows."

I won't be daunted where I live. "As long as you've got my name I should know yours, shouldn't I?"

They consider this as if they've forgotten how to blink, and then the dented man says "Maddock."

"Wrigley," says his colleague.

"All right, let me play you the tape."

As I follow my wet footprints, which I'm furious to realise do indeed start and finish at the wet patch by the entrance, Maddock says "Must cost a packet to live here."

"What's his game again?" Wrigley wants to know.

"He's an escort."

I carry on padding upstairs until I feel I'm trying to outdistance the sense of pursuit very close at my back, and then I swing around at the half-landing. "Who did you hear that from?"

"Try looking in the mirror," says Maddock.

My forehead has recommenced throbbing by the time I realise what I told them in Whitechapel. "I said I give tours of Liverpool."

"Seeing to our image, are you?" Wrigley says. "See it's all true."

I won't bother to respond to this, not least because I've realised that in my haste I forgot to bring my keys. I feel as if the police and my headache left me unable to think. My rage is approaching the point at which it will explode into words, however carelessly selected, when I see that my door is ajar. That was thoughtless too, but at least I'm not shut out, and I follow the blurred wet tracks into the apartment.

Wrigley bumps the door shut with his bulky shoulders. The policemen stare along the corridor, at or past the old views of Liverpool, until I move to stand outside my workroom like a butler. "It's in here."

Maddock tramps past me, only to turn a scowl on me. "It's not working."

"I switched it off to save the messages."

Wrigley adds his frown to the proceedings. "All right, give it here. We'll take it and give it a listen."

As Maddock stoops to unplug the answering machine I protest "You can't take that away."

He stays in his hulking crouch and screws his head around on its thick ridged stub of neck. "Who says we can't?"

"My father might call."

"He can if you don't go out."

"How long are you likely to be? I've a tour this afternoon."

Both men glower at the prospect or at the inconvenience they apparently think I'm causing. Wholly as a ruse, and a feeble one at that, I say "Can I get you gentlemen something to drink?"

They exchange a look, and Wrigley shrugs. "I could do with some water."

"Same here, out of the tap," says Maddock.

"Give me a minute and I'll play you the tape."

As I make for the kitchen I feel more in charge, though my nakedness under the knee-length towel in the shape of a robe doesn't help. I fill two tankards at the granite sink, and an afterthought is gurgling in the plughole when Maddock says "Can you see how this fucking thing works?"

I hurry back so fast that water spills out of the tankards, splashing my feet and adding to the marks on the carpet. He's hunched over the machine, his stubby fingers hovering over the keys. "I'll do that," I protest. "Take these."

Wrigley accepts both drinks and hands one to Maddock, who plants it none too gently beside the machine. As he wipes a scattering of drops off the keys he says "Tell me what I'm doing."

He has already switched on the machine. "Press R," I resign myself to advising, "and then P."

"Ah and then pee," Wrigley seems to feel required to convey or translate.

"Not both," I shout as Maddock jabs two fingers at the keys, because I'm afraid this will damage if not erase the tape. "Do what I said."

Wrigley lifts his tankard so deliberately that I could imagine he's testing its weight as a weapon. Instead he takes a sloppy mouthful and wipes his chin. "That's the stuff."

I've never known anybody so enthusiastic about a drink of water. I even feel its spray on my face. Meanwhile Maddock leans on the rewind button and barely waits for the small shrill voices to finish gabbling in reverse before he knuckles the key to play the tape. As it reiterates Moira Shea's appeal for my father's return he drains half his tankard while gazing at me. "Sounds like someone's after you," he says. "Don't be letting a lady down."

"She's on my tour this afternoon."

"Keep it shut," Wrigley warns as my father begins to speak.

I'd like to think the policeman is rebuking his colleague as well as me. My head throbs with the alternative throughout my father's call. "So what was he supposed to be worried about?" Wrigley says.

"I don't know. If I did—"

Maddock jerks a hand up as the machine starts clattering. "Is this buggered?" he says and reaches for it.

"It's fine. Leave it alone. Just listen."

Both men stare at me while my father tries to talk above the noise of the drill, only to be overwhelmed by the collapse of scaffolding. "Sounds like he was in someone's way," says Maddock.

"I'd say no use."

Surely Wrigley is referring to the message, not my father. "There's one more," I blurt.

As I fish out my mobile, a hiss of static announces Lucinda on the tape. "Just to say I'll see you later," she says. "Looking forward to our bath."

"Not that," I interrupt or try to. Though I've no reason to feel guilty, the message and especially its continuation were just between us. I brush against Maddock's unexpectedly rubbery torso as I poke the rewind key. "He's here," I say, brandishing the mobile.

The room feels not just crowded but humid, and I retreat into the corridor before bringing up my messages and switching the phone to loudspeaker mode. The policemen don't blink as my father shouts over the thunder of the train and is cut off by the clink of the brick. "That all?" says Maddock.

"Tried calling him?" Wrigley contributes.

"Of course I have, but I can never get through. I take it you have, tried, I mean."

"We've got his number sure enough." As I pocket the mobile Wrigley says "If that's the latest we didn't need to come all this way. You could of brought it in."

"What about the first one? He might have told whoever he was speaking to where he was going next."

"You don't know where he was to start with."

"It was somewhere he wasn't meant to cycle, and he was looking at bones or stones. That sounds like a graveyard to me."

"Shouldn't have been cycling," says Maddock.

"I know that. He said so himself." Frustration drives me to plead "It's worth seeing if I'm right, isn't it?"

As if at a signal I fail to identify, they lift their tankards to their large loose mouths, and I can only assume they resent advice about their methods. They gulp the rest of the water and thrust the tankards at me. "Tell your ma you're waiting to hear," Wrigley says.

Is he warning me not to attempt any investigations of my own? If I hadn't been considering it in the light of their behaviour, I certainly am now. "You can see yourselves out, can you?" I say to regain some authority.

"We can do a lot more than that," Maddock says. They leave me with a stare each, and he leads their heavy way to the door. I stand in my doorway until the backs of their almost neckless heads have jerked down out of sight, and then I follow the damp trail to the bathroom. I have to give my tour, and then I'll decide where to search.

Chapter Thirteen

ANOTHER INTERRUPTED TOUR

Of the people scattered on or around the steps that lead up to Queen Victoria—tourists, office workers taking a late lunch, lawyers or their clients due in court across the square—just two advance to greet the sight of my peaked Pool of Life cap. They're Moira Shea and her male companion. "What have you been doing to yourself?" she cries.

Even if I could bear to pull the peaked cap down, it wouldn't hide all of the bruise on my forehead. "Knocked down in the street," I tell her, suppressing the rest of the memory or rather spending time with it inside my head. "It was just about where someone brought up the atrocities."

"You don't mean all that Ripper stuff again," says her companion.

"Some of us like it, Gerry. You ignore him."

Is the advice for me or about me? "Not the Ripper, no," I say. "Frog Lane. You'll remember somebody mentioned that business."

"That was you," Gerry says as if he wants to laugh. "You said it was Whitechapel."

"Not the place, the atrocities. Did you see who that was?"

They gaze at me until I fancy that's their answer, and then Gerry says "It couldn't have been your dad. He wasn't with us then."

"Is he going to be now?"

"I wish he was," I say too fervently for grammar. "We don't know where he is."

"I expect he can get a long way," Moira says, "on that bike of his."

"So you didn't see who mentioned the atrocities," I say and raise my voice. "Anybody else for Pool of Life?"

Two people step forward—considerably fewer than have booked. Perhaps the rest are daunted by the likely weather; the sky above the river looks pregnant with night and rain, which is why I'm wheeling a golf bag stuffed with six umbrellas, an assemblage I bought on my roundabout way here. One newcomer is a man whose wide dull eyes and thick straight lips appear to be challenging the world to alter their expression. By contrast the slim girl, who clearly isn't with him, seems close to dancing with eagerness to start the tour. I might be more inspired by her if I weren't trying to determine which if either of them is here on Waterworth's behalf. Asking would seem paranoid at best, and so I call "Tour just beginning. Pool of Life."

An unshaven scrawny man in an expensive suit and tie looks tempted to use this as a reason to skip court, but that's the most positive response. "Never mind, you've got us," Moira says. "Blame the wet."

"Are we off to see the pool?" the slim girl says.

"Maybe the one Jung dreamed about," I tell her.

"That's when he saw the pool in all the rain and knew he was in Liverpool." Since the others look blank she adds "It was where all the streets led in his dream. It was lit up with a tree on it and he thought the light was coming from the tree."

The straight-lipped man doles out a voice that's little better than expressionless. "What's that about?"

"He thought it was him."

"Some of us think it's about creativity," I intervene. "There's plenty of that here."

I don't just mean where we're standing, though it's where plays were first performed in Liverpool—the earliest on record, at any rate. A Pace-Egg play was staged at Easter in the Castle, if staging isn't too strong a word for drawing a circle with a wooden sword to contain the performance. *St George and the Serpent* was the title, and I wonder if the monster called Slasher was meant to have come from the sea, since Neptune was among the characters, along with Toss-pot and the King of Egypt and Beelzebub. By now the girl is eager to interrupt. "They think they've killed Slasher," she contributes, "but they forget there's still the egg."

Is this true? It feels like a dream she has planted in my mind. My lack of sleep distorts the image, making me imagine not an egg but a mass of spawn, and I do my best to expel the notion by continuing to speak. Strolling players were so popular in medieval times that one of the seven original streets of the town was named Juggler, although by 1571 the corporation was prohibiting the display of "monstrouse or straunge beasts, or other visions voyde or vayne." On the other hand, four years earlier a theatre down towards the river doubled as a cockpit by order of the corporation "for further and greater repair of gentlemen and others to this town." None of this enlivens the thick-lipped man, and I push my golf bag downhill away from the river.

I wouldn't be surprised if people think I'm selling the umbrellas. Above Lord Street the dark sky looks ready to collapse, and the tubular concrete tower that houses a radio station is supporting a cloud like the nest of a great bird. A few brave tourists flourish cameras on the upper deck of an open-topped bus that passes my party and turns left along North John Street, narrowly missing a phalanx of young mothers pushing buggies and impatient with the traffic lights. The south branch of the street was once Love Lane, leading to the custom house at the oldest dock, where yet another stretch of water was subsequently drained. The dock became Canning Place, where in 1840 creatures with too many limbs or eyes or heads or alternatively too few were exhibited. South John Street is presently a trail of rubble above which helmeted workmen perch on scaffolding that sketches an imminent mall, and I wonder if my father talked to any of them. Perhaps I should ask, but not now. Instead I conduct the party past the stores on Lord Street to Whitechapel.

I do my best to douse the lurid flare of memory by turning to Paradise Street, formerly the Common Shore, across the intersection. Most of it is fenced off by builders, and shops and a pub have occupied the Royal Colosseum. Known to its friends as the Colly, it put on a play written by the stage manager, *Prince's Park and Scotland Road; or, Vice in Liverpool*. Before its theatrical years it was a Unitarian chapel. Theatregoers had to enter through the old graveyard, and a vault was used as a dressing-room. Bones could be found in its depths beyond a flimsy partition, and some of them were used as props in plays. "That's what you call recycling," the eager girl says, stoppering a flask from which she keeps sipping water. "Trust Scousers not to let anything go to waste."

The Sheas, if that's what they both are, seem dutifully amused, the straight-lipped man not at all. I lead the way along Church Street, past a block of shops that has erased Church Alley, the birthplace of James Maybrick. The narrow lane bordered the churchyard of St Peter's, where his brother Michael became known as a precociously youthful organist. When the church was demolished about a century ago, the contents of some of the coffins were found to have turned to stone. How soon did James become jealous of his musical brother? The family lived in the alley until James was thirteen, and perhaps he was one of the children who had to be chased away from Joseph Williamson's grave, whatever made them play some forgotten version of hopscotch on the slabs around it. Williamson died on May Eve in 1840, less than two years after James was born and a year before Michael's birth. The mysterious builder was buried with his wife in a crypt of St Thomas's Church at the far end of Paradise Street, less than five minutes' walk from the Maybrick house. Two minutes would have taken James to Whitechapel or the Colly or the Liver Theatre, originally the Dominion of Fancy, on the upper floor of shops on Church Street. Might this have helped him develop a taste for playing roles? "Maybe he played with the bones," Moira Shea says with a delicious shudder.

I've let myself be diverted by Maybrick on her behalf. This isn't my night tour, and I'm not sleepwalking, whatever Waterworth said. Beyond the site of the Liver Theatre, Bold Street leads uphill to the district where poets of the Beatles era dwelled and wrote and drank. Around the corner in Hanover Street is the Neptune Theatre, which sounds as if it ought to be beside the Pool. Other theatres were—at least, beside the ground that supplanted it—which is why I guide my party past a stone eagle pinioned by a wire cage on the corner of a store to Williamson Square.

Stalls like remnants of the vanished markets are selling football shirts and other symbols of Liverpool's pair of teams. Children run through shivering arcades of water that the pavement raises like instruments of an aquatic ritual. Of the theatres and concert rooms that surrounded the square, only the Playhouse has survived. Its greatest rival, the Theatre Royal, had a pit approached through passages as good as subterranean and "choked with a foul and pestilent congregation of vapours," perhaps from the drained marsh. I can't recall which theatre staged *Water, Water Everywhere!*, a comedy by a local Victorian playwright that included characters such as Captain Squelch and Mistress Trickle. Next to the Playhouse a shop full of aquariums has been replaced by the Fall Well pub, although the real well was farther up the slope of Roe Street. On our way to the site we would once have passed the Parthenon Music Hall, where in 1850 *Daughters of the Deep* was among the staged tableaux. The well was filled in at the end of the eighteenth century, and the Royal Amphitheatre was built opposite. Among its circus acts were the Guising Gorsutchers, a pair of Scouse contortionists so bonelessly supple that they used to challenge the audience to name shapes they couldn't take. These days the theatre is the Royal Court, where one of the earliest productions was the 1888 *Wraiths of the Well* by a Liverpool writer. As I push my burden in front of the theatre I could imagine somebody is mocking me; he's certainly shading himself with an umbrella as he disappears around a plinth behind St George's Hall. Riots in theatres weren't uncommon, and one in the Hall was caused in the 1860s by the Davenport Brothers from London, who claimed that spirits helped them escape from any bonds. Cries of "We've got spirits of our own" were heard, perhaps referring simply to enthusiasm. The straight-lipped man refrains from betraying any, and I feel as if I'm not sufficiently awake to engage his attention. The tour turns along Lime Street beside the Hall and opposite the station, which occupies Waterworth's Field. The man doesn't react to the name, and I manage not to suggest that the place must have been called after some wet character or somebody just worth a dunk. Less than two hundred years ago, when the street was Limekiln-lane, a cock would be turned loose in the field on Shrove Tuesday so that boys with their hands tied behind their backs could run it down and overpower it with their teeth. A bull was baited at the excavation of one of the first docks in some kind of primitive inauguration ritual. A cockpit in Cockspur Street became a place of worship, and a baited bull was once dragged into a box at the Theatre Royal to watch the play, but how does any of this fit together? I'm glad to be distracted when my pocket starts to sing about love, love, love.

I've changed the ringtone yet again. "Excuse me," I say and halt beside a stone lion that looks as if it's ignoring the railway tunnel beneath its feet. The caller's number is withheld. "Hello," I demand, "who's this?"

"Isn't it you?"

Presumably Lucinda means this as a joke, but I'm not in the mood. Before I can say so she wonders "Have I done it again?"

"I don't know what you've done."

"I thought I might be calling while you're on a tour."

I can think of only one reason why she would. "Is my father there?"

"Not this time, Gavin. I've got other reasons to want to speak to you, you know."

How awake am I? I've had no chance to tell her "He went off somewhere yesterday and we haven't heard from him since."

"Oh, Gavin, I'm sorry."

"No need to be that much, I hope."

"Have you told the police?"

"I've a few stories for you about the police. Keep an eye open for him," I say, and to my party "I shouldn't be long," even if I don't know this until I learn "Why were you calling?"

"Is that the river?" I'm about to tell her that she heard a wave of pigeons rising from the paved plateau when she says "I was going to ask if the names out of the book are some kind of joke."

I blink at the quartet who are watching me with various degrees of interest or patience or neither. "Joke," I say but don't invite.

"And who's Waterworth?"

"He's one of your lot. Employed by the council, not the libraries." I slap my forehead, making Moira Shea cry out on my bruised behalf. "You mean an account book," I say. "I don't use one."

"I know. Not that kind of book. I don't expect he'll realise."

I turn away from my party, to be confronted by the building in which Virginia Woolf's uncle went mad. I'm surely not that close to knowing how he felt as I say "Which book, then?"

"Broadbent."

I shut my eyes, because I'm staring so fiercely at the pillars in front of the Hall that they appear to stir like trees in a wind. "Who?"

"R. J. Broadbent. *Annals of the Liverpool Stage*, 1908."

At once I realised where the names I listed came from. The book was part of my research for this very tour, and they're all connected with Liverpool theatres. The book has never been reprinted, but will the names seem as obviously historical as I'm starting to find them? "Try not to worry about it or Deryck either," Lucinda says. "I expect he got carried away by his research."

I'm trying to be reassured by this when she says "Was he on his bicycle?"

"He should have been."

"People might have noticed it, mightn't they? You could put it out on the radio if you need to, but I hope you don't."

"I'd better get back to my routine. Will I see you later?"

"I hope so."

As I pocket the mobile, Moira Shea looks ready to be sympathetic. "Was that your girlfriend again?"

I wish Waterworth's man weren't hearing me confess "It was."

"Say there's no trouble between you. You've already got enough with us."

"You're no trouble."

"We weren't meaning to be. We didn't know about your father. You ought to have put us off and gone looking for him."

"I don't want to keep letting people down."

"How have you been doing that?" says the straight-lipped man.

"His tour went a bit wrong the other night, that's all, and he's giving us this one for nothing."

"I wanted to come when there'd be less murders," Gerry says.

"I hope I haven't been too savage this time, Mr Shea."

He stares at me before declaring "I'm no Shea."

I can only move us onwards, though the slim girl has planted a foot by one paw of the petrified lion to flex her leg.

"Aren't you taking that?" the straight-lipped man says. "You'll have them thinking it's a bomb."

I look back to see the abandoned bag of umbrellas. "I'd have brought them," the girl says.

She isn't helping any more than Moira Shea and her companion did. I grab the handle and shove the bag past the statue. To our right, where buses swing past a trio of derelict cinemas that may dream of lighting up their screens, we could visit the site of St James's Hall, in which Florence Maybrick of Alabama was made to feel at home by the American Slave Serenaders, "the only combination of genuine darkies in the world." I spare Gerry the reference, and I don't know whether the chamber of horrors in the waxworks on the ground floor ever featured the Ripper, although the pale gleeful inhuman faces of plunderers boarding a wrecked boat became famous for giving children nightmares. Instead I lead the party past the Empire Theatre, which is offering Aristophanes in Scouse, opposite the Hall. When the theatre was the Alexandra, Henry Irving played Prospero in a production of *The Tempest* so vigorous that the auditorium was flooded, some said from beneath. Beyond it, at the foot of the Everton slope, the Adelphi Theatre—Delly to its friends—was known for local plays. One bill included *The Bride of Everton; or, Liverpool in the Olden Time* and a curtain-raiser, *Led by a Light; or, The Marsh Maiden's Suitors.* The Delly was built as a circus, sometimes flooded by the upper reaches of the Pool. An unsigned reminiscence in the *Liverpool Porcupine,* a Victorian satirical journal, suggested that some of the circus performers "took more to the water than they did to the ring." I'm making for the site, past the old law courts at the top of the hill where the library stands, when my pocket recommences chanting about love.

"I have to take this," I announce, because the display shows my parents' number. "Hello?"

"Gavin? You'll be busy, won't you? Have you got just a few moments?"

"As long as you need," I say, because my mother isn't as calm as she's trying to sound.

"I won't take much of your time. I don't suppose there's anything we can do." Nevertheless she seems to have taken me at my word, since she falls quiet until I'm close to prompting her. "The police have found something," she says, and then there's another silence.

Chapter Fourteen

Gangland Wake

When I tell the taxi driver on the rank in Whitechapel where I want to go, he lowers his stout head to peer at me. "That where you live?"

"I'll just be visiting."

He gives his head a shake that would disarray his hair if he had any. "Wouldn't, mate."

Is he one of the drivers who won't accept a fare unless they think the distance makes it worth their while? "I'd like to all the same," I tell him.

His shrug resembles the preamble to a fight. "Your funeral."

At once I remember why he would prefer not to take this journey, but I'm not about to be deterred. I've already had to conduct my party back to Derby Square, since I couldn't risk cutting another tour short, and take the bag of umbrellas to my flat, where no message was waiting. I climb into the taxi before the driver can change his mind.

The taxi swerves away from Whitechapel but not my memory of it. It speeds up Stanley Street, past a seagull pecking at an abandoned Frugoburger in the lap of a statue of Eleanor Rigby on a bench, and veers into Victoria Street towards the Haymarket, where the end of Dale Street used to house the Mechanical Exhibition Rooms, renamed the Penny Hop. The place exhibited working models—the Storm at Sea, Napoleon the Fortune-Teller, Neptune and His Brood Rising from the Pool. Why am I bringing this to mind while I have no audience? We cross the tunnel entrance and follow Islington towards the ridge, where my mother is staying close to the phone. As the house comes in sight the driver says "Who's going to do it, do you reckon?"

The question unnerves me until I grasp what prompted it—hordes of red-shirted football fans marching beneath the dark afternoon sky down to the Liverpool ground. I feel as if I've become trapped in the past as well as in anxiety, because the crowds seem as unreal as a dream the landscape is having. I don't even know which team is playing Liverpool, and I can only tell the driver "I've no idea."

"Aren't you from round here?"

"Very much so. I'm just not interested in football."

He stares out of the visor of the mirror as if I've revealed I'm worse than foreign. I might wonder by way of retort whether he's aware that Thomas de Quincey had an opium reverie up here that transformed the waters of Liverpool into an enormous consciousness. The spectacle of the red horde tramping past a disused library near where he had the vision makes me yearn for the past as the taxi swings inland.

Along Breck Road the uniformed matchgoers thin out like the highest reach of a stream, clogged by shoppers and gossips bunched in front of dozens of small shops. A pub is advertising the Scouse alternative to Toad in the Hole, a sausage casserole called Frog in a Bog. Past Anfield the road broadens and grows domestic with houses before it crosses Queen's Drive, the wide avenue that describes an arc through much of outer Liverpool, linking the riverside at Bootle— the farthest reach of High Rip violence—to Aigburth, close to another stretch of waterfront and the house where James Maybrick died. Beyond Queen's Drive is Norris Green, across a roundabout under a bridge. Goods wagons clank overhead like links of an enormous chain, but this isn't where my father called from; there's too much traffic, and the acoustic isn't hollow enough. I try not to be distracted by the memory as the taxi ventures into Norris Green.

A grassy strip planted with trees divides the long straight road lined with houses, the public face of the suburb. Soon it's interrupted by a crossroads, the left branch leading between two crescents of shops with signs as faded as old photographs or displaying ghosts of letters stolen from their names. All the shops are shut out of respect, however enforced, for the funeral of a teenage gangster shot by another suburban gang. The driver swings the taxi across the intersection into the other half of the estate.

Mounds in the roadway—not ancient graves but hindrances to speeding—slow us down at once. We're surrounded by boxy twin houses with steep red roofs pulled low over their bedroom windows, and I could imagine that the dark sky is weighing the roofs down. Many of the houses have sprouted ornamental lamps or stained-glass porches or acquired windows meant to seem antique, but others are boarded up. Another four streets radiate from a roundabout, and they're all as deserted as wasteland. The only sign of life is a thickset dog that glances up nervously from licking its wounds beyond the elaborate wrought-iron gate of a front garden flattened by concrete, but I'm more concerned with the roundabout. It's apparently the one across rather than around which my father's bicycle was ridden like a machine tougher than it is, buckling the wheels.

The rider still managed to pedal several hundred yards into Swinebrook Crescent, where he abandoned the bicycle in the middle of the road, presumably to obstruct the police car that was chasing him. Most of the crescent is derelict, although a few windows among all the tinned ones are defiantly curtained. The houses face a semicircle of grassland that may have been intended to recall a village green. It's overgrown now and occupied by dozens of seagulls, some of which raise their wings at our approach as if they're claiming the territory. We're miles from the sea, and I can't help feeling that, just as the gangs have regressed to savagery, the green is reverting to a marsh. As I wonder if this underlies the streets the driver says "Which house?"

"Can we drive around there while I see?"

I peer at the houses as the taxi coasts forward. If we're being observed from the occupied properties, the watchers are staying unseen. Several of the sheets of metal nailed across front doors have been wrenched loose. Perhaps the cyclist fled into one of the reopened houses, but how does this help? Did I fancy that visiting the area might give me some insight into my father's activities? I've seen no reason why he would come anywhere near. I feel less awake than ever, so that the deserted estate has begun to resemble a dream of habitation. Eventually the driver says "What are you looking for?"

"I don't really know."

He brakes so abruptly that my head rediscovers its ache. "Better pay up and get out."

"Sorry, do you think I'm here for something illegal?" When he only stares at me in the mirror I protest "I'm looking for my father."

"Make your mind up. Don't you know where your own dad lives? That's no way to treat your family."

"Of course I do, and it's not here. His bicycle was stolen and this is where it ended up."

"They use them for deliveries." No doubt the driver has drugs or guns in mind. "Stolen where?" he says.

"That's what I'm trying to find out."

"Funny way to do it if you ask me."

I'm afraid he's about to insist on my leaving the taxi. "I think I've seen all there is to see," I tell him.

He sends the taxi out of the crescent with a screech of wheels. The seagulls rise as if the wilderness has heaved them up to circle shrieking overhead. They might almost be signalling our presence to the crowd that confronts us on our way back to the main road. The funeral and its aftermath must be over, because the streets are suddenly full of people, most of them using mobile phones, even the drivers and cyclists. All of them stare at the taxi, and every pedestrian turns to watch it pass. Stones clatter against both sides of the vehicle, and then one cracks the window behind my head. I fumble for my mobile, gasping "Shall I call the police?"

"Leave it. They're not interested," the driver snarls and accelerates over the speed bumps, almost thumping my head against the cracked window.

He keeps glaring in the mirror at the damage or at me as he leaves the estate behind. He doesn't speak while he retraces the journey, and I don't until the taxi turns along the ridge of Everton. "This is fine," I say.

"What's fine about it?"

"It's where my parents live."

"I thought you were supposed to be looking for one."

I might have offered to pay for the damage, but I've had enough of his suspicion. I hand him exactly the amount on the meter and wait for him to release the door. Once he finishes thinking about it I emerge beneath a sky as black as the cab. The wooden For Sale flag shivers in a wind as I open the gate with a clang of the latch. The colours of the house—bright red walls, yellow door and windows, orange curtains framing nets—seem determinedly cheerful, positively forced. So does the floral dress that my mother is wearing again, though surely not all the time since my last visit. Is it tighter on her? Perhaps she has been eating for comfort; she looks almost bloated. She blinks past me at the taxi that's belatedly departing, and then she watches me approach between the rockeries, on which I'm taken aback to see weeds. Her face is owning up to so little expression that I'm apprehensive before she speaks. "I don't think they're looking for your father any more."

Chapter Fifteen

WATERED DOWN

The kitchen is resolutely bright as well. The fluorescent tube is switched on, and much of the small room gleams white—the walls and the cupboards on them, the cooker and the refrigerator, the round table and its rounded chairs. Although the sun is behind black clouds above the river, the kitchen feels as if it's lit up in the middle of the night, and I imagine my mother waiting sleeplessly in here, gazing down the slope towards the giant birds perched at the Pier Head while she yearns for the sound of the gate. On her way along the hall she says only "You'll have a hot cup, won't you? Kettle's on." I hope she's trying to contain her anxiety rather than too distracted to concentrate, and so I don't speak while she takes two Cavern Not Tavern mugs from the cupboard beside the tinny sink. I manage to keep silent while she's handling the kettle and then a bottle of milk. Once she replaces that in the refrigerator I risk asking "Why do you think they've stopped?"

She hands me a mug of coffee and sits at the table to sip while she ponders her answer. "They seem to think it was him on the bicycle."

"You're joking," I protest and am dismayed to see her lips begin shaping a smile in response. "I mean they must be. That was never him."

"They said the man fitted his description. They didn't see his face."

"I don't care what he looked like. Why would he have been running away from the police? I'll bet they didn't tell you bicycles round there are used for guns and drugs."

"They did actually, Gavin." She looks apologetic as she says "I think they think that's why he was there."

I've run out of expressions of disbelief. I take a gulp of coffee and demand "They're accusing him of what exactly?"

"Of buying something like that, and that's why he ran off."

"They said that to you?"

"Pretty well. They gave me that impression," she says, looking sorrier than ever. "They did say he's been behaving strangely lately."

"How can they know that?"

"From someone at the library, apparently."

I open my mouth and shut it again, feeling stupid as a fish, before I say "Someone."

"They didn't tell me who. I'm sure it couldn't have been your girlfriend."

I see that she can't bear to think so. She doesn't need to add "I liked her, Gavin. I think she's right for you. Don't fall out with her over this, will you? We don't want to lose anyone else."

"I hope we haven't lost anyone." This leaves her comment ominous, and so I ask "Just what did they say?"

"He made such a scene over something that didn't exist that the library had to call someone to take him away. That sounds like drugs, doesn't it? And the way he's been behaving about water."

"Come on, you'd know if he was taking any drugs."

"He has changed, Gavin. Some of the ideas he's been having recently I can't follow at all. And some days I've hardly seen him. Suppose he's been going out to take something? Then I wouldn't know."

"You've only started thinking like this since the police came, haven't you? Don't let them get to you. You're tired, that's all."

"You look as if you are, Gavin. I don't want to tire you out when you've got so much to do." With some pride and more doubtfulness she adds "I did ring up the radio station to ask if anyone saw where his bike might have been taken from. That was before the police came."

"And had anyone?"

"They'll give my number to anyone who rings." She has started to let herself look hopeful when she glances upwards. "What's that?"

I've been hearing the soft regular sounds for some time. I thought it was raining again, but the sky is suppressing its downpour. "It's upstairs," my mother says. "It's in his room."

"I'll see."

I hold up a hand to forestall her, but she follows without bothering to be quiet. From the hall the sounds suggest that someone's pacing on tiptoe upstairs. I grab the unsteady banister for extra speed and run up two stairs at a time as noiselessly as I can to switch on the light in my father's workroom.

It's empty apart from the desk and the clutter that covers and surrounds it. There's barely a path between stacks of books and papers from the door to the chair in front of the desk. The room is silent, not least because I'm holding my breath. Then the noise emerges from hiding, and I see movement. Several words of a print-out on top of a pile of books swell up as if they're being magnified for my attention, and then they spread into a stain, blackening the page.

Another drop of water starts to dangle from the ceiling. As I step forward it elongates and detaches itself. Surely I'm hurrying, and only lack of sleep makes me feel as oddly sluggish as the drip looks. It wins the race and splashes on the page, turning the words in the midst of a description of a hunt into soggy nonsense. I seem to glimpse a reference to some fluid transformation of the hunters' quarry, no doubt a legend, as I snatch the unstable pile out of the way. "All right," I tell my mother. "It's just—"

"It isn't," she cries and lurches into the room. "Help me."

She stoops with a groan to gather more than an armful of

my father's research and staggers onto the landing. She's heading for their bedroom when she falters. "Where's it coming from?"

"It's been raining so much that it must have collected under the roof."

She darts to the stairs and teeters on the topmost while she swings around to watch me. "We need to take everything down."

I'm close to grabbing her to steady her. "Shall I take some of that for you?"

"Don't worry about me. I can manage." She demonstrates by tramping down several stairs, faster than I think she intended. "You bring his computer," she says.

She's pressing her cheek against the top of the pile to hold it tighter if not from displaced affection. While I can't grasp her concern for his ideas so soon after she was criticising them, I shouldn't judge her when she's so anxious. I disconnect the various leads on the computer tower and hug it as I make my careful way downstairs. The metal feels clammy, unless that's me. My mother has dumped her burden in a corner of the front room. "Might the damp get to it there?" I wonder.

She drags the stack a few inches away from the walls and stands up panting. "I must need someone else to do my thinking for me," she says, "I'm in such a state."

I plant the tower beside the television and dodge her on the landing as she returns with another rickety stack. I grab the computer monitor and plod to the front room, where the accumulating clutter reminds me of my previous visit—I could fancy that my mother is willing the disorder to magic my father home. Soon she resorts to piling books and papers in the hall. "They'll be all right there for now," she assures me or herself. "I don't mind where they are so long as they're safe."

Is she applying the same thought to my father? I run upstairs in an attempt to head her off from carrying too much.

As I lift another stack, the latest drip catches my wrist. It's larger and thicker than I would expect, and retains a shape like an amoeba on my skin until I set off downstairs, at which point it trickles onto my hand, extending tendrils towards the gaps between my knuckles. This maddens me, and I almost sprawl headlong in my haste to get rid of the papers before the water can reach them. "What's happened to you?" my mother cries.

"Just wet," I say and hurry to rinse my hand and wrist under the bathroom tap. I use soap as well and towel my skin vigorously, which only aggravates the tingling I wanted to assuage. We finish clearing the workroom, and the mocking sound of an irrepressible drip follows us into the hall. My mother releases a protracted sigh and leans on the creaky banister while she rubs the small of her back. "Thanks for being such a help," she says. "Do you want to make me a promise?"

"What about?"

She seems disappointed by my wariness. "Don't have an upset with your girlfriend over us. We've enough to worry about," she says, and upstairs a drip punctuates the end of her sentence as if she has called the water forth.

Chapter Sixteen

STRONG MATERIAL

As I tramp down Folly Lane or rather Islington, away from my parents' house, the weight of the sky laden with darkness appears to press layer after layer of the cityscape into the river. The students at the university halfway down the slope have gone home for the summer, but delegates at a conference on the history of seaside resorts are converging on a campus theatre opposite the Collegiate, which looks more like a stage set than ever. In the middle of the eighteenth century Liverpool was a seaside resort, bringing actors up north to entertain the holidaymakers while the London theatres were shut for the season. I'm struck by the notion that everyone was enticed here by water. Quite a few of the delegates are anticipating some of that and carrying umbrellas. As the sun glares through a crack in the darkness I seem to glimpse the blossoming of one before its shabby owner vanishes around a corner.

Thirst is making my throat feel as rough as my skin where I wiped off the drip. I'm alongside London Road now, and I imagine drinking from the Moss Lake stream that fed the Pool. The thought brings an image of silhouettes lapping at the Pool or raising handfuls of it to their faces. The vision is lit by a moon, but I can't distinguish how many of the drinkers are human, nor whether the forms rising to meet them are their reflections. The image is so vivid while it lasts that I could think my thirst is giving me a fever.

Two hundred years ago I would have seen stalls in the Welly Market ahead, between St George's Hall and the old law courts. I assume the nickname originated with the well around which the market flourished until outbreaks of violence led to a ban, and perhaps Wellington kept the name alive. He's perched on a towering column beside a fountain, where children are dancing around the inside of the stone bowl as if they're performing a ritual to summon up water. The sight exacerbates my thirst as I trudge down Shaw's Brow, where a lunatic asylum faced whatever was to be seen on the heath—"lights which belong on the marsh," according to one inmate, who also spoke of hopping figures lit by them or from within. The asylum was demolished by the time Shaw's Brow became William Brown Street. The library halfway down the slope contains a cafeteria, but my thirst can wait until I've had a few words with Lucinda.

The automatic doors wince aside, and the lift carries me up to Local History. Lucinda isn't behind the counter or among the tables mounted with microfilm readers. She isn't in the inner room, where tables are overlooked by token shelves of books. The counter is staffed by a plump youngish man in a pinstriped suit and narrow rimless glasses. His round face surmounted by pale cropped hair seems determined to appear older than its years, with a pallid rectangular moustache to compensate for its paucity of eyebrows. No doubt he's preparing to unleash a query as sombre as his expression until I say "Where's Lucinda?"

"She's quite busy just now."

"Can you let her know I'm here? I need a word."

"What about, please?"

"She'll know, or if she doesn't she soon will." When this fails to shift him or his expression I say "So can I see her?"

"She's nowhere you can go, I'm afraid."

She must be in the stacks. "Then you'd better tell her I'm here."

"And who would you be?"

"Say Gavin."

"Gavin . . ."

"Meadows," I resent having to tell him.

"Ah." Even more meaningfully he adds "Yes."

"Yes what?" I say fiercely enough for several readers to frown in my direction.

"You were here the other night, weren't you? And your father was. I hope there'll be no repetition of the incident."

"I wish there would," I blurt and have to explain "If it means he shows up. We don't know where he is."

Perhaps the librarian thinks I'm bidding for sympathy, because he owns up to no emotion. "So are you telling her?" I rather more than prompt.

"About your father."

"She knows about him. About me."

"I'll be dealing with it."

Presumably he means when more staff appear, since he can't leave the library unattended or contact her by phone. "I'll catch up on my reading till you do," I say.

Even once I've given him my reader's ticket that Lucinda made, he's in no hurry to release the barrier that admits me to the inner room. Beyond it a few readers are poring over books and maps that they've requested. More in search of distraction than for research I make for the shelves and find a book of local curiosities. It's published by Philip, Son & Nephew, the bookshop where my mother worked. The author is Richard Whittington-Egan, a local journalist who wasn't averse to embellishing his material. Here's "Cylinder of Horror," which confirms the tale of the Victorian corpse found in a tube on a bomb site. A librarian returns from wherever she has been, and another wheels a trolley out of the stacks, at which point their bespectacled colleague leaves the counter without glancing at me. As I wait for his reappearance or rather Lucinda's I read about a Liverpool wrestler called Malleable Mal. He became a legend of the Stadium, which was built over the site of St Paul's Churchyard off Tithebarn Street, a short walk from James Maybrick's office and close to Cross's Trading Menagerie ("Largest Trading Zoological Establishment on the Earth—Send for Requirements—No

Species so Rare that It Cannot Be Obtained"). The wrestler's detractors called him Flabby Mal, apparently because of his fondness for smothering opponents by falling flat—no, hardly flat—on them. He never lost a match, since no amount of twisting and wrenching his limbs could force him to submit, while he seemed able to slither out of any hold and bounce back from the severest forearm smash. He ended his career as half of a tag team, though his partner Brutal Bertie refused to share a dressing-room with him, supposedly because he found the sight of a naked Mal too repulsive. The public only ever saw Mal fully clothed or, in the ring, dressed in a rubbery white fabric from his neck to his wrists and ankles. As a boy Whittington-Egan saw him wrestle, and describes Mal's body as resembling "tripe wrapped up tight so that it wouldn't burst in a housewife's bag of shopping." After Mal's retirement the young journalist set out to track him down, but the only address he could trace proved to belong to an abandoned cellar near the oldest dock. Shouldn't the man with the narrow glasses have returned by now? I leave the book on the table and make for the counter. "Excuse me, what's happened to your colleague?"

The younger and taller of the girls turns with a ready smile. "Which one would that be?"

"Whatever his name is. The fellow with the windows." When squinting between two pairs of my fingers fails to signify him I say "Glasses, what there was of them."

Perhaps my father could make this funnier, but her amusement has begun to look dutiful. "He's gone home," her workmate says.

"Can someone else help?"

The younger librarian is still amused. It may be her natural state, though I suspect it would change if my anger broke loose. Antagonising the staff might waste time or achieve worse, and so I say "I'll fill in a slip."

Part of the problem may have been that the staff visit the stacks only to fetch books, and I've thought of one—the work of the local occultist my father was discussing with Lucinda. I take a squat elongated boxy catalogue off the shelf once I've managed to dredge up the name.

Strong, John. The form of the listing makes him sound like a wrestler, but he's the author of *Glimpses of Absolute Power*. Did he publish anything else? Presumably not, since the neighbouring pages refer to other authors—and then I notice marks on the back of his solitary page, like the faint reflection of another entry. The traces of print are unrelated to the next listing, and they aren't the reverse of his. Nevertheless when I hold the catalogue up to the overhead light I see that the first of the mirrored words are Strong, John.

The rest of the traces are even fainter. They've begun to twitch, or my eyes have, by the time I decide that the next words are "Unpublished papers." I would fill in a request slip if I could decipher the classification number. Instead I take the catalogue to the counter. "Excuse me, can you tell me what this is?"

The tall girl settles her amused gaze on me before saying "A catalogue."

I could easily find her humour infuriating. Several readers are disturbed by a loud hollow knock—the sound of the catalogue striking the counter. "This," I say and dent the wad of pages with my finger.

She eases the catalogue away from me and starts to read the entry opposite the traces of print. "Not that," I protest and point at them. "There."

I feel as if I'm trapped in an unbearably lethargic dream as she makes to turn the page. "There, where I'm showing you," I don't quite shout, poking at the page again. "Here, on the back."

When she leans forward to examine the sheaf, two translucent drops dangling from her ears sway as if the earrings are about to fall. "It's this," she says, indicating the adjacent entry. "It's some of the ink."

"No, it's from something else that was there."

Her colleague joins in peering at the sheaf and jabs a stubby finger at the opposite page. "It's from that, no question."

The entry is for Strong, Johanna. Unreported rapes: thirteen case studies from Liverpool's docklands. The book is published by Liverpool University Press, but none of this convinces me. "I'm sorry, you're both wrong," I insist, "and I want to know—"

"Let me." The elder librarian slides the catalogue towards her and underlines the reversed words with a clipped fingernail. "Johanna Strong," she reads as if she's dealing with a child. "Unreported, you can see what else it says for yourself."

"It's nothing like that," I say, recapturing the catalogue. "For a start, that's not rape."

"May we ask what makes you say that?"

I feel accused by both of them—her colleague is abruptly unamused—and so I say "Can't you spell?"

"I'm afraid I don't appreciate the relevance. If you'd kindly—"

"That doesn't say rape. It would be epar, don't you see? This says papers. Unpublished papers by John Strong."

The tall girl parts her lips, but it's her colleague who says "May we know your name?"

"Gavin Meadows. Pool of Life, that's me, and yes, my father was asking about this. One of you told him it didn't exist."

She doesn't quite look at the tall girl as she murmurs "I think you'd better call—"

"No need to get security. I'm just asking about your stock like he did, for God's sake. Asking you to do your job." I pick up the catalogue but refrain from brandishing it in case it resembles a weapon. "Lucinda knows about it," I tell them. "Where is she?"

"I'm afraid I couldn't tell you. Now could you please give me—"

"I'm keeping hold of it. I want to show her." I gesture with the catalogue at the door to the stacks, and the pages flap wide. "I'll wait till she comes out," I announce.

"I'm sorry, that won't be—"

The woman falls silent as I turn on her, waving the catalogue. I've noticed what I should have seen at once. Between the inner edge of the page for John Strong and the one for Johanna is a torn scrap of paper. "Tell me you can't see that," I say, no longer knowing how loud. "Someone's ripped a page out. Who did that? When? What for?"

Well before I finish, the women are looking at each other. "Call security now," the elder woman says.

I stalk across the library, past readers who flinch as I flourish the catalogue. I hammer with it on the door to the stacks. "Lucinda, you're in there," I yell. "Come out. We have to talk." She hasn't responded when a uniformed guard appears behind the counter. "All right, you win. I'm going," I inform him and drop the catalogue on a table with a thud that resounds through the room. I grab my ticket from a box on the counter and vault over the barrier to march through the lobby and down the stairs. As I emerge from the building, leaves in St John's Gardens start to twitch, and the trees shake. The sky sets about delivering its darkness, and if I had any thoughts worth the name they would be drowned by the storm.

Chapter Seventeen

SOME HELP

I ought to phone the police as soon as the door shuts behind me—if the mobile in my sodden pocket has survived the downpour, surely I can—but I'm desperate for a drink and a shower. I gulp handfuls of water from the tap between peeling off my clothes in the bathroom, and then I climb into the bath. The shower aggravates my confusion; the onslaught of water does, and the idea that I'm using it to wash away water. As I perform the slow ritual dance that it entails, a sentence I leafed past in Whittington-Egan drifts back to me. It was in one of his rants about uncommon sex, a subject that appeared to fascinate as much as it disgusted him. He spends an entire chapter in deploring gay men or at best pitying them for their failure to conform, but I wish I hadn't been so quick to pass over the next chapter, where I read "As late as the nineteenth century, the detestable vice known as 'frogging' was rife in the cellars of Whitechapel." He meant the street in Liverpool, and perhaps that was all he could bring himself to write about the practice. The Internet may be less reticent about the meaning of the term.

As I reach for a towel I'm troubled by the reflection in the steamy mirror. I wipe away the condensation in time to see a trickle of moisture run down my face. I could almost think my bruised forehead is exuding the fluid—and then I realise what's troubling me. Was my mother too worried about my father to notice the injury? I mustn't blame her, and I should be doing more on their behalf. I towel myself fiercely and grab the mobile from the floor outside the bathroom and redial the police.

An operator takes the occurrence number in exchange for a generous helping of silence. I'm about to ask whether anyone's there when a familiar but hardly friendly voice demands "Yes?"

"Is that Constable Wrigley?" Since this earns no answer, I offer "Constable Maddock?"

"Something like that." As I wonder if I've demoted them he says "What's it about this time?"

"The same as last." In case he thinks I mean Whitechapel I add "My father."

"We said we'd let one of you know."

"Is that what you've been saying to my mother?"

"Yes, her."

"That's not the way I heard it." When this falls short of provoking a response I say "She thinks you don't think he's worth looking for."

"What else does she reckon she knows?"

"That you're treating him as some kind of suspect, which is ridiculous."

"Why'd we give up looking if we think he's one of those?"

I ought to have wondered about that. Is my mother more confused than I realised? Rather than admit the possibility to the policeman I say "I thought that's why you think he was in Norris Green."

"So why do you reckon he was?"

"I can't see any reason to assume he was at all. We don't know where his bicycle was stolen from, do we?"

"If it was pinched why didn't he report it? He'd got his mobile on him."

"Maybe it doesn't work where he is." I'm even less happy to have to suggest "Unless he was attacked and they took the phone too."

I remember the shrill clink that put a stop to his last call. Was he hit with the brick? I imagine my father lying somewhere, surely no worse than unconscious. Could the assault have damaged his brain? Perhaps he's wandering the city, having forgotten where he lives and I do, if he hasn't taken refuge somewhere. Perhaps he doesn't know who he is. These feel like dreams I'm trying not to have in case they come true, visions that hardly seem to belong to me, but of course the idea itself is no more than a dream. In an attempt to bring myself back to reality I ask "Where is the bicycle, by the way?"

"We're keeping it for evidence."

"Fingerprints, you mean?"

"Something like that."

I assume he's saying that detection has become more sophisticated. "Have you followed up the messages you came to hear?"

"Thought you were at home," he says so triumphantly that I feel observed and uncomfortable with my nakedness. "Trying to keep out of the wet, are you?"

This is followed by a rush of static I could mistake for a wave on a shore. Is he on a mobile somewhere in the open? "The messages," I prompt.

"Still looking."

Since he conveys no enthusiasm I'm provoked to say "How hard?"

"How hard are you after?"

"As hard as we ought to expect."

"You'll be seeing us when we've got something to give you."

With this he's gone, apparently washed away by static. I hurry to the bathroom for my towelling robe, and then I head for my workroom. I've already checked that there are no messages on the answering machine, but I've yet to look on the computer. All the new emails are impersonal, and can't distract me from remembering the names I sent Waterworth. Perhaps he'll think they're simply British.

The Frugoget search engine reveals that frogging can refer to ornamental lace or the corruption of a text, neither of which helps. My gaze wanders to the window, outside which the night has overtaken the dark of the storm. Raindrops are still trickling down the glass and the windows opposite, so that I can't tell whether anything is moving in the dimness of the office. When I strain my eyes I seem to glimpse at least one large figure writhing deep in the gloom, as if performing a sluggish dance that appears to involve changes of shape. As I grip the sides of the desk and lean forward, eyes stinging, my mobile strikes up its band.

I straighten up, and the dancing shapes sink into the darkness and vanish. I interrupt the ringtone before it can go on too much about love. "Where are you?" I want to know.

"Just outside," Lucinda says.

"Then come up. We need to talk."

"Let's, but you come down. I know where's best." Through a rush of static, unless it's a wind along the street, she says "We'll go to our place by the river."

Chapter Eighteen

AT THE MOUTH

Slamming the door of Lucinda's car dislodges rain from the roof, so that half a dozen ropes of water wriggle down the windscreen. Beyond them, at the end of the street, a dim blurred figure appears to swell up before vanishing towards the river. Lucinda gives me a tentative smile and reaches out a hand but, observing my mood, doesn't quite touch me. Instead she drives along the street and turns downhill.

This takes us past the oldest theatres, all of them unnamed—one in Cockpit Yard, another along the Old Ropery, a third in Drury Lane, where a popular eighteenth-century play would end with "a procession of a human sacrifice after the manner of the ancients." Theatre audiences, especially sailors, were so liable to grow violent that an armed soldier would be stationed at either end of the stage to keep order. During a riot at the Drury Lane theatre an actor costumed as an aquatic creature was shot, though one report insists he was a member of the audience and the cause of the disorder. Some of these streets no longer exist, and a fountain constructed of dozens of pivoting buckets stands where a theatre once stood. The buckets are dormant though dripping with rain, and somebody homeless or drunk is squatting under them. I lose sight of the bulky glistening shape before the car swings onto the Strand opposite the Liver Building, where the metal birds perched on the pair of clock towers are rigged like masts. Histories of Liverpool suggest that Coleridge had the ancient Liver Bird in mind when he conceived the albatross. He certainly visited Liverpool, and we may imagine him deep in a reverie on the Birmingham coach—the "lousy Liverpool," as it was known, on which he did indeed catch lice. One biography suggests that he imagined more of the *Ancient Mariner* in Liverpool—the slimy creatures from the sea, the nameless dweller in the ocean with power over all the creatures of the water—but why am I swamped by these thoughts? They must be conjured up by Lucinda's silence and mine, but they feel as if I'm not thinking so much as being employed to think.

Since Victorian times there has been a walk upriver from the Pier Head, but building work has cut off the route. Lucinda drives along the dock road, which used to be divided by an overhead railway that was torn down more than fifty years ago. Several boys ride their rearing two-wheeled steeds along the central reservation, pedalling towards Aigburth. Another demolition has exposed the location of the first dock, where an animal is prowling amid the debris. Most likely it's a dog, however it defeated the high fence. Perhaps it swam along the river; the whitish form, which elongates as it leaps several feet, looks wet, and there's no water in the dock. I lose sight of it as Lucinda steers the car off the main road, towards the warehouses surrounding the Albert Dock.

They've been converted into apartments above shops and restaurants. One block houses the Tate Gallery, where a Dada exhibition is outraging sensibilities with the long-banned *Three Persons of God*, a trio of urinals. Lucinda drives around the warehouses and parks at the edge of the promenade, beside a ship's mast rigged to the pavement. As I climb out I hear a soft but enormous lapping beyond the sea wall. Did I once imagine that the waves in the river were calling to those in the dock? I must have been young or asleep. Apart from the ripples there's silence except for a radio presenter's voice beyond an apartment balcony until Lucinda says "Are you going to tell me what's wrong?"

"I'm not the only one who hasn't been talking."

"I didn't want an argument while I was driving, Gavin."

"So you knew there was going to be one."

She locks the car and gazes wistfully at me across the wet roof. "Let's walk," she says and then frowns. "What have you done to your head?"

"Nothing." I don't want to be reminded of Whitechapel just now, let alone to talk about the incident. "It's fine," I tell her, though the question has quickened the ache in my forehead.

The promenade extends behind the warehouses. Beyond railings festooned with occasional lifebelts, a second fence composed of chains strung between cones is silhouetted against the restless water. Lucinda steps through a gap and sets off between the fences, towards skyscrapers multiplying around the Pier Head. She likes to walk close to the water, but there isn't room for two abreast, and so I pace her on the landward side of the fence. The slopping of dark water below the promenade seems to pace her too. When she looks away from the advancing tide I say "Why didn't you come out when I needed you?"

"Aren't I allowed to be busy sometimes? Maybe even too busy to come as soon as you call?"

"Like expecting me to answer my mobile whatever I'm doing, you mean." Before I've finished speaking I see how irrationally unfair this is, which only aggravates my anger. "I did a lot more than call," I object. "You must have heard how important it was."

"As a matter of fact I didn't. I was on my break."

"I'd have thought you'd have heard me wherever you were."

"That isn't something to be proud of, Gavin." She halts and turns to the river, so that she appears to be confiding in it. "We did hear some noise in the staffroom," she murmurs. "We thought it was more demolition work."

When she doesn't move I hurry to the next gap and tramp back to join her. She seems intent on the river, where innumerable ripples glint as if a vast underlying pallid mass is showing through the blackness. A buoy rocks in their midst, and alongside the opposite bank a ferry ploughs through the reflected lights of Seacombe towards the bay, but the view is largely of wakeful whispering blackness. I feel as if I'm distracting Lucinda from it by saying "I'll bet your colleagues had fun telling you all about it when you got back to the counter."

"Why do you say that? It was no fun for anyone."

"Tell me what they said, then."

"No, I want you to say, Gavin. I want you to tell me what happened. What was it all about?"

She still hasn't looked away from the water. I know she finds it peaceful at night, but now the river feels oppressively lulling. I could almost fancy that her speech has borrowed a surreptitiously hypnotic rhythm from the waves. My lack of sleep must be to blame, because I feel as if the insistent ripples are drawing me down, robbing me of balance, until I retreat to the gap in the barrier. "Let's sit down first," I call.

Metal benches are spaced along the promenade within the shadow of the wall in front of the apartments. I'm making for the nearest bench when I see another couple on the one next to the mast. Perhaps they didn't want us to realise we were being overheard, since they've made so little noise. I move to a further bench and don't speak until Lucinda is seated, an arm's length from me but not touching. "Did they show you what I found?"

"You still aren't telling me. You're asking."

"You should have listened to my father. There was an entry in your catalogue for the papers he wanted."

"Gavin," Lucinda says so quietly that it's almost swallowed by the repetitions of the waves. "There wasn't, honestly."

"You looked, did you?"

"Certainly I did, when he came in, and there was nothing at all."

"How about this time?"

"Gavin," she repeats, and the water seems to. "Why would I look again?"

I'm distracted by the slopping of the river. I could imagine that the sound isn't just beyond the promenade—that it's to my left as well. At this distance I'm easily confused into fancying that the occupants of the other bench are making some of the noises. All I can distinguish is that they're embracing with their faces pressed together, and I concentrate on saying "You could see the print on the back of the other page, and there was a bit left of the one somebody wants us to think wasn't there."

"Nobody else saw them, Gavin."

"No need to keep saying my name." Instead of this I retort "Who are you going to believe, people who won't admit what they're seeing, or me and my father?"

"My own eyes, Gavin. Please don't go the same way as Deryck."

The couple on the other bench must be anticipating a downpour. As far as I can see they're waterproofed from head to foot in shiny black material that even covers much of their heads, concealing their ears. Could it be some kind of fetish? This might help to explain the passion that thrusts their faces together so fiercely that they appear to have flattened, merging the heads into a single roundish mass. I attempt to ignore the illusion while I say "That's exactly what I will be doing."

"Why would you want to do that?" She sounds worse than disappointed. "You've got your tours," she says. "They're you."

"I'll have time for both. I'll make time. If the police can't do their job, it's up to me."

"What are you saying they aren't doing?"

"Finding him. Seems as if too many people can't be bothered looking at evidence."

I turn towards her, not least to lose sight of the couple on the bench. Of course I didn't glimpse the substance of their heads clinging stubbornly together as the figures moved apart. It could only have been a lingering kiss, and the loud wet noise came from the river, not from their features stretching like rubber masks before the faces separated and sank back into place. "Shall I tell you what I think?" says Lucinda.

"I hope you always do."

She gazes at me, but I'm wondering what she sees beyond me as she murmurs "How much sleep have you been losing?"

"About as much as my mother, I'd imagine. No, probably not nearly as much."

"I'm off work tomorrow. You catch up on your sleep tonight and if there are any calls I'll take them."

"You think I'm imagining things, is that it?"

"I'm not blaming you, Gavin. Nobody should."

I'd be more provoked to argue if it weren't for the Whitechapel incident—for the way the memory has begun at some indeterminate point to resemble a dream I can't shake off. Surely I'm not imagining a copious splash in the river behind me, even if Lucinda doesn't look away from my face. "Shall we do that, then?" she says.

"If you're sure you don't mind. I mean, thanks."

As I stand up I'm confronted by an empty promenade all the way to the bench by the mast and beyond it too. Unlike its neighbours, the bench looks wet. "Did you see them?" I blurt.

"What, Gavin?"

"You mean who," I insist, pointing at the bench. "The couple who were there."

"I was looking at you. I didn't see anyone else."

Rather than argue I trudge to the car. The radio beyond an open window is bringing "Criminal Record" by Rachel and the Rehabs to an end. I'm still behind the apartments and walking over the buried mouth of the Pool when I falter. "What's that?"

"What now, Gavin? I can't see—"

"Not see," I protest. In a few seconds the radio presenter repeats the information. "That's it," I almost shout. "That's what my father meant by stones." The trouble is that I've been brought so nervously awake that sleep seems more remote than ever.

Chapter Nineteen

THE OLDEST STONES

As we enter Calderstones Park two adolescent girls in ankle-length white dresses greet us with a wreath each. My head prickles, less with the flowers one girl has placed there in imitation of her own adornment than from insomnia. She and her friend produce more wreaths from the cardboard boxes on either side of the avenue to await the next newcomers, and I notice that the boxes originally contained bottles of Frugorganic spring water. We're advancing between trees decorated with drops of this morning's rain when Lucinda blinks at my preoccupied frown, which feels weighted by the wreath. "I hoped you'd sleep," she says.

Eventually I did, which is why it's now the afternoon. Once we left the bath that she insisted would help me relax I lay awake for hours, sleepless with attempting not to betray that I was and unable to yield up my vigilance to her. I couldn't help trying to imagine how she would answer the police or my mother if they called, or suppose my father did at last? Suppose he distrusted her too much to speak? The idea felt dismayingly close to distrusting her myself, and all this felt like an uneasy dream I was having without benefit of sleep. At some point I lost consciousness, but this doesn't seem to have done me any lasting good. "You did your best," I tell Lucinda. "And you're here. Maybe you'll spot something I miss."

The avenue leads to a green shaded by trees, recalling the ancient woodland that once surrounded much of Liverpool. Among the trees dozens of robed figures are celebrating Druid Day. In the distance actors are performing a play beside a solitary goal for football practice. Children have tied ribbons to some of the trees, around which they dance with the colourful tethers. A woman in a pointed hat topped with streamers is telling fortunes at a picnic table as she gazes into a bowl of water. A girl similarly garbed is leading people with forked sticks in their hands across the green, and I wonder if she has mistaken what the druids were supposed to have meant by divination. I'm reminded that a stream used to start from the park and join the river miles away, close to James Maybrick's house. It's dry now, or has it gone underground? It has nothing to do with why I'm here. I need to find whoever spoke to my father.

I can't see any park officials. A sign directs us to the Calder Stones, which are housed in a roundish but angular building opposite the green. They're half a dozen brownish irregular lumps of rock, some of them incised with obscure symbols. At least one of the rocks is almost my height. Though they're arranged in a circle, not everyone thinks they're druidic. Historians have concluded they belonged to an ancient tomb, and the circle was constructed just a couple of hundred years ago, during the druid revival. I peer through the reinforced glass of the locked door at the stones, one of which sports a mark like a large misshapen handprint, and wonder why my father would have cycled all the way here, twenty minutes' drive from the city centre. I'm noticing more blurred marks that suggest some bulky person has been fumbling wet-handed at the stones when Lucinda says "Excuse me, do you work here?"

She has accosted a man in muddy trousers and a shirt as green as much of the park. Once he admits to the connection she says "Do you happen to remember a gentleman on a bicycle? When would it have been, Gavin?"

Although it seems much more remote I have to say "Two days ago."

The thick-limbed man looks ready for amusement. "What am I going to remember about him?"

"He's a lot like his son."

Lucinda indicates me, which apparently fails to recall my father. "Maybe you remember the bicycle," I say.

"Doubt it."

With by no means all of my frustration I say "It has a slogan on the frame and a web address."

"Oh, that one. Him."

The man is openly amused now, but I manage not to react to it. "You talked to him, then."

"You want Davey. He was telling us about some old—" The man thinks better of continuing and produces a mobile from his pocket. "You're wanted by the stones," he informs someone, and advises us "He's on his way. Don't go anywhere."

He retreats into an ornamental garden, where the shade beneath the shrubs is darkened by patches of lingering rain, and vanishes towards a greenhouse. My forehead is prickling with the wreath now, and I hang the flowers on the nearest tree while several garlanded suburbanites gaze at me as if I've forsaken a halo. I'm awaiting Davey when I wonder if I should have recognised someone across the green, and I hurry back down the avenue. The large robed man booming and gesticulating in front of the football net is indeed the leader of the Histrionic History troupe.

They've acquired an extra player. Before I can identify which of them is unfamiliar, Lucinda calls "Where are you going? He's here."

Beside her is a new green-shirted man as brawny as his workmate but untouched by mud. His tattooed arms and rolling gait put me in mind of a sailor. He halts near the fortune-teller and watches my approach. "No mistaking him," he says.

Perhaps I look as if I need Lucinda to explain "For Deryck's son, he means."

"So you remember my father. Was it you that told him to get off his bike?"

"He never moaned to you about that, did he?"

"He didn't have to. I'm the person he was calling." As my aching forehead loses its grip on a frown I say "Why did he need to get off when the stones are locked away?"

"They weren't. Open to the public once a year."

"That must be why he came," Lucinda says. "Did he take a look at them?"

"More than one of those, love. More like a feel and a snog. We had to tell him to stop. Maybe he was trying to make out the stuff that's carved on them, but he was bothering the public."

I'm unnecessarily reminded of the marks on the stones. "He's the public too."

"Do you know if he found anything?" Lucinda says.

"Nothing we could make any sense out of."

The shrug that goes with this enrages me, but I manage to say only "See if I can."

"He wasn't here, you know. He'd gone in the greenhouse."

"I take it you followed him."

"Somebody had to, the way he was carrying on."

Lucinda heads off my anger by saying "Could you show us where?"

"It'll have to be quick."

His walk isn't. As he heads for the ornamental garden he reminds me more than ever of a seaman who hasn't quite regained his land legs. I follow him and Lucinda until I'm distracted by a child's shrill protest. "There's someone in the water."

He's by the fortune-teller, and just tall enough to stare into the bowl. "That's me, sweetheart," she tells him and the rest of her audience.

"No, a lady."

She gives a laugh that does its best to stay polite. "I hope that's me as well."

"The other lady. The one with the watery hair. She was talking to me."

"What did she say, Bevan?" his mother wonders, less to him than to the bystanders.

"I don't know," he says and gives her a patient although supercilious look. "I couldn't hear. She was under the water."

"Is she still?" the fortune-teller enquires.

He cranes over the table and shakes his head. "You must have scared her off."

"I hope I'm not that scary." This gives the listeners an opportunity to laugh and the mother a cue to usher him away as the fortune-teller blinks at the bowl. "Maybe I'm better at magic than I thought," she tells her next customer.

When I catch up with the park-keeper, Lucinda is saying "Did he have his cycle when you last saw him?"

"Rode off on it." As he opens the door to the greenhouse he adds "I told the police after it was on the radio about it."

I hold the clammy doorknob while Lucinda follows him in. The long narrow building is full of jungle, as if a strip of the landscape has reverted to one of its earliest states. Amid the mass of vegetation, leaves grow restless as condensation drips from the peaked glass roof. A path not much broader than our guide leads down the centre of the greenhouse, and he halts on the far side of a small bridge. "There you are," he says as I step on the bridge. "You're him. Stopped there and spouted, and then he went off."

I do my best to control my anger in advance. "Do you remember what he said?"

"It came this way."

"What did?" Lucinda says.

"You tell me." With a stare that renders the directive literal he adds "He was looking down there when he said it. That's all I know."

I gaze into the water where he indicates and see ripples reshaping my reflection. "Didn't he say anything else?"

"Said they must have too. Don't ask me what. We'd had enough. Didn't want him going on and on about stories we were supposed to know."

"Which stories?"

"Old ones about round here. I just told you, we don't know."

"There are some."

For a moment I think Lucinda is the speaker. The woman behind her is robed from head to foot in white, and her hair isn't much less devoid of colour. She's pressing her large hands against her thighs as if to keep them in shape. "Will you tell us?" says Lucinda.

"What do you have in mind?"

A ripple under the bridge reminds me where my father stood. "Any about water," I say or ask.

"I like the one about the stag."

"Then I expect we will," Lucinda says.

"It's the earliest legend we have, from when there was forest all the way down to the river. The story tells there was a stag the king's huntsmen could never catch. They'd see it through the trees and then it would be gone as if it had sunk into the earth. In most versions it was by a stream, and in some a knight sees it turn to water."

"It goes to the water, you mean," I say.

"No," the woman says and seems delighted to continue. "The stag turns into it. In the best version the knight sees its horns are a fountain, and then the sunlight shines through it and it's transformed into a wave that vanishes downstream. Sometimes he follows it to the river, or in some versions he waits by the stream in the hope of seeing it again and eats only fruit that grows there and drinks only from the stream. We take that to refer to fasting in order to achieve a vision, but it isn't clear when it dates from. Some commentators date it much earlier than King John, but there's nothing in Baxter to support that."

"That's William Baxter." Once this is confirmed Lucinda tells me "Early eighteenth century. Wrote the *Glossarium Antiquitatum Britannicarum*. He thought he'd discovered that the lost Roman town that's mentioned in Ptolemy was the earliest settlement around the Pool."

As I'm reduced to reflecting that my father might have made a joke of the initials of the title, Lucinda says "You were mentioning commentators."

"They say, not many of them, that there may have been a pre-Roman settlement."

"How's that supposed to fit in with your stag?" I ask.

"Just that if we're talking about Mesolithic times the settlers would have had to travel a long way. The argument is they would have had to be led."

"Someone usually does that, don't they? I wouldn't call it new."

"In this case it was more like something."

"That'll be the stag again, will it?"

"Something of water. Maybe something older. There used to be a Christian tradition that the first settlers were brought to the Pool by an angel or a saint. In some versions it's St Cuthbert. There was a dockland church with windows that showed him leading his flock, and the last window had him descending into the river. It was all destroyed in the blitz, sadly, but it sounds like a Christianised pagan tradition."

"Are you a historian?" Lucinda says.

"I lecture at the university."

"If you're a lecturer," I'm provoked to ask, "why are you dressed like that?"

"Because of my skin."

The little that's visible does look odd—not just unhealthily pale, which may be an effect of the unseasonable weather, but coarse and moist, perhaps with the humidity inside the greenhouse. "Sorry. Sorry," I say and turn to the keeper. "Did my father give you any idea where he was going next?"

"Off to pester someone else is my guess."

I'm at the edge of my anger but succeed in saying only "Who?"

"All he said was it was all fitting together."

That's the opposite of my experience, but I'm not reluctant

to leave the greenhouse. So much moisture has gathered on my skin that I feel close to steeped in it. "Where do we want to go now?" Lucinda says.

I lead the way through the garden to the green. Children are listening to storytellers under the beribboned trees while the diviners straggle in the direction of the distant river. The actors have produced a giant egg from the football net where they've stored props. It's a druidic symbol, but it reminds me of something else, and it isn't the only aspect of the play that abruptly seems familiar. "Let's see the show."

I haven't time to explain my tone. I set off so furiously across the green that the fortune-teller's customer sidles out of my way. He must have jarred the table, because the face I glimpse in the bowl of water squirms and appears to swell, especially the eyes. As I reach the far side of the green the egg splits jaggedly in half, pulled apart by two of the girls, to disgorge a multicoloured rubber serpent. The bulky actor and his female trio dance hand in hand around it, and the play ends to a small storm of applause, though none from me. As the players begin to gather up their props I call "So where do you get your ideas?"

The leader of the troupe swings to face me while the girls grapple with returning the expanded serpent to its egg. "Why, it's—" he says and then "Remind me."

"The competition."

"I don't think I got your name."

"Your friend did."

"Which friend is that?"

"Why, haven't you got any?" This conveys my rage but little else. "Either Mr Waterworks," I say, "or whatever her name is."

I mean the slimmest and least shaven of the girls—the only one who isn't wearing a wig or doesn't appear to be. For the moment the dance seems to have used up the energy she kept being unable to contain when she took my last tour. "Gavin Meadows, isn't it," she says. "Thanks for coming to see us."

"And I wasn't even sent to watch."

The man cocks his massive head as though its weight has tipped it sideways. "I don't think I quite—"

"She does," I say and turn on her. "Were you just keeping an eye on me for Waterworks or looking for ideas as well?"

"Neither." She shakes her head, setting off a movement like the start of a dance or of a bid to escape. "I was trying to make sure we didn't copy you," she says, "and nobody sent me but me."

"Then who—" At once I remember the man who seemed determined to be unimpressed. "The bastard," I declare. "That's who it was after all."

My profanity startles a couple of giggles out of the audience that has lingered for the encore, and somebody murmurs "Is he part of the show?"

I assume this is intended as a joke, but it's too much for Lucinda. "Try not to mind him," she says to the troupe. "He's lost—"

"Don't say I've lost my father. He's lost at the moment. I haven't lost him. Not lost as in lost, as in lost lost."

I'm babbling. I could wonder if she was about to say I've lost something other than him. The performers have begun to look as awkward as the audience, which is wandering away. I've had enough, above all of myself. "Forget it," I tell anyone who should be told, and make for the car.

Blackness as wide as the sky is heaving itself up from the river. The trees along the avenue seem to intensify the darkness, as does the throbbing of my head. I'm advancing almost blindly when Lucinda catches up with me. "Where now?" she says.

"Home."

At once she looks worried. "Aren't you feeling well?"

"I'll cope. I should have thought to bring a photograph."

"Of Deryck, you mean?" She peers at me in the gathering afternoon gloom and says "You just need to show people your face."

I don't want to feel as if I'm trying to replace him. At least it will save time, and so I say "Then let's go to the tunnels."

Chapter Twenty

In the Tunnel

When we step into the visitors' centre we're confronted by a squat figure with a spectacularly protruding stomach. Beneath a stovepipe hat his face is grey and blind, as good as eyeless. I assume the statue is meant to suggest why Joseph Williamson was known as the mole of Edge Hill, but the appearance of a creature that has seen too little daylight is excessively convincing for my taste, and the motley clothes in which he's dressed don't help. The plump middle-aged woman in a Friends of Williamson's Tunnels T-shirt behind the counter opposite seems bent on ignoring his presence, but she glances up at my approach, and then does rather more than glance. "May I help you?" she says as though she's addressing someone in another room.

"If this looks familiar," I say, indicating my face.

She frowns at it—more accurately, continues to do so—before sidling from behind the counter. "Please excuse me a moment," she says and retreats down a stone corridor into the museum.

It isn't very large. Most of the exhibits—clay pipes and china fragments and skulls smaller than human, all retrieved in the process of clearing the tunnels—are housed in glass cases on either side of the corridor. Beyond the blind figure that guards it, placards display information about him. As well as the apparently haphazard labyrinth of tunnels he built houses above them, and some of the rooms had no windows. During a period of thirty-three years he lived in at least eight of the houses, as if he was engaged in some kind of search, but after his wife's death he made his home in a windowless cellar. He died of water on the chest, I read as I'm distracted by a muffled voice. Is it a religious broadcast? The voice seems to be chanting in an irregular rhythm, though if it's on a radio, it's so far off the station that I can't make out a word. It's beyond the tunnel entrance beside the corridor, but the door is locked. When I lean towards it the voice begins to sound as if it's singing underwater; I could imagine someone drowned and celebrating the experience. The thought must be born of too little sleep, and I'm about to press my ear against the door when a man calls "Excuse me, may I help you? That's shut."

He's the woman's age and rather bulkier, and looks determined to impress me with both. "Will you be opening it now?" I ask her as much as him.

"I've just finished explaining to you that the tunnels are closed until further notice."

"I don't think you quite did," Lucinda says as I protest "What, all of them?"

"Even the latest one. Somebody ought to be pleased."

He's staring at me, and I know he means my father, but I demand "What do you mean?"

"Someone who objects to them," the woman says. "He even said the people who blocked them up with rubbish knew what they were doing."

"He put off several of our customers." Quite as accusingly the man adds "Have you been in a fight?"

"Something like that," I admit and give up fingering my bruise once I realise this may suggest a threat. "You haven't told us why you've shut the tunnels."

"You haven't asked." Barely in time to head off my retort the man says "Water."

"How badly are they flooded?" says Lucinda.

"Never this badly. It must be the weather."

"It can't be that bad," I object. "There's someone in there. I heard them."

I haven't since I started speaking outside the door, but the friends of the tunnels compete at frowning. "There certainly shouldn't be," the woman says.

Lucinda seems about to speak until I send her a quick grimace. As the woman inserts a key in the lock I hear a sound like surreptitious wallowing beyond the door. She throws it wide, revealing an arched sandstone passage at least twelve feet high, illuminated by spotlights that leave stretches of darkness untouched. A rough stone ramp slopes down from the entrance, to be cut off by a drop of twelve feet or more, over which a catwalk of planks on scaffolding extends to a cleft through the back wall. "Is anybody in here?" the woman calls.

"Here."

The muffled answer sounds mocking, but it's just an echo. She advances down the ramp, followed by her colleague. The shapes swelling up to meet them are their deformed shadows. Though Lucinda tries to restrain me I hurry after the pair, who turn to me as I reach the catwalk. "Would you mind—" the woman says while the man contributes "Could you please—"

They're interrupted by a large loose splash in the deep pool that has gathered under the scaffolding. I venture onto the catwalk in time to see dark ripples spreading through the gloom. The water is too murky for the floor of the pool to be visible. "What was that?" I gasp.

"Something someone left fell in," the man says. "If you would—"

"What, though? I didn't see it, did you?"

"We didn't have to. It couldn't be anything else," says the woman. "Will you please go out now. This area isn't for the public."

Of course it is, and I don't move, because I'm trying to free my mind of an illusion. Half a dozen trickles of water glisten on the sandstone at the far side of the subterranean pool. There can't be any question that they're streaming down the wall, but the glimmers that the ripples cast on the stone make the trickles appear to be crawling upwards, reaching for the surface of the earth. The glimmers subside, drawing my attention to the ripples themselves. Am I seeing a pale object through them? Surely it's part of the floor of the pool, though it appears to be changing its irregular shape more thoroughly than the distortions of the ripples can account for. I could think it isn't alone down there, and I'm craning over the edge when the man's shout almost overbalances me. "Will you both—"

"I'm just taking him away," Lucinda says, having caught my arm. "Come on, Gavin. That's all there is to see for now."

"You heard it, didn't you?" I'm close to pleading.

"I'm sure it's what this lady and gentleman said."

"Not that. Someone singing in here before."

Perhaps it's because I'm staring into the water that she sounds uneasy. "I didn't, Gavin."

Are the pallid blotches in the depths not just changing shape but growing? I clutch her hand on my arm and lean out further from the catwalk. "Can't you see that?"

She hasn't responded except for gripping my arm harder when the woman says "Kindly leave or we'll be forced to call the police."

"Shall I give you the names to ask for? Wrigley or Maddock. They love hearing about me."

"Gavin," Lucinda says and steers me away from the edge. "Sorry," she tells the staff as they tail us to the door. "He's worried about his father."

I barely manage not to warn her to stop bringing him up. As we emerge into a cobbled yard that's darkened by the imminence of rain she says "Shall we go home?"

I feel as if the glimpses in the tunnel are lying dormant in my mind. Perhaps they were only ever there, which suggests that I may not be much good just now at searching for my father or identifying clues to his whereabouts. I'm also thrown by remembering "I thought you thought I didn't need to."

"Home to my house."

I've never seen it. Besides, I wouldn't mind a drink. "I'd like that," I assure her.

A wind twitches the windscreen wipers as we climb into the car outside the yard. Lucinda drives uphill past tenements that have overwhelmed the site of the village of Edge Hill. Until the city surrounded it the village had a clear view of the river, which may have distracted the villagers from the labyrinth under their houses. We must be passing over it as Lucinda turns the car across the slope. Another street of tenements, where the dark sky transforms dozens of small windows into slates, brings us onto the brow of Edge Hill.

A terrace from Williamson's time stretches along the brow to St Mary's Church, where one of his tunnels is rumoured to have opened into the churchyard. That's the tunnel the restorers think they're clearing from the far end. Lucinda's house is in the middle of the terrace. Its door and window frames and the railings of the small neat garden all gleam black. She parks in front of the spiky gate, and as I climb out I see two large blind eyes at her bedroom window.

In a moment I see they're binoculars. They must give her a fine view across the river, although just now they're slanted towards the church. She makes for the house with her key at the ready, and I'm on the path when my mobile starts to sing about love. I silence the song as she opens the door. Close to the ground the high white hall is green—the carpet, the pots of ferns along the party wall. Some of the ferns are restless, and I'm reminded of leaves jerking with moisture in the Calderstones greenhouse. There's a draught along the hall, and my mother is on the phone. "It's getting in," she says, her voice ragged with sleeplessness. "It's everywhere. It's destroying all your father's work."

Chapter Twenty-one

SOMETHING UNEARTHED

Even with the boot loaded to capacity and the backseat and the floor in front of it piled high, there's nothing like enough space in the Spirita. At least we still have plenty of the cartons we fetched from shops along Breck Road. I'm not just dismayed by how much the damp has affected the books and loose papers, I'm angry with myself for not ensuring they were farther from the walls. Wherever print's visible it has blurred, and quite a few items are stuck together. I've little chance to examine the damage, because my mother keeps urging us to carry out our burdens as fast as we can, now that she's convinced nowhere in the house is safe. She bustles around us with an umbrella in case it begins to rain, but she's so distracted that most of the time she holds it over herself. My final cargo on this journey is the computer tower, which Lucinda hands me once I'm strapped into the passenger seat. "Hurry back as soon as you can," my mother pleads and then delays us. "I forgot to ask, did he call you? Not Deryck."

"Who?" I say less gently than I should.

"Whatever his name was." She appears to be inviting me to supply it until she adds "The workman. He rang me and I said he should ring you."

I hug the computer tower in case this lets me feel less inclined to throw my hands up. "But what about?"

"Your father, of course. You remember, I asked on the radio for people to get in touch."

"Couldn't you have found out what he had to say? If he wouldn't even give his name he mightn't want to ring twice."

"I did find out, Gavin. I only wanted him to talk to you as well in case I'd missed anything while I was so worried about Deryck's things."

"I'm sorry," I say, which falls well short of my feelings. "Where was he when dad saw him?"

"He wouldn't say, and he didn't know where Deryck rode off to." She leans forward, and so does the umbrella that's shading us from a momentary flare of sunlight through a rupture in the clouds. "I did get something out of him," she murmurs. "I'm not completely useless."

"Nobody thinks you are, Gillian," Lucinda says. "What did you learn?"

"They've been digging up things all over town but they've been told to keep it to themselves," my mother says and looks even warier. "Be careful what you say about it, won't you? You don't want to make any enemies who could harm your work."

I suppress more than one thought and say only "What things?"

"Some of them looked like bits of poles for holding houses up above a swamp, but he wouldn't say where."

"That sounds like a Mesolithic settlement," Lucinda says.

As I wonder how anyone except an archaeologist could know, my mother pleads "You won't tell anyone, will you? It could put him out of a job."

I'm not sure who she means, and so I say "Anything else they unearthed?"

Something claws at the roof of the car—the tips of spokes of the umbrella. My mother jerks it up, adding to the darkness inside the vehicle, and blurts "What he saw."

"What would that have been, Gillian?"

"People standing up."

"You're not saying they stood up when they were dug up," I protest and try to laugh.

"I'm saying they were buried that way." My mother's eyes drift from side to side before she adds "Alive."

I don't want to believe it. "How could he tell?"

"Because even though they were so old he could see they'd been trying to claw their way out."

As I attempt not to imagine the burial Lucinda says "How old?"

"He said very because of how deep they were digging, the contractors, I mean, but they were told not to hold the work up."

"That's disgraceful," Lucinda says. "They shouldn't treat our history that way."

As my mother visibly regrets having spoken, I ask "Did he say anything else about dad?"

"Just that Deryck said it sounded like another sacrifice."

"Another." When my mother seems equally bemused I say "I can't imagine him saying anything like that."

"He has been." More optimistically than seems entirely rational she adds "At least he'll know where they found those bodies."

I'm at a loss for an answer that would feel anything like safe, and it's Lucinda who says "Had we better be moving?"

"I'm sorry. It's my fault for keeping you. I should have thought."

"Someone will be back before you know it," says Lucinda.

The car speeds along the ridge and downhill, past a maze of narrow streets cut off from the main thoroughfare. They're crammed with houses, some of which are boarded up and sprayed with illegible weather-beaten graffiti, but in the days when windmills flanked the main road, one side street harboured a circus. Even though it was several hundred yards from the highest reaches of the Pool, it was flooded around the time Lucinda's house was built, and an infestation of amphibians delayed the reopening, which in any case was unsuccessful. During its decline the theatre in Christian Street became known as Croaker's Circus, though the proprietor's name wasn't Croaker. The main road leads us onto the Dale Street flyover, and as we pass Waterworth's office a face blurred by breath on the pane appears at the window, so that I have to resist an absurd impulse to crouch low over the computer tower. The halting homebound traffic eventually lets us pass the town hall, and soon Lucinda leaves behind the fitful descent of vehicles towards the river.

The basement puts on its lights to greet us as she drives down the ramp. A few vehicles occupy their spaces on the stone floor of the car park that serves all the buildings on this side of the street—the apartments, a sandwich shop, a tobacconist's, an employment agency. Lucinda parks within the outline beneath a giant's handiwork—my apartment number stencilled on the bare brick wall. "You carry that up and I'll be unloading," she says.

I plant the computer tower on the top step while I unlock the door to the lobby. It thuds shut as I climb the stairs. I have to dump the tower again in order to open my apartment. I leave the tower in the only empty corner of the main room and, having closed the door, hurry downstairs. Lucinda is waiting by the car, beside which are the boxes of material. "I could drive back if you think these are safe to leave here."

The basement is meant to be secure. Once the street door has tilted shut I heft the nearest carton and make for the steps. It's too much of a struggle to let myself into the lobby without setting down my burden, and I only just save it from toppling into the basement, since there's so little room on the step. I block the door with the carton and fetch the next. By the time I've trudged upstairs with it and lowered it to the floor so that I can unlock my apartment again, I'm sweating with frustration as well as exertion. I hold my door open with the second carton and head for the basement once more.

The energy-conscious lights have gone off, and I wave my arms to alert the sensors as I descend the steps. I clutch another box to my chest and plod upstairs, where I leave the carton next to the computer tower, then hurry down to gesture at the lights. That's the way it continues to go:

tramping upstairs only just ahead of exhaustion, dropping my burden, sprinting down to magic the light out of the subterranean darkness, grabbing the next box with my clammy hands . . . I don't rest until the task is almost done, and then I sit on the floor with my back against the wall that bears my number.

On top of the carton next to me is a copy of half a dozen lines of verse. My father has scribbled William Colquitt's name beneath them. Colquitt was an early Victorian poet, but hardly a good one. Apparently I'm looking at part of his epic poem *Description of Liverpool*, including these lines:

> "Behold the Pool, where Neptune's kin doth dream
> Of antic life in marsh and secret stream.
> Nay, though the Pool be buried furlongs deep,
> This stifles not the maggots of its sleep . . ."

My father has scrawled a ring around the second couplet and written in the margin *Record Office copy, not later one*. The Record Office is the other name for where Lucinda works, and there's a further note: "John Strong?" I'm pondering this when the page goes out as if it's a dream from which I've wakened into blackness.

I wave my arms, to no avail. The sensors can't detect movement so close to the floor. I try to stagger to my feet, but my legs are too busy prickling to support me. I can just distinguish the walls and the vehicles by the dim glow that leaks around the door at the top of the ramp, because the door to the lobby is no longer blocked. Did it edge the carton aside without my noticing? In that case, why hasn't the carton fallen down the steps? Someone in the lobby might have moved it, but they would have had to be exceptionally surreptitious. I'm struggling again to rise to my feet when a light comes on.

It's in my pocket, accompanied by the song about love. I snatch them out and see Lucinda's number. The display

blinds me, but I didn't glimpse a figure in the corner farthest
from the ramp. "Hello?" I urge, pressing the clammy mobile
against my face.

"I'll be on my way back in a minute. I tried to persuade
Gillian to come away from the damp but she's insisting she
has to stay by the phone."

"Good," I'm sufficiently distracted to respond, having
barely heard her second sentence, as I turn the mobile towards the walls to prove that nobody is hiding in the corner.

Perhaps nobody is. The light is too feeble to illuminate
much at that distance. The blurred object, if it's even there,
resembles a growth—a huge pallid fungus with stalks like fat
limbs and a lump that's only something like a head. The lump
does have features, even if too few: a pair of holes that might
suggest irregular nostrils, and beneath them a wide gap from
which an item surely too large for a tongue is dangling. That's
the only sign of movement. As the dangling object squeezes
out it grows larger still—bigger than the orifice—before it
drops to the floor with a moist flat thud.

As I sprawl backwards I glimpse it hopping away into the
dark. I must have cried out, because Lucinda's tiny voice
calls "What's wrong?"

I scramble to my feet, and the sensors turn the lights on.
The carton I planted on the top step is balanced at the edge.
The corner farthest from the ramp is empty except for a
misshapen stain, and in a moment I'm not sure I even saw
that. I retreat to the steps, lying as I go. "Nothing," I do my
best to hope.

Chapter Twenty-two

SINGING TO SLEEP

Lucinda scrutinises my face as she climbs out of the car. "What was wrong?"

I glance past her at the corner, where any trace of moisture has vanished into the bricks. I'm sure of that, having ventured close, and I couldn't see or hear a creature hopping or lying low beneath any of the cars, the only concealment. "Just the light," I say. "It went off."

"You sounded as if it was something worse. Didn't you sleep?"

"When? What are you talking about?"

"Last night, Gavin. Did you get any sleep at all? You seem so on edge."

"What do you expect with everything that's happening?"

"Maybe I shouldn't expect it, but I'd like to take some of the pressure off you if I could."

"You can. You have. Think how long I'd have taken to bring all this stuff here by myself."

She seems disappointed that I'm being so impersonally practical, but I'd rather not discuss my fears down here. "Let's finish unloading," I say, "and then we can relax."

Perhaps that's unrealistic. I lift a carton out of the boot and loiter with it until Lucinda says "You go ahead or we'll be in each other's way."

I can't avoid leaving her in the basement without inviting questions I don't want to answer. I labour upstairs and dash back as soon as I've dumped my burden, slowing in time not to collide with Lucinda on the stairs or, I hope, for her to wonder about my haste. For the rest of the operation I contrive not to be much more than a flight of stairs distant from her. At last all the cartons are in my biggest room, where we've stacked some on top of others. "Now we can do what you said," Lucinda says.

Once she heads for the bathroom I realise she has relaxation in mind. "I just want to ask you about this," I tell her.

She watches me heave cartons off cartons, turning the floor into as much of a maze as my father's workroom was. Eventually I have to say "Did you bring the one with William Colquitt on top?"

"I'm sure I would have noticed. Do you need to find it now? You're getting yourself into more of a state."

No, I'm tipping up carton after carton to determine which of them has the page stuck underneath. "Come for a bath," Lucinda says.

"Not until I show you." I tilt the last carton and let it thud to the floor, where it puffs out a fungoid smell. Did I miss a carton? I wipe my damp hands on my trousers and rub my moist forehead and set about looking again. I'm so tired that when I peer at some of the topmost documents they look more blurred than they were—too blurred for me to decipher. Straining my eyes only aggravates the illegibility. "It was a verse that was only in the first edition of the book," I complain. "Some kind of metaphor for filling in the Pool. It's in the poem about Liverpool. My father found it in your library and thought it had something to do with John Strong."

"If you don't find it I'll have a look tomorrow when I'm at work." She helps me stack the cartons again and displays her hands, which look so discoloured that someone uninformed could think she has been underground. "Shall we have our bath now?" she suggests.

I linger to gaze at the boxes. If they're damp I ought to replace them, but none of the nearby shops will be open now that night has fallen, and so I follow Lucinda. The bath is foaming with her favourite salts, Sea Whispers. As she stoops to ruffle up more waves, her spine is outlined all the way down to the small of her back. While the sight and the hidden wings of her shoulder blades are as delectable as ever, just now the bones put me in mind of a fossil brought to light by excavation. Guilt at the thought is one reason why I trace them with my fingertips, but she straightens up before my hand reaches the firm curves of her bottom. "You aren't even undressed yet," she objects.

I strip in the bedroom and drop the dirtiest items in the wicker bin before returning the next dirtiest—me—to the bath. Lucinda is already in it, and rises like a mermaid from the foam, holding out slim arms scaly with bubbles. When I start to climb in facing her she makes a pass in the air with one hand to indicate I should turn around. Once I've lowered myself between her legs she massages my shoulders so gently that her hands almost feel as if they're merging with me. She soaps and rinses my back and then nestles against me. Before long her warmth and the almost imperceptible movements of water and foam are closer to lulling me to sleep than anything has been for days, so that for a while I scarcely notice she's murmuring a ditty in or behind my ear:

> ". . . *The mermaids down below*
> *Would give their crystal kingdoms*
> *For the love of Gav, I trow . . .*"

"What's that?" I mumble sleepily.

"Something from the archive," she whispers, and at some point continues

> ". . . *For all the landsmen lovers*
> *Are nothing after Gav . . .*"

By now we're in bed, and I could take the words as an invitation, but I'm sinking into the infinite depths of sleep. I can only hope she's as content with our spoony embrace as I am. Is this what they used to mean by spooning? The thought floats away to join whatever else I might feel or think. Some indeterminate time later I'm not entirely wakened by her or a voice resembling hers, which is murmuring more of the song. Perhaps it's her mobile, which I'm surprised to realise I've never heard. Isn't knowing your lover's mobile tone an index of intimacy these days? The idea and the surprise are too distant to rouse me any further. Nevertheless, though far from immediately, it's the notion of answering a phone that fishes me out of my sleep.

The room is full of daylight muted by the curtains, and I'm alone in bed. When I blink the clock into focus I see it's almost noon. Lucinda must have left for work hours ago. I retrieve my mobile from the bedside table, but there's no record of a missed call. I rest the landline receiver against my upturned ear while I stay supine, and then I rear up sideways. There has been a call from a withheld number.

I kick away the quilt and stumble to my workroom. The answering machine has recorded a message, if it isn't just the click of somebody failing to leave one. The single digit resembles an I, a symbol of my insufficiently vigilant self. I fall to my knees and press the button, and wait while a shrill voice babbles backwards. As soon as it regains its usual sound I recognise it without welcoming it. "Mr Meadows?" it says, barely a question. "Hank Waterworth. Please contact me as soon as you pick this up."

Chapter Twenty-three

HANK'S REPORTS

"Gavin Meadows for Hank Waterworth."

The vague trace of reassurance that his first name seems to offer me—a name that a Liverpudlian might have adopted to sound as American as many British pop stars try to seem—vanishes as the receptionist raises her head, withdrawing her expression. She stays remote from me in every sense as she tells the phone "Mr Meadows is here" before advising me "Mr Waterworth is coming to get you."

Is this a threat she's enjoying behind her blank face? I feel as if I'm less awake than before I listened to his call, because I can't think up an explanation for the list of names I sent him. In the shower the water drummed all thoughts out of my head, and then the crowds and the noise of traffic and renovation kept them at bay. Now they're unable to reach through the tangle of languages that fills the hall where council tenants make their payments. None too soon I see Waterworth emerge from his office beyond the glass doors and outdo the receptionist in concealing any expression. When I step forward to help him with the last door, he gives me a frown and an equally brief shake of his head. Once the door is officially opened he says "Thank you for finding the time, Mr Meadows."

"Call me Gavin," I say, though only as an excuse to call him Hank.

"Please follow me," he says and barely holds the door.

As I imitate his measured tread I recall that there used to be a circus on this site. His pace is theatrical, but what kind of act are we in? It feels more like being led into the Bridewell prison in Cheapside across the road outside his window. He sits in Rhoda's chair between views of an unrecognisably if not optimistically futuristic Liverpool and doesn't quite wait for me to take a seat before he says "I've been talking to the library."

"You've found me out, then. I had to get them from somewhere. I can't remember everything and I can't make that sort of thing up. There's nothing wrong with my figures, though."

Waterworth gazes at me as if he's watching a performance, and then my resignation lets me see what I should have wondered sooner. "What made you get in touch with the library?"

"They got in touch with me."

There's only one question I want to ask, though I equally don't. "Who did?"

"Who would you expect? The local history people."

"Which of them?"

"I've told you before that I can't discuss employees of the council with you."

"Then just nod or shake your head," I say as I imagine my father might. "Was it Lucinda Wade?"

"Once again, I've told you—"

I began by only needing confirmation of my disbelief, but that's on its way to leaving me alone and worse than bewildered. "In other words, it was."

"It was nobody like that. Please don't pursue the matter."

"So why did they get in touch?"

"You aren't going to tell me you don't know. About the scene you caused there, which sounds like the trouble they had with your father."

"Are you telling me they called you about a bit of an argument with a couple of librarians? That's worse than pathetic."

"Among other incidents, Mr Meadows."

"Gavin." It's partly his lack of response that provokes me

to add "If they say I did any more than disagree with them they're lying and I'd like to know why."

"I shouldn't be too eager to accuse anyone of that. There's quite a bunch of them."

"Bring them on."

"Let's start with the Williamson tunnels. I'm told you made a scene there too and forced your way into an area that wasn't open to the public."

"Christ, have you got people everywhere? I didn't force anything. The door was open and all I did was follow someone. Who told you different?"

"One of the people you harassed," Waterworth says and scowls as if he has revealed too much. "Don't try doing it to me."

"Come on, I don't harass people. If that's what they call harassment I'm surprised they haven't got a notice up about it. People used to be able to handle a bit of criticism of their work. Customers could be difficult without being made to feel like criminals." I'm sounding more than ever like my father, which may be why I add "Pretty soon I wouldn't be surprised if it's all against the law. If you so much as complain in a shop they'll call security and then they'll have to get counselling for stress."

Having waited none too patiently for me to finish, Waterworth says "You disagree with Tasha Bailey, then."

"I might if I knew who she was."

"A member of Nicholas Noble's historical troupe. I believe you interrupted a performance they were giving in a park and accused her of stealing your ideas and even swore at her in front of children in the audience."

"Not at her." I leave it there, though I'm even angrier than I was then. "I don't think any children heard," I say, "and I'm sure it was a lot milder than they hear in the schoolyard."

"You're supposed to be educating, not lowering yourself and your audience." Waterworth gives me a moment to feel abashed and says "At whom, then?"

Perhaps my gaze makes it clear who I might have called a bastard. It halts the conversation until I say "I thought you had a man on my tours."

"He's filed his report."

"Let me read it if you like."

"I'm sure you know that won't be possible." With no lessening of reproof Waterworth says "He thought your script was incoherent and gave too much information."

"Well, I certainly haven't heard that objection before."

At once I realise this may sound as if people have complained about a lack of substance, but Waterworth is already saying "Information some of your customers made it clear they didn't want. I believe they were treated to more of your obsession with the Ripper business."

"It isn't my obsession. It's nothing to do with me. Somebody wanted to hear about it. You met her."

Now I recall that Moira Shea didn't raise the subject, but Waterworth says only "I'm also told your tour was interrupted yet again while you talked to your girlfriend."

"What are you on about, yet again? All right, it happened when you were there, but it's only ever been twice."

"And what was so important that you had to keep your customers standing around for three and a half minutes?"

Barely in time not to own up I remind myself that he's unaware of my trick with the names I sent him. "My father," I tell him.

"And did you learn anything helpful?" When I shake my head Waterworth says "You should realise your customers were left feeling guilty for taking up your time when you could have been searching for your father."

"I certainly didn't mean them to and I'm sorry if they did, but I'm starting to think your man was just looking for things to complain about. Did he have anything good at all to say?"

"I'm afraid he confirmed my impressions."

"Maybe you shouldn't have sent such a miserable bugger."

This is out before I can anticipate it, but I hurriedly add "Everyone else seemed to have a good time. Tasha Bailey especially did."

"She said nothing about it to me, and we've still to deal with the police."

"I wish somebody would," I'm provoked to declare, and then I demand "How do they come into this?"

"Your attitude to them. I'm informed you let that be overheard on your tour. And there's also how you behaved."

"What's anyone saying I did now?"

"Try putting on someone else's voice."

"Why would I want to do that?" I say and laugh in case this fits. "What's wrong with mine?"

"I'm saying," Waterworth says and underlines it with a stare, "you called the police using an assumed voice."

For a moment I'm so speechless that I might as well be underwater. "Have you got a spy on the force as well?"

"I guess it must run in the family, looking for conspiracies." Before I can spit out a retort he says "Didn't you tell them you organised tours for us?"

"So what if I did? Why should they go telling tales to you?"

"Maybe they thought you were pulling a publicity stunt, and I'm inclined to agree."

A row of faces so high up they might belong to circus giants peers through the window behind him. As the bus moves onwards I protest "What are you saying was a stunt? Whatever's happened to my father?"

"No need to make me sound unsympathetic, Mr Meadows, though there's a limit to the allowances I'm prepared to make. I mean the act you put on in Whitechapel."

I point at my forehead so fiercely that I jab the bruise. "You're saying this was an act."

"It surely sounds like one. You told the police the road was called Frog's Lane, didn't you? That's what you called it when you were telling us your tale about atrocities as well."

"It isn't mine. I don't know whose it is. And I was confused when I was talking to the police. Didn't they tell you I was knocked out?"

"I heard they saw you injuring yourself. I believe you did on your last tour, and I just saw you do it now. Maybe you're so desperate to make a name you don't much care what kind."

"That's ridiculous," I say and laugh, but neither seems to work. "Why don't you accuse me of being on drugs while you're at it?"

"Is that what the police said?"

I'm determined not to betray any uncertainty by glancing away from him, and so I can't be sure what I just glimpsed. Another bus has cruised by, leaving me the impression of a face pressed against a window on the upper deck. Of course the face wasn't flattened by the glass, at least not enough to turn it grey and enlarge it, especially the eyes and mouth. I hardly know I'm saying "Didn't they share that with you too?"

"I think we'd better put an end to the discussion, Mr Meadows. Under all the circumstances—" A frown narrows his eyes, and he says "Wait a moment."

"I wasn't going anywhere."

"Don't until you've told me this. What were you saying you got from the library?"

"Not much. That's why I had the argument with them."

"We aren't talking about that and I believe you know it. I—" Waterworth thrusts his wide snub-nosed face forward above his folded arms and jerks up the forefinger of his right fist. "Don't answer that," he orders. "I'm speaking."

The mobile has twitched in my hip pocket and emitted the shrill notes that signify a message. I would ignore his prohibition if I thought this might give me time to invent a story, but he's saying "I mean what you assumed I meant when you came in. You thought I was referring to your accounts, didn't you? You've neglected to keep records and so you made the information up."

"The names aren't as real as they might be. My earnings from the tours are, though."

"I'm afraid, Mr Meadows, I don't think you have much of an idea what's real."

"Gavin," I say, which sounds desperate even to me. "Let me tell you—"

"No, because I'm telling you. If I had any doubts before you arrived, I haven't now. I'm taking the decision to withdraw our support with immediate effect. For all sorts of reasons we can no longer advertise your tours or recommend them in any way."

"I'll do without your support, then. Just so long as you keep quiet about my tours, Hank."

"Mr Waterworth," he says and rises to his feet as if honouring the name. "I'll see you out. We don't want you getting lost in here."

Is that a gibe about my father or the state Waterworth supposes I'm in? I trail him out of the office and overtake him in time to open the last glass door, not that it's much if any of a triumph. He blocks the door with a foot while he calls to the receptionist "Mr Meadows is no longer with us."

I don't look at either of them, or at the faces gazing down from a bus that cuts off the sunlight, flooding the lobby with gloom. I take out my mobile as the glass doors meet with a sound like the solitary note of a bell. The next pair echoes it, sounding submerged by the distance, as I decipher the message, and then I glare along the corridor. I'm close to pounding on them so that I can show Waterworth what he delayed my seeing. There are four garbled words: **Imjm nokay jim hdere**. However clumsily keyed, the message—I'm okay, I'm here—is from my father's number.

Chapter Twenty-four

No Sale

There's no point in blaming Waterworth. However irrational he made me feel—confused enough to imagine a face spread across the window of a bus—I shouldn't have let him prevent me from reading the message at once. At least it was sent only a few minutes ago, and I reply so hastily that some of the letters fall over themselves. **Whes,** I nearly ask, and then **Wherd,** and at last send **Where** too fast to add a question mark.

I return to the opening screen, which shows Lucinda asleep in my bed, and wait for a response. Soon the image fades to conserve energy, and I'm drawn to peer at it so hard that a shadow on the far side of the bed appears to stir. I've never previously wondered what cast the shadow, and it's impossible to tell from its undefined shape. Before long an angular 8 relinquishes a segment to denote the next minute, and I'm still watching when the 9 reduces itself to zero while the digit in front of it seems to writhe like a worm to turn into a 5. I'm not just observing, I'm being observed, and the receptionist looks ready to ask me to leave. In any case the tangled languages that echo in the payment hall are gathering in my brain, so that I feel close to incapable of thinking in English.

I hurry out of the building and loiter on the steps. Traffic crowds down the flyover into Dale Street or lumbers up from the depths of Whitechapel. Although it's early afternoon, many headlamps are lit. How dark may it be where my mother is? I would call her to tell her I've heard from my father if that mightn't delay his next message. Why doesn't he just call? Why haven't I? Perhaps for fear that someone else will answer, even if only with silence, or am I not awake enough to think? I bring up his number, and hear the bell in the midst of waves of static and traffic. At last it gives way to his voice.

"I've got on my bike or I'm otherwise engaged. State your name, rank and serial number . . ." Knowing that he can't be on the bicycle dismays me, and the theatrical British accent he adopts makes me wish I'd never seemed impatient with any of his jokes. "I'll ring you back," he promises, and I will it to be true. Surely anyone who'd stolen his mobile would have deleted the answering message.

"I got your text, dad. Did you get mine? Why aren't you answering? Let's talk. I'd rather talk. There's no reason we can't, is there? Remember you said you wanted a word, so let's have it. You didn't want to worry mother, but we're both worried now. We will be until we hear from you properly. I know you don't want that," I say and would continue, however incoherently, except for realising that he can't interrupt my call to speak. "I'm ringing off now," I tell him, "so you can ring back."

A bus confronts me with two tiers of spectators before carrying them onwards. A 5 on the miniature screen rounds itself and infects its neighbour with the process, but that's the only life the phone shows. I'm alone with memories of my father's voices, and I remember the impromptu tours of Liverpool he gave me when I was a child. Even when my mother came with us, he did most of the talking. Sometimes he introduced me to places that no longer exist—the miles of gardens that adorned a landfill site for a few years by the river near the Maybrick house, the narrow lanes off Church Street that were soon to be buried under department stores—but usually I had to imagine the locations he was evoking. He liked to stroll along the grassy midways of suburban boulevards and reminisce about the trams that used to clank and spit electricity all the way to the Pier Head. Once we took a succession of buses along the dock road from Garston to Seaforth so that he could show me the route of the overhead railway. He had fun with challenging me to guess which suburban buildings he'd watched films in—an undertaker's premises, a nightclub, a car showroom. If I succeeded I would be treated to a re-enactment of a scene from the film, especially if it starred Cagney or Bogart or James Stewart or John Wayne. He enjoyed taking me on the Mersey ferries to watch hordes of homebound businessmen walk widdershins around the decks. Didn't he once suggest they were unconsciously reviving an ancient ritual connected with the river? Was my head ever filled with the harsh smell of coffee that greeted you at the doors of Cooper's that used to occupy the corner of Paradise Street, or are these dreams my father gave me? I'm dismayed that just now I can't recall more from our life together; I'm even struggling to visualise his face, as if it's losing its shape in my mind. I feel as if my chance to locate him is retreating, but haven't I overlooked a way of tracing him? I dash down the steps and around the building towards Whitechapel.

I'm clammy with rage at my thoughtlessness. Am I ever going to wake up? As I sprint down Stanley Street I pass someone sitting on Eleanor Rigby's bench. Are they homeless or in some other unfortunate condition? My glimpse suggests that their face is as grey and baggy as their outfit, and I'm not even sure it's a hood that renders their cranium hairless and carelessly shaped. I'm quite glad to be on the opposite side of the road. The drain beyond the kerb in front of the bench utters a splash, and I suppose the person must have disposed of some litter and fled, because when I glance back they're nowhere to be seen. All that matters to me is the Frugone store on Whitechapel.

It's on a corner of the street leading to the Playhouse, and my head begins to throb as if it's raw with memory. It throbs more vigorously as I find the shop is locked. Beyond the window full of pink phones and striped ones, not to mention leopard-spotted mobiles and others spattered with cartoonish drops like magnified negative rain, employees with buckets are doggedly mopping the floor. At the back of the shop, water looks inches deep. One man greets the sight of me by spreading his arms wide, which displays the Frugosh special offers logo on his sulphurously yellow shirt. As I start to move away the gesture turns into a promise of an embrace, and he strides to open the door. "Don't run off. We're not underwater yet," he cries, shaking his head and the jowls of his expansive mottled face. "You look like my kind of customer."

His enthusiasm comes with cigarette breath. "What's happened here?" I feel bound to wonder.

"Must be a burst somewhere with all the weather. What can I get you? If it's anything the water's done for we can organise it overnight."

"I was hoping you could trace a mobile."

"Nothing simpler. Let's have the details."

"It's my father's."

"Needs an eye keeping, does he? I know what they can be like. You don't want to put them on a leash but you can't have them wandering off all hours God knows where. You've got his agreement, yes?"

It must be at my parents' house. "You don't need to see it, do you?" I hope aloud as I take out my mobile. "I can show you his number."

"He gave it you is what I'm asking."

"Why wouldn't he? How else would I know it?" I retort before my bewilderment begins to clear. "Sorry, you mean—"

"He signed up to let you track him."

"I'm sure he would, but he's, he's disappeared. That's why I need to trace the text he just sent."

There's a sound of wallowing behind the salesman, and his eyes flicker sideways. As I identify the noise as the action of a mop he says "Looks like your best bet's the police."

"Oh," I say, which is mostly a sigh. "Well, if that's all you can offer . . ."

I'm turning away when he steps outside and shuts the door as a preamble to murmuring "What's it worth to you?"

I'm ashamed to be wary. "Quite a lot," I compromise by saying.

"I won't ask what's up between you and the authorities. Have you got another phone?"

"At home."

He glances both ways along Whitechapel and leans close enough for me to smell smoke on his mutter. "Give us your mobile and fifty and your other number and I'll give you a bell tomorrow."

"Can't you do it any sooner? He might try to get in touch with me again."

"I'm already taking a risk for you. That's my best deal."

I'm painfully tempted to give him the phone before he can abolish the opportunity, but it would feel like yielding up my father to the unknown. "Thanks anyway," I murmur. "I'd better try elsewhere."

"Suit yourself, but I'm telling you for nothing you won't find a better offer."

I wouldn't be surprised if, like his employers, he undertakes to match any price I'm quoted by a competitor. Instead he raps on the shop window and clouds the glass by pressing his forehead against it. "Paddle over, someone," he says, which turns the window greyer. "You won't drown."

There's no point in trying any of the other phone shops. As I tramp up Lord Street I call the police. I've invented a mnemonic that represents the ten digits of the occurrence number. Oh Eustace oh God oh, it begins before degenerating further into nonsense, and I wonder if I only dreamed that St Eustace was somehow related to changes in sea level. Apparently giving my father's number over the phone isn't permitted. "We'll send someone out as soon as we can," a woman informs me, not without sharpness.

In any case I should be home and making certain my father's research doesn't suffer any more damage. There's a branch of Frugo Corner, the shop-sized version of the supermarket, at the Castle end of Lord Street. A supervisor sporting a Frugoal football supporter's shirt, which is striped red and blue so as not to take sides in Liverpool, loses his enthusiasm for helping me once he discovers that I'm after empty cartons. When I produce a crumpled receipt as proof I often shop here he makes with some reluctance for the stockroom.

A succession of hollow thuds puts me in mind of trapdoors before he reappears, kicking cartons in front of him as if he wants to live up to his shirt. I nest as many as I can inside one another and stumble almost blindly out with the pile of them. I have to rely on the crowds to move out of my way as I tramp past the regal monument and down towards the river. In my street more people than ordinarily use it to retreat into doorways or otherwise vanish from my path. In more than one instance their footsteps sound loose and rubbery—boots for the weather, of course.

I return to the lobby to collect half the boxes. Once they're all in my apartment I gulp handfuls of water from the bathroom tap. I'm on the way to the main room when I abandon the boxes in the corridor. I've yet to check that my father's computer has survived the damp.

I disconnect my computer tower and plug in his. The monitor flickers like the first hint of a storm, and after the usual computer preamble the opening screen fades into view. I've never seen it before, and it takes me off guard. It's an image of my parents on either side of me, somewhere by the river. We're decades younger; I've yet to reach my teens. The opposite bank of the river is smudged by fog, which also obscures a large vessel in the middle of the water. The blurred reflection helps produce the illusion of a vast dark shape rearing up into the fog. It can only be a ship, though perhaps my father reshaped the image—but as I reflect that he must have scanned the old photograph into the computer, the screen grows as black as the bottom of the sea.

Chapter Twenty-five

AN AUTHOR DISINTERRED

Computer Combinations wouldn't be able to deal with the problem for at least a week. Computer Shooter might have time to examine the system within five days, but I'd have to take the computer to their premises several miles away in dockland. Computer Mission offers me the same wait, but they're even more distant, all of which is also the case with Computer Commander and Compurity. I'm close to calling a taxi to transport me and the lifeless monolith of a computer tower to dockland until I speak to one more from the yellow pages, PC Tec. They can collect the computer within the hour and attend to it tomorrow.

I wish this were more of a relief, but too much else is wrong. There hasn't been a message from my father while I was busy on the landline, and I feel as if he has vanished as utterly as his web site. Will the computer experts be able to retrieve his work? I tried switching the system on and off half a dozen times, but the screen remained as blank as dreamless sleep. At least I can save his research from any further harm, and I take the new cartons into the main room, only to falter. Last night I thought my tiredness was rendering the material illegible, but every visible document is so smudged by moisture that I can't decipher a word.

I snatch them off the cartons and strew them about the floor. The pages they were covering up are blurred too, but with some effort they're readable. Where the topmost item is a book, the pages have become a pulpy mass. There's no point in letting despair creep any closer. I line up the unsalvageable books and pages along the hall, and then I set about transferring the contents of the soggy boxes into the dry ones. Bits of information snag my mind. The women who made cords along the rope walks were known as the hempy girls, apparently a reference to visions some of them gained from the cannabis in the hemp. The commonest vision was of a giant rope or umbilical cord that could draw forth a creature hidden under the land. In the early fourteenth century performers of miracles that involved the Pool—healing people by immersion in it, especially cases of possession or mental states perceived as demonic—were banned from the town. In 1775 a society was formed "for the recovery of persons apparently drowned." Couldn't the rescuers tell? As I empty another box my mobile starts to sing about love.

The display leaves the caller nameless. That can't be my father, and so I don't speak until Lucinda asks "Gavin? Are you on a tour?"

"Do you know, I'm not."

"Good," she says, which exacerbates my bitterness. "You were wanting to know about William Colquitt."

"Are you at work? I'll ring you back."

As I grab the landline phone it occurs to me that one of her colleagues may answer. How much of an argument will that involve? After my encounter with Waterworth I'm more than ready for one, so that my eagerness takes some relinquishing when Lucinda says "Record Office."

"William Colquitt."

If my abruptness takes her aback, she stays professional. "There's nothing in his poem about burying the Pool."

"Nay, though it be buried furlongs deep . . ." I sound as if I'm making this up and growing antique too. "It's only in the edition you've got," I insist.

"Nothing like that. I read the whole poem. There was only ever one edition. He wasn't that popular." With barely a pause she adds "Did you say your father copied it and wrote something about John Strong? Maybe he—"

"If you haven't got it, tell me where else it could be."

"I don't think I can, Gavin."

"In his head and mine, you mean. You don't need to say it."

"I wasn't about to. I'm just trying to tell you the truth."

"You're pretty fond of doing that, aren't you."

"I hope so. Honestly, Gavin, you sound—"

I'm even angrier for having made such an apparently idiotic comment. "Telling your colleagues about me, for instance."

"Who says I did that?"

"Hank Waterworth."

"I've no idea who that is."

"The man behind our image. One of that mob. The tourism organiser. The character who decides what the city's going to support, and that doesn't include me after your people complained to him."

"Gavin, I'm sorry. I didn't know they meant to."

"What did you think they wanted, to send me a get well card?"

My retort is too close to suggesting one might have been appropriate, an idea Lucinda exacerbates by saying "I just tried to tell them how you are."

"Which is what?"

"How much you're adding to the city and how Deryck has to be preying on your mind."

"So which vindictive sod called Waterworth?"

"I couldn't say. I can't talk any more now. Let's wait till we can go to our place by the river." When I mutter less than a word she says "Don't you want to see me later?"

"Just not there for a change."

"I'll see you soon," she says and is gone before I can ask where. Presumably she means to come to the apartment. I take both phones into the hall and hobble along it on my knees. I could imagine that, like some spectacularly malleable circus performer, I've turned into a dwarf, but I'm scrutinising

the blurred documents. None of them looks like the remains of verse, and I didn't see the poem in any of the cartons. Could it be online?

I stumble to my feet and into the workroom to disconnect
my father's computer. I substitute mine and watch the icons
float up from the blackness. Having logged on, I send the
Frugoget search engine after William Colquitt. It seems Lucinda didn't exaggerate his unpopularity, because there isn't
a single reference to him.

Staring at his name in the search box won't dredge him
up, and I'm about to quit Frugonet when I think of something else to look for. While it isn't urgent, I wouldn't mind
a few moments' break from emptying and loading cartons. I
type "mermaids down below" in the box and start the search
engine. I've hardly drawn a breath when I have the source,
and the breath comes out loud and harsh.

Of course I knew it was unlikely that the name in the
song Lucinda sang could originally have been Gav. Perhaps
I should have guessed the name it supplanted. ". . . For all
the landsmen lovers are nothing after Jack . . ." The song is
called "They All Love Jack," set to music by Stephen Adams. I could think he was trying to dissociate himself from
some aspect of his family, because his real name was Michael Maybrick. He was James's brother.

Chapter Twenty-six

Passed Down

The site is called *James Maybrick Is Jack the Ripper*. As I stare at the lyrics, which first saw publication three years before the Ripper made his name, an accompaniment on a piano more tinny than tuneful starts up. It sounds like the kind of enthusiastic amateur performance you might hear in a pub, and I imagine drinkers chanting the song and swaying in time with the waltz. The notion isn't too appealing. No pub would be so dark that the figures reeling back and forth like underwater vegetation appeared to lose and then regain their indistinct shapes with each reiterated movement while they sang so lustily that their mouths opened far too wide. I'm striving to expel the image from my mind—perhaps I need to turn off the computer, since the tune I first heard Lucinda sing feels as though it's acting like an uninvited lullaby—when my reverie is punctured by a bell.

I shove the chair backwards so fast that it ends up in the hall. The waltz continues tinkling as I poke the button of the intercom, to be told "Police."

The voice is all too familiar, even if I don't know which name to give it. I hold down the button to admit the caller and am heading back to silence the waltz when there's a knock or at least a thump at the door. The fist sounds not just large but unexpectedly soft, and he must have pretty well leapt upstairs. I open the door to see the policeman with the dented nose—Maddock, if I'm not mistaken. His face does look damp, but there's no other evidence of his exertions unless I count his scowl. In a bid to lighten the mood I remark "On your own today?"

"He went to the bog."

I suspect they feel entitled to use whichever toilet is convenient, and I'm glad his partner didn't choose mine. As I shut the door behind us he says "Got visitors?"

"Not that I'm aware of."

"Don't want anybody wet, is that it?"

It takes me an uneasy moment to recall the bag of umbrellas beside me. "They're for my tours," I tell him.

"Having a singsong?"

Perhaps I'm supposed to acknowledge his attempts at jokes, but the shrill piano is picking my thoughts to bits. "Just the computer," I say and make for it. Before I can quell the waltz he comes into rather too much of my workroom. "Let's have a look," he says as I grab the mouse.

I feel suspect for stepping back and furious as a result. He flattens one large leathery hand on the desk and lowers his head, swelling the ridged stump of his neck. "Research for your job, is it?" he says and begins to sing to the accompaniment. "The mermaids down below . . ."

His singing voice is a sepulchral croak. I remember Lucinda murmuring the lullaby, and find I'm reluctant to learn what name Maddock might substitute for Jack. Of course that's absurd to the point of grotesqueness, but I cut off the music by closing the page. "Anyway, that isn't why you're here."

As he steps into the corridor a bathroom tap delivers a gout of water that it must have been storing up. He frowns along the corridor before heading for the main room. "He's not, is he?"

"Who?" I have to ask, and "What?"

"Here." With as little patience Maddock adds "Your old man's not come back."

"If he had I wouldn't have called you."

"Could have since. This looks like his mess."

I take a deep breath that keeps in quite a few words and say "Would you mind showing a little more respect for my family?"

He turns among the cartons to stare at me. "We'll be doing our job. Anyone complaining?"

"Not without a reason." I cross the room and sit in a chair to demonstrate whose home this is—whose castle. I won't have it invaded by threats that can't even own up to their nature. "Be careful there," I tell him.

He takes a hefty step towards me, and I wonder how much he and his partner are creatures of the night, used to dealing with the kind of violence that takes place after dark and with the breed of people responsible. It seems I'm less courageous than I would like to dream. As my forehead begins to feel like an omen of an injury I realise how disinclined the authorities will be to take my word against the one of even this policeman. "Would you want anyone to talk about your family like that?" I try asking.

"What are you saying about my family?"

"Nothing. That's what I said."

"Don't be fucking clever. You've got no audience now. What are you thinking about them?"

"Still nothing. I don't know the first thing about them. All I—"

"I'll tell you the first thing," he says, and a grimace that may conceal some kind of humour widens his mouth. "They lived beneath you."

Does he mean socially? His hostility suggests it. The safest response I can find is "Who?"

"Weren't you listening? The first ones. The sort you and your old man are supposed to be interested in."

"Then I am if you want me to be," I say in the hope of placating Maddock. "Tell me about them."

"Like I say, they lived down below."

It isn't just the echo of the song that disconcerts me. "Where?"

"Not in your basement. That'd be a laugh," Maddock says without demonstrating what kind. "Some cellar round here, though."

"How long ago are we talking about?"

"When the old bitch was on the throne who didn't want to know what women had to do to feed their kids."

I hope his fury is directed at the past, not at me. "Victoria," I risk saying.

"That's the twat. Long as they stayed underground the city pretended they didn't exist. That's except for the sods that used them, like your mate Maybrick."

"He's not my anything." I'm suspicious enough to add "What makes you say he is?"

"You were looking at stuff about him and his brother."

"You're saying James went to, to people like your ancestor."

"That's the tale my cousin got. Know what I reckon is the worst?"

I'm by no means sure I want to, but there seems no way to avoid saying "I don't."

"They made them leave the lights off."

"Out of hypocrisy, you mean? I believe the Victorians—"

"Not that crap," Maddock says and looks capable of spitting in the nearest carton. "So they couldn't see people like my gran's gran."

"Wouldn't you call that hypocrisy?"

"Don't you want to know either?" Maddock says, wiping his wet mouth with the side of his fist. "They couldn't stand looking. And maybe it let them make her into anything they wanted."

His entire face writhes as if it's seeking a new shape, and perhaps I'm too anxious to speak. "Is that why you do what you do?"

His face settles on an expression or at least an ominous blankness. "Like what?"

"Working for the police so you can save other people from being exploited."

"She did it herself. All she could do. That's what she was. There's still plenty—" He glares at me, widening his eyes as if he has wakened from talking in his sleep. "That's it," he says, which sounds like a warning until he adds "That's why we joined up."

"Not just you, then."

"Me and my cousin." When I fail to grasp the point that he apparently regards as obvious he says "Terry Maddock."

"So you're Constable Wrigley or whatever you are." This isn't too well put, and I stumble onwards. "You two must be very unusual."

Wrigley's glare is back. "What're you saying about us?"

"Just that there can't be many relatives together on the beat. I'm surprised the city hasn't made something of it."

"Who's going to tell them?"

His confidences aren't just unwelcome, they're menacing, especially when he takes several heavy steps towards me. "So what did you get from your old man?" he says.

When he extends a large hand that still looks moist from wiping his mouth I show him the mobile. I bring up the inbox and display my father's message. "What language's that meant to be?" Wrigley objects. "Looks like he doesn't want to be found."

However painful it is, I have to suggest "Maybe he doesn't know what he's saying."

Wrigley widens his eyes until they bulge while, I assume, he memorises everything about the message, and then he makes for the hall. "We'll see," he says. "We've got his number."

I'm still worried that the message may leave the police less inclined to search. I wish I'd tried harder to put them off from coming here, especially since there seems to be no reason for the visit. "How soon will you be able to track it down, do you think?"

"Depends. If we come up with him we'll let one of you know." As I shut the door and follow him to the stairs he says "You can stay up. I know the way."

"I need more boxes."

"Still taking after your old man, are you?" Wrigley says and doesn't wait for an answer. He turns the first bend in the stairs with a fluid movement that looks close to reptilian. As he stumps down to the lobby the ridges of his token neck seem to swell, and I could imagine that he has grown broader and more squat, as if the weight of his thick torso has redistributed his flesh. He doesn't bother holding the street door open, perhaps because a harsh voice from the car parked on the pavement is summoning him. As I emerge the car screeches away, swerving riverwards while I head for Frugo Corner.

I tramp back hugging cartons, through crowds of office workers hurrying home ahead of the rain that has brought the black sky low. The side streets are emptier, and mine is entirely so apart from a dark shape I glimpse slithering under the door to the basement. It's a shadow cast by headlamps, which swing away from the intersection as I fumble for my keys. I struggle upstairs with the boxes and drop them in the main room, and then I take out my mobile. Too much is unresolved just now.

I don't want to disturb Lucinda more than I have to while she's at work, and so I text a solitary word: **Later**? I add a jolly face and send the message, and am separating the Chinese boxes I've brought home when the phone on the table jerks and chirps. Presumably she's busy, because her message is almost as terse as mine. **Mabybe not tonight**, it says, and I take the extra consonant to indicate her haste. I needn't think it shows that she doesn't care enough to correct the word. I still need to call my mother. I should have done so earlier, but for various reasons I'm afraid to raise her hopes too much.

Chapter Twenty-seven

THE NIGHT'S THOUGHTS

When my eyes grow too hot to be soothed by handfuls of water I abandon trying to make sense of my father's research as I box it up. I trample the empty cartons until I see this leaves faint stains on the carpet, and then I have to make several trips to the basement bins. On the middle floor someone is singing a muffled song in the bath, but otherwise the building seems as good as deserted. At least nobody sees me keep waving my arms at the underground lights to ensure I'm not left in the dark. The frantic shadow that vanishes under a parked car belongs to my hand, of course. At the top of the ramp the metal door clatters as tendrils grope beneath it, but that's just the latest downpour.

It's too late to expect to see Lucinda, and it's her turn to get in touch. I've told my mother about my father's message, and she seemed to do her best not to feel too immediately hopeful, despite having answered the phone before it could ring twice. I lock the apartment and take a shower, though I'm close to having had enough of water; my labours gave me such a thirst that I feel bloated with drinking from the tap. Perhaps I miss Lucinda more than I'm willing to admit, because I find the caresses of the shower unexpectedly intimate; I wouldn't need to be much drowsier to imagine that trickles are fingering my back. As I towel myself a blurred shape moves back and forth behind the condensation on the mirror—my own face.

I return as much water to the plumbing as I can expel, and then I trudge to bed. The window above it is swarming with rain. Even with the curtains drawn, the dimness that fills the room at the tug of a cord appears to shift like the depths of a river. When the movements begin to infect the outlines of objects in the room or rather my perceptions of them, I close my eyes tight and pull the quilt up over my face.

Rain fumbles at the window, and then I hear an outburst of yapping and shouts. Nobody is hunting in the streets; some drunks must be setting off car alarms, unless they have dogs with them. An intermittent raucous noise is harder to identify, but however much it resembles croaking I conclude that it's made by rusty hinges and a wind. Perhaps it's a door in the building opposite. It doesn't matter so long as I can sleep.

I still feel bloated. As slumber starts to close around me I could fancy I'm drowning in my flesh. I'm drifting in the midst of a flotsam of thoughts salvaged from my father's research. In Mesolithic times the coastline shrank inland two hundred metres every day; no wonder the tribes were desperate to placate the water by any means they thought might work. I'm reminded of the bull that was baited at the inauguration of the first Liverpool dock. In 1780 a doctor and his wife had themselves buried up to their necks in Colquitt Street, presumably to demonstrate some cure, but did they see how they resembled an ancient sacrifice? At a dinner in 1806 for the Prince of Wales at Liverpool Town Hall, the toasts included the Lancashire Witches and Neptune's Maggot. In those days criminals were still incarcerated in the dungeons of the tower at the foot of Water Street, though it was soon demolished. More than one prisoner ended up in the asylum opposite the heath where Lucinda's library is now. Whenever they were forced to bathe they would rant about how the dank cells had let in not just water but its denizens. No doubt ducking was part of their treatment, and my father thought it was almost a city tradition: in 1777 Mary Clarke was flung into a dock, apparently because the assailants had mistaken her nature, and decades later female prisoners in

the House of Correction on Mount Pleasant, up the slope
from the home of the young Maybrick brothers, were rou-
tinely pumped upon or subjected to the ducking-stool. There
were seawater baths where the docks are now, and bathers
complained that intruders were gaining entry to the private
cubicles and using them as hideouts—lairs, as one bather
oddly put it. The High Rip violence started opposite the
Flashes, the vanished pond that used to serve a ducking-
stool. In the days of the Rip and the Ripper, pits full of water
beyond Everton Brow were used as public baths. The on-
slaughts of rain that shake my bedroom window remind me
of the storms that repeatedly flooded the town less than two
hundred years ago. Back then house numbers and street
names were painted on the buildings, and I imagine someone
wandering the unpaved muddy streets in a storm. He's blinded
by water, and in any case the signs have been rendered illegible by rain. The dream feels like my haphazard attempts to
find connections in my father's research. Perhaps in some
sense the processes are the same.

   The notion troubles me until I struggle out of bed to check
whether his web site can help me put all the details together.
I'm in the corridor before I recall that his computer is useless
and not even here—PC Tec collected it hours ago. There's
something else to see; the windows across the street are lit,
however dimly. I'm close to my desk when I see that the floor
opposite mine is no longer used as an office. Silhouetted figures are performing pliés in a dance class, bending their legs
wide at the knee and then rising to their full height. I haven't
previously realised how froglike the exercise looks, and I'm
quite glad not to have drawn their attention by switching on
the light, even though the rank of figures is at the back of the
long room. Their shapes are dismayingly various and rather less
than constant, and I have an unpleasant suspicion that every
eye, none of which I can distinguish, is watching me. I've taken
a pace backwards when the tallest silhouette—dauntingly
tall—rears up and springs across the room. In a moment it

has thrown open the window directly opposite me and leapt onto the sill. It crouches low and launches itself across the space between us. Before I can retreat, its body is flattened like gelatin against the glass while its splayed limbs cling to the wall. Its face slithers back and forth on the pane, dragging out of shape whatever features it has. At least it can't get in, I think desperately until its substance seeps and then floods under the sash.

The spectacle jerks me awake, or the frantic movement at the window does. It's a burst of rain, the sound of which must have caused my dream of Springheel Jack. I don't need to turn over in bed to confirm that the window is keeping the rain out; I'm just grateful to find Lucinda beside me. Except for her I would be alone with the residue of the nightmare. I wouldn't have minded her wakening me when she let herself in or when she joined me in bed, but of course she wants me to catch up on my sleep. Presumably it was raining whenever she arrived, since the indistinct mass of her face appears to be glistening, although if she drove into the basement garage, where would she have been rained on? Perhaps she had a shower and left her face wet. This seems unlikely, and I strain to distinguish more than the silhouette of her head on the pillow. My vision adjusts to the gloom, a process that makes her features seem to rise out of the silhouette rather than simply growing visible. Her eyes are opening to greet me, however much they resemble round lumps that are swelling up from the substance of the head. There's no further chance of mistaking the face for Lucinda's. Apart from the eyes and the grinning mouth, which is far too wide and lipless, it isn't much of a face at all.

I have a dreadful sense that the intruder will move before I can, unless it's waiting for me to try. I'm struggling to decide whether to inch away as surreptitiously as possible or to fling myself backwards, assuming I'm able to do either, when something starts to rattle at my back.

I almost lurch away from it, into the arms of my companion.

As I recognise the vibrations of my mobile I flounder towards it off the bed. I make a grab at the light cord and knock it out of reach as an object sprawls on the floor beyond the bed. I capture the cord and tug it almost hard enough to wrench the socket out of the ceiling. The light reveals that the bed is empty even of the quilt, which lies in a heap on the floor beyond it. By this time the phone is declaring its love. I clutch it and poke the key to accept the call and press the mobile against my face. "Hello?" I plead, hardly caring who's there so long as I hear a human voice.

"Gavin, I'm sorry. I've woken you, haven't I."

"It's all right." Indeed, it's considerably better if my mother actually has. I risk crouching to peer under the bed, where there's no sign of an intruder. "What's happening?" I say as calmly as I'm able. "Is there news?"

"You won't have heard from anyone yet." When I admit as much she says "I didn't want to disturb you, but I don't think I can stand it by myself."

I venture around the bed, and as I take hold of the quilt with my free hand I say "Don't worry. If you need to talk—"

"It isn't just that, Gavin. Something's getting in."

I almost lose hold of the slippery quilt, but I succeed in throwing it one-handed on the bed. There was nothing under it. "Water, you mean? How bad—"

"Not just water. Worse than that." My mother has lowered her voice so much that straining my ears seems to attract a rush of static. "It's here now. It's downstairs," she whispers. Even lower, as if she doesn't want to hear her own words, she says "I thought it was your father."

Chapter Twenty-eight

No Longer Alone

I wait in the street for the taxi I called on the landline. I want to be sure I don't miss it, but I'm also glad to be out of my apartment, having failed to convince myself beyond any doubt that the shapeless mark as large as a man on the carpet by the bed was just a shadow. The building opposite is dark, and no matter how often I glance at it to take any watchers off guard, none of the windows shows me anything like a face. The streets are quiet except for a gutter somewhere, which is reminiscing about the latest downpour and anticipating the next one. Eventually a rising wave proves to be the hiss of wheels as a black taxi turns the corner. "Home?" the driver says as I climb in.

"Used to be," I tell him, and the address.

He says no more while the taxi swerves into Tithebarn Street and heads inland, past Maybrick's office and the Flashes. It swings away from Deadman's Lane and speeds uphill towards the ridge. At nearly four in the morning there's no sign of anyone awake besides us, and I wonder how many dreams surround us. At the end of a side street a lanky shape rears up beyond a garden fence, and I think I hear baying, which falls behind like a hunt that has lost the scent. The thin eager figure has reminded me that the introverted maze of narrow streets the pavement cuts off from the main road is supposed to have been one of Springheel Jack's playgrounds. Could Thomas de Quincey have seen the creature in a vision? Hardly, since de Quincey died decades earlier. Time can't work like that except in dreams, however much opium he took in Everton.

As the taxi speeds along the ridge I see my parents' house but not my mother. The house is surrounded by a sulphurous aura, and I'm afraid it's on fire until the mist recedes from our approach and grows dark. Only that house is lit—every window. "That's you, is it?" says the driver.

I could imagine that it's doing duty in place of the lighthouse that used to stand on the ridge. What might it attract out of the dark? That isn't how lighthouses are meant to work. When the taxi halts I say "Can you wait while I see what's happening?"

The driver's hooded eyes peer at me in the mirror. "Not thinking of hopping it, are you?"

"I'm not that kind."

His eyes narrow as though the lids are growing heavy with the late hour. "Hop out, then, and let's know the score."

The light through the orange curtains flares on the For Sale sign and adds lurid highlights to plants and weeds in the front garden. The bars of the gate gather orange outlines as I step on the path. The clang of the latch brings my mother to the front door so fast that she seems about to flee the house. "Oh, Gavin, I'm sorry for bringing you," she cries.

"Don't worry," I tell her, however inappropriately. She's wearing her flowered dress again or still. In the dogged light from the hall it looks paler than it should, and so does she. An armchair has been moved from the front room to the foot of the stairs. Presumably she wanted to stay by the old-fashioned phone that my father insisted on buying, which is perched on its rest halfway up the stairs, as far as the cord from the wall stretches. I assume that's where she retreated to, and I raise my voice. "Where's the problem?"

"I'm not sure any more. Down here, I think."

I do my best to stride into the front room as challengingly as I spoke. It and its contents are steeped in tired light; I can't tell if they're dusty or just faded. Nobody is to be seen, and the windows are locked. All of this is equally the case with the back room and the kitchen, where the outer door is locked and bolted. "I can't see how anyone could have got in," I say, though not entirely with relief.

"It came through somewhere. I heard it, Gavin," my mother calls. "Maybe it went the same way."

"What did you hear?"

"I thought it was water at first, but it was too . . ." After quite a pause she says "Too slithery. That's how it got."

How much has my father's disappearance affected her mind? As gently as possible I say "Has anyone been to look at the roof?"

"I should have called someone, shouldn't I? You've more than enough on your plate." She seems to need to pause again before saying "It wasn't that, though."

"Did you see anything?"

"Something. I told you I thought it was Deryck, but I wasn't thinking straight. It couldn't have been him."

"But what exactly?"

"Just the back of his head. I thought he was squatting. I'd had to go to the bathroom," she says with a hint of embarrassed defiance. "I was coming down because I'd heard that noise, and there it was in the hall. I even called his name because I thought nobody else could have got in, and then I saw it wasn't squatting, it was really like that. And then it went away."

"Where could it have?"

"Maybe there if there's nowhere else."

She's pointing at the cupboard under the stairs. As I make for it she takes a step forward and then retreats. I grab the doorknob, which may not be moist if my hand is, and fling the door open. My mother cries out as an object lurches at me. It's a spade that my vehemence has disturbed. The cupboard is full of tools and a damp smell, perhaps brought in from the garden. No, there's a patch of moisture in the darkest corner, and I'm peering at it when a voice demands "What's up, love?"

The taxi driver has stepped into the hall. Most of his

stature must be in his torso, because he's shorter than his height while he was driving led me to assume. His broad face looks jowly with somnolence, but he keeps a sharp eye on my mother as she says "I thought I'd had a break-in."

"Did you call the law?"

With more pride than I feel entitled to she says "No, I called my son."

There's a hole in the far corner of the cupboard. At first I took it for the wettest section of the patch of damp. It's no larger than a mouse or something of that girth. I can do without the additional thought, and I slam the door as if this may shut up the idea. "I'd better check upstairs," I tell my mother.

"I'll stay with your mam," says the driver.

What sounds like a handful of water greets me as I reach the top of the stairs. It must have been gathering in a bath tap. My father's workroom looks even more deserted for being occupied by several plastic buckets, none of which contains enough water to justify their presence. The windows are locked, and the same is true of the bathroom and my parents' bedroom, where the bed is made as neatly as you could find in a hotel. It's evident that my mother has been sleeping or attempting to sleep in the chair in the hall. "I've been praying I never see anything like it again," I hear her say. "I don't like to think it might still be in the house."

The driver gazes up the stairs at me while addressing her. "Are you living on your own, love?"

"Only since his father's gone away. Not for much longer, I hope."

The driver holds out a hand to me. "Do your best, mate."

I'm sufficiently confused to think he wants to shake my hand until I realise he's waiting to be paid. "Can you hang on a few minutes?"

"You aren't going anywhere, are you?"

"He can't be expected to stay with me," my mother says. "He's already got so many things to do."

"His mam ought to come first. If he isn't staying maybe he should take you home."

"You wouldn't have room, would you, Gavin?"

"It's more a question of beds."

"Don't worry about that. We've still got sleeping bags from when we were your age."

"That's fixed, then," the driver informs me. "I'll wait like you said."

"Will that be all right, Gavin? You don't want a silly old woman imposing on you on top of everything else."

It seems clear that she wants to be contradicted. As I make a tentative attempt the driver says "You're not, love. I'd have you for my mam."

"I'll just get a few things, then," she tells him as much as me, and hurries to rummage upstairs. When she reappears she's preceded by a plump object that wriggles out of her embrace before slithering down into the hall as she fails to grip the sleeping bag between her chin and a laden canvas hold-all. "You shouldn't be carrying all that," says the driver.

I've already slung the sleeping bag out of her way and am hurrying to relieve her of her burden. As I carry it downstairs she brings the phone to the hall table and hesitates. "Where's some paper? I'll leave him a note."

"You stay exactly where you are, love."

The driver returns from the taxi with a pad of Dockside Cabs receipts and hands one to my mother along with a stubby ballpoint. She lays the paper on the table blank side up and regards it for some seconds before writing *Gone to Gavin's. If you're here, please call. We just want to know you're safe.* She adds half a dozen crosses that resemble stitches in the page and pins it down with the receiver she has taken off the hook. "He'll have to call you if he can't get through here, won't he?"

While I mumble in agreement the driver grabs the sleeping bag as if he's determined to give her no chance to change her mind. I linger in the doorway with the hold-all while she switches off the lights. As she shuts the front door, something stirs in the dark hall. I'm reminded of the flutter of a bat in a cave, but the pale object that waves like an underwater leaf is her note, enlivened by a gust of wind. She watches it subside and pulls the door shut, launching herself along the path. "Let's go if we're going," she says.

The driver has unrolled the sleeping bag across the back seat. He bows my mother into the taxi, where she almost slides off the quilted bag before securing herself with the seat belt. She greets the mishap with a laugh that sounds anxious for company, and the driver obliges. I do my best while inadvertently imitating the incident as the taxi swings away from the dark house.

West Derby Road shows a distant hint of dawn above Tuebrook, but we leave the glow beyond the ridge. We're in sight of the central library when my mother gasps. "What will Lucy think of another woman in your flat?"

"If I see her I'll ask."

"Oh dear, aren't things right there either? Will I make them worse?"

"I shouldn't think so. It's not important just now."

She looks ready to argue, but instead says "I'll make it my business not to get in your way. Just try and carry on as if I'm not there."

"Ought to be glad he'll have his mam looking after him," says the driver.

Perhaps she feels bound to suggest how. "I'll be able to answer your phone if anyone calls while you're doing your tours."

"That's if I am. The city's had enough of me, or the man who decides has, anyway. He thinks I'm bringing it into disrepute."

"How dare he say that? I've never heard such, I won't say the word. What's his name?"

"No point in worrying about him as well. There's nothing we can do about him."

"Don't be so sure," my mother says, but nothing more as the flyover takes us into Dale Street. The headlamp beams glint in flooded gutters beside the deserted pavements and send shadows fleeing into the old dark lanes. In Trident Street the beams sweep a shadow away from the basement entrance or under the metal door. "You're home," says the driver.

While I pay him and retrieve the hold-all, my mother releases herself and the bag. By the time I unlock the lobby door and prop it open with the hold-all, the driver has taken the bag and ushered my mother to the threshold. "Want me to come in?" he asks her.

"He'll look after me."

"See you do," he says and, having handed me the bag, pushes the hold-all into the lobby to shut the door behind me and my mother.

She insists on carrying the hold-all upstairs, but drops it as I switch the hall light on. "Oh, Gavin," she says. "Are you feeling invaded?"

"Not at all."

She's gazing at the material lined up along the hall beyond the umbrellas, and tramps heavily forward to crouch in front of a page. "What happened to this?" she says in dismay.

"We didn't manage to save those in time."

I'm afraid she may ask about the computer, but she heads for the main room. Once she has finished staring into the cartons she says "Can I see Deryck's message?"

She stares at this too as if she hopes it will grow clearer. "Why has he typed it like that? It looks like some kind of code. Was he trying to tell us something? Why would he have to do it like that?"

Imjm nokay jim hdere. "I should think he was just in a hurry," I say, though this isn't as reassuring as I would prefer.

"He must be all right really, mustn't he, or he wouldn't have sent it at all." Perhaps as a further attempt to be positive she says "Shall I make us a cup of tea?"

"I wouldn't mind seeing if I can get some sleep."

"You're right, we should while we're able. You snuggle into bed."

I've followed her with the bags, but I wonder "Where will you—"

"I'll be fine in here. I'm not too old to make myself comfortable on the couch. The bed isn't just yours, is it? You have it and don't worry about me."

Even when I grasp that she's thinking of Lucinda I'm reminded of the intruder that had to be a dream. It makes me grateful not to be alone in the apartment, even though I feel inhibited in the bathroom. I run the tap into the sink while I use the toilet, and then I reward myself with several mouthfuls of water. "Good night," my mother calls as I head for my room. "Try and sleep."

The quilt is too flat to be hiding anything, and I refuse to look under the bed. I switch off the light and shut my eyes to intensify the dimness while I do my best not to listen to my mother in the bathroom. I'm drowsing when I hear her in the main room. I think she's on the phone until I remember that both are on my bedside table. Who's she talking to? Eventually I deduce from her tone that she's reading aloud. She must be looking at my father's research, but I can't distinguish a word. Her voice seems so blurred that she might be talking in her sleep.

Chapter Twenty-nine

ON THE AIR

It's daylight, and my mother is still talking. I have the impression that her voice took some time to waken me. Perhaps she hasn't slept at all. Has she been reading my father's research in the hope of deducing where he is? I've yet to distinguish a word, and I wonder if she's trying to decipher the items in the hall. Suppose the blurring that has overtaken them spreads to her brain? I can't be quite awake if I imagine that it could. I raise my head and strain my ears, and then I hear my name.

She isn't calling me, she's talking about me. The landline receiver is gone from the bedside table, but the mobile is next to the clock, which shows me that it's early afternoon. I hop none too efficiently into yesterday's trousers and pull a Liverghoul T-shirt over my head. I haven't time to choose a less contentious item—I want to hear what she's saying, and to whom. Easing the door open, I pad along the hall.

My mother is on the couch beside the sleeping bag, which is propped up like a companion without much of a shape. She strikes her lips with a finger and covers the mouthpiece of the phone. "I'm going on the radio."

"What are you—"

"Don't distract me, Gavin," she says and ducks her head as if the phone has dragged it down. "I'm on now. Will you be able to hear?"

"If you put it on loudspeaker."

"Can you?"

As she hands me the phone I'm tempted to take the call or even cut it off. I switch the receiver to its hands-free mode in time to hear a presenter say "Gillian? We seem to have lost Gillian from the city centre. It's all quiet on the Gillian front."

"I'm here," my mother cries.

"You sound a bit remote."

"Is this better?" she says and, before I can warn her, presses the receiver against her ear.

Even with the side of her face in the way I hear the presenter. "We've got you now."

"No need to shout," she says. "And I'm not from the city centre, I'm in Everton."

"I'm sure you know best where you are." In much the same indulgent tone he says "I believe you want to talk about tours of the city."

"I most certainly do. The ones Gavin Meadows gives."

"They're the criminal tours, aren't they? I don't mean criminal in the sense of—"

"Maybe the city would like you to think they are. They're trying to stop them."

"Who's doing that, Gillian?"

"What's his name, Gavin?"

I was anxious for a chance to intervene, but now I'm less willing to speak. "It doesn't matter," I have to say. "He thinks he's responsible for the image of the city."

"He can't be more than you are. Maybe he's jealous because nobody knows who he is."

Before I can decide how to reply the presenter says "Is that Gavin Meadows? What are you saying the problem is with your tours?"

"He's isn't saying there's one because I don't believe there are any," my mother interrupts. "This man who spends his time criticising the people who do the real work, what was he trying to say, Gavin?"

"I expect he does real work too. I think he thinks I'm giving the public too many tales and not enough history, or maybe not the kind he wants."

"That's rubbish too. I want everyone to know that Gavin's always told the truth."

"Storytelling can be a kind of truth, can't it?" the presenter says. "May I ask if you're his mother?"

"I am, and proud of it. And I hope anyone who's listening with any imagination will support his work. Show the bureaucrats they can't take the soul out of the city just because it doesn't suit their idea of the place. His tours are keeping Liverpool alive."

"Have you been on many of them? Ten seconds."

"I'm going to," my mother says with some defiance.

"Gillian from Everton and Gavin from I'm not quite sure where."

"What does he mean by that?" my mother apparently feels I should know. "Shall we listen to the radio in case they talk about you?"

A young woman reads the news in an accent so Irish it revives one of the ancient ways Liverpool was pronounced, and I think she's saying inspectors have raided a school until I deduce that they gave it a rating. While the newsreader informs us that some of the oldest buildings in the city centre are inexplicably unoccupied, my mother wanders into the hall. "Have you tried to read these? I did but it made me feel—"

"What?" I'm forced to prompt.

She shakes her head, dislodging an uncertain laugh. "I can't describe it, unless that's what they mean by water on the brain."

I have an unhelpful random notion that the incomprehensible documents on the hall floor resemble explanations of the images of old Liverpool above them—interpretations I've no chance of understanding. The newsreader is saying that an application to exhume James Maybrick and compare his DNA with a sample taken from the supposed diary has been turned down, and I feel as if the authorities are making sure the legend stays alive. The news ends with a jokey item about a party of clubbers who saw a horde of frogs last night in Whitechapel. My mother giggles at this through the weather forecast—more and worse rain—and the travel report, which mentions that the railway loop under the city has been closed because of water. Her mirth trails off and dies of a hand over her mouth as the presenter says "Before the news we were hearing about tours of the city. Hank Waterworth, you're in charge of them, yes?"

"How dare he say that? You are all by yourself," my mother declares, almost drowning the presenter's voice. "I believe you want to talk about Gavin Meadows and his crime tours," he's saying.

"I don't know that I do. Mr Meadows and his tours are no longer included in our tourist package, and they don't carry our recommendation."

"You don't need it," my mother assures me while the presenter says "You used to support them, didn't you? What's changed?"

"I didn't, no. My predecessor did, but I can't talk about her." Having given the listeners a moment to imagine why, Waterworth says "I didn't find they were up to the standard it's my job to expect."

"Anything specific?"

"A whole lot too much. Mr Meadows is liable to cut his tours short because he hasn't planned them right, and he doesn't seem any too sure of the information he's trying to put over. Some of it you can't tell if it's real or he's making it up, and I don't know if he can tell either. Visitors to our city deserve better than that for their money."

"He doesn't deserve ours," my mother protests, so that I only just hear the presenter say "Have you had any feedback from the public?"

"I guess the word is out, because his tours haven't been too popular lately. Some of his customers are saying what I've told you, and we're hearing other criticisms as well. The property owners who live where he's been taking his High

Rip Trips, they don't care to have their neighbourhoods turned into criminal districts. The way I hear it, some of them mean to find out if the law can stop it."

"Is that true, Gavin?"

While I open my hands and the distance between them the presenter says "I wonder if any of our listeners have been on the tours."

"I'd welcome hearing from them if they have. Let me take this opportunity to publicise a tour we recommend. It's the Histrionic History Hunt, and it starts every day from the square behind the town hall. If it's wet there's a bus."

"Did you hear the call before the news?"

"I won't comment on it, except it sounds as if Mr Meadows is desperate for publicity, and maybe that reflects on the kind of service he's offering."

"I don't think we can say he asked his mother to ring on his behalf."

"I'm not saying that. Are you?" When the presenter stays silent Waterworth says "The item on your news sounded like a stunt to me."

"Which was that?"

"About frogs in Whitechapel. The only person I've heard talking about them is Mr Meadows. Maybe it's some kind of tale he wants the city to swallow. Can I give out the Histrionic History number?"

"They didn't broadcast yours," my mother complains, and she barely waits for Waterworth to depart before she says "What a hideous man. Some of the time he didn't even make sense. What was all that about frogs?"

"It doesn't matter now."

I can live without the memory her question threatens to rouse, but the radio does that as well. The presenter plays Paul McCartney's "Frog Song" as a preamble to saying "Now here's Pen from Page Moss. Is it right you saw the frogs last night in Whitechapel?"

"Two of us did."

"What did you think you saw?"

"We didn't think," Pen objects. "My friend Teeny said it was one thing but I told her she was mad. It was people dressed up."

"That does sound like a stunt. We'd heard you saw actual frogs."

"Not that big," Pen says with a titter that incorporates a shudder. "I told Teeny they must been partying like us, only fancy dress."

"And what did she say?"

"She'd had more than me," Pen finds it necessary to establish. "She saw them first and she thought there was a circus in town. Thought they were a parade. They wouldn't have been hopping along and I wouldn't even call it walking in all sorts of ways if it was a parade, would they? You wouldn't have one that late either. And she said stuff like they were bigger than she thought or not so big, and she wasn't even sure what they really looked like. I told you she'd had a lot."

"I won't ask of what. So how are you saying they looked?"

"They were all sorts of sizes. She was right about that. You'd have thought some of them were babies, only it must have been how far away they were. They had to be kids, though. They shouldn't have been up so late." On the far side of a pause she adds "I don't think they were all meant to be frogs. Things out of the sea, some looked like, only they were more like out of your dreams."

"Not mine," the presenter wants us all to know. "And where were they again?"

"Going down into the underground parking off White-chapel. We stuck around to see them drive out, but it came on to rain again and we never."

"So long as you had a good time. I hope you weren't driving. I should say we've been told there was nothing on CCTV."

That's the end of Pen, whose place is taken by a woman advertising boat tours of the docks. My mother gives me a look that seems to be waiting to find an appropriate expression and says "What did you think of all that?"

I'm by no means sure I want to. The anecdote has left me aware how reassuring I found the idea of having only imagined the body in Whitechapel and the creatures spilling forth from it. Now the memory feels capable of rising up to acquire reality, and I'm looking for an answer to suppress it when the landline rings. "Mr Meadows?" the caller says. "Finbar here at PC Tec. We've got your computer on the bench. You'd better come and have a look."

Chapter Thirty

DISAPPEARING SITES

The monumental monarch appears to be ignoring the fugitive who dashes out of the law courts. I barely glimpse the figure, who's clad from head to foot in shiny black and hooded too, before half a dozen policemen close around him, if it's a man. They have so much trouble keeping hold of him that I can't see their captive for the mass of them as they drag him back into the courts. "Slippery customer," one remarks.

The white concrete building looks muddy under the storm cloud that has reared up from the sea. Behind the courts there's a short cut past a rickety wire fence around a few acres of overgrown mud like a revival of the ancient marsh. As I dodge around a corner of the fence the mud begins to hiss and glisten and seethe. It's enlivened by the latest downpour, and I sprint for the bus station where the first dock used to be.

It gives by no means enough cover, since the imaginative architects omitted a roof. Would-be passengers huddle at the backs of glass shelters, where the wind and rain easily find them. At least a bus I want is waiting in its bay. Some of the windows must have been open recently, since many of the seats upstairs are wet. The left-hand front seat isn't, and as I sit down I take out my mobile. "This is Gavin Meadows. Any news of my father?"

"Gavin Meadows. Any news of his father." Though this rouses no answer I'm able to hear, Wrigley or Maddock says "We can't tell you where he is."

"How is that possible? You're the police."

"Can't work miracles. Either his phone's dead or he's somewhere there's no signal. Him or it, all right?"

It's far from that. "But you know where the message came from, surely."

"Working on it."

I should have accepted the Frugone salesman's offer. "You'll let me know as soon as you do, won't you?"

"We'll be telling somebody. You're not the only one that's interested."

I could retort that I'm a damn or a stronger sight more than interested, but I need to say "Don't try to reach my mother at the house. She's staying with me."

The bus moves forward with a jerk that unravels skeins of water on the window in front of me, and I end the call. As the bus swings into the triple carriageway at the mouth of the Pool I wipe greyness from the moist chill glass. Rain washes rain off the windows to replace rain with rain, so that the south docks—Albert, Wapping, Queens—are reduced to vast unstable hulks of brick or granite, and I can barely distinguish the grey conical tower like the gnome's house my father once assured me it was—the policeman's lodge at the Wapping gates. On the landward side the bus is paced by the reddish sandstone bulk of the Anglican cathedral on the ridge above a quarry that became a graveyard. The docks give way to a casino and a marina opposite a rank of small commercial buildings cut off at the pavement. Past them the blocks seem increasingly temporary, little more than oversized prefabs left over from the years after the blitz. Some of them exhibit signs that swim into legibility, and the sight of a P and a C sends me to the stairs, jabbing the bellpush.

At least the storm is on its way upriver. As the cloud unlids the sun the bus stop rediscovers its shadow, which puts me in mind of a drowned flag that has risen to the surface of the pavement. Opposite the Herculaneum, the southernmost dock, a tunnel gapes in a sandstone ridge crowned with Edwardian terraces. It's a remnant of the overhead railway. A minute's walk back towards the Pier Head brings me to the boxy premises of PC Tec, where the first initial of the logo perches on the last letter of the word. Beyond the white metallic door that contains the only window, a wide room is scattered with wire stands full of computer accessories. The stands jingle as I make for the counter, and the oldest of the men behind it—Finbar—greets me. "Thanks for coming so quick, Mr Meadows. I didn't want to do anything till you'd had a gander."

I recognise his long wrinkled leathery face and greying ponytail, but not the outsize horn-rimmed spectacles in which his eyes appear to float. "What have you been doing to it?" he says so reprovingly I'd like to believe it's a joke.

"Such as what?"

"You'd think you'd been giving it a bath," he says and unbolts a flap in the counter. "See for yourself. It's exactly how I brought it in."

His ponytail wags at me like an extra rebuke as I follow him into the back room. Numerous computers, variously eviscerated, are laid out on benches against the walls. Some are connected to monitors, and Finbar leads me to a tower that's lying on its back below a calendar of naked women rising from the waves. I think he means to show me something on the monitor to which the tower is hooked up until he points an accusing finger at the exposed innards. "How did that happen?"

The hard disc glints and dulls as I step closer. It isn't a trick of the light; the disc is glistening with moisture, patches of which appear to shift within the metal and subside. "That's what I was trying to save it from," I protest. "It's this insane weather."

"Nothing crazy about rain. Only people can be that."

I seem to have offended him in some unidentifiable way. As he takes a drink of water from a paper cup that was standing beside the computer I have to ask "Is everything lost?"

"There was something when I powered it up. Don't ask me how that's possible. Your web site, was it?"

"It wasn't mine."

"Some kind of aquarium, was it meant to be? Something was swimming, or somebody was. And some of them were climbing out, if you call that climbing. Maybe it's the state it's in that made them look like that."

I'm not entirely certain that I want to learn "Like what?"

"Show him."

Some of Finbar's colleagues have left the counter now that they've finished or at least interrupted their discussion of last night's local football matches. Though he looks unconvinced by the suggestion, he switches on the computer. For an instant the screen seems to flicker like an omen of a storm, but the impression vanishes before I can be sure I glimpsed it. "It was there," Finbar insists.

"Maybe you were dreaming on the job again," a workmate says.

I try to head off Finbar's anger. "Will you be able to salvage anything?"

"Can't say yet. We'll be in touch, but it won't be today."

As I head for the exit he comes after me, draining the paper cup, which he flings into a bin. He's bolting the flap in the counter when he says "I know what it looked like."

I find I'm reluctant to ask "What?"

"I was just thinking it could be a swimming pool, but it was too rotten all around it. I think it was an old dock like the one they're digging up."

There's no point in wondering until the information is retrieved, if it can be. A bus bears me towards the Pier Head and, closer, the building work that has uncovered remains of the original dock. As the bus swings across the carriageway into the bus station, it leaves behind the sight of workmen who have congregated beyond the metal fence to gaze at some object they've unearthed.

A breeze shivers puddles in the bus shelters. Beyond them Hanover Street has been reduced to a narrow lane by the wall around a redevelopment. Cars progress in single file along the dusty lane to an unsignposted dead end. Side streets climb towards the Moss Lake as the rope walks did, but the only one that doesn't bar the disorientated traffic is opposite the radio station, in front of which is a shelter that has never seen a bus. Inside the shelter three boys barely in their teens are smoking a version of the substance that gave the hempy girls their dreams. When the doors of the radio station part at my approach the boys turn their pale roundish faces to me, stretching their mouths and their eyes so wide that I could imagine I'm sharing their delirium.

In the performance space beyond the reception desk a folk group is singing a shanty about nymphs. "Can I speak to someone?" I ask the receptionist. "I'm Gavin Meadows."

A burst of applause greets this, but the enthusiasm is for the folk group. "Who are you here to see?" the receptionist says and gives me a pretty blink.

"Someone from your phone-in. I'd like to get in touch with somebody who called."

"I'm afraid we never give out numbers. You'd have to ring and ask them to get in touch with us."

I'm about to object to the delay when I grasp that going on the air will let me advertise my tours and my number. "I will tomorrow," I say while the folk group begins to sing about a maritime storm. As the doors creep shut, the refrain ("Sup water, lads, sup water—We'll dream beneath the sea") follows me, but I'm distracted by the sight outside. Three men with whitish faces loosened by age are waiting in the shelter, apparently trusting it to attract a bus. Perhaps their bulging eyes and moist grey nostrils and expressionlessly thin lips scared the boys off.

Hanover Street brings me to Church Street, and I'm abreast of the caged stone eagle when a glimpse beyond it stops me. I peer through the afternoon crowd to see a prancing shadow vanish into Williamson Square. Dodging through the crowd, I hurry along the side street, only to halt at the corner of the square with something like a laugh.

The bloated bodies are why the dancers look so spindle-legged. They're dressed in puffy costumes that may be meant as a joke or a historical reference to one. The outfits seem close to misshapen, or the performers do—Tasha Bailey and her fellow thespians, of whom Nicholas Noble appears the most batrachian. They're handing leaflets to anybody who will take one. "What are they trying to be?" I say rather more than aloud.

Noble stares at me and adopts an appreciative grin. "We're Histrionic History," he announces. "Just now we're the Hop Troupe. I thought you were meant to know your history, Mr Meadows. They used to go round advertising the theatre before this place was built up."

Does he mean while the area was a marsh? Surely that makes no sense, and I'm about to say so when a couple of middle-aged women beside me start to chant a Beatles phrase as if they're counteracting his dive into whatever past he has in mind. They're joining in with my ringtone, and they aren't helping me to know how to react to the number in the display window of the mobile. It's my home number.

Chapter Thirty-one

A Traditional Dinner

The phone is still off the hook, but the note my mother left is on the floor. I finish hoping that my father has come back once my shouts to him and then to anyone fall flat in the empty house. The sight of my mother's lonely chair standing guard beside the phone makes the place feel even more deserted. I put the note back on the table and then check for any calls. Nobody has rung since we abandoned the house. I hang up the phone and call the estate agent on my mobile, but no potential buyers have been in touch.

The house smells stale, close to mouldy. I leave the kitchen window open while I go upstairs. The buckets in the workroom don't appear to have collected any more water, and as far as I can tell the stains on the ceiling haven't grown. My parents' bedroom is as forsaken as it was last night, and the bathroom is silent, without even the hint of a drip. I take my time over going down to shut the window, because the staleness hasn't dissipated. As I return along the hall I grow aware of the cupboard under the stairs. My mother only asked me to check for phone calls, but perhaps the cupboard is the source of the smell. Grasping the rickety plastic doorknob, I pull the door wide.

Does it send a mouse fleeing into the wall, or just a trick of light and shadow? Obviously the latter, since the glimpse resembled a gelatinous member recoiling like a mollusc into the corner stained with moisture and dimness. The damp of which the cupboard smells doesn't appear to have spread, though I don't look too hard or too long. I shut the door and am laying the receiver on the table when I'm distracted by marks on the stairs. They have to be blotches of damp, how-ever much they remind me of tracks of various sizes and shapes or lack of shape. I must have overlooked them earlier because the light has changed. They aren't enough to keep me in the house, and as I slam the front door I'm quite glad to see a bus.

The city sinks towards the river as the bus carries me down-hill, so that I could imagine that the land beneath the thin pale sky is reverting to marsh. I disembark at Castle Street and head for Frugo Corner. On my way home the bagfuls of provisions my mother asked me to buy lend me a sailor's gait. The merman above the threshold looks misshapen by the weather, as do the glistening contents of his cornucopia, or ready to assume new shapes. The bags thump and slither against my door as I let myself into the apartment. "Is that you this time, Gavin?" my mother calls or cries.

"It's me all right. Who else came?"

"Someone making noises like you just did. They didn't come in. Were they drunk, do you think?"

"How would I know?"

"They sounded as if they were trying to find their way in somewhere. I expect they live across the corridor."

It doesn't sound much like my cellist neighbour, but per-haps he's had something to celebrate. My mother is sitting in the main room, surrounded by papers and books, and holding a magazine that's little more than a pamphlet. "Was there anything at the house?" she says with an attempt at carelessness.

"There weren't any calls, and I'm sure nobody had been there either."

"I wasn't really expecting anything," she says but ducks her head as if it has acquired a burden. "Just put the bags in the kitchen while I finish reading this and then I'll see to dinner."

I unload the bags, which contain enough provisions for at least a week, into the refrigerator. I haven't finished clearing space in there when my mother waddles to the sink to gulp more than a glassful of water. "You should read that," she says. "Or you could peel the potatoes if you like."

She seems to have infected me with thirst, and I drain a mug of the water that wriggles and then pours out of the tap. It leaves me feeling bloated, though surely not as much as she's begun to look. "I'll help," I tell her.

"Ham steaks and bubble. You always loved that. I hope you still do."

"It'll be fine."

"How long has it been since I made your dinner? Remember when Deryck convinced you you'd hear it bubbling and squeaking when you put your knife and fork in? I had to tell him to stop. He had you not wanting to touch your food in case it did something it wasn't supposed to." As her reminiscence flags she adds "Or would you rather have fish?"

"Whatever's best for you."

"Let's have that, then. The ham will keep. Fish is good for your brain, isn't it?" She laughs, but not at this. As she consigns the gammon steaks to the refrigerator she produces the joke. "And I expect he'd say you need a bit of ham in your job."

She's doing her utmost to believe that our lives will return to normal. I sense that her behaviour and her conversation are determined not to acknowledge how desperate they are to bring my father back. I mustn't shatter the pretence, and so I concentrate on scraping the potatoes until she says "I should have told you right away. Lucy says she'll call back."

"When?"

"She wasn't saying. She doesn't know where she'll be. I'm glad she called, anyway."

"Why did she, do you know?"

"Oh, Gavin, does she have to have a reason? She'd heard about you on the radio, or someone had. She doesn't need to feel guilty about anything, does she?"

The parer catches on an eye of the potato in my hand, and I feel as if the conversation has snagged too. "I couldn't say."

I mean I'd rather not, but my mother says "I didn't think so. I told her she shouldn't. We don't want any more of us splitting up, do we? I said I'd get you to call her, but she said you can't."

"Why not?"

"Will she be somewhere you can't reach her? Or maybe she's at work and they don't like her taking calls. I know she didn't want you trying."

"Then I won't."

"Don't be like that, Gavin, not with everything else. You go and sit down now. Thanks for helping." As she drops the potatoes in a saucepan with a series of knells like the notes of a gong too rusty to resonate she says "You could read that story and tell me what you think. Lucy might be interested in it as well."

The magazine is lying on the armchair my mother has vacated. It's the third issue of *Weird World*, published by Gannet Press of Birkenhead. On the cover a gleeful befogged skull hovers above a marsh. While the issue isn't dated, my father has pencilled 1956 at the top of the contents page, which lists "The Rime of the Ancient Mariner" and Poe's "Ms. Found in a Bottle" and two tales by authors I recognise as local, Eric Frank Russell and G. G. Pendarves, born in 1885 of a Cornish family that had been drawn to Liverpool. Russell's contribution is "Vampire from the Void," in which a voracious extraterrestrial lands in Liverpool, devouring its first victims outside James Street Station before feasting on drivers in the Mersey Tunnel. The victims are said to have "gone where the good niggers go," and the brittle yellowed pages also emphasise the historical nature of the tale reprinted from a 1939 pulp magazine, but I don't see why this should interest Lucinda or me. Or did my mother mean the story by Pendarves? The editorial says it was an unpublished story found among her sister's papers. The sister was a lecturer at the oldest—indeed, then the only—university in Liverpool, and the tale was based to some extent on her research.

It's called "The Portrait of Jacob Williams." He's a Victorian engineer who builds a railway system under his home town of Vivilake. As the work progresses he spends more and more time underground, but is it his concern for security that keeps him there when his employees have finished their shifts? Some wonder what he finds to eat, while others speculate that he may have reverted to his ancestral state, since he's said to have been born in a cellar and spent his childhood there. The workmen especially dislike the way his appearance seems to be taking on what they suspect is the family look. One day the excavations release a subterranean lake, and he's among those carried away by the flood. All the bodies are retrieved except his, though a searcher swears he heard someone floundering beyond the limits of the lights. The diggings are bricked up, and Williams is largely forgotten by the time the narrator—his grandson—investigates his heritage. He has been inspired to do so by a painting of his grandfather, from which some of the paint is flaking away. On an impulse more narratively convenient than plausible he scrapes off fragments to reveal that sections of the portrait have been painted over. In the original the subject's hands were slightly but unmistakably webbed, while his round eyes were far too large and his mouth unpleasantly wide. Worse, with every detail that's exposed the narrator feels more as if he's gazing into a mirror.

I'm not surprised the tale wasn't published during the author's lifetime. It isn't very well told, and why should I feel defensive for thinking so? As I close the magazine my mother says "It's ready if you are. Do you think that's about who I thought?"

"It's a story."

"But it's about the tunnels Lucy lives near, don't you think?"

"I imagine so."

"You keep on imagining. It's still your job." From the kitchen my mother says "Stories about a place are part of it, aren't they? They're like what it dreams."

Is she quoting my father or something she found in his research? I'm tempted to look for it, but she's waiting, so visibly eager for me to be pleased that it feels like a last hope. Two platters of grilled sea bass and potatoes grace the table, along with sets of my best cutlery and glasses for a jug of water. "Is that all right," my mother says, "or are you having something stronger?"

"Maybe we both should."

"We ought to stay alert in case . . ." Instead of going on, perhaps because her hope is greater if it remains unexpressed, she says "I expect a glass won't hurt us."

I fetch two from the cupboard and a bottle of Muscadet that has been chilling in the refrigerator for days. It's Lucinda's favourite, but it has waited for her long enough. "That's nice," my mother says, having followed a sip of wine with a gulp of water, but seems distracted. "I feel as if it's watching me."

More reluctantly than I care to understand I ask "What?"

"My head. I'm going to cut it off. Shall I do yours as well?"

She means the fish, of course. "If it bothers you."

The dead eyes encrusted with blindness do look rather large and wide. Perhaps they're reminiscent of the portrait in the story, and she may be assailed by that memory too. I'm also reminded that the early Liverpudlians lived mostly on fish from the river and the Pool. As she severs the heads and consigns them to the kitchen bin my mother says "What do you think they've seen? You'd wonder if we're putting it inside us."

I'd prefer to wonder nothing of the sort. Once I've enthused about the meal and we've filled some time with nervous smiles whenever our eyes meet, she says "Shall we have the radio on?"

We're just in time for the news, but not of my father. Dozens of cellars are being used to grow cannabis. Several pet animals have been slaughtered in back gardens near the docks. A gang beat up three men last night as they left Club Rubadub, which—though the newsreader doesn't mention it—becomes the Happy Spanker, formerly the Slap and Tickle, once a month. Animal rights activists are picketing the new Korean restaurant, the Good Dog. My mother greets this with a laugh that she seems to want to take back, then drinks from both her glasses. Either the wine or the fish is making me thirsty too, and soon I have to replenish the jug.

The wine hasn't relaxed her as much as I hoped. After dinner we finish the bottle, but it hardly helps. At her suggestion we watch television, comedy shows that become increasingly outrageous as the night advances. She meets the jokes and oaths with tentative smiles or determined mirth. It seems important to her that I share her merriment, and I make an effort, though it feels as if we're both striving to ignore my father's research all around us. As the vulgarities multiply she tries to seem up to their date, but she can't hide her restlessness. When we run out of dutiful laughter at the sight of men apparently tying their genitals in knots she says "Don't feel you have to stay up just for me, Gavin. I'll be fine on my own."

"What will you do?"

"I may go to bed as well. Shall I have the ordinary phone? Then we'll have one each and you aren't so likely to be disturbed. I'll try not to be in your way much longer."

"Who said you were?"

"I do. Yours and Lucy's. Maybe she doesn't even like to call you while I'm here."

"I hope she's not like that."

"I wasn't saying anything against her." My mother continues to look apologetic while she says "I expect I was just being stupid, don't you? I'm too old to behave like that."

"I don't understand what you—"

"At the house," she says impatiently, though it isn't clear with whom. "I must have dreamed it. Some dreams don't feel like dreams, do they? I've been having quite a few of those."

That's hardly a good basis for her to be on her own. Perhaps sensing my objections, she says "I'll go home soon, and that's a promise. Let's see if I can tomorrow."

She switches off the television as I head for the bathroom. I run a tap to drown the sounds of urination, and so does she when it's her turn, unless she's having yet another drink of water. "Good night," she murmurs along the hall. "Try and sleep."

I'm nowhere near succeeding when I hear the radio. She's playing it so quietly that I could almost be dreaming the faint surges of music, which must be why some of them seem capable of turning into Michael Maybrick's waltz. Can I also hear the rustling of documents? Eventually the melodies are interrupted by a newsreader, but I can't distinguish a word. Since my mother doesn't call me or come to me or otherwise react so far as I can tell, it seems clear that there's no word of my father. Once I give up striving to listen my mind begins to sink into itself, but I've no idea how long I've lain in its depths before my mother says "Are you awake? I've found him."

My mouth feels shapeless with sleep, and that's how my question sounds. "Where?"

"Not Deryck. Sorry. Were you asleep?" It's unclear which mistake she's apologising for: probably both. "The person he asked Lucy about," she says. "John Strong. I've found what he copied of his."

I feel weighed down by all the water I drank, however much of it I returned to the land via the bathroom. As I struggle to sit up or at least to waken fully my mother says "You stay there if you're comfortable. Shall I read it to you?"

I blink my watery eyes into focus and see her standing in

the bedroom doorway. The light from the main room glimmers on a sheet of paper in her hand. "If you like," I mumble.

She plods to switch on the light in the hall and then fetches a kitchen chair along with a handful of pages. Planting the chair outside my room, she perches on the edge of the seat. "Tell me when you've had enough," she says, and all at once I wonder if she prefers not to be alone with what she's found.

Chapter Thirty-two

STRONG DREAMS

"If we dream gods they dream us," my mother intones to show she's reading, then returns to her ordinary voice. "Do you think he means only if we do, or has it got to be both?"

An unenlightened mumble is the best I can produce. The material she's reading and the comments she interpolates make me feel like a child in bed in the dark. She and my father often used to read to me as I drifted off to sleep. Sometimes my father would tell me a story instead. I must have been very young when he convinced me that a mermaid was someone who helped you to speak up. On that occasion and others too, my parents' disagreements over how to tell a bedtime story resembled a comedy routine they were performing on my behalf. My mother's version of the tale wasn't much more traditional than my father's joke about aid, since she ended with the little mermaid's painless transformation into a human girl rather than the agonising process to which Hans Andersen subjected her. Presumably the amphibious creature had enough control over her shape that she was able to pass for human, though I didn't think that then. "I don't know why Deryck copied all this," my mother is saying. "What did Lucy say he was?"

"I didn't know she said he was anything."

I'm not sure how much if any of this I pronounce. "Not Deryck," my mother says. "The man I've got here. Mr Strong."

"An occultist."

"You didn't say an octopus. He seems to have plenty to do with water. All life is in the pool, and all comes forth."

I'm preparing to ask whether the pool has a capital P

when she adds "Its spawn stalks the streets and thinks itself the purpose of creation. I suppose he's talking about evolution. Everything came from the sea."

Even if she's clarifying the text to herself, I could fancy she's addressing a child until she says "The townsfolk and their maggots are creatures of the pool. A maggot used to be an idea, didn't it?"

Given the writer's contempt for humanity, I think there's another interpretation, but my mother is saying "The magician is borne up on its dreams while the mob wallows in them. He'll be the magician, won't he? I wonder what tricks he got up to." She abandons the question to add "The mob look down upon the products of the congress in the depths, but are they not themselves as low a form of life?"

She isn't asking, and it doesn't seem to bring an answer. "The parturition in the dark is shaped by the pool," she says. "I don't know what Deryck could have wanted with all this. You can't even tell if it was like this to begin with or he just copied bits of it."

"Don't read any more if you don't want to."

She hears this, unless she's simply pursuing her thoughts. "It could help, couldn't it? It might show us the kind of thing he was trying to look into, your father."

"Then let's leave it for the morning if you think you'll be able to sleep."

I don't know whether this reaches her, because she says "They who tell fables or act them out, no less than composers of airs or of verse or bedaubers of canvas, give their flesh to the dreams of the pool."

When did the author of all this obscure incoherence write it down? It sounds as if he's speaking from a past far more distant than his own. Perhaps this was intentional— one element of the insufferable pretentiousness of his prose. "Thus the town has sprouted theatres like fungi rooted in the marsh."

My mother laughs at this, however uncertainly. "He did

have his way with words, didn't he? I feel as if I'm praying, reading all this out. It gets inside your head, doesn't it?" She may mean to prove this by intoning "Is a sports arena a theatre or a circus? Does a demon enter into men that makes them savage, or does their savagery call forth the demon? The god becomes the sacrifice."

I thought Strong had football hooligans in mind, but the final observation throws me. In her normal voice my mother says "I'm thirsty again. Would you like some more water as well?"

"I've plenty."

"Replenish?"

When my answer falls short of sound her slow heavy footsteps recede along the hall, to emerge from a downpour—at least, they return from the bathroom once the tap has been hushed. A rustle of the pages she left on the chair brings her footsteps to an end, and then it's silent long enough to let me sink towards slumber, so that I can't help resenting the intrusion of her voice. "I don't think I like this bit."

"Then don't read it."

I can't tell how much of this trickles out of my mouth, but apparently the thought is clear. "I already have," she objects. "Don't you want to know?"

"If it helps."

"It's in hell," she echoes or interprets, and pauses before saying "Some of its dreams shape the dreamer that shares them, others enter the world. Some show what is to be while others seek to obviate the worst. The blackest dream conjures its subject rendered more monstrous still."

I'm put in mind of the vision, if that's what it was, I experienced in Frog's-lane—in Whitechapel. As I struggle to restore it to the past, my mother's soliloquy floats into and out of my consciousness, and I have the odd notion that she's trying to compete with me at storytelling. "A god is parasitic on the mob but symbiotic with its equal, the magician . . . The mass are but vessels it uses to dream . . . He who does not dance a demon to his tune must dance to the tune of the demon . . ." Why is she continuing to read if she's as nervous as she seems? She sounds as though she's being forced to read—as though the text is forcing her. I would ask her or help her to stop, but her words seem to be weighing me down. "Those that need eyes shall produce them . . ." I could imagine that mine are vanishing like globules of liquid into my porous head. I'm nearly asleep, that's all, and my mother's voice is retreating—staying on the surface of the dark.

I'm the dark. No, I'm spreading through it. It's earth, which is very little hindrance to me in my transformed state. I seep through the soil and through the rock, groping into crannies with my infinitely fluid tendrils. Burial can't stop me, however much it darkens my nature. As I extend my territory I sense life multiplying overhead. I can reach it by rising into the open; sometimes I drift through the air. However separate from my body portions of me may become, they simply expand my realm before returning to me. I'm vast and as old as the world, but my dreams are older still. They're as infinite as time, that human illusion, and able to reshape it. I'm in the process of containing a dream in a vessel of flesh and observing how each changes the other when a voice interrupts my pastime. "Aren't you awake yet? Sorry if I woke you, but you need to speak."

I can only assume John Strong's notions and his language infiltrated my sleep. Whatever they planted there seems to shrink into my brain as I blink my eyes wide. My mother's face swims into focus and regains its shape while she says "You're on the radio."

This brings me a good deal more awake, but I've left some of my voice behind. "How?" I croak.

"Not yet," she says and hands me the landline receiver. "You're next. I rang up. Someone needs to put the story straight after what that man said about your tours. They won't let me on again so soon, but I've got them to have you."

"Gavin from the city centre," a voice in my hand is saying. "Are you there, Gavin? Somebody was."

I work my lips until they feel more familiar as I raise the phone to my face. "I am."

"I believe you want to respond to the comments we had yesterday about your tours."

"I'll just give my number for anyone who wants a tour. Maybe the city ought to let people decide what's true for themselves." I feel as if the residue of the dream is hindering my thoughts, and if I started talking about Waterworth I don't know where I might stop. Having intoned the digits, I'm anxious to add "If anyone's seen my father Deryck Meadows in the last few days, could they call that number?"

"Can you say why?"

"He's, he's missing. Hasn't it been on your news?"

"Not to my knowledge. I'm asking my producer. I take it you'll have told the police."

"Of course we have, but we've heard as good as nothing. They're supposed to be tracing his mobile but they're taking longer than, than someone else said it would take."

"They have to prioritise. You'll have heard they're understaffed." After a pause he says "The newsroom say we haven't had the story."

"Then someone needs to do their job."

"We'll look into it," the presenter says, and not quite as briskly "I hope your father turns up safe and well."

It's the end of the conversation, and my mother is waiting to speak. "They ought to be able to phone the house about Deryck as well. I should stop being silly and go home."

"You aren't being silly. Nobody could blame you for not wanting to be on your own just now." I've left the reasons ominously undefined, and so I say "You do whatever's best for you."

"I'll think, then. Shall I keep the phones while you have your bath?"

In the kitchen she turns on the radio as well. I'm not long

in the shower; the water seems too eager to invade my eyes and mouth, and it distorts the muffled voices on the radio, and a scrap of Beatles music too. I towel myself in front of the mirror, where I look not just blurred but puffed up by condensation, and dodge into my room to dress. On the radio a woman is complaining that there are too many Scouse criminals in films, and I assume I haven't missed much until my mother plods into the hall. "Someone rang," she says.

So the Beatles song was my ringtone, but her expression makes me reluctant to ask "Don't you know who?"

"Oh yes, I know," she says, and her face grows unhappier still.

Chapter Thirty-three

DON'T LET HIM IN

As the woman who has opened the front door parts her lips, a voice somewhere in the small rectangular two-storey house cries "Tunnel congested."

"All right, mother," the woman calls while half her mouth shows me a resigned wry grin.

She's broad and short—lesser than me by a head plus a forehead. Her roundish face is framed by waves of greying hair that aren't quite symmetrical. Before she can speak again, a lorry laden with containers not much smaller than the house thunders by on Vauxhall Road and turns along a street to the north docks. Even once the main road lost the name of Pinfold Lane, the speeding vehicle might have been a stagecoach desperate to outrun highwaymen. The hiss of rain that's lingered on the road fades beneath the wheels as I say "Beverley Sharples?"

"Guilty as charged, and you'll be Deryck's son. It's like turning the years back. You look more like him than him." Perhaps her gaze isn't considering just me, because she adds "I didn't know if Gillian would tell you I called."

"Why shouldn't she?" I feel disloyal for asking.

"Maybe I'm a bit of his past she'd rather not know about."

"He came to see you, didn't he?"

"You're right, that'll be another reason."

Though I didn't mean to imply this, it may be the case. Beverley gazes harder at me and says "Has someone been knocking you about?"

I'd almost forgotten the bruise. It feels like a soft spot on my forehead, though I can't define its boundaries. The question seems so pointed that I retort "My mother never has."

"I was thinking of the people who don't like your tours."

"Not them either. I don't know who, if it was anyone."

Before she can pursue the issue, the other voice complains "Aren't you coming in?"

"I was just going to ask him, mother," Beverley says and steps back.

The terse hall is brightly papered in an Oriental pattern. More sunlight than we've grown accustomed to this summer is reaching through the upstairs rooms for the pine staircase. All this is overwhelmed by dozens of smiling painted clay faces that cling like limpets to the walls. No doubt they're designed to seem friendly and welcoming, but on closing the door I feel as if I'm shutting myself up with an onslaught of mirth, so relentlessly concerted it's worse than theatrical. The click of the latch prompts Beverley's mother to call "Is that Frank?"

"He'll be down at the docks still. He's my husband," Beverley confides to me and raises her voice. "It's—you'll see who it is, mother."

She moves aside to let me enter the front room, which boasts an expensive fawn leather suite that's grouped around a grey slab—the wide screen of a home cinema system. Two pine dressers display china, and the walls swarm with faces, fossils of jollity. A woman who may have been Beverley's size until she spread, a process that appears to have drained all colour from her skin and shaggy hair, sits facing the screen and the window. Above the houses opposite, the grassy slope of Everton is scattered with huntsmen or at least men accompanied by unmuzzled Rottweilers, but her eyes don't acknowledge them. As I venture into the room she turns her head, dislodging an antimacassar from the back of her chair and flailing her hands at it. "Is he back again?" she wonders aloud.

"It's his son, mother."

The old woman continues to regard me with suspicion until Beverley murmurs "Sit down and I'll bring us a drink."

Without giving me time to respond she tramps off to the kitchen. Her mother gropes ineffectually at the antimacassar, which has lodged like a ruff no paler than her skin behind her neck. She seems incapable of other movements—certainly of raising herself from the armchair into which she's wedged, let alone using her legs, which are twice the width of her feet. "Let me," I say and retrieve the antimacassar, only to find that it's as damp as any towel. I drape it over the top of the chair and rub my hand surreptitiously on my trousers, though perhaps I don't need to be discreet, since she has reverted to staring out of the window. "Don't drink and drive," she advises.

"I wasn't planning to. I can't."

She watches me sit in the chair opposite hers. I have the notion that she means to ask if it's damp, since I can't be sure, but she says "Do you like my faces?"

"Are they company for you?"

I might have produced a better answer if I didn't find them disconcerting. While looking at her I'm equally aware of the faces—a sailor's and an eye-patched pirate's—that flank hers. "They aren't all mine. I can't do that," she says and pulls at her cheeks as if to demonstrate their lack of malleability, though the effect is closer to the reverse. "They always stay the same, that's what I like."

I'm some way from interpreting this when she says "Are you talking to Frank?"

"He won't be home till teatime," Beverley shouts along the hall.

"Your dad was," her mother informs me. "Frank told him about them robbing from the docks."

Since she has lowered her voice, I don't know how incriminating the anecdote may be. All the same, she appears to expect me to ask "Who?"

Her eyes flicker as if to check that the one-eyed face can't hear. "More like what," she mutters.

"What, then."

"They've always said there's something fishy down there. My dad used to when he worked on the docks. Things go walking off the ships."

"I've heard that. There was even a case in the eighteenth century when a ship was supposed to have sailed out of the old dock with nobody on board."

"Meat's the favourite. That does most of the walking."

She's referring to theft, and I do my best to repel the image—more like an unwelcome dream—of raw meat lumbering or hopping or wriggling maggot-like away from the docks. "And nobody knows what happened to it," I say.

"Yes they do, only nobody believes them. It isn't the dockers if that's what you're getting at. Maybe some of them rob and no wonder with their wages, but they couldn't do all that. It's the others that they can't stop coming in."

"Forgive me, but why can't they?"

"Slimies, that's what he called them." She and the sliced-off faces fix me with their eyes as she says "In and out of the containers like a circus act, but how do you think they could open those big locks?"

"I've no idea."

"They never," she says in gleeful triumph. "They eat it all in there."

As she waits for my reaction I hear water pouring into a jug. When I don't speak she says "They're meant to be like they might have crawled out of the river, only they didn't. They're from round here and come back this way too, and that's too close to home."

There may still be a chance of reducing all this to the truth. "Has anybody seen them?"

"Just their marks. They leave plenty, but he says the dock police have given up." She ducks her head to mutter "He says you can't tell from the trails they leave behind what they look like from one moment to the next."

"Is she telling tales again?" Beverley wants or may want to know.

The old woman's face grows as immobile as any of the faces on the walls, and considerably blanker. Beverley must have taken some care over keeping quiet in the hall, especially since she's pushing a trolley. It bears a jug, three glasses and a decanter two-thirds full of an amber liquid. "Are you having water with it?" she asks me. "We always do this early."

"What is it?"

"Scotch from the docks."

If this sounds like a joke, it also suggests that pilfering does take place and needs a cover story, though the old woman's sounds unlikely to convince anyone who matters. Perhaps hers is a distorted version of tales the dockers tell, but it makes the offer of a drink welcome. "Half and half," I say, "thanks."

I have to say when twice to prevent Beverley from drowning my whisky. Once her tumbler and her mother's are topped up almost to the brim with water, she sits in the middle of the sofa. "You'll be wanting to hear about Deryck," she says.

"Do you mind telling me why he came to see you?"

"Of course I don't. You might, though." She takes rather more than a sip of her drink—I can scarcely taste mine for water—and says "He wanted me to talk about the times we used to have down in the shelter."

"Think," the old woman urges and stares out of the window. "Think."

"Sup up, mother," Beverley says and waits until she's obeyed. "He'd forgotten till he heard me talking on the radio."

"That's not what he said," her mother objects.

"All right then, mother, you tell the story."

"He said he'd got so he didn't know if he'd dreamed them up till he heard you on the wireless. I'm getting that way myself."

"We all will." Beverley celebrates or otherwise greets the prospect with a drink. "Is that why he's gone walkabout?" she asks me. "Has he been forgetting a lot?"

"Gone walkies like the meat," her mother seems to enjoy saying.

"Mother."

Once they've finished I admit "I don't know what he may have forgotten."

"He'll be in our prayers, won't he, mother?"

"Dreams as well, if there's a difference."

"Thank you both," I feel bound to say. "What did you talk about?"

"Just the shelter," says Beverley. "He used to have me thinking he could hear things worming around behind the walls. I thought he was attracting them by going on about them. He didn't seem to like that idea much when he was here."

"Shouldn't have dreamed it up in the first place."

"I don't think he did, mother. I think it was one of his grandfather's tales." Largely to me Beverley adds "Maybe Deryck was trying to forget some of the stuff he thought he remembered. Maybe he gave his wife the wrong idea about what we did down there and that's why she's taken a dislike."

"Like the froggies," says her mother.

As the old woman and the limpet faces observe my confusion Beverley says "The which?"

"The girls that used to be kept in cellars. Only they weren't girls, more like things that had to live down there. Men liked them because their mouths were so big and they could stretch their legs and puff themselves up and do all sorts of other tricks, everything anyone could dream of. Some men went to them because they were cheaper than girls and some got the taste, and then they had to pay a lot more."

By now Beverley has tried to interrupt more than once. "Mother."

"Don't blame me. It's not my tale. My grandpa used to go

on about them, the dirty old reprobate," the older woman seems delighted to inform me. "Do you know what else he said?"

"I don't," I say and rather wish.

"If they had babies the men that owned them would take them and chuck them in the docks. That wouldn't do much, would it? Even if they were dead they mightn't be once the water got into them. He said that, and about the philanthropists."

Her monologue appears to have foundered on her triumph at pronouncing the word, however much this misshapes her mouth. Then she says "They saved some of the babies before they got dumped and gave them to families to look after. He used to say there's a fair few folk living in the town that mightn't like to know where they came from."

"Old people," Beverley says halfway between indulgence and reproof. "They were like that in the shelter."

The interruption is so relatively welcome that I'm anxious to prolong it. "Who were?"

"My gran and grandfather and Deryck's."

The old woman is already opening her mouth, and I hold my breath like a swimmer until she speaks. "My dad used to get everyone singing."

"Even if they didn't know the song."

"Even the Cuthberts. That's what we called men that were too soft to go and fight. I remember one of his songs," the old woman declares and treats me to an excerpt—the words and the waltz rhythm and a sally at the tune. "I'm not composed of loot, old boy. I'm not composed of loot."

As I refrain from thinking of a song I'm glad she didn't sing, she tells me "And Deryck's old feller, he'd take off all the Liverpool comedians. Arthur Askey and Tommy Handley and the one who played Constable Unstable." Having pronounced the words of the name like each other in two different ways, she says "And the other one, who was that? Hardly Yardley."

By the time I grasp that it's a catchphrase rather than a name, Beverley is saying "Whenever he was down there he'd say 'Don't let Jack in.' It used to scare me, but I expect it was some old comedian's line."

"Hardly, Yardley," her mother says with glee. "People were always saying the thing about Jack, but maybe Deryck's grandpa meant one of them behind the walls."

"You sound like you believed in them," Beverley protests. "You used to clout me for talking about them."

"That's why I did, because you and Deryck talking about them brought them."

I'm about to point out that she's as good as contradicting what she said earlier—at least, the objection will do for me—when Beverley complains "You're not saying you ever heard one."

"Saw one too. A bit of one."

Beverley utters a laugh that sounds more determined than mirthful. "Which bit?"

"A hand. A big wet hand, or that's what it wanted to be. It was feeling for Deryck's grandpa like it was going to get hold of his head or stroke it or something. Only people started flashing lights about and it went back in its crack in the wall."

"Behave yourself, mother. How could a hand come out of a crack?"

"Squeezed," the old woman assures me.

Surely they're competing for the most extravagant reminiscence, and I think I've heard enough; I can't see how any of this would lead to my father. I drain my glass and set it on the trolley. "Well, thank you both for all—"

"Aren't you going to show him what Deryck saw, Beverley?"

"I don't think it would help him."

"Then I will. I want people to see."

The old woman clutches the arms of the chair and struggles to heave herself forth. As the effort squeezes moisture from her brows—surely not from the rest of her—Beverley sighs. "All right, mother, if it means so much to you. Don't go getting yourself in another state."

Is she reluctant to make for the kitchen or only slow? At least the wide room harbours not a trace of an observant head except for those outside the window. The three men are fishing from the opposite bank of a canal at the end of the back garden. Beverley unlocks the door and plods out of my way. "There you are," she says loud enough for her mother to hear.

As I step out of the house the edge of a mass of black cloud engulfs the sun. The unnatural dusk appears to soak into the houses across the water, turning the red bricks the colour of disinterred clay. Above the roofs, cranes along the docks resemble prehistoric skeletons in a museum. What else is there to see? The small lawn is occupied by a pair of loungers mottled with patches of damp, and it's bordered by rocks overgrown by ferns glistening with moisture. If they were much wetter they would resemble underwater vegetation. I'm wondering why my father would have found any of this significant when I notice the path to the garden gate.

It's composed of six flagstones, the farthest of which extends beneath the gate onto the towpath. A tendril of water snakes from the chink between the third and fourth stones to vanish into the canal. I'm put in mind of the many springs that used to feed the townsfolk, though the more prosperous had wells in their grounds. Even if the path has sprung a leak, I don't know what it would have meant to my father. Is it moving? Perhaps only my efforts to distinguish it make it seem to writhe. I turn back to the house, to be confronted by Beverley. "He didn't know there was a canal," she says. "Too much water everywhere, he said."

She's stepping back when I hear a sound behind me. It's liquid, and so close to a whisper that I could think it surreptitious. It ceases as I swing around. Has anything changed? The three men are still squatting on stools beside the canal, and of course they're fishing, even if I'm unable to focus on the rods. I've no business fancying that the lines that trail from the wide-eyed trio bear any resemblance to umbilical cords. I'm more concerned with the water on the garden path, or rather with my previous misperception. The trickle must already have begun halfway up the third flagstone from the house; it can't have sneaked closer, since the path slopes slightly but unmistakably downwards to the towpath. "Something the matter?" Beverley says low.

I presume she doesn't want her mother to hear. "I don't think so," I murmur, but at once there seems to be: her mother is telling someone to keep their hands off.

I'm at least as disturbed that Beverley doesn't react. As she locks the back door I whisper "Nobody's with her, is there?"

Beverley shakes her head without looking at me. "It's just a sign."

Of what? I'm in the hall, between the watchful but in-effective faces, when the old woman cries out again. "Don't phone and drive," she exhorts, and at last I understand that ever since I arrived she has been reading advice for drivers aloud from the matrix sign ahead of the junction outside the window. She didn't tell anyone not to touch her—she was saying that drivers should keep their hands free. My relief lasts until she catches sight of me and bulges forward in the armchair to demand "Have you seen it?"

"The canal," I try assuming. "I expect you like sitting by it."

"Used to. He put me off. Too wet." As Beverley joins me the old woman says "He came back."

"I told you before, mother, this is Deryck's son."

"I know that, Beverley. I'm not completely off my head yet. I'm saying his dad came back."

"When?"

Once the old woman has finished laughing at my question and her daughter's overlapping one she says "This morning when you were at the shops. It wasn't all of him. Just his face."

This time only Beverley speaks. "Where?"

"Right there."

For a moment I'm able to believe she's pointing outside, but her pudgy finger with its ragged bitten nail is indicating the floor in the corner to the left of the window. More of the premature dusk appears to have gathered there than in the rest of the room. As I peer at it, part of the darkness appears to swell towards my gaze, and then I recognise that it's a discoloured patch above the skirting-board. "It's just more damp," Beverley says. "We'll get it seen to."

"No, it's where his head came through." When Beverley frowns at me, perhaps to remind her that I'm there, the old woman says "I hope you'll still want to find him."

This sounds like my cue to leave, which I would have preferred to do sooner. I mumble a shapeless answer and make for the front door. Beverley sidles past me to open it and murmur "Her and her faces. She just likes telling stories. They keep her alive." As if there's some connection she murmurs "Good luck with finding Deryck."

"Thanks," I say. "Let me know if you hear anything." I shut the wet wooden gate and walk away without looking back or caring for the moment where I'm bound. I just want to leave the house behind, and far too much that I've heard.

Chapter Thirty-four

Three Minutes on the Train

I haven't walked far—I'm still in High Rip territory—when my mobile tries out its new ringtone. I thought it sounded nostalgic, but the day has grown so dark that I could imagine the song about the blackbird is summoning the dead of night. The maze of streets designed for cheerfulness alongside Vauxhall Road may have ousted the grim Victorian lanes where gangs lay in wait for intruders, but they aren't much less narrow or secretive. Perhaps they're just as introverted—focused on the canal—and certainly able to hide any of their denizens who don't want to be found. Though I'm at the edge of the area, I feel as if the warbling of the mobile has identified me as an intruder. The caller's number is unidentifiably familiar, and so is his voice. "Gavin Meadows? We've got your computer."

I'm distracted by a figure that appears at a junction ahead and immediately shrinks out of sight. "What are you doing with it?"

"Not a lot. It did Fin's head in. He had to go home."

"I'm sorry," I feel expected to say. "What happened?"

"He kept thinking he'd got it running, but there was never anything when he shouted us to look. You want to be careful what you bring in to be fixed. Good job there's no girls here and we're all broadminded."

"I don't know what you mean. It isn't my computer."

"That's lucky, isn't it? Tell it to the law." Having celebrated the threat with a pause, he says "The kind of stuff you'd watch by yourself when you're sure there's nobody else about. Fellers having it off, and not just with people. Someone must have messed with the images, he said. Nobody could really look like that." As I remind myself that my informant didn't see any of this he says "What do you want done?"

"What can you do?"

"The hard disc's shot. Can't retrieve a thing. Two of us have tried since Fin went." He sounds as if he's holding me responsible for some or all of this, even when he says "Do you want a new disc putting in?"

Some element of my concern for my father makes me say "Better not, thanks."

"Suit yourself. No charge since we couldn't fix it. When can we drop it off?"

"Any time. Someone's in now."

"On the way, mate."

I could imagine he's so eager to clear the workbench that he can't waste even another second. During the conversation I've turned along Blackstone Street, one of the wider roads leading to the docks. It predates the High Rip era, and so does the railway bridge halfway down, beyond which the perspective has wedged a cargo vessel between the buildings at the end of the street. The bridge is where a sailor was kicked to death, having strayed into territory a High Rip tribe regarded as exclusively theirs. Now the figure I saw turning the corner is under the bridge.

Almost everything is in focus—the aggressively new houses that have claimed both sides of the street, the brown brick arch that spans it, the cranes raising skeletal snouts towards the clouds above the docks, the sun opening a luminous fan through a gap in the blackness across the river, where a windmill on a ridge gleams like a bleached bone. The only detail that I seem unable to see clearly is the squat figure in the gloom beneath the arch.

I take it for a man. Although his face and the rest of him is steeped in shadow, I have the impression that he's watching me, perhaps even waiting for me. As I head downhill, the dark fabric in which he's dressed appears to glisten like the rain that lingers on the pavement. It must be the change in perspective that makes him look even more dwarfish, both broader and shorter. Perhaps I'm better able to see his eyes because they're widening, though surely not as much as I imagine. I'll be able to discern him better once the light that's slanting through the clouds reaches the bridge. The cargo vessel brightens and the dockland cranes blaze, and the road beyond the arch glares like scraped tin. The figure shrinks against the left-hand wall, and then there's nobody under the bridge.

He must have dodged around the wall. In less than ten seconds I'm on the far side of the bridge. The wall of the railway embankment stretches for hundreds of yards to the next arch. The bricks are unbroken except for the occasional crack, but there's no sign of the figure I saw—at least, none apart from marks on the pavement under the bridge. They have to be wet footprints, though they must have begun to dry to be so seriously misshapen. I'm staring at them and at the absence of their maker when a man's voice addresses me, loud enough to suggest that his mouth is enormous. "Looking for something?"

It's amplified by the bridge. He's on the opposite side of the road, where he has emerged from a house on the corner of a side street. His wide low scalp is shaved as if to make up for the hairiness of his body, most of which is left exposed by sandals and capacious shorts. His black pelt glistens like a mass of wire, and the shorts glare a fiercer red, as the sunlight reaches him. "I was trying," I admit.

His heavy footsteps resonate under the bridge, and his voice does. "What's stopping you?"

"Well, nothing," I say without amplification. Presumably he has himself in mind. "Have you noticed anything odd around here?"

"Bloody right I have." By now he's close enough that I can see beads of moisture decorating his chest hairs. "Like what, for instance?" he demands.

"Anyone, I don't know, behaving oddly. Someone who doesn't belong to the neighbourhood."

"I'm looking at him."

"I don't think I've done anything particularly odd, have I? I'm just searching."

"For what?"

I'm about to bring my father up when a new voice shouts "Trouble, Des?"

A man has emerged from the house opposite my interrogator's. He's hairier on top but otherwise less hirsute, for which he appears to have compensated with tattoos. "Caught this feller snooping round and asking questions," Des informs him and scowls at me. "Hang about. Were they saying about you on the radio?"

"That was my father. He's missing."

"Forget him. We're talking about you. It was you, wasn't it? By Christ it was." Des turns his back on me to yell "Know who this is?"

"Never saw him before as I know of."

"He's been here enough. Likes digging up stories we don't want dug. Brings his customers round to oggle the animals in the zoo. That's us, Mick."

I've begun to feel he's using the archway to dwarf my voice, and so I step beneath it to say "I've never done anything like that. I just take people through your history. Not yours, this area's."

"Like I said, digging up the dirt and chucking mud," Des insists as a third nominally dressed man stomps out of the house next to Mick's to bellow "What's all the row?"

"Des caught him hanging round our houses, Bill. Looking for stuff he can say shows we're throwbacks."

"Not at all," I protest with a laugh, which the archway exaggerates more than seems helpful.

Bill reaches behind the front door to produce a baseball bat. "I'll be showing him who's a throwback."

"Look, it's got nothing to do with anyone living round

here. I just run a tour about the Victorian gangs. You can't deny history. It's part of us."

"Never mind saying who it's part of," Bill says and deals his garden path a clunk of the bat.

"They were just taking care of their patch," says Mick. "They didn't want anybody else acting like they belonged here."

"Anybody blame them?" Des enquires.

I'm compelled to speak up on behalf of the victim and of history itself. "Do you realise somebody was kicked to death right here?"

Des swings to face me. "And what was he up to, I'd like to know."

"Who's he saying gave him a kicking?" Mick shouts.

"Fellers like us, he means," says Bill.

"Excuse me, you don't know what I mean."

"He's saying we're too thick to understand his crap," Des declares not far short of my face.

"Try to understand I'm only looking for my father."

"Well, you won't find him round here or any bastard else we don't know."

"What's he saying we done now?" Bill bellows.

"Sounds like he thinks we done his dad," says Mick.

"I wouldn't be surprised."

This is said for me alone to hear, but it gets to Des. "You want to watch what you're saying about us," he says, and so does the archway. "You heard him right, Mick."

"Not at all. Really, if you'd like people to think you've evolved . . ."

I shouldn't have said that. Any remark seems potentially dangerous, but so does keeping quiet once Des calls "We don't want him going home disappointed, do we?"

It's the cue for his neighbours to advance. As Bill lifts the bat in my direction and lets it sink like a dowser's wand, I step back. "I've a train to catch," I say and walk not too cravenly fast downhill.

Even if I was doing my best not to sound scared off, I shouldn't have told them where I was going. Immediately beyond the bridge a branch of the road angles towards the station past a tract of industrial land, but it's deserted and too remote from any traffic. I head for the docks until I reach the next main road, and glance back from the corner. Des and Mick are standing like sentries on the near side of the bridge, but there's no sign of Bill.

I want to think he's satisfied with warning me away. Surely he wouldn't have used the short cut I avoided, which joins the main road a few hundred yards ahead. However little traffic there is, would he really attack me in daylight—even in the meagre light that penetrates the clouds, which are unbroken again? I mustn't let apprehension hinder me, and I hurry towards the station. Perhaps a bus will come to any rescue that I need.

Nobody is at the junction with the short cut or beyond it. The main road leads past industrial properties, behind which are side streets Bill could use to head me off. Whenever I give in to looking back, I'm alone on the pavement. The occasional lorry hurtles past, but I can't help thinking the drivers are perched too high to find me of any significance. I meet no buses; I don't even see a stop. At least I haven't seen Bill or the rest of the gang—do I need to think it's one?—by the time I arrive at the next side street that passes under a bridge.

I hear water trickling as I hurry beneath the arch. Although it's loud, I can't locate the source; it must be amplified by the acoustic. Beyond the arch a ramp leads up to Sandhills Station, which consists of little more than a couple of empty platforms, open to the sky. Nobody can sneak up on me, and I'll hear anyone who climbs the ramp unless they're bent on silence.

I'm in the midst of High Rip territory. Many of the massive warehouses along the dock road belong to that period, and so do most of the streets between them. Might any of the surfaces retain a trace of blood? At least one historian speculates that the disinterred object from which Blackstone Street took its name was a primitive altar. As for the streets that have cleaned up the slums on the inland side of the railway, I'm not far from fancying that the timeless gloom that's inundating them has risen from the canal.

My reverie is interrupted by a train to Liverpool. As the staccato of the wheels eases towards silence it almost covers up another series of sounds. I would take them for footsteps if they weren't so soft and wet. There must be some kind of spillage on the ramp. As I board the train, the platform at the top of the ramp darkens and begins to glisten. The whole station does, with a downpour that veils the windows of the train.

The carriage is unoccupied except by a remnant of cigarette smoke. The journey to Moorfields—on this line, the station nearest my apartment—should take less than four minutes. As the train gathers speed the wind rakes threads of water on the windows close to horizontal. The glass remains not much better than opaque, so that I imagine more of the landscape than I'm seeing. To my right across the aisle is a parade of dockland warehouses interspersed with boxy industrial units, but before any of this was built the sandhills gained a reputation for nude bathing. Washington Irving described the swimmers he once watched there at twilight as "resembling seals or some unrecorded form of marine life." Originally the area was covered by an ancient forest through which a stream flowed down from Everton, close to my parents' house. A pale object is taking and losing shape out there, and for a moment that shows I'm less than fully awake I wonder if it could be a face. It's another gap in the clouds above the river, but there is indeed a face. One is peering at me from the next carriage.

Is it Bill with his bat? When I twist around on the seat, nobody is visible. The carriages are swaying in and out of alignment, but not enough to hide a watcher. I grip the back of the seat and stand up as steadily as the train will allow. Beyond the unlatched doors, which are inching open and shut, the next carriage appears to be deserted. Surely the likes of Bill wouldn't feel any need to hide, and I'm sinking onto the seat when a figure begins to rise to its full height beyond the glass.

While it isn't silhouetted, I'm unable to distinguish much about its shape, except that it's so hulking that it still looks crouched. Its face is pressed against the farther window, but this doesn't bring the features into focus. I hope only breath has turned the window moist within the outline of the head, because the sight is too reminiscent of the underside of a snail flattened against glass. The arm that's supporting me has begun to shiver with tension or worse, and I'm about to move without any idea of how or where until my body robs me of the chance. I've gone blind.

A blaze of sunlight through the clouds has found the train, that's all. As I blink my eyes clear I seem to glimpse the shape beyond the doors recoiling from the light, shrinking from it in the fullest sense. In another moment I'm able to see, even if my vision is as faded as an old photograph. There's nothing at the window between the carriages other than a smear on the glass—a broad grey roundish patch of moisture, unnecessarily reminiscent of mould. It's featureless except for an elongated horizontal crescent of unmarked glass low down on the patch. If that's the outline of a mouth, it's as wide as one in a bad dream.

My arm is trembling again. I grab the seat across the aisle and dig my fingers into the upholstery on either side of me. Apart from the grey smear, which has grown teeth composed of moisture trickling across the empty grin, I can see no sign of an intruder. Perhaps the light is keeping it back, I dare to think, however irrational the notion is—and then darkness rushes up behind me to engulf the train. We've entered a tunnel.

The route is underground now all the way to Moorfields.

We'll be there in less than two minutes—in as unbearably long as that. I'm about to retreat towards the driver's cabin, even if I stop short of seeking refuge with him, when I recall what I hardly noticed as the train arrived. It's being driven from behind. The intruder is between me and the driver. There's still no visible activity, and I wonder if the artificial light is enough to hold my fellow passenger in check. Then the lights flicker, and in a moment the train is as dark as the tunnel.

I know these electrical failures are common and never last more than a few seconds. They're the equivalent of a missed heartbeat or two, even if mine feel as if they've stopped for good. As I hold my breath or lose the ability to breathe, I hear a noise besides the insistent clatter of the wheels. It sounds as if a large object has slithered into the carriage.

I gasp, not only because the lights have come on. The doors between the carriages are swinging shut, and the nearer one bears a wet mark. Despite its shape or lack thereof, it could have been left by a large hand. I let go of the seats and back away, struggling to be ready for a figure to spring into view on one side of the aisle or the other. But it's darkness that pounces as the lights fail once more.

It brings the slithering closer. I throw out my hands for support, because I'm in danger of losing my balance, and my fingers sink into two objects—the tops of seats. I've just realised that I'm presenting myself like a target held in place by my own hands when the lights flicker. Do I glimpse a squat form dodging out of view? The lights steady again, revealing a trail of marks along the aisle. If they're footprints, the kindest word for them would be unequal. The trail ends where I thought I saw movement, halfway between me and the next carriage. There's only that much space behind me. Before I can retreat, the carriage is flooded with twice the light. We've arrived at Moorfields.

I don't look away from the aisle as I back and then sidle towards the exit doors. I've seen no further movement in the carriage by the time the train finishes coasting to a halt and sets about parting the doors. The instant they're wide enough I bolt onto the platform. I very much wish it weren't deserted, especially since the nearest passage to the world above is at least fifty feet away. The train shuts its doors, and I really don't need them to twitch open again as encouragement for me to run. Nothing has emerged from the train by the time I reach the rudimentary corridor. As I dodge into it the train moves off, and I can't be certain that a shape squeezes out between the doors I used. I'm even less sure amid the racket of the train that the glistening object flops onto the platform like an expulsion of mud before it starts to reform.

I don't look back. I dash for the stairs midway along the corridor between platforms. Was I wrong about the light? Has the pursuer adjusted to it, perhaps out of determination not to let me escape? I sprint up the stairs two at a time—I try to make it three and almost miss my footing. They bring me to a bank of escalators with daylight at the top. Though the light is a hundred feet or more away, it emboldens me to glance downwards. I immediately regret the error, not least because I'm transfixed by my attempts to distinguish what's below.

It's a hand, or rather part of one. It's clutching the tiled corner of the passage as though about to haul the body into view. Once more I'm put in mind of a snail, and not just by the colour and texture of the flesh. The fingers are extending along the wall—they're visibly lengthening. Only the prospect of seeing their owner in any more detail lets me dare to turn my back and reel onto the escalator.

I've barely set foot on it, grabbing the rubber banisters as the metal step almost leaves me behind, when the sunlight far above me dims and goes out. As I sprint up the sluggishly ascending steps I feel as if I'm trying to overtake the light or call it back. I'm six steps up, having taken them in three precarious strides, when a weight lands with an expansive leathery thud at the foot of the adjacent escalator.

I can't look. I seize the banisters again—they're crawling upwards at two different speeds—and risk trying to clamber three steps at once. My foot skids off the topmost, and only clinging to the restless banisters saves me from sprawling backwards. Two steps at a time will have to suffice. I climb a pair, and then another. Then I hear footsteps—at any rate, the large soft impacts of objects doing duty as feet—that have begun to mount the next escalator.

Although it's descending, it seems not to matter. Perhaps the pursuer is little better than brainless, or perhaps it has been relishing my attempts to escape. Its spongy tread sounds more than able to match my pace. It's springing up the stairs with a terrible effortlessness despite their contrary motion, as though its legs are abominably long. Any moment now it will overtake me, and I'll have to see it on its way to head me off, unless it plans to stretch its arm across the division of the escalators and capture me with an elongated hand.

I can only flee upwards as the stairs and the banisters threaten to leave me behind. The pursuit is almost at my back—I have the sudden awful thought that it must be capable of leaping from escalator to escalator—when I hear voices, which I take to be violently arguing until I grasp that only their language, or at least the repetition of redundant words that makes up much of it, is fierce. In a moment the speakers appear at the top of the escalators: three girls shouting to be audible above the stereos plugged into their ears. While I wouldn't like to share a train journey with them, just now they're as welcome as the sunlight that has returned beyond them. As they loiter at the top I hear a body floundering down the next escalator. There's a large loose thump at the bottom, and almost immediately one at the foot of the stairs. The pursuer may have retreated into the subterranean tunnel, but as the escalator brings me abreast of the girls I feel bound to call "Better watch out. There could be something nasty down there."

"Left something, did you?" one girl shouts, and another offers "Dirty sod."

Perhaps I'm as unreliable as they seem to think. Certainly I have an odd sense of climbing away from a dream or its source. I might feel more as though I'm returning to the real world if the sunlight weren't so intense as to border on blinding, especially where it's reflected from the rain that coats the streets. I'm walking straight into the light, which gives me very little chance to discern faces or even shapes in the homebound crowds. I'm anxious to be home myself, both for refuge and to see how my mother is. Once I'm reassured in those ways I may be able to ponder what I've just experienced, if it was anything more than my lack of sleep run wild.

The shadows in my narrow street give me back my vision and some nerve. A drip catches the back of my hand as I unlock the door beneath the merman. Shutting the door makes me feel on the way to safe. The old desk greets me with a rattle of its inkwell while I make for the stairs. As I climb them I hear a radio, and by the time I reach my apartment the news is audible along the hall. I let myself in time to hear the final headline. "Police are becoming increasingly concerned about the whereabouts of Deryck Meadows from Everton."

"I hope that helps," a voice calls—not the voice I'm expecting. I shut the door behind me and wait for a response. None comes, but it takes me some moments to wonder if the comment was addressed to me. "Lucinda," I say, "where's my mother?"

Chapter Thirty-five

Home Again, Home Again

"I was going to ask you that, Gavin."

Lucinda has appeared at the end of the hall. She looks doubtful and somewhat concerned, and not only those. As I go to her I see that my father's computer tower has returned to my workroom, where the eye of the answering machine is lidlessly alert—the number of messages. Beyond the bag of umbrellas the trail of waterlogged research leads to the main room, where more of the contents of the boxes are scattered on the carpet. "Have you been looking at those?" I'm prompted to ask.

"A bit. I'm glad you're back," Lucinda says as if this follows, then seems to contradict herself. "I thought you might be Gillian."

As we share a soft embrace that grows firmer I say "How long have you been here?"

"Twenty minutes?"

"And there wasn't any sign of her? She didn't leave a note."

"I can't see one, can you?"

"Then I don't expect she's gone far. Maybe she wanted something from the shops."

Lucinda lifts her head from resting it against my neck and meets my eyes. "So long as she hasn't gone because of me."

"Did she know you were coming?"

"I didn't say when we spoke."

"Then it can't have been you, can it? It wouldn't have been anyway," I add, ashamed of my clumsiness. "She'd like you to be here."

"And where have you been?"

"Just to see an old friend of my father's. Her mother did most of the talking but I don't know how much was made up. I think I ended up as confused as she was."

How eager am I to rationalise the incident on the train? It already feels like a waking dream, and what else could it have been in any world that makes sense? It's even more absurd to think it wasn't my own dream. I need to feel rational—not just feel but be. The newsreader finishes a report about flooding in Liverpool—the loop line beneath the city centre has been drained, but engineers fear this won't last—and returns to the subject of my father. She repeats her headline and reminds me that he has been missing since last week, then adds that until recently he worked at the art gallery and issues a description that sounds disconcertingly like me. That's all, not even a mention of his bicycle. As the newsreader forecasts further downpours Lucinda says "The radio was on when I got here."

"Then she can't be far away."

"Shall I make dinner for the three of us?"

"If you could."

It isn't that I lack enthusiasm for the idea, but rather that I feel as if our embrace and our murmured conversation is trying to maintain a sense that all is or will be fine. As Lucinda turns towards the kitchen she says "Are those Gillian's?"

She's gazing at the table, which is strewn with bits of research. There's the score of an early sixties hit, "The Froggy Hop" by Liverpool band Davy and the Divers, as well as their later ballad "I'd Swim the Mersey for You." Next to these is a reproduction of Adrian Henri's painting *Christ Feeds the Multitude in Paradise Street*, hardly a realistic depiction of the place, since the crowd is overlooked by posters for John West and the signs of fish and chip shops. Some of the beneficiaries of the miracle resemble the seafood they've been handed. Soon the street will be part of the Paradise Project, a development that sounded to my father like a science fiction horror film. Beside the page are photocopies of John Lennon's satirical sketch of a blackbird fly and his cover rough for *Sergeant Leper's Bony Parts Club Band*, and I see what Lucinda had in mind; the image of misshapen Liverpool worthies is pinned down by my spare set of keys. "She didn't take them," I protest.

"She'll ring then, won't she?"

"You'd have heard if she did, wouldn't you." This prompts me to ask "Did you check for calls in case anybody didn't leave a message?"

"I didn't," Lucinda admits, and I hurry to fetch the landline receiver from its stand. I'm keying the digits as I tramp back along the hall. The automated voice tells me I was called and pieces the number together. It's among the ones I know best. The call was made almost an hour ago from my parents' house.

I haven't time to answer Lucinda's anxiously enquiring look. I jab the key to connect me with the number and strain my ears to hear more than the repetitions of the distant bell. For a moment I think it has been interrupted, as if somebody is fumbling at the receiver, but then it goes on, and on, and still on. I don't realise I'm holding my breath like a victim of drowning until my head begins to swim. The phone has been ringing for minutes now, and isn't it simply delaying me? "Someone's rung from the house," I tell Lucinda. "I've got to go up."

"I can't take you."

My brain feels close to incapable of absorbing any more complications. "Why not?"

"Won't someone have to be here if Gillian can't let herself in?"

"I should have thought. Can you call me a taxi?"

My father might have responded with the old joke, but she must realise the situation can't be lightened that way. When she holds out a hand I feel frustrated by having to explain "On your mobile. I want to keep these clear."

Once she has called a number she remembers Lucinda tells me "Ten minutes."

That's at least twice as long as I would have hoped. I'm sure that my mother was called to the house, but why hasn't she rung to let me know what's happening? In search of distraction I glance over my father's notes about Hope Street, which was built along the edge of the Moss Lake. Some of the residents used to steal corpses from the graveyard that supplanted part of the lake and smuggle them in barrels down to the docks. In 1826 the practice was discovered when, according to a no doubt superstitious sailor, the contents of a barrel bound for Glasgow tried to get out, or perhaps he was just talking about some preservative. Before Hope Hall in that street became a theatre it was a chapel, where a sect conducted secret rituals in the basement until a journalist revealed the activities, supposedly designed to regain some kind of closeness to the ancient earth. The doorbell brings some relief from all this, which has set history jabbering in my skull again, and Lucinda is first to the intercom. "He's coming now," she tells a blurred voice and gives me a swift hug. "Let me know what's up."

A black cab is squatting opposite the merman. As I climb in, the latest rain starts to thump the roof like a soft but relentless pursuer. "Where you going?" says the driver.

Her voice is still blurred—thick with Liverpudlian and perhaps compromised by the looseness of her wide lips. She's wearing a combat outfit that tones in with the camouflage-patched baseball cap yanked low on her broad head. She stares big-eyed in the mirror while I tell her the address, then seems to expand—at least, her shoulders do—as she crouches towards the wheel, muttering "Ever going to stop?"

She means the rain, which looks capable of washing away the streets or at least the sight of them. The windscreen wipers struggle to dash it aside, so that her ability to see ahead seems close to miraculous. The Victorian streets have been transformed into a liquid impression of massive architecture, but the downpour slackens as we swing uphill beyond the edge of the old town at Deadman's Lane. Last year a tenant of one of the houses dreamed so vividly that undiscovered victims of the plague still infested the muddy earth that he complained to the council. It seems I'm not the only one beset by history and whatever it breeds.

Sunlight cuts the clouds open above the bay as we climb the road to Everton. Off to the right is a bridewell still used by the police. Previously it was the site of the house of a man called Harrison, though some of his neighbours declared that he wasn't a man after he invited them to share his diet, consisting entirely of insects. His guests said he belonged in the zoological gardens beyond the ridge. Dogs were often set to fight in the fields around the zoo, or to hunt anything that ran, and in its latter days the zoo attracted drunks who set animals free, unless they escaped. One large ungainly creature was seen in the nearby pits used for public bathing, though what kind of animal would have taken refuge there? More to the point, can nothing put a stop to the chattering of history in my bruised head? I feel as if it's even invading my language. But the taxi is speeding along the ridge, and I have a reason to speak—indeed, to repeat it when the driver doesn't react. "We're there."

The house is dripping as though it has been dredged up into the temporary sunlight. It looks repainted by the rain to help the sign attract potential buyers, and I'm able to hope that its cheerful appearance may be an omen of things within. Nobody comes to the door or the windows as the taxi backs up and halts outside the gate, however. "Can you hang on?" I ask the driver.

"Picking someone up?"

"I don't know what I'm doing."

This is more inadvertently eloquent than I like. As I hurry along the garden path I feel as if the house is yet an-other of the places to which I seem compelled to keep re-turning. How disloyal is it to think of my parents in the same context as Williamson or Maybrick or the High Rip or the Pool? Surely the weeds flanking the path and beginning to sprout from it can't have visibly grown since my last visit, even given all the rain. I shove my key into the lock and push the front door wide.

Someone is or has been here. The hall is more deserted than last time; the armchair that was standing sentry by the phone has returned to the front room. The phone is on its hook, and the note my mother left is lying on the stairs. It flutters a little to greet me, but otherwise I'm met only by an intensified smell of damp if not of mould. "Mother?" I call. "Father? Anyone?"

The words drop like stones into an empty well. I glance at the taxi driver, who seems close to pressing her face against the window of her cabin, and then head for the stairs. Damp patches mark the carpet all the way up. Despite their irregularity, the trail could have been made by someone with wet feet. Perhaps their hands were wet too, because half a word of my mother's note is distorted by moisture; it looks as if she wanted to be reassured that my father was sane rather than safe. I pray, however aimlessly, that both of them are both as I call "It's me. It's only me."

Why am I nervous of looking in their room? I grasp the clammy plastic doorknob and ease the door open. At first the sunlight through the window dazzles me, and then I make out a dark shape, if it can be described as a shape, crawling towards me across the bed. It's the shadow of a cloud that is lowering itself towards the river. Otherwise the room is deserted, and there's no sign of life up here apart from a single drip that falls into the bath or into one of the buckets in my father's workroom.

The smell that the house has acquired rises to meet me as I tramp downstairs. It puts me in mind of lightless places and of a reptile house at the zoo. There are even traces of damp on the telephone receiver—of moist fingerprints, at any rate, so blurred that I doubt they would be of use to the police. Should I ring Wrigley or Maddock about the latest developments? My mind seems unable to focus on the situation. Once I've removed the phone from the hook I open the door under the staircase.

Nobody can be hiding there—certainly not my parents. Perhaps the patch in the darkest corner has grown, and the smell is stronger, but that's all. If a shape appears to surge out of the corner as I close the door, it's a shadow, and I refuse to look again. I need to concentrate on the rooms, though they feel drained of memory, more lifeless than museum exhibits. Mustn't I phone the police? If I do, will they intensify their search or scale it down? I haven't decided when I notice an item on the chair that was moved from the hall.

It's the photograph my father scanned into his computer to use as the opening screen. He did indeed manipulate the image. My parents are still holding my younger than teenage hands, but he looks harassed; perhaps he's nervous that the timer of the camera will be too quick for him. The object in the river at our backs is even harder to define, and the fog makes it look composed of water, but it must be one end of a vessel. I take it for the prow, because there are suggestions of a face—domed forehead, great round eyes, a mouth wider than the three of us. Would any ship have had a figurehead like that just a couple of decades ago? Perhaps it was part of some historical celebration, but then why can't I remember it? I could fancy that my parents are trying to ignore whatever's behind us and distract me from it, in which case they seem to have succeeded. I pick up the photograph, though it feels almost as damp as the scene it depicts, and lock the house. "Got what you came for?" says the driver.

I've no answer except to display the photograph as I resume my seat. Having twisted her head around on no great length of neck, she says "That your wife?"

"My mother," I say and then catch up with her mistake. "That's me in the middle."

"And what's that behind you?"

"You tell me."

"How should I know?" She turns away, tugging her cap down as if the hairless nape of her neck feels exposed. "Looks like something I used to dream about when we lived by the river."

I'm by no means sure of wanting to learn "What?"

Her eyes widen in the mirror—bulge, even—with some kind of disbelief. "It was a dream. I was a kid."

The taxi swings towards the river, above which the tethered metal birds blaze like a brace of phoenixes as the clouds train the sunlight on them. I rub my fingers dry and take out my mobile. Her number has barely rung when Lucinda says "What's happening, then?"

"My mother isn't there."

"Oh, Gavin, I'm sorry. Anything at all?"

"No, I mean she hasn't come home."

"I gathered that much, but is there—"

"My home. My home now. Where you are." Is my brain so overloaded that I've lost control of language? "You're telling me she isn't there," I manage to say without snarling.

"She isn't, so I have to."

"I know. I know." Repeating this makes me aware how little else it's true of. "Let me know if she turns up," I say. "I'll be back soon."

As I lower the mobile the driver says "Are you in a rush?"

Only to contact the police, and I shouldn't put it off; suppose my parents are still near the house? Perhaps my mother is trying to stop my father from wandering, unless she has succumbed to it. I resent having to take time to say "Why do you ask?"

"If you're not I'll just get a wash. I'll knock it off your bill."

She means the car wash by the road ahead, where once there was a pond. "I can use my phone in there, can't I?"

"I won't be stopping you."

I key the police number as the taxi turns off Islington. I'm waiting for the switchboard to connect me when the driver inserts a token in the slot and moves the car forward to await the machinery. "When I was a kid," she says, "I used to call this going under the water."

The gantry advances and begins to spray the taxi, solidifying the dusk that the clouds have brought forward. The windows are swimming by the time a voice says none too positively "Yes?"

"Sergeant Maddock?" Since this proves unproductive I offer "Sergeant Wrigley?"

The promotion doesn't seem to please him. "No trace yet," he says.

"Yes there is. He phoned not much over an hour ago."

"From where?"

"He was at the house."

"Took your time, didn't you? What'd he say?"

I'm distracted by someone who must work in the car wash. The windows are virtually opaque with soap now, so that I can see only a blurred shape near my side of the taxi. "I didn't speak to him," I say. "My mother did."

"And he said what?"

"I don't know." Three massive brushes close around the vehicle to wipe away the soap, revealing nobody. "She went out," I say. "All I know is he definitely called from the house. He's the only one who could have got in."

There's silence except for a soft thud against the window at my back. It's a brush. As the apparatus starts its return sweep the policeman says "We'll come and have a word."

"Is that necessary?" Since he apparently feels this doesn't deserve an answer I say "I'm on my way home, but—"

"That'll do us."

I would say more if it weren't for the sight outside the taxi. The spray is blurring the glass again, but I'm almost sure that a figure is standing utterly still outside my window, within reach if it were to extend a long arm. The water has lent it some qualities; the head looks wet, and its rounded outline and vague features seem as uncertain of their shapes as the turbulence on the window. Surely just the water is distorting the squat figure, but when I say "I'll be out of here any moment" it feels akin to a wish.

As the spray droops and the pipes glide away with a farewell hiss I realise that the policeman has cut me off. I peer through the window while a blower reduces trickles to drops and lines them up in the process of raking them off the glass. Long before they've gone it's plain that nobody is near the vehicle. It's cruising out of the car wash when the driver says "You could imagine all sorts in there."

Even if she's reminiscing about her childhood, I feel compelled to ask "What sort of thing?"

"That'd be telling."

I'm less anxious to know than I am to be home, but a tailback halts us on the flyover behind the library. The central barrier prevents us from taking another route. I can't even pay and walk, because there's no pavement. Surely Lucinda will ring if she has any news. The trinity of traffic lights controlling the junction at the end of the flyover releases vehicles two at a time, and at last we pass the obstruction. Half the road at the foot of Cheapside is flooded and has been coned off. Is Waterworth watching the thoroughfare revert to its historical state? Someone's at his office window, turning the glass grey with breath.

Two minutes later I'm outside my door. "Call it ten," says the driver.

I add a pound and let myself in. The pen in the inkwell seems eager to communicate as I run to the stairs. I'm not sure why I should be in such a hurry—at least, until I hear a man's voice beyond my door. As I twist the key I'm able to believe he's my father. I'm stepping into the hall when I realise he's a policeman, but that isn't why I falter. He's talking about Operation Ripper.

Chapter Thirty-six

A Troglodyte

As I leave the photograph on my desk Lucinda calls "Is that you, Gavin?"

"Who else is it going to be?" I do my best to leave this behind by demanding "What was that about the Ripper?"

"We weren't talking about him."

I don't know why she should laugh, and I'm further thrown to see that the other person in the room commandeered by boxes is Maddock. He's seated at the table and drinking from a glass of water. His flat undented nose and indeed his face in general still look like invitations to a fight, so that I'm provoked to ask "Where's your cousin?"

He lingers over a gulp and puts the glass down beside a document. "Who's been blabbing?"

"Careful you don't spill that on there. Who do you think?"

"I'm asking you," says Maddock, leaving the glass where it is. "You want to be careful what you stick your snout into."

He won't daunt me, especially not in front of Lucinda. I cross the room and move the page away from him. "It was your cousin who opened his mouth. He didn't need much coaxing from me."

It's clear I could have phrased this better, which may be why Lucinda intervenes. "It was ripple, Gavin."

"What are you talking about?"

"Operation Ripple. I thought you might be interested."

An audience might find it comical that Maddock and I have the same response, though his is harsher. "Why?"

"It was on the news. There were dawn raids around the docks and up in Marsh Lane and Aigburth. The Marsh Lads and the Eggy Gang have been fighting over drugs that are shipped over in containers. That's why there were all the shootings in the spring."

Having grasped that she's referring to the season, I'm left to wonder "What's that to do with me?"

"Marsh Lane was as far as the High Rip went, wasn't it? And the Eggy Gang meet on some waste ground down by the river at the end of Maybrick's road. I thought it sounded like material for you."

"First I've heard that's why you asked," says Maddock.

"It isn't why you came, is it?" I remind him. "Have you still not traced my father's mobile?"

"Show us someone that'll do it quicker."

I'm on the edge of mentioning the Frugone salesman when Lucinda says "Is it likely to take much longer, do you think, Inspector Maddock?"

I've no idea whether she has established his rank or elevated it to placate him, and his scowl isn't telling. "His signal's down the last I heard. Might be dead."

"We know where he was an hour ago," I protest, "and now my mother's with him surely they'll be easier to find."

"Maybe they don't want finding."

"I'm absolutely sure my mother will. Just because my father called her—"

"You don't know that," Maddock says not far short of triumphantly. "You got it before. You tell him."

Lucinda takes a moment to look apologetic. "Don't we only know somebody called from the house, Gavin?"

"Someone who didn't have to break in, so it had to be him."

"Unless it was Gillian. Could she have phoned to say where she was and not wanted to talk to the machine?" When I don't immediately argue Lucinda says "Did you find any sign of Deryck at the house?"

"Not that he's been there recently, no."

"So all you know is his wife went out this afternoon," says Maddock, "and already you're calling us again."

"You can understand why he's concerned," Lucinda says. "The situation with his father and now not knowing where his mother is or what frame of mind she's in."

"He's still got you, love. Maybe you can calm him down. We don't like him wasting our time."

As Maddock stares at me hard enough to revive a twinge from Whitechapel I blurt "Aren't you doing that by coming here?"

His stare doesn't relent, and I won't slacken mine, even when Lucinda murmurs "Gavin . . ."

"How long would you suggest I leave calling you next time?"

"If you don't hear something," says Maddock, "just wait and remember what I said."

"I don't think you're being entirely reasonable," Lucinda tells him.

"You wouldn't want to see me when I'm not, love," Maddock says and stands up. "Thanks for the water."

I follow as he loiters in the corridor, frowning at the sodden documents. "You want to get her to tidy up a bit," he advises. "Never know who's going to come visiting."

He halts again outside the door. "I'll see myself down," he says and produces what I take to be his version of a grin. "Watch out you don't end up sunk in the tunnel with this weather."

For various reasons I'm disinclined to respond, but I say "Which tunnel?"

"The Mersey one. The Queen's hole. Didn't they tell you when they sold you your digs? It goes right under you."

He means Queensway, the road tunnel that goes underground close to the upper reaches of the Pool and leads beneath the river to Birkenhead. The best I can do in the way of a parting shot is "Where's your car today?"

"Don't need a car to get to the bridewell."

His thick neck seems to grow yet more undeveloped as he drops out of sight stair by stair, and then I listen to his soft but heavy tread until a door brings it to an end. As I return along the hall Lucinda says "Has he gone?"

"I made sure."

"What a, I honestly don't know what to call him. No wonder you're on edge with somebody like that investigating."

"I should be. I ought to be out searching."

"Would you like me to drive? It'd cover more ground."

"How can you? Somebody needs to be here."

Presumably she realises my harshness is directed at the situation, not at her, because she says "I meant I could drive around by myself."

"Can I borrow your phone first?" I don't want to block mine, but the precaution seems to be redundant; there's silence from the house and just my father's message on his mobile. "Call me," I tell it. "Just please call."

"So shall I go?" Lucinda says. "I've made dinner. A big casserole. I found some nice fish."

"Thanks. I'd be in a worse state without you," I say, which seems comprehensively inadequate. "A lot worse."

The afterthought earns me a wry smile and a swift hug. I listen until I hear the door to the basement shut behind her—I've never noticed how much it sounds like the street door—and then I watch from the window as her headlights crawl up into the premature twilight. As the beams swing away a pale object appears to dodge back into the abandoned offices—a reflection, of course. I wash Maddock's clammy glass, which seems to rouse my thirst, so that I have to fill one for myself. I'm rather more than sipping from it as I switch on the radio in time to hear the latest bulletin.

My father isn't included, and it's too soon for my mother. The final item relates to a study conducted by researchers at the oldest Liverpool university, demonstrating that the emotions of the subjects—Liverpudlians—display patterns very similar to waves and tides in the Mersey. It sounds more like a story than a study, and the newsreader jokes about taking water with it. As the presenter of the evening show begins an interview with the curator of an exhibition of objects washed up on the Mersey shore—a stone knife, an ancient medallion depicting an eroded shape walking on water, a skull so distorted by the actions of the river that its species has yet to be identified—I shut off the radio and look for distraction. My father's research is all I can find.

The table is strewn with information about Joseph Williamson. During a period of just over thirty years he lived in no fewer than six of the houses he built above his tunnels. Some of the houses were at least as deep as they were high, four storeys with four basements. The historian James Stonehouse described some of them as "built as if by a blind man who felt his way." At least one contained a room with no door or windows, and the chaplain of the local blind asylum lived in the first house Williamson built. The blind had their own Liverpool church, and I'm reminded that members of the congregation used to pray to be saved from activities only they could hear beneath the church, originally located behind the Empire theatre in Lime Street and later housed in Hope Street, by the margin of the Moss Lake. My mind is chattering with history once more, and I drain the glass to have an excuse to go and refill it. Soon enough I'm back to Williamson, however.

I know he lived in the cellar of the last house he inhabited, dying of water on the chest ten years after he lost his wife. Stonehouse wrote that a tenant heard "very unaccountable and strange" noises beneath her house, but I haven't previously encountered the suggestion that Williamson began tunnelling because of sounds he'd heard beneath his own first cellar. Another tenant complained of damp in her house and was startled soon afterwards when a head appeared through the floor. It must have belonged to one of Williamson's army of workmen, some of whom surprised the diggers of a Victorian railway tunnel by appearing from an unsuspected subterranean passage. Still, I can do without imagining how an intrusive head might look.

My father has underlined sentences from Stonehouse. A woman who met Williamson in the street described him as "not walking but stumping." His habitual outfit might have belonged to a tramp. He referred to his father as "the greatest rip that ever walked on two feet," though how else would the elder Williamson have walked? Some of the tunnels led to "yawning chasms, wherein the fetid stagnant water throws up miasmatic odours." Why would the builder have left these sections accessible while bricking others up as soon as they were excavated? Stonehouse says that Williamson seemed "driven to play the explorer and yet fearful of his goal." He never let anyone tour the excavations, a point my father has underscored twice, until in the year before he died Williamson gave a letter of authority to a physician. "Dr. Watson is not to be interrupted in his walks on my premises, either on the surface or under the surface." It was signed J. W., E. H., beside which my father has scribbled "Eh?" and "One for Sherlock." Williamson believed that his employees "worked all the better for their throats being wetted." Stone from the excavations was used for building his houses and St Jude's Church on the ridge, midway between the highest of his tunnels and my parents' house.

Why has my father marked these references? Was his mind wandering, as it may be now? Surely my mother can appeal for help with him, or could she be too embarrassed? The silence of the phones that are lying on the table feels like news I may not want to learn but need to know. All I can do while I wait is read, and here's another piece about Williamson.

Although it's by Stonehouse, it wasn't published in his lifetime. Apparently Cornelius Henderson, an artist who was a tenant of Williamson's and painted his portrait, threatened to sue, and so the essay didn't see print until 1916, in the *Transactions of the Historic Society of Lancashire and Cheshire*. What was the problem? The only significant difference between the two pieces—certainly the only one to which I can

imagine anybody objecting—is that in the posthumously
published article Stonehouse refers to Williamson as a troglodyte.

My father has ringed the word three times and written
"Strong" next to it. Is that an adjective or a name? When
I've finished staring at the word I put the page aside. Underneath are reproductions of a painting and an old photograph. Without the accompanying text on each page, I
mightn't grasp that they're portraits of the same man. The
painting is by Henderson and shows little more than the
subject's head and shoulders; the frame cuts off the arms and
the trunk well above the waist. The head seems rather too
large for the eyes, which are gazing to the left as if a vision
has engaged them. The image is a good deal more idealised
than the photograph of Williamson seated splay-legged in a
chair, a walking-stick under one hand, a clay pipe in the other.
In his crumpled suit and misshapen tall black hat, he looks
as if he may well have spent time underground. The large
eyes in the broad leathery face are narrowed at the spectator, who could think they aren't used to the light. The photograph was found under the floorboards of Williamson's
last dwelling.

Some commentators doubt that it's a photograph of him.
The first photographic studio in Liverpool didn't open for
business until the year after his death. If it's a fake, why would
anyone have made it, let alone hidden it under a floor? It reminds me of the discovery of the Maybrick diary, if only to
aggravate my confusion. I could think that the city has buried
not just secrets but products of the imagination, although
whose? As I examine the portraits side by side, the painting
watches the photograph as if that's the vision Williamson
experienced. The narrowed eyes of the photograph trap my
gaze until they seem to twitch as a preamble to widening. I'm
not far from seeing the frame of the image as a bath in which
the grotesque figure is supine. The idea that it could bob up
towards me won't let me move, even when I seem to distin-

guish a dark glint between the eyelids where I hadn't noticed one before. My imagination is taking hold, or is something taking hold of it? When I hear Williamson's fingernails scrape the sides of the bath I gasp as though I've come to the surface of whatever medium has engulfed me. The scrape is the sound of a key in the lock.

Chapter Thirty-seven

Night and Water

"Come in, Gavin."

"Shouldn't somebody stay out?"

"I wouldn't have thought so." Lucinda gazes up at me from the bath as she murmurs "Why?"

"In case we need to hear."

"What would we?"

"The phone. The other phone. The bell."

"I'm sure we won't miss them. I just thought a bath usually helps us to relax."

Perhaps that's meant to remind me I'm not alone in being tense. She's had to put up with my preoccupied silence over dinner, even if it was preferable to my stumbles in and out of conversation. Then there were my attempts to wash up, punctuated by the clang of dropped utensils and the smashing of a plate from the set my parents bought for the apartment. The local news interrupted the evening every hour, but never with a mention of my parents, and I felt as if the programmes I tried to watch on television—a report on how inadequate British flood defences are, a documentary about unsuspected forms of subterranean life discovered by potholers after examples were washed to the surface—were marking time until the next bulletin. I couldn't open any wine in case Lucinda had to drive, not that her searching my parents' neighbourhood and its outskirts for an hour had produced a result. Eventually we tried playing the City of Culture board game, but the questions on cards that the dice turned up—asking us to identify the work of Liverpool artists and composers and poets and writers, occasionally of books—made me feel threatened by the chattering of history and imagination. I still do, and perhaps the bath will be a refuge, or surely Lucinda's embrace is. "I'll leave the door open," I tell her.

"Suppose someone comes in?"

"I hope someone does," I say and then realise our mistake. "They can't with no keys."

Once I've undressed in the bedroom, I have to leave the phones in the hall. Lucinda sits forward as I return to the bathroom, leaving the door minutely ajar. She's certainly entitled to a massage. The water redoubles its ripples while I climb in behind her and splay my legs on either side of her. I'm kneading her shoulders and kissing boss after soft boss of her spine when she says "You haven't asked about last night."

"What about it?" I say, moving my hands towards her neck.

"Where I was. I expect it's not important with everything else."

"You are," I say and grip her shoulders. "Where?"

"Not quite so hard, Gavin. The new tunnel."

I'm conscious only of asking "What were you doing there?"

"That really is a bit hard." She squirms in my grasp until it slackens, and then she says "Taking pictures."

"Since when have you been involved?"

"You don't have to stop. I only said too hard." Once I've recommended massaging she says "I wasn't there for the Friends. I'm just a librarian seeing to the record."

"So what's it like down there?"

"They had to row me in a rubber boat. I'm back, though, and you didn't have to fetch me from the underworld."

I seem unable to judge how soft her neck is within my grip. "What did you see?"

"We couldn't go too far because it's partially blocked and they can't clear it until the water goes wherever it has to, but there's definitely another section that leads towards the church by my house. That's enough now, thanks. Do you want me to change round?"

"If you like."

She rises with such suppleness that I could fancy she's about to vault over me like a circus performer. As I shuffle squatly forward, she sidles past and then closes her legs around mine. Her touch on my shoulders is so gently lingering that her soft grasp feels larger than I know her hands are. I'd like to relax into the rhythm of her fingers, which seems to be adopted by surreptitious ripples in the water, but perhaps I need an extra element. "Aren't you going to sing tonight?"

"I'm feeling a bit hoarse. You don't want me croaking in your ear."

"Shall I see if we've got some medicine?"

"I expect it just needs watering. I'll have a glass before we go to bed."

I'm beset by ripples as she flexes her legs, distracting me from the impression that her massage has adopted the tempo of a waltz, although it reminds me to ask "Where did you hear the song you sang last time?"

"The score's in the archive. I thought you might like it. One more buried bit of Liverpool for you to use."

I'm not sure how, even if she has my tours in mind. "You know who wrote it, then."

"Stephen Adams, wasn't it? Liverpool's most prolific songwriter before the Beatles."

Is she suggesting he wrote the words? That's another local myth to be blamed on James Maybrick or the version of him that has been kept alive. I shouldn't make Lucinda talk when her voice does seem to have acquired an undercurrent of hoarseness. I devote myself to extracting any stiffness from her shoulders, and then we lie quiet until I feel close to falling asleep. A chill from the water or from the prospect sends me out of the bath.

Lucinda climbs out with a whisper of ripples, and I'm

ready with a towel. Once we've finished drying each other I retrieve the phones while she carries glasses of water into the bedroom. By the time I follow she's under the quilt, which bares her erect nipples as she stretches out her arms. "Are you sure?" I murmur. "If your throat isn't in such good shape . . ."

"If you're going to end up in my condition you will anyway, Gavin."

I only meant she might prefer to sleep in case that helps her recover. Perhaps she's run down from working late last night, unless she caught something in the tunnels, but she hasn't lost her energy; in fact, she puts me to shame. Am I distracted by hoping to hear a bell? I feel as if she's opening her legs too wide in an attempt to compensate for my flaccid performance. As she entwines her limbs about me, I'm impressed by how much of me she's able to encompass, unless that's my imagination. She digs her fingers into my shoulders but takes care not to use her nails, which I can't even feel. Her eyes widen with a plea or an exhortation until my thoughts seem to be drawn into their depths, leaving my mind empty of anything but her. Her tongue is unusually eloquent tonight, however silent; it seems to have a message for every part of my mouth. I've no sense of how long we rock together like victims of a storm at sea, but at last the waves of her soft firm flesh conjure forth my miniature flood. She holds me tight—it feels as though she's attempting to render her limbs sturdier—while I gasp like somebody rescued from drowning. Eventually she releases me and turns over. Once I've tugged the cord to let the darkness down she takes my hand and guides it around her waist and slips her fingers between mine.

Her body feels almost as soft as sleep, and soon they're one. How can I follow her into unawareness when my parents are at the mercy of the night? If they were together and anywhere safe they would let me know, or might they think it's too late? Surely the police have to be searching for them, and I've no idea where I could; I would simply be another wanderer in the dark. Can't I at least make a call? When I start to inch away Lucinda's fingers grow firmer, increasing their hold on me. She needs her sleep before she goes to work, especially since she was up so late last night, or rather down. She has more of a job than I have just now, and I should keep still on her behalf.

At some point, and then more of them, the stillness closes like deep water over my mind. Whenever I waken I feel reprehensible for having dozed, and lie straining my ears until sleep overtakes me afresh. Sometimes I hear howls of pursuit—the sirens of police vehicles—or the shrill barking of car alarms. Once I'm roused by a harsh rhythmical noise as it passes the apartments, and I imagine a squat shape croaking in time with its ungainly waltz along the street, though it must be the sound of some mechanical fault. More than once I hear rain assailing the window, reawakening my concern for my parents. Lucinda strokes my palm until the storm sinks away, and I feel as if her long fingers are playing the instrument of my hand, performing a silent lullaby to coax me to join her in sleep. I must be well on the way, since her fingers aren't nearly as long as that, and fish aren't swimming in and out of my mouth; it's just the lingering taste of dinner. The thought of unseen depths seems capable of rendering them not much less than palpable, and they swallow up my mind.

Breathing wakens me—no, its absence does. At least Lucinda is still clasping my hand, however attenuated her fingers have grown. Even this is a memory that must have been misshapen by a dream, and I'm alone in bed. When I turn over to reach for the glass on the bedside table, I see the phones have gone. This sends me stumbling out of the bedroom, calling "Where are you? Where's—"

"I'm just about off to work," Lucinda says from the kitchen. "Would you like any breakfast? We're out of milk, but we could have porridge the old way with water."

"It's all right, thanks," I say, because I feel bloated and

tense. Part of this will be anxiety, but I wonder if I've caught her illness. "Should you be going in if you aren't well?"

"I think it was just an overnight thing." Her voice does sound restored to normal. "It seems to have taken itself off," she says. "Anyway, I can't give in to it at the moment. I've too much to do."

"Where are my phones?"

"I've got them safe," she says and takes them out of her pockets. "I'd have put them back on my way out. Perhaps you'll hear today. I'll be thinking my hardest about it."

Does she mean as a substitute for prayer or in case she comes up with an idea we've overlooked? Suppose some reference buried in one of the cartons is the key to my parents' whereabouts? As I peer at the nearest box Lucinda says "I'll leave you to it, then."

She hugs me as hard as she can, and I respond even more forcefully, but my attention stays on the topmost document. "There he is again," I mutter.

Lucinda lets go as if I've betrayed her affection. "Who is?"

"John Strong. You can't honestly believe my father could have made all that stuff up."

"I'm saying nothing, Gavin."

I have the impression that she doesn't want me to go after her or the remark, but I follow her along the hall. "Say whatever you need to. Say what you're thinking."

"I looked in the stacks." She opens the door and leaves me with a kiss that may be meant to compensate for any disappointment. "We've got nothing by him, not even a book," she says. "He might as well be another Liverpool legend, just something else the city dreamed up."

Chapter Thirty-eight

Deontu Klnok

I listen until the basement door cuts off Lucinda's footsteps. The stairway looks as empty as my mind. I know writers have concocted tales of Liverpool—one even claimed that a fictitious anecdote of Arthur Machen's was true and attributed it to a Scouser—but John Strong was a writer, not a tale. I can't imagine anything that could have got into my father to make him invent all that material. I'm struggling to make sense of Lucinda's comments when my mobile bursts into its nocturnal song.

I slam the door and dash to grab the phone from the table. The caller is unidentified, and apprehensiveness is one reason why I'm short of breath. It dismays me how feebly I gasp "Hello?"

"Hank Waterworth."

I don't exert myself much to say "Yes."

"Have they been in contact with you?"

I'm anxious to learn more after all. "Who?"

"Whoever wanted to take one of your tours." Quite as disapprovingly he says "I didn't speak to them."

Before I can respond he says "Has there been any news of your father?"

The reminder turns my throat dry. "I'm expecting some," I croak.

"I apologise if this is upsetting for you. May I express my hopes that you'll hear something soon."

He's mostly conveying his attempt to be more human. "Thank you," I say with as much of an effort and break the connection.

It's nearly noon. I need to hear the news, and I switch on the radio to be met by a football crowd chanting "You'll Never Walk Alone." The song has been adopted by the city for its own use, and it occurs to me that Jack the Ripper was as well. As I gulp a glass of water I'm urged not to fear the dark when I walk through a storm. Somehow I don't find this reassuring, and I can use some distraction. Perhaps I can do something for my father while I'm waiting—prove that he copied the thoughts of John Strong.

I dump the carton by the table and fish out the topmost document, several photocopies stapled together. The first reproduces a page from the *Liverpool Mercury* that includes an account of the Thomas Cosgrove case. Cosgrove was discovered in Cheapside just before dawn on 22 February 1815, after having tried all night to force his wife to swallow a corrosive poison. As dawn approached he choked her to death with a finger and thumb before taking the poison himself and cutting his throat. Despite all this, he was described as conversing in "a collected and rational manner." He refused to give a reason for his actions, pinching his lips together with a finger and thumb whenever his motives were raised. He died a fortnight later in the bridewell opposite his house. My father has scribbled Strong's observations in the margin—Strong's, not his own. "How muscular a brute, or how malleable a mate! Did he make an end by daylight so that he would never see her face plain, or the one in the mirror?"

The next page of newspaper gives an account of Cosgrove's burial at the crossroads where the first High Rip murder would take place. Surely Strong could only have been speculating that among the mob watching the burial were the families of all the Tithebarn Street thugs. "Did the spectators dream that they were witnessing savagery submerged? To cast it into darkness is to add darkness to its power." The third sheet is a page from the *Liverpool Echo* dated decades later. One paragraph reports how Cosgrove's body was disinterred during the construction of a sewer, but who is my father quoting to the effect that the corpse seemed barely human? Supposedly it was swollen and distorted by the water that had brought it closer to the surface in an attitude suggestive of a bid to worm its way to freedom. I don't care to imagine the spectacle or entertain the fancy that the Flashes had resurfaced—the pond that used to sport a ducking-stool. I'm glad to be diverted by the one o'clock news.

A man has been arrested for drugged driving in the Queensway tunnel, having swerved a bus to avoid an obstacle he can't describe. The police are having to protect street cleaners from attacks by clubgoers in the early hours. A television reporter surveying her hometown of Liverpool has been pelted with bottles and threatened with a gun. Some football supporters object to the use of "You'll Never Walk Alone" as an anthem for the city, since it's sung by fans of the rival team. My parents' disappearance is the final item of the bulletin. A phone-in caller sets about accusing the television reporter of bringing the city into disrepute, and I switch off the radio, to be disconcerted by the next page of John Strong as transcribed by my father. Strong might almost have been predicting the call.

He believed Liverpool was founded on denial. The construction of the town and in particular the draining of the Pool have been attempts to deny the nature of the place. "That which is buried shall rise up darker," he wrote, and I wonder if his style was designed to reach into the past. "The jealous spirit of the Pool shall cast down spire upon spire." Even the old spellings of the name were acts of repudiation: Lirpole, Litherpool, Leverpule, Laverpole . . . "The men who shape the town are blind as any troglodyte. Never did the laver name the seaweed which the bird holds in its beak. The bird is not the emblem of the city but the symbol of the vision which the builders tether to the earth, and what is the liver if not that which lives in the Pool?"

I've no idea, and none of how this could lead me to my parents. "The city cloaks its nature in borrowed names, names risen south." It has indeed lifted street names from London, and I'm reminded of a passage in the supposed Maybrick diary: "Whitechapel Liverpool, Whitechapel London, <u>ha ha</u>. No one could possibly piece it together." The diarist also rants about cutting people open and eating their offal, even if he never mentions the liver by name, and seems obsessed with destroying a church—St James's, whether in London or Liverpool. The Merseyside church is above the docks, close to Prince William Street, from where a letter signed by the Ripper taunted police for failing to locate him. The narrator of the diary often addresses himself and even questions why he can't bring himself to destroy the journal. It reads like the work of someone dreaming he's a writer, and I'm dismayed to feel that's true of the annotations on the photocopies. Need I care? My father didn't think them up, he only wrote them down.

"Have the names the power to send dreams southwards?" I could take this as a reference to Maybrick, but why has my father added the next sentences? "Those whose ancestry lies in the mud are drawn back to the dark to breed. Men have been driven mad by discovering their parentage or the nature of a mate. Some families cannot bear to have an album." I can't help recalling that the Ripper scribbles were found in a Victorian scrapbook, the first forty-eight pages of which had been removed with a knife but were shown to have held photographs. My father has stapled a sheet to this one. It's a photocopy of a crude handbill, which I deduce is early Victorian, advertising a mock trial at the York Hotel in Williamson Square. The title is *Jack Myprick and his Miraculous Stalk: The "Cellary" Champion Caught on the Hop in Whitechapel.*

Presumably the pun or puns meant more at the time. I don't have time to speculate about the name—to wonder if their reactions to some family secret sent Michael Maybrick one way, James another. As I stare at the handbill, a tapping at the window grows larger and more shapeless. The rain makes me aware that I'm thirsty once more. I'm filling my empty glass at the kitchen sink when I catch sight of a figure through the window. The beads and equally restless threads of water on the pane let me distinguish only a squat blurred glistening shape outside the abandoned offices. Instead of taking refuge in the doorway it's standing in the downpour without an umbrella. Is it in its element or too preoccupied or not intelligent enough to move? I plant the glass with a clank beside the sink and unlatch the window. As I heave at the swollen sash the figure comes to life with a swift but ungainly movement that the water on the pane must be enlarging and distorting. By the time I raise the sash the street is deserted.

I lean over the sink and out of the window, to be rewarded with a faceful of rain. Where could the loiterer have gone so fast? Craning out simply blinds me with rain, and I massage my stretched neck as I slam the window. In the bathroom I towel my head until it feels as if I'm rubbing it bonelessly soft, and then I retrieve my drink. I'm back at the table when I notice the page that's now uppermost in the box.

The content may be rambling if not incoherent, but that doesn't matter. It's a photocopy of a page of typescript, some of which is annotated or rewritten. The handwriting isn't my father's, and the type is so primitive that I wouldn't be surprised if the machine was a century old. There's no question in my mind that I'm looking at the actual work of John Strong. So much for Lucinda's strange mistake.

"Before it was invaded by a river, the Mersea was a pool." Some geologists think this may have been the case in the Mesolithic era, but I doubt they would go any further with Strong. "While the earth dreamed of evolution, the Pool shaped spirits with its dreams . . . The god takes on the aspects of the sacrifice . . . Do the god's dreams inspire the tributes of the savage, or must the savage tributes shape the god? . . . Some of its dreams rise as mist, and some are trapped in mud to take on the flesh of the dark . . ." I'm beginning to feel as if Strong was compelled by the landscape or something beneath it to piece together a secret tale of the city—a labyrinth that gives only glimpses of sense. That sounds like Williamson's problem, but was my father overtaken by a similar compulsion? Has it infected me, preventing me from thinking properly about him? "The Pool yet dreams of the light beyond light . . . Its dreams confound the tyranny of time and space . . . Sometimes it finds a worthy vessel for the dreams it stretches forth. Carl Jung was touched by one, and Strong became its ark once Strong drank from an ancient well." Some old wells were recommissioned during the blitz, but that's all I mean to believe— certainly not "The deeper it spreads through the dark, the more vessels it sets dreaming. Even the dead may become its receptacles and regain a form of life. What are ghosts but the dreams of the dead? Those who live by the dead may share their dreams . . ."

The last word swells up before my eyes and changes shape. The page has been spattered with rain—with water, at any rate. The landline phone is ringing, and my nerves jerked the glass in my hand. I let go of it and grab the receiver. "Hello?"

"Hello."

The voice is too hoarse for me even to sex. "Gavin Meadows," I tell it. "Who's this?"

"You'll be the tours, will you? All by yourself?"

I could imagine that the caller's ascertaining whether I'm alone. "It's always been a one-man show."

"Can you fit us in the next one?"

"I'm sure I can," I say but think it best to add "How many are you?"

"We're a big family, us. Some little ones and a few old things as well. Don't worry, you won't leave any behind. We can all keep up."

"I'm just wondering about umbrellas with this weather. I try to provide them, but I've just got six."

"Don't bother bringing any if you don't need one. We've got plenty. Never know when it'll change. We'll see you then, then."

Despite the inexpressiveness of the voice I sense enthusiasm, even urgency. "Sorry, when?"

"Two o'clock, isn't it? We'll be round the old witch in her temple."

This is the first time I've heard Victoria described that way. "I don't know if I'll be running that tour."

"The council said you were. It's now or nothing for us. We're only up today."

"Could you wait until tonight at least?"

"The youngsters need to get their heads down. They want more sleep than us."

"I see, only—"

"Better let them have their dream time. They're the future." As I mumble not much of a response the caller says "He wants to know what we think."

Does that mean Waterworth or his colleague? I don't want to hear any more from the monotonous voice just now. I could imagine that it has lulled me into saying "All right then, two at the monument."

"Lots more than two. You won't believe it. So long as you can cope."

"Certainly I can," I say without meaning to end the conversation. I should have asked for the number in case I need to cancel, but it's withheld. Can't I go out? If my parents are together, surely they'll call my mobile rather than or at least besides the landline if they call, whyever they haven't yet. The phone at the house is still off the hook—blocked, at any rate. I've more than an hour before I have to leave for the tour, and I can hope the situation will be resolved by then. I shouldn't live down to Waterworth's opinion of me, especially when I would be disappointing a good many more people than him. I still need to earn a living; I've little enough put aside for a rainy day. Meanwhile one of Strong's thoughts has caught my attention, if the fancy can be called a thought. "Some will not learn their own nature until they find the Pool."

I don't know why this bothers me, but I look for something else to occupy my mind. "The Pool reaches for the light through the magician but is retarded by every inferior vessel, by the mass and their dead and by the troglodytes its lesser visions spawns . . . Every native of the city is its creature, and every one of their creations strives to set down a dream of the Pool . . ." Mustn't that include this rigmarole? "History consists of tales men tell to bring the past to an end, but legends are its life . . ." I'm instantly prompted to wonder which kind of tale the Ripper diary was. Hasn't the Ripper become a legend, and one that stays alive by being unresolved? All at once I'm sure that the truth about the diary will never be established—that the whole point of the document is to remain mysterious. The notion seems to lead deeper into a labyrinth as well as proving how possessed by history I am, so that even the muffled throbbing among the papers on the table—a sound suggestive of an intruder trying to dig itself forth—comes as a relief.

The mobile is throbbing, and my skull. The screen displays one message received—just that information. As I jab the key to reveal the message I'm afraid it will prove to be an automated sales pitch. But it's a personal communication, however garbled, and as I translate it my mouth grows parched with urgency. **Deontu klnok fnor uvs** means **Don't look for us**. It's from my father's mobile number.

Chapter Thirty-nine

THE SAME DEAL

If I ring back on my mobile it might delay another message or at least my reading of it. My father's number isn't stored on the landline receiver. Although typing it in takes just a few seconds, the delay sets my forehead aching with a wordless reminiscence of Whitechapel. I poke the key to call the number and add another bruise to my face by fiercely pressing the receiver against it. At last the mobile gives up ringing, and I hear my father's voice.

He has seldom sounded livelier or more cheerful. The trouble is that he's recorded. "No, you aren't on your bike," I protest. "I know you're otherwise engaged, or are you just not answering?" I'm shouting over him, and I have to moderate my tone as he falls silent. "Don't tell me you aren't still there," I plead and try to appeal to his sense of the ridiculous. "Or go on, tell me that if you like. Just speak to me, that's all. You must know how worried I am. I'm certain mother does. I need you to tell me what's going on. If you don't I'll have to come looking, and you say you don't want that. Tell me why. For the love of whatever's still sacred, tell me what's happening."

My words are growing as uncontrolled as Strong's appeared to be. I'm saying everything that comes into my head, even when this puts me at some distance from the truth. Have I really implied that I won't go to find them if I learn where they are? Perhaps my father sees through the ruse, because once I finish babbling he doesn't respond. In a few minutes I have to accept that he has no intention of calling back.

I'm wasting time. I should have the message traced. I dash to the bedroom and grab the first clothes that come to hand—yesterday's, though they're so crumpled by their night on a chair that they make me look close to homeless. I've no time for a shave. I plant the landline receiver on its stand, though it feels like abandoning a connection with my parents or at least the chance of one, and run down the hall.

The pen in the inkwell clatters like a faulty alarm as I tramp to the street door, outside which I'm tapped softly on the shoulder by a drip from the merman's cornucopia. The sky is growing as dark as deep water. On Castle Street the remnant of the sanctuary stone inset in the roadway gleams like an exposed trilobite as a cloud toys with the sun, but nobody in the lunchtime crowds appears to find it worth a glance. A pair of green men offer me protection as I cross opposite the old Bank of England branch. A stream beside the pavement races me down Cook Street, and as I hurry through the lanes to Whitechapel a blackbird starts to sing. It isn't the dead of night, whatever the sky imagines, and the melody is trickling out of one of the shrines to the Beatles. The notes continue to twitter in my skull as I dodge through the mob on Whitechapel to the Frugone shop.

As soon as I open the door the salesman I spoke to last time steps forward, raising his arms. He's still advertising special offers with a Frugosh shirt. His arms subside once he recognises me, and the scaly tail of a tattoo withdraws its fin into the yellow sleeve. "Can I help?" he says loud enough for his colleagues to hear.

He must be hoping it will shut me up. "Can I have a word?" I murmur. "About the deal we discussed."

"That's expired, sir, I'm afraid." At least none of his colleagues is looking, and he has lowered his voice. "If you'd like me to show you anything else . . ."

"Whatever you like, but I need to talk about that. You were right, I couldn't find it anywhere."

"We're the buddies of your budget," he says, quoting the

new Frugo slogan, and ushers me away from his workmates. "Have you seen our latest Frugosh? Mobiles you can watch six free films a month on."

"Sounds good, but I really need to get that other deal."

"You should have got it while it was going. You were in the right place for it then."

"This is as well. Nobody's listening." When he widens his large eyes but leaves them blank I say "Can't I just give you the number to trace? I mustn't be without my phone."

"Keep it down." His expansive face has grown so mottled that it seems in danger of puffing up, though his jowls stay pale. "Give us your number," he mutters.

"It's my father's. It's—"

"I'm saying give us yours and I'll let you know if I can do anything."

"When will you?"

"Should be after work."

"I can't wait that long. It's too urgent. It could be a matter of I won't say what. It's desperately urgent, I promise."

"Not so desperate if you went looking somewhere else. Take it or leave it. If you're giving me your number, make it quick."

"Let me give you this first." I reach in my hip pocket, and my mouth dries up. Have I been a victim of that Victorian survival, the pickpocket? No, the notes have taken refuge in the folds of my handkerchief. I crouch towards a shelf of mobiles, their little screens as featureless as slates awaiting chalk, while I count out fifty pounds to plant in the sales-man's hand. "That's what we agreed, yes?" I remind him.

He looks both ways before slipping the money into his back pocket. "It'll do," he says and unclips a ballpoint. "Let's have your number, then."

He's about to turn away, having inscribed it on his wrist, when I murmur "You'll want my father's too."

I bring up the message onscreen, covering it with my thumb so that he can read just the digits. The police would insist on reading the message, one reason I'm wary of contacting them. "I need you to let me know where that came from just as soon as you possibly can."

"Something up with your lugs? I said—"

"I'm begging you, all right?" Perhaps he finds this absurdly old-fashioned, and certainly deserving of no more than a stare, which provokes me to add "You don't want me making a row. We're being watched."

His throat works—it bulges, and so do his eyes. I have to decipher his question from the shapes his swollen lips adapt. "Who by?"

"The security cameras," I say and nod at the monitor above the counter. "We're up there. I won't have to tell the manager why you took my money, will I?"

I'm belatedly assailed by the notion that if he wasn't smart enough to avoid the camera he may not be much use in tracing my father's number. As he yanks his sleeve down, surely not so hard that he smudges the information on his wrist, I murmur "Don't keep me waiting any longer than you absolutely need. You don't want me coming back or ringing the shop."

Is this too threatening? Alternatively, is it convincing enough? I can't think of anything else I could risk saying. I leave him before he has time to respond, but I sense his distended gaze on me all the way to the street. When I glance back through the glass door, he lifts a finger to his lips. I don't know whether he's musing on how to deal with me or enjoining silence.

I have less than an hour to my tour, but I mustn't simply kill time, and I need to take my mind off waiting to hear from the salesman or, surely better, my parents. Even showing the librarians that the unpublished papers exist would be something to do on my father's behalf, and then I realise I haven't brought the photocopied typescript with me. "Use your head," I blurt so fiercely that people seem to think I'm haranguing them as I tramp across the road. Why are so many people wearing a badge? It depicts a drop of water hovering above or falling on a word. At first I think it's WADE, and then I see it's WAD. No doubt it refers to yet another event designed to publicise Liverpool.

The blackbird has been silenced, whichever cellar it was in. As I hasten along the lane I hear a subterranean rumour of someone living in a nowhere land. Above Castle Street the sky has grown so dark that the sanctuary stone is indistinguishable from the road. I dash across as the green men start to gutter. Darkness presses the waterfront buildings low as I descend towards the river, and I could imagine the giant birds have been hooked by lines that are dragging them into the depths.

Somebody is taking a late bath in one of the apartments. As I pad fast upstairs I hear water sloshing above me. It subsides as I reach my floor. The afternoon is even darker than it seemed; I have to switch on the light in my hall, even though most of the inner doors are ajar. I'm in the main room and reaching for the page on the table before I realise why the apartment is so dark. Has my parents' disappearance robbed me of awareness? When I left, all the curtains were open, but now they're drawn as close as they will go.

I snatch the page from the table on my way to let the meagre daylight into the room, calling "Who's here?" That's thoughtless too. Only Lucinda could be, but why would she shut out the light? I'll ask her when I see her. I'm in the hall, where the discolouration of the pages looks as if large damp hands have been fumbling at them, when I hear water sloshing again. It's beyond the only inner door that's shut—the bathroom door.

I repeat my question, which brings silence except for a watery gurgle that might belong to the plumbing or express stifled mirth. I take hold of the doorknob, which is as wet as a stone in a marsh. "I'm coming in," I announce, which feels more like an attempt at a vow. I twist the knob and fling the door wide. The shower curtain flaps, and surely that's the reflection I glimpse in the mirror, not a pallid figure with far too little notion of its shape ducking low in the bath. As I venture unwillingly forward, isn't that just my shadow slithering along the wet green trough towards the plug that's half out of the hole? Surely I don't see the glistening tail or some other section of an intruder squeeze into the hole and disappear like a snail into a shell. I can't be certain of any of this, because I'm out of the apartment at a speed that leaves behind most of my breath.

Chapter Forty

At the Monument

I don't quite slam the door of my apartment. At the last moment I block it with one foot, because I'm almost too furious to think. How can I let myself be scared out of my own home in broad daylight, or at any rate today's version of it, by nothing more than suspicions of an interloper? I won't be much use to my parents if this is the best I can do. I'm acting too much like my mother. I take a breath and then a deeper one to hold while I inch the door wide.

The lamplit hall leads past the darkened rooms to the solitary uncurtained window. Beyond the golf bag bristling with umbrellas the illegible documents are lined up on the carpet like eroded slabs in a churchyard. The stillness makes my ears and the bruise on my forehead ache, and arrests my breath until I have to gasp, and turns my mouth as dry as paper. I won't move until the trespasser betrays its presence, although my immobility feels as if I'm paralysed by a waking dream. But I am moving—I'm inadvertently crumpling the photocopy in my hand. I fold it small enough to fit into my hip pocket, and then I grip the doorframe and take a single stealthy pace into the hall.

I've no idea how long I may have stood with one foot across the threshold when it occurs to me that the electric light could inhibit any trespasser. I let go of the doorframe and feel absurd for covering the switch with my hand to mute the click. Darkness returns to the apartment, taking refuge in the blacked-out rooms, but there's no sign that anything else does. I support myself with the doorframe again and glare at the section of mirror that's visible in the dim bathroom. At last I glimpse movement—a shifting of the shower curtain, but it's just a flicker of eyestrain. As I blink my eyes wide I feel as if I'm wakening or not quite, and glance at my watch. Somehow it's nearly time to start the tour.

I won't leave the apartment dark, not least because it puts me in mind of the way a death used to be signified. All the curtains of a house with a corpse in it would be drawn, as if any light from the world outside could bring about some kind of revival. Only water can, except that's one of John Strong's deranged notions, and what is it doing in my head? The intrusion enrages me, and I stalk along the hall.

Are the kitchen curtains wet? I haven't time to be sure, nor whether there are faint damp almost shapeless tracks in the hall. I'm in the bedroom, tugging the curtains as wide as they'll go, when I hear a noise in the bathroom. It's only a trickle of water, but is it leaving the bath? It's beginning to sound larger and heavier too. Quite a weight seems to be groping forth and gaining far too much substance as it extends towards the hall. It's between me and any escape other than jumping from a window, which is such a nightmarishly ridiculous idea that I'm furious again. Have I let in enough light to keep anything back? "Come out if you've got the guts, you—" I shout, but the rest of my breath is needed for a dash along the hall. Is that my shadow—the blurred shape that rears up as I pass the bathroom? It's as much as I glimpse on the way to slamming the apartment door so hard that the impact seems to end up in the cellar.

As I hurry downstairs I'm seized by a kind of hysterical glee, like a child running away from a prank he's committed. It seems grotesquely inappropriate, more like an emotion in a dream. Until I reach the outer door the pen rattles in the inkwell as if it's amplifying my panic or eager to transcribe it. When I step into the street the mossy cornucopia bestows a drip on me like a warning of a storm.

I've forgotten to bring an umbrella again. I don't know whether I'm more infuriated by the oversight or by its pettiness in the midst of so much else. My lightweight jacket is meant to be waterproof. The narrow street appears to have squeezed most of the light from the strip of sky, but when I emerge into James Street, which is several times as broad, my surroundings simply expand the dark. As I hurry uphill to the monument that rises where the Castle used to stand, however, the pillars elevating the dome above the bronze queen blaze white and their shadows topple onto the statue. I could imagine that the dome is about to collapse like the church that was its predecessor, undermined by water lurking beneath the site. The pillars have been shaken only by a glare of light above the river. A reverberation suggests that a portal as wide as the sky has opened at my back. In a moment the slope behind me breaks into a hiss so fierce that it's on the way to convincing me the Mersey has burst its banks. Then the storm falls on me, and although it takes just a few seconds to sprint to the monument, I'm drenched before I reach the shelter.

As I rub my wet scalp with my wet hands, which has little effect beyond making my skull feel softened, the buildings around the square grow as falsely bright as a diorama—a display of architecture spanning more than a century. The light vanishes with a prolonged rumble like an earthquake, and I'm reminded that two Liverpool churches were struck by lightning in a great nineteenth-century storm. People are fleeing through the afternoon dusk to whatever refuge they can find. Policemen in daffodil jerkins retreat into the law courts as pensioners shuffle and hobble down James Street to the underground station. All along Castle Street to the town hall workers dodge into offices while shoppers race down Lord Street to Frugo Corner and the neighbouring stores, pursued by a miniature flood that might almost be seeking to revive the Pool at the Whitechapel crossroads. Within a minute not a single human being is to be seen.

Where are my customers hiding? Perhaps they're sheltering in the Moat House at the corner of the square. It's the oldest building, a mid-nineteenth-century bank that is now a hotel. Because it was built over a stretch of the moat the cellars are unusually deep, and I'd prefer not to think that anyone feels at home down there. I pace around the giant tenant of the dome to find that the bunches of pillars don't afford much protection from the downpour. The orb in Victoria's hand drips like a treasure she has just found in the river or an internal organ she's offering to Whitechapel and the Pool, and she gazes towards the crossroads as if she's mocking my fruitless search for customers. One plodding circuit around the hem of her bronze robes shows me only drenched deserted streets. I wouldn't blame anyone for failing to show up, perhaps on the assumption that I won't. I'm huddling behind the queen's massive skirts, the best in the way of shelter that the monument can offer, when a jagged lurid rip appears in the black sky above the river.

The buildings around me seem to lurch forward as though they're eager to be photographed by the flash, and I glimpse a movement that's more real. For some reason it puts me in mind of a creature retreating beneath a stone. As the untimely twilight returns with a crash as vast as the sky there's another movement—more than one. Someone's wielding an umbrella at the near end of Lord Street, and somebody else is holding one outside a pub on the corner of James Street, among tables and chairs spitting rain.

For a moment I wonder if the newcomers are associated with the Histrionic History troupe. It isn't just that they've grown so theatrically still; their costumes could well be described as historical. Indeed, the outfits look not just so haphazard that they might have been chosen in pitch darkness but positively ancient, close to mouldering, certainly glistening with moisture. However much of that is rain, it's hardly reassuring. Despite the downpour, the loiterers aren't holding their umbrellas up. They're leaning on them.

I'm reminded of the photograph of Joseph Williamson gripping his stick like a blind man. Their motley clothes are reminiscent of his shabby crumpled garb. I can't distinguish much else about the watchers in the twilight veiled with rain, and perhaps I'm glad. Though their large round greyish heads are bald, this doesn't seem to guarantee their gender. Surely the outlines of their wide-mouthed expressionless faces are unstable only with streams of rain, but in spite of the downpour their big eyes don't blink. I'll feel less threatened if I wait in the entrance to the law courts. Before I can head that way there's another vicious flash.

I see what made me think of creatures beneath stones. The umbrellas jerk up to fend off the lightning, inevitably not fast enough. I'm facing the watcher in Lord Street. Its eyes don't simply wince at the light—they don't even close so much as shrivel, retreating into the head. The umbrella hides the figure from its rudimentary neck up, but not until I've glimpsed two wrinkled indentations in the pallid rubbery flesh where the eyes were. The sight seems as paralysing as the worst nightmare, but I have to move while I'm not being watched. I stumble around the monument towards the law courts, only to lean against the statue like a child clutching at his mother's skirt. The rain outside the courts seems unnaturally amplified, and now I see why. The drumming lessens as two figures in faded voluminous dresses lower their umbrellas and raise their hairless globular heads to the rain.

Can't I shout for help? The police may be deep in the courtroom building by now, and I don't know who else would respond, let alone what may have happened by the time they do. I twist around and wish I hadn't, though ignorance might be even worse. A fifth watcher has appeared on the corner by the Moat House, and another is crouching over an umbrella on the opposite corner of Castle Street. I'm surrounded, and I have a sense that there's more of the gang I've yet to locate.

If I can see just one person as human as myself I'll cry for help or even company or perhaps no more than their awareness, which ought to let me make my escape—surely my captors won't risk being noticed by anyone else. I cling to this hope until several figures in yellow jackets cross the far end of Lord Street from Paradise Street to Whitechapel. They're too distant for me to determine whether they're workmen or police, and suppose they're neither? So many people wear that sort of item these days it's no longer a uniform, and how easy is it to obtain? The figures don't seem bothered by the downpour, and could they hear me at that distance? Before I can find out they vanish into Whitechapel.

While I was preoccupied with them, reinforcements have arrived. Two newcomers in crumpled sodden dungarees are leaning on miniature umbrellas in the gloomy corner between the law courts and the concrete offices at the top of Lord Street. The smallness of the figures is no comfort. They're too squat, and the lower sections of their unnecessarily large heads are sunk in the unbuttoned collars of their ragged shirts as if they're neckless. Even if they're children, this suggests they belong to the family I was lured here to meet. What do they all want of me? In the midst of my panic, which has made me dry-mouthed and so breathless that it feels like drowning in the storm, I wonder if they only mean to keep me here, since they aren't closing in—if they're preventing me from going somewhere else. Then, as though my fancy was an inadvertent summons, the watcher on Lord Street advances at a slithery pace.

Every one of its companions follows suit. Half of them I only hear, but the sounds are unpleasantly detailed. The figures take another lopsided step like the next move in a sluggish hopping dance, a ritual rooted in the history of the place, and then they falter. As the umbrellas jerk up in unison, spraying raindrops, I could imagine that I'm watching some nightmarish musical number. The lightning has already faded, and in a few seconds the umbrellas droop, revealing that some faces have eyes again while others are less immediately venturesome. The spectacle pins me where I am, one hand clutching at the queen's chilly metal robes and finding no hint of security. I'm appalled to realise that however briefly the cordon was halted, I might have had time to dodge through it. I flinch at a belated peal of thunder, which seems to have used the delay to gather extra violence and which the loose circle of figures takes as a cue to advance in various ways as grotesque as they're inexorable. The one outside the pub crouches over its umbrella to drag itself forward, which makes its misshapen approach seem even more determined. The scrape of the ferrule on the pavement as the ring of figures closes in sounds like eagerness rendered solid. It ceases as the umbrella swings up, and I hear a dilapidated flapping all around me. The noise makes me think of reptiles stirring in a cave as I bolt down the steps of the monument.

The umbrellas have sunk again, and their bearers have started to peer out of hiding, by the time I reach the top of James Street. The crash of thunder feels like an insubstantial pursuer leaping on my back. The pursuit is altogether more substantial, and I seem to hear at least one participant bounding after me. I'm dashing downhill and across the flooded road to the station when I realise how horribly wrong I've gone because of panic. Underground is the last place I want to be.

Nothing would be more welcome than an exodus of passengers, but there's nobody in sight ahead. Mustn't there be staff inside the building? As I sprint for it I skid on the streaming pavement and almost collide with the first of a rank of bus shelters, but the leaps behind me don't hesitate—indeed, I think they're growing longer. I've just regained my balance when a bus swings uphill from the Strand.

Its headlights don't quite touch me, and by the sound of it they don't slow down my pursuers. All the same, the bus is a refuge—must be. I stumble around the shelter and thrust my arm out as far as it will stretch, but the bus doesn't lose any speed. I'm at the wrong stop—I need the lower one. I dash for it, waving my arms, and as the outsize wipers flail the rain they seem to be imitating me or gesturing me away. Before I reach the middle shelter the bus is past the lowest. I'm almost desperate enough to stagger in front of the vehicle, hoping I'm less of a blur to the driver than he is to me. Instead I lurch at it as it speeds alongside. I'm about to pound on the doors when they fold inwards. "Slow down, pal," the driver says. "I didn't want you getting any wetter than you are, that's all."

I clamber on the platform and am immediately afraid of being followed by a final leap. "Shut them, then," I gasp, "or you'll let it in."

His wide but low forehead breaks into furrows that appear to squeeze his eyes small. Perhaps he's offended by being told how to do his job, and I'm close to renewing my demand by the time he shuts the doors. As I fumble for money I croak "Did you see all that?"

"Just saw you, pal," he says and sends the bus uphill.

Chapter Forty-one

The Key

The bus is climbing James Street when the driver says "Good one." He's enthusing about the latest flash. As far as I can distinguish through the sweeps of the wipers and the constant renewal of rain on the windscreen, the square around the monument and all the roads that lead to it are utterly deserted. Has the lightning sent the creatures back where they came from? Traffic lights halt the bus at the corner of the square, and the driver stares at me until I wonder if he expects me to go back under the dome. I retreat in confusion and return in more of it once he says "Don't forget your change, pal."

I grab it from the metal trough beneath his window as the bus turns along Castle Street. Another glare of lightning displays figures huddled in doorways of offices and banks and restaurants. Quite a few are clutching dormant umbrellas, but they all look reasonably normal. "Some that strive to quit the darkness are indistinguishable from the mundane mob, even to their own eyes." Did I read that among my father's extracts from John Strong, or did my mother read it to me? I feel as if I dreamed it, and I want to believe that's the case with my encounter at the monument, because my mind does seem unable to escape some kind of underlying darkness. I don't think it's only the gloom of the storm.

I perch on the edge of the front seat, brushing trickles of water out of my eyes again and again. The bus swings into Cook Street and speeds downhill to Victoria Street, where buildings of Victoria's vintage seem to blanch at my approach.

An onslaught of thunder backs up the lightning and sets car alarms twittering in Mathew Street, alongside the musical cellars. I wish I were hearing my blackbird, however much night it evokes; how long will the Frugone salesman take? The headlights of the disturbed cars blink a warning, which I feel I've understood once the bus turns down Sir Thomas Street to Whitechapel.

Yet again I'm back where I saw whatever I saw. I could imagine that I'm compelled to keep retracing the past—not only mine. The city is exerting the compulsion through its layout and the smallness of its original boundaries, but how reassuring is that? The entrance to the underground parking gapes like a cave as the bus swerves up Roe Street, where passengers crowd out of a shelter. I scrutinise every wet face, especially those that widen their eyes at me. Do they think I'm as irrational as I've begun to feel? I have to struggle not to look back at them once they sit behind me, so close together that they might all know one another. The bus climbs past the site of the Fall Well and turns along Lime Street, and I'm at my stop.

The moment I alight between two stone lions that stream as if they've just risen from the well, the bus shuts its doors and moves off with a swish of water. Have all the passengers turned their waterlogged heads to observe me? Of course they look drowned because the windows are. I dash across the flagged plateau to shelter beneath the portico of St George's Hall, which revives the chattering of history in my head. The first building on the site was an infirmary that housed a lunatic asylum, close to the location of the courtroom in the Hall—the courtroom where Judge Fitzjames Stephen lost his mind. What may have entered his head overnight that turned him from sympathising with Florence Maybrick to condemning her as a poisoner? He used opium, and perhaps he dreamed of her curious comment that "James took arsenic not to pale his skin"—which Victorians often did—"but to excuse his inhuman pallor." How could this have driven the judge mad? A flash of lightning urges me onwards, and so does a sense of the railway underfoot. While I didn't use the underground, that needn't mean nothing else did.

As I sprint around the side of the Hall I blink at St John's Gardens. The only figures I can see are the dripping greenish statues on their plinths, and so I'm pursued just by the thought of the sentries with halberds who used to guard the entrance to the courtroom. What aspect of the past were they meant to conjure up? "All rites have their inception in terror," John Strong must have written. "The mob enacts them daily, never glimpsing their significance. The more their ancient meanings are forgotten, the more the ignorant shall be compelled to perform the rites." I feel beset by history or a dream of it, whatever the difference may be, and it's a relief to leave the Victorian evocations of a bygone era behind at the library entrance.

A guard frowns at me from behind his counter. With my unkempt hair and stubbly face and sodden crumpled clothes I must look little better than homeless. No doubt I leave wet footprints on my way to the lift. As it bears me to the fourth floor I run my hands through my even wetter hair and shake rain from my fingers, spattering the close grey metal walls. A prolonged muffled rumble seems to reverberate beneath me, but the foundations aren't subsiding into the heath. The absence of lightning before the thunder reminds me how cut off from daylight I am.

Two more frowns greet me across the local history desk. "Sorry about last time," I say, though only to head off any threat to call security, and then I notice that both women are wearing the badge that says WAD under a hovering drip. "What's that all about?" I'm determined to discover.

"Today," the younger woman says. "It's Water Awareness Day."

Presumably I would know this if I weren't so preoccupied or so much in need of sleep, although it sounds like a joke about my drenched state. In any case I should be learning "Where's Lucinda?"

The younger woman opens her mouth, but her colleague is faster. "Not here, I'm afraid."

"I can see that," I say and dilute it with a laugh. "So where?"

The woman folds her arms so hard that her torso bulges under them. "Shouldn't you know?"

"Why, what's it to do with me?"

"That's what I'm asking. Wouldn't you know if she wanted you to?"

Rain begins to trickle down to my left eye, and I almost splash the women in my haste to brush away the distraction. "We didn't have much chance to talk before she left for work. We had a good night but I'd only just got up."

I don't care how intimate this is so long as it confounds my interrogator, who presses her lips together as hard as she's hugging herself. It seems to find more favour with her colleague, who murmurs "She's down in her tunnels again."

I rub my streaming forehead. "What do you mean, hers?"

"It was her idea. Her dream, if you like."

I don't, and her colleague visibly dislikes my being informed, which provokes me to say "But she's down there for you. For the library, I mean."

The younger woman intertwines her fingers as her workmate says "She isn't, no."

My wet clothes feel like a sudden chill rendered solid. "How can't she be?" I protest. "She works here, doesn't she?"

As I'm reminded how my father kept quiet about his dismissal, the younger librarian says "She's taken a few days off."

I stand as if I'm stuck in a marsh until the older woman says "Can we help you in some other way?"

Although it sounds more like a challenge than an offer,

I'm equal to it. "As a matter of fact," I say, reaching in my pocket, "you can."

My hand closes on the page of John Strong's thoughts, and I feel as if I'm rescuing them from a swamp. "Let me show you this," I say. "I'd be interested to hear your comments."

Perhaps this isn't the best way to talk about the sight of me groping in my trousers. The older woman in particular seems to find the proposal unattractive. "Here you are," I declare, planting the photocopy on the counter.

Both women recoil as though I've presented them with something monstrous. I've no idea if they're reacting to whatever word I may have said aloud. The page is no longer a page; it's a soggy mass of pulp. When I attempt to unfold it, the folds come apart like dough. All the print has seeped through, filling every surface with a tangle of blurred symbols; there are even some on my fingertips. "It was him," I insist and clutch my throbbing forehead. "It was John Strong."

The librarians stare at the ragged scraps of paper exuding rain onto the counter. I'm vainly attempting to locate a single identifiable fragment of text when the older woman says "Do you want those?"

I hardly know what I'm saying or how hysterically it may make me laugh. "They're all yours with my compliments."

She scrapes the sodden fragments into a waste bin and uses a tissue to dab with distaste at the moisture they've left behind. "Better collect the requests," she says.

There's a box of slips of paper at the far end of the counter. Most of the books are kept behind the scenes, and readers have to request them. As the younger woman empties the box and picks up a key on a wooden tag I have a desperate inspiration. "Can you let me through?"

The older woman frowns as I advance to the barrier that guards the inner room. "You'll need an admission ticket."

"Lucinda made me one." As I grope in my breast pocket I'm appalled by the possibility that the storm has reached in there too. No, the pocket is relatively dry, and the mobile and the wallet containing all my cards are safe. I slip the reader's ticket, which is doing without an apostrophe, out of its plastic sheath and lay it on the counter. "See," my nerves goad me into saying, "I didn't make that up."

She waits for me to sign the admission book and lingers over comparing my signature with the version on the card, unless she's disapproving the drop of water that my head let fall on the page. I worsen matters by dabbing at the damage with my thumb, which turns the first letter into a C and renders the end of Gavin indecipherable. I'm wondering whether I should sign again by the time the librarian pushes the button to release the barrier.

Her colleague has trundled a trolley into the stacks and locked the door behind her. Just three tables are occupied, each by a solitary reader. Two are facing the stacks, but one has a view of the counter. How observant is he? I need an excuse to be in this section, and I head for the catalogues, only to find that the solitary name I can think of is John Strong. I need to ask for something else—any book will do. My gaze snags on Cod, having drifted over the spines of other stumpy catalogues: Ado to Ago, Are to Ask, Ate to Ave, Bed to Beg, Bog to Boo . . . William Colquitt will provide me with some cover, and I copy the details of his book of poetry out of Cod to Come. As I turn away from laying the request slip in the box, the man who's facing the counter pushes back his chair.

Though it feels unappealingly moist, I sit on the chair as he lumbers to the barrier. Whatever books he's left, they'll help me not to seem unduly watchful. Perhaps they can hush the clamour of syllables in my skull, fragmented words I must have glimpsed: Frog to Front, God to Gog, Moat to Mob . . . Perhaps the books will even stop me wondering too much about Lucinda's whereabouts and why she's there, since I'm not supposed to use my phone while I'm in the library. I drag the nearest book towards me and open it with too much of a thump.

It's a book of Scouse slang and colloquialisms. I turn like a schoolboy to the chapter about sex. Getting off at Edge Hill means withdrawal prior to orgasm, while slowing down for the tunnel and going under the Mersey require no elucidation. The Beatles smuggled a reference to fish and finger pie into a song, though hardly anyone outside Merseyside understood its significance. In the seventies phrases from their lyrics became sexual references, however jokey: fixing a hole, nobody came, a ticket to ride (a condom), rubber soul (a black condom), and every girl knew what a boy meant by saying "Let me take you down." Just now I don't care to be reminded of a place where nothing is real, and the book hasn't distracted me from the spawning of syllables: Pond to Pool, Rip to Rite, Seek to Seep . . . I shut the book and open the next one—an anthology of several centuries of Liverpool art—with a thud that earns a frown from the elder librarian.

I feel as if I'm miming readership. As I lean forward a wet object wriggles off my scalp onto my forehead. I brush back the drenched lock of hair and wipe my hand on the underside of the seat, having straightened up as though I've been struck by a revelation. Here's *A Memory of Everton* by George Stubbs, depicting a hunt along the ridge. The horses and their riders are painted in his usual naturalistic detail, but their prey is nowhere to be seen. An untypical trick of perspective makes a small pale cloud appear to be fleeing along the grassy brow against a metallic sky. How close was the location to my parents' house? There's no sign of the old beacon, unless its presence is suggested by a hint of greater brightness at the left edge of the picture, towards which the elongated pallid mass is gliding, not leaping. When I start to fancy that the mass looks more solid than a cloud I turn the page.

The Scientists was painted by Joseph Wright of Derby during his years in Liverpool. In some ways it's uncharacteristic of the eighteenth-century artist. The title isn't as precise as usual, nor the activity that's shown. As with much of his work, figures in a dim interior are only partly lit by candle-light. All three faces are intent on an object almost entirely concealed by their bodies. Is that a flabby whitish elbow on a slab? Is there the gleam of a knife? Perhaps it's the dim-ness that makes the eyes in the plump preoccupied faces bulge so much. The picture involves one of Wright's favou-rite effects—background details that only gradually become visible. I wonder if the painting is unfinished, since some of the details are so obscure. Whatever they're meant to sig-nify, those must be masks in niches on the wall, even if the round-eyed wide-mouthed faces appear to be worming out of it to watch whatever operation is in progress. The wall itself is barely visible, though its glistening suggests the place is wetter than a laboratory ought to be. In the top left-hand corner of the canvas a clouded moon may symbolise a light to strive towards. Not only the height of the glassless win-dow leads me to believe that the room is underground, and I'm reminded that the laboratory of the hospital where St George's Hall now stands was in the cellar.

I'm glad to be diverted by a muffled rumble at my back. It isn't thunder, it's the trolley emerging from the stacks. The librarian delivers books to the readers and returns to the counter, where she leaves the key just underneath. She isn't due to make the trip again for a quarter of an hour, and I'm watching for my chance when her colleague murmurs to her. They must be eager to get rid of me, because the younger woman retrieves the key and takes my request slip out of the box.

Won't recent art let me feel less besieged by the past? Here's a modern sculpture by Arthur Dooley, one of his stat-ues of Christ. Not just the thin arms but the entire grey metal figure reach heavenwards, straining unnaturally tall. Its joints are as spiky as the sunburst of thorns that encircles its cranium, and so is the ground in which its bare bony feet are rooted. Is that meant to be a swamp? The piece is called *Reaching for the Light*, which fails to quiet the litany of syllables in my brain: Try to Tup, Up to Vale, Wed to Well . . . Before I can look to see if they're on the spines of the catalogues, the librarian brings me the Colquitt book. "I've finished with these, thanks," I tell her.

She watches me dab my forehead and rub my wet fingers together. "Will you be careful, please?" she says. "This is our only copy."

"Don't worry, I always treat books as if they're my own."

For some reason I'm reminded of the sodden items in my hall. I leaf through the slim volume until she makes for the counter with the other books, and then I think of a reason to read rather than simply pretend while I'm biding my time. I turn to Colquitt's *Description of Liverpool* and see lines I recognise:

"Behold the Pool, where Neptune's kin doth dream
Of antic life in marsh and secret stream . . ."

The trouble is that they're followed by a couplet I've never seen before. I feel as if another trace of my father has been erased. When is the Frugone salesman going to contact me? I'm glancing surreptitiously at the counter, behind which the women are stooping to a computer, when I realise that the book has given me some help after all. It's my excuse to go to the counter.

There's no need to attract attention if I don't have to. I lift the chair before I inch it backwards, lowering it to the floor once I've room to move away from the table. I've paced more than halfway to the counter when the older librarian becomes aware of me. She frowns and turns back to the screen, and I almost sprint to the counter while she's ignoring me. I'm there and starting to inch my hand across it when her colleague glances at me. "I'll be with you in just a moment," she promises, unless she's resigning herself.

I manage not to snatch my hand back. As a hint of mois-

ture outlines it on the wood I say "Are you absolutely certain
that's your only copy of the book?"

"We certainly are," the older woman says. "It was never
reprinted."

Both women seem bent on taking no more notice of me,
unless they're trying to distinguish the image on the monitor. Is the aerial view of Liverpool blurred by fog or rendered incomplete by bombing? I could imagine that the
tops of the visible buildings are rising out of a drowned
landscape. The women's attitude is all I need—it has to be.
If I stay here much longer one of them is bound to look. I
take a breath, which is surely audible only to me, and reach
over the counter.

In a moment my groping fingers find the key. Before they
can grasp it and the wooden tag, the key shifts on the ledge
beneath the counter with a faint scrape amplified by all my
nerves. The key ring rattles against the tag, and the younger
librarian begins to turn towards me. No, she's only leaning
closer to the monitor, but my efforts to hold my breath are
making my head swim—they've already squeezed every trace
of moisture out of my throat. Then my fingers close around
the key and the tag, and I lift the silenced handful across
the counter.

I'm sneaking away until it occurs to me that I don't need
to move stealthily—in fact, it looks suspicious. I glance back
from the table where the Colquitt book lies beside a faint
stain. The librarians are still crouching towards the monitor. I have to pass the other readers, and I'm making to hide
the key in my hip pocket when I remember how sodden that
is. I clench my fists, and the ring clicks against the tag like
the sound of a sprung trap.

I can't look at the librarians, and I avoid glancing at my
fellow readers as I stride past them. I have to seem entitled
to do what I'm doing. I've reached the door to the stacks
when there's a muffled noise behind me. It isn't pursuit, it's
an afterthought of the storm. I slip the key into the lock and

twist it and push the door open, to be met by movement in
the corridor beyond. Only my feeble shadow is there, and
only tension captures me by the nape of the neck as I step
into the corridor.

I'm closing the door when the reader nearest to me looks
up from a book of maps. Her eyes meet mine, and I press my
lips wide in an expression that isn't quite a smile but implies
it has no reason not to be one. I don't let my breath out with
a gasp until the door is shut. Is that the scrape of a chair? Is
she on her way to ask the librarians whether anyone who
looks the way I do just now is authorised to enter the stacks?
I have to use whatever time I've stolen, and I hurry along
the short corridor.

It leads to a room that, to judge by the section visible
through a glass door, must be huge. The nearest shelves are
full of bound newspapers, yellowing fragments of which
are scattered like ancient leaves in the narrow passages between the shelves. How far will I have to search? I'm scarcely
conscious of raising the wooden tag like a wand to ward off
hindrances or to aid me in my quest as I leave the corridor. I
could fancy that it helped, because to my left, occupying most
of a lobby outside the main storeroom, are several smaller
bookcases. By the look of it they hold the rarest books and
manuscripts.

A request slip is protruding from a gap between two books
about the local slave trade, *Ebony Cargo* and *Chained in a
Cellar*. The key rattles against the tag as my shadow dodges
down the twilit alley between the wall and the musty shelves
to the occult section, but there isn't one; it seems to have
been crushed to nothing by a mass of religious tomes that
don't even tolerate a gap. Something like a pointed fingernail is trapped under the weightiest, however. I shove the
key and tag into a sodden pocket so as to use both hands to
extract the leathery volume, which is wedged between its
portly neighbours. As it tips off the shelf, dragging my hands
down, it dislodges the item it wasn't quite able to hide,

which flutters to the floor. It's a request slip, of which I saw a corner. I manhandle the book into place again and stoop to pick up the crumpled form. I've only begun to smooth it out when I recognise the handwriting. The slip is my father's request for the unpublished papers of John Strong.

Chapter Forty-two

THE SLIP

I don't stride to throw open the door and brandish the form and shout for an explanation. I don't even march to the counter for one. Should I show Lucinda first or confront the pair of women with the evidence? Suppose they call security to take it off me? I mustn't risk losing it, and I fold it to fit in my breast pocket. If I loiter much longer I may still be here when a librarian enters the stacks.

I stop at the end of the corridor, because the trolley is rumbling across the library. I'm about to do my best to hide among the bookcases when I realise the sound is receding. It isn't even a trolley—it's the retreat of the storm. I have to overcome my anger at the mistake before I can ease the door inwards.

The two readers at the tables raise their heads like animals scenting an intruder. Beyond them the younger librarian is examining the Colquitt book. She's beside the table I vacated, and her colleague is out of sight. I'm about to close the door, at least enough to hide me, when she shuts the book and turns away with it. I steady the door as it wavers indecisively, but I'm too late. She sees me at once.

Her lips part, and her eyes widen so much that they send a fleshy ripple up her forehead. She holds the expression while I step forward and pull the door shut. I'm wondering how long she means to keep her challenge silent—whether she may be too shocked to speak until I'm past the exit barrier—when she says "What do you think you're doing?"

Her voice is so muted that it might be reminding me where I am. I don't speak until I'm abreast of her, by which time I've thought of some kind of an answer. I take the key out of my sodden pocket and lay it on the table, just out of her reach. "Returning this," I inform her.

The table amplifies the rattle as she grabs the key, and her workmate rears up from crouching behind the counter. "Is anything the matter?"

"I'd say so," I declare, but her colleague speaks over me. "He was in the stacks."

"I'll call security."

The older woman is heading for the phone when my elongated strides bring me to the counter. "And tell them what?"

"That area is clearly signed staff only."

"So people can't find out what you're hiding, is it?" As she turns to the phone I protest "I haven't stolen anything. I care as much for the past as anybody here."

Her colleague holds up the Colquitt book as if it's an exhibit for the prosecution but says "Then why were you in there?"

The readers have turned around on their chairs and are awaiting my answer as well. "I tried to show you," I say. "You didn't believe me, so I had to find some proof."

The older woman is reaching for the phone. "Don't you want to see what I've got?" I rather more than ask.

I grope inside my jacket, only to discover that a fold of the paper has snagged on the mobile. I mustn't damage the solitary item of evidence. I pull out the request slip and the mobile, which catches on the edge of the pocket and flies out of my hand. It hits the floor with a decisive thud that earns a gasp from a member of the audience. Have I harmed it? Suppose I can't receive the Frugone salesman's call? The impact hasn't activated the display. I shove the paper into my pocket and jab a key at random, which brings up the wallpaper image—a close-up of my own sleeping face. Lucinda must have added it, and I haven't time to wonder when. "It's all right," I announce.

"Is it indeed," says the older librarian. "May I ask whom that belongs to?"

"He's pinched a phone," someone whispers at my back.

"Of course I haven't. It's mine, look."

The librarians peer at the somnolent image until I begin to wonder what they're seeing or even what I saw. I'm about to examine it afresh when the older woman says "Are you expecting us to believe you found that in the stacks?"

"I'm not, no." I unfold the request slip beside the mobile on the counter. "That's what I found," I say in a desperate kind of triumph.

As she reaches for it I pin it down with all my fingertips. I'm not letting it out of my possession. She draws back as if she's recoiling from the sight of my extended fingers and says "Perhaps you would care to explain."

"It's John Strong after you said he never existed. You said this didn't, anyway. You said his papers didn't, and this was on the shelf where you got them for my father."

"I most certainly did nothing of the kind. Did you?"

Her colleague leans forward as if she's wary of venturing too close to me. "I'm sorry, I didn't put it there."

"Then who did?"

As she gives me a look that may contain some element of distress, the older woman intervenes. "I think that's best left to the imagination."

"It won't be staying there, believe me." Was she suggesting I'd imagined some if not all of the situation? I needn't grow angry when I'm able to say "I hope you can see why I was in there at least. I'm sorry if I broke the rules, but I don't think it was too serious, do you? Maybe I've shown you how easy it is. I've helped you take more care of your security in future."

I shouldn't have mentioned security. I hope I haven't said too much about it or in general. As I pick up the form and start towards the barrier the older woman says "Will you give me your word you've done nothing else?"

"Absolutely. It's yours. Go and check if you like."

"Then considering your relationship with Lucinda I'm prepared to overlook the incident, but I would ask you to remember that your behaviour reflects on her."

"I'll do that." I give the barrier a push and then a harder one, but it continues to confront my groin. "This isn't working," I protest.

"Just as soon as you've returned the slip."

I fold it and hide it in my pocket before saying "I'm afraid I have to take it. It's all I've got."

"We can't allow that. It's council property."

"I'm certain the council won't miss it, but I would. It's something my father left. I need to keep everything I have of his."

I'm ashamed of using him this way, but surely it's justified. The younger librarian widens her eyes, and my appeal seems to have worked until her colleague says "While I appreciate your situation—"

There's no point in waiting to hear why she still can't let me go. I plant my hands on the uprights flanking the barrier and vault over it. I feel as if I'm dreaming of agility, but it's real enough; someone gasps behind me like a circus spectator. I dash into the fourth-floor lobby and am heading for the lift until I dodge to the stairs. If a security man is called, I'm betting he will use the lift. As I run down two and three stairs at a time I feel lithe as water.

Indeed, my legs are growing wetter. My drenched trousers are to blame. On the ground floor the mechanical doors defer to me barely in time. I slow to a walk as I come in sight of the security desk at the exit. Behind it a guard is putting a phone down, and stands up as I stroll closer. "Excuse me—"

"I'll do that," I tell him and sprint for the exit, so fast that I nearly collide with the unhurried automatic door. As soon as it slides out of enough of the way I dash through the gap and squeeze through the one the outer door sets about offering. Has the rain only just stopped? The flagged path looks molten with sunlight and water, and a solitary figure in the entrance to St John's Gardens across the road is holding up an umbrella. She's wearing spectacles that remind me of John Lennon until I notice that the large round lenses are opaque with rain. Either she's blind or they're some kind of disguise or camouflage. I can barely see for the brightness after the storm; I'm struggling to keep my watery eyes open. Just in time I realise where I can take refuge from any pursuers. I veer left, away from the figure in the shadow of the umbrella, and spring up the steps to the Walker.

I try to act like an average visitor to the art gallery as I push the door open, but the charade seems not to work. Behind the information desk in the middle of the extensive marble lobby, a young woman glances up and then stares wide-eyed at me. I mustn't let her drive me out. I'm striding past the desk when she says "Sorry, I was rude."

I risk glancing back, but there's no sign of the guard from the library. If he had to wait for someone to take over his post he won't have seen me come in here. "I know I'm as wet as it gets," I say and catch sight of the badge she's wearing. "That's what you call water awareness."

"It's a joke, isn't it? They say we still need to be careful about using water." She gives her head a quick shake as though to free drops from her shoulder-length hair and says "I wasn't looking at that. I thought for a moment you were, well, it doesn't matter."

At once I'm sure it does. "I was what?"

"Someone who used to work here. It was only because the sun was in my eyes."

"It still is. I'm the son."

"You are, aren't you? That's the sort of thing Deryck would say. He was always kidding." She gives her lip a pretty nibble and murmurs "Is he all right? We heard the police were looking for him."

"Because he's missing. I'm waiting to hear."

"I hope you do and everything's as it should be." Even lower she says "I hope it's not that he doesn't want people to see him."

For some reason my mouth grows parched. "Why shouldn't he?"

"If he's ashamed, I meant. I think he was when this place got rid of him."

"I think you're right. Do you know why he was fired?"

She looks around to ensure we aren't being overheard and then leans on the counter. "He kept telling people the city was trying to cover things up."

"Which things?"

"I heard a big argument he had with his boss. I should think everyone did. It was one of the reasons they asked him to leave."

I wait, but then I have to prompt "What kind of argument?"

"I expect most people wouldn't think it was worth making such a fuss about. He was saying one of the portraits we have in storage, it's a painting of Joseph Williamson, the man who—"

"I know all about him." Even if this is an exaggeration, I'm anxious to learn "What was my father saying?"

"That it wasn't real."

"Not real how?"

"The painter was a tenant of Williamson's, and Deryck said he was trying to make him look more ordinary. Not ordinary, human, that's the word he used. There's supposed to be a photograph of Williamson, except most people think it isn't, but Deryck said it's the photograph that's real."

"I've seen it. I don't know how he would know."

"I shouldn't think you'd understand what else he said either."

"I might." All the same, I feel irrationally reluctant to ask "What was it?"

"It was when he lost his temper. He was shouting, and I don't know if he really knew what he was saying." She shakes her head again as if to dislodge the memory and murmurs "He said he was sure it was a real photograph because it was like looking in a mirror."

Chapter Forty-three

WILLIAMSON'S WAY

I remember the supposed photograph of Williamson, apparently found under the floor of the house where he died—the coarse wide-mouthed almost circular face with its eyes slitted to show only the black pupils, so that you could imagine the pupils were elongated and horizontal. "It's nothing like him," I protest.

"That's what I said. Nothing like Deryck, I mean."

"So what would have made him think it was?"

"Maybe he dreamed it." While she plainly intends to be comforting, she fails even before she adds "You'd think he'd know the difference."

"Sometimes you don't, I can tell you."

She waits as if I've led her to expect a tale and then says "Maybe it runs in the family, then."

I'm not sure how this makes me feel, but peace of mind isn't involved. "I hope you find him very soon," she says, "and I promise I'm not the only one here."

"Thanks," I say before she can trouble me further, and move away from the desk.

Talking or nervousness has left my mouth as dry as the drought that her badge predicts. The café beyond the desk sells bottled water, but I need to be frugal just now. As I climb the expansive marble stairs, a wave of humidity that smells of weak tea follows me from the café. Since when have the stairs been dominated by an enormous painting of a storm at sea? The billows that look set to drag a sailing ship into the depths resemble a giant hand with spume for fingernails, unless that's yet another dream I'm having while awake.

I push open the imposing Victorian door to the Gents and cross the white marble room to the nearest sink. A handful of water just about moistens my arid throat, and half a dozen more do away with my thirst for the moment. As I straighten up with a gasp from gulping so much liquid, a shape rears up in the mirror above the sink. It's at my back.

It's nobody but me, in a mirror beside the door. As I swing around, sunlight glares through the window into my eyes. For some moments I can see only a blurred shape in a full-length frame, which puts me in mind of an impressionistic portrait. I slit my eyes and crouch towards it, rendering the figure squatter but no clearer. Why am I wasting my time like this? There are far more important issues to clarify. I grasp the brass doorknob and haul the door wide, to be met by stares from several visitors to the gallery. I'm no painting, and they've no right to look at me that way. Before I can begin shouting like my father I stalk to the stairs.

I take out my mobile as I emerge from the building. I'm in the shade of the portico and about to call Lucinda, if she's above ground, when a movement on the far side of the road catches my attention. While nobody is in the entrance to the gardens, at least two figures with umbrellas are to be seen. One—the woman wearing spectacles that might as well be opaque—is leaning on hers at the foot of a statue, in the shadow of the plinth, while the other is beneath a tree just inside the wall. Though the lawns must be as waterlogged as a swamp, the loiterer on the grass seems entirely at home. She has lifted her umbrella to observe me—that was the movement I saw. Despite the shade of the foliage, she seems to feel too much sunlight has reached her, because she jerks the umbrella down and her head up. As she does so, a large object falls to the ground. Her whitish dress—spotted brown with mud, I think, as well as an intentional pattern—bulges far too shapelessly while she stoops to retrieve the item. For a moment I have the unappealing fancy that she's clapping a sodden divot to her cranium. Certainly the wig she plants

on her naked greyish scalp isn't much less muddy and be-
draggled than the grass.

As the umbrella tilts forward and wrinkled shrunken eyes
peer from beneath it I have to resist the impulse to retreat
into the gallery. You can't use mobiles in there or in any
building along the row. I step back until the watchers are
just visible between two pillars, and manage to control my
shaky finger enough to key Lucinda's number. It rings and
rings again, so that I'm preparing to be answered by an automatic voice when she says "Yes, Gavin."

She sounds uneasy, but all I need to learn just now is
"Where are you?"

She doesn't respond immediately. I'm about to repeat the
question when she says "Up near my house."

"How long are you going to be there?"

"How long do you want me to be?"

"Till I get there."

"Yes, but how long are you likely to take, do you think?"

I squint between the pillars. The figures with the umbrellas are standing utterly motionless—I could imagine their
feet have sunk into the mud they seem to like so much—but
I won't be using the path through the gardens. "As long as
the bus takes when I get it," I tell Lucinda.

"I'll meet you at the stop. The one by, the one at the top
of Edge Hill."

"I'm on my way," I promise her and myself.

I could have been while we were talking. I used our conversation as an excuse not to venture out of the meagre refuge of the colonnade. I tramp down the steps to the street in
a rage. If anybody were nearby I would point out the watchers, so long as they weren't the same breed, but there's nobody close enough to accost. The figure beneath the tree
lowers its large head without benefit of a neck to watch my
progress, but that's the only movement in the gardens as I
stride uphill and around the corner of St George's Hall.

All the way along the pillared building I'm aware of the

tunnel underfoot. I feel as if each of my footsteps is being imitated in the dark down there. I hurry past the stone lions and around the far end of the building. A convoy of buses, some dwarfish and others twice their height, is mounting the hill that descends from the site of the Fall Well to its licensed namesake. I have to pass the entrance to the underground to reach the bus stops, but at least a horde of commuters is emerging from the main line station across the road. I hurry past the tiled corridor, along which I seem to hear a heavy body stirring as if my footsteps have awakened it—someone homeless, perhaps. I'm nearly at the pedestrian crossing that leads to the buses when an object nods out of hiding above me, around one of the stone posts that flank an entrance to the gardens. Despite or rather because of the sunlight, it's a raised umbrella.

I want to laugh hysterically at it. I want to shout, despite the renewed dryness of my mouth, and point until everybody within earshot is aware of the lurker. Suppose it has fellows I'm unaware of? Suppose some of them are capable of mingling with the crowds around and inside the bus shelters? I might feel safer avoiding that area and staying as much in the open as possible until I catch the bus. I retreat uphill, where a single-decker to Edge Hill has been halted by traffic lights. When I thump on the door the driver turns his head away on its thick neck and gazes along Lime Street as if he's looking for the vanished waxworks. Before I can redouble my assault the lights release the vehicle, and I'm all the more furiously frustrated by having to wait to cross. As I glare at the entrance to the gardens, the umbrella sinks like a shell protecting a mollusc.

Once buses finish ignoring the red light I dash across the junction. It used to be nicknamed the Bay of Biscay after the winds that often carried refuse up from the market, unless some kind of marauder did. On the far side Lime Street appears to be sinking into history—at least, the kebab shops and cheap outfitters are interspersed with disused cinemas, one of them transformed into an equally derelict night-club, and an abandoned amusement arcade. The sorry block comes to some point in the extravagantly florid façade of the Vines public house, beyond which stands the Adelphi, just a few years under a century old but the third hotel of that name to occupy the site. The enormous ground-floor lounge was based on the stateroom of the *Titanic*. I don't want to be reminded of aquatic matters, even when a glance over my shoulder reveals no pursuers with umbrellas, only the odd ill-dressed pedestrian shambling after me. I hurry around the corner and up Brownlow Hill to the nearest bus stop.

The hotel blocks my view along Lime Street. Before any Adelphi was built, the Ranelagh Pleasure Gardens occupied the place. Strolling players would perform there, which puts me angrily in mind of Nicholas Noble's gang. I'm within a minute's walk of both a Maybrick residence by a lunatic asylum and Blake Street, the home of a man who died in 1883 of being kicked in the stomach by a policeman. No motive was recorded, though the practice was known as bursting or wellying your victim, terms still in use. I'm grateful to be rescued from history by a double-decker bus that swings around the corner. I've paid my fare and am clambering the stairs when the blackbird in my pocket starts to sing.

I sprawl on the left-hand front seat upstairs and snatch out the mobile. The caller's number is withheld, and I keep my answer neutral. "Gavin Meadows."

"You're still available, then."

It isn't Lucinda. It isn't either of my parents or the Frugone salesman. It isn't Wrigley or Maddock—it's not even as welcome as either of them. "I haven't gone underground if that's what you mean, Hank."

The retort is less satisfying than I'd like, and so I demand "Why, are you planning to send me another crew?"

"Rest assured we shan't after your latest behaviour."

"Well, that's something." My rage has fallen short of my

response, and I'm provoked to add "What behaviour, may I ask?"

"Letting down the party it was never my idea to send."

"So whose were they?"

He's silent while the bus passes the main university building. The terracotta Gothic frontage has developed an exoskeleton of scaffolding and canvas, above which a clock tower and a spire indicate the latest onset of black clouds. Students flock across the road to a rudimentary block of shops—a coffee bar, a sandwich shop, a Frugo Corner. I'm about to repeat my question when Waterworth says "I've told you more than once that I won't discuss council employees with you."

"You can tell me who's saying, saying I did what?"

"Your tour group waited and you never showed."

"That's a lie. I was there. I'm still drenched." With rising fury I enquire "Where were they?"

"Where they were asked to be, and all of them say you weren't."

"You've met them all, have you?" I feel as if I'm dreaming aloud. Perhaps he doesn't think I expect an answer, and I have to prompt "Met any?"

"There was no need for me to meet with them. We spoke and that's enough."

"I'm not surprised they didn't show their faces. You'd know why if you saw them."

The bus has climbed past boxy outposts of the university to the upper margin of the Moss Lake. As it turns along Crown Street Waterworth says "I've no idea what you mean by that. This city believes in inclusiveness. So you did see your party and chose to let them down."

"I don't think so. More like I called them up." Perhaps I'm dreaming aloud again, and I add "The bunch I saw didn't want the tour."

At once I wonder if they could have—if following the historical route and hearing my anecdotes would have affected them somehow. In that case, what may it have been doing to me? I mustn't imagine that I've been as driven by occult impulses as Williamson was. The thought gags me while Waterworth says "I'm ending this discussion. I just wanted to advise you that all employees involved with tourism will be making it clear we don't support or recommend your tours."

"I thought you weren't supposed to talk about your personnel."

The retort is more automatic than angry, because I have a sense that my tours have become redundant, perhaps just by comparison with the search for my parents. The bus has swung up West Derby Street and is climbing towards the swift black sky that lours above Edge Hill. "Thanks for the spank, Hank," I say as I imagine my father might, and stow the phone in my pocket. I'm hauling myself to my feet as the bus reaches the top of the hill.

A set of traffic lights turns red to greet it, but it swerves so vigorously into Lucinda's road that I'm flung back onto the seat. As I grab the bar across the front window again, the bus speeds past the terrace of houses opposite the church. It isn't slowing for the bus stop, and I'm opening my mouth to shout to the driver when the sight ahead interrupts my breath.

A triangular flagstoned island occupies the middle of a three-way junction in front of the church. Four police cars are nesting on it around a bench. For a moment I think the bench is the location of the problem, but it's deserted. The police are in the churchyard. It stands six feet above the road, and I crane to see what's wrong.

To the right of the single path, which is flanked by shrubs pruned almost to their roots, policemen waistcoated in yellow are erecting a fence of tape and metal stakes around a pond among the mossy gravestones. A tilted greenish obelisk pokes up from the water, which also contains a pair of rounded stones covered with mud or mould. There are sticks in the water as well, and larger chunks of wood. I'm assuming all these belong to the shrubs until I notice that one of the stones has teeth. So has the other, along with jagged sockets where the eyes and nose were, and the bundles of scrawny items to which the rounded objects are attached aren't sticks. Are the two incomplete shapes endeavouring to crawl out of the water? Surely the movements, however much they suggest feeble attempts to hop, are simply the effect of ripples a policeman sends through the water by driving a stake into the earth. I'm staring in reluctant fascination at the spectacle when the bus swings away from the church, and I glimpse Lucinda inside the bus shelter beside the terrace.

"Wait," I shout and stagger into the aisle, but the driver doesn't respond. The bus continues downhill towards Edge Hill station, from which the city's first railway tunnels extended to Lime Street, encountering some of Williamson's workers in the process or the man himself—someone who came out of the underground dark. As I clatter downstairs the bus crosses a junction and halts at a stop, where the driver delays opening the doors to say "There's a bell, chum."

As soon as the doors fold open I see Lucinda on the far side of the crossroads. She must have been quick—have sprinted, even. A few long-legged strides bring her across it. Her eyes are wide enough to contain a good deal of anxiety, and the pupils are enlarged by the gathering darkness. "Gavin," she says and somewhat less welcomingly "What were you doing this time?"

"Shouldn't I be asking you that?"

She falters, though I don't think my question was especially aggressive. "Why should you?"

I feel as if we're accusing each other of having caused the situation in the churchyard, which my mind seems unable or unwilling to recall with more conviction than a dream. I'm about to be more specific when Lucinda says "They called me from the library, Gavin. They said you stole the key to the stacks."

"I borrowed it. Did they tell you what they told me about

you?" I give her more than a moment to respond, but when she only blinks before widening her eyes as if to exhibit their innocence I say "You aren't here for them. They don't know what you're up to any more than I do."

"Is that what they said? I suppose they had to." She sounds inexplicably wistful, and turns to gaze towards the church. "What's happening up there?"

"Don't you know?"

Perhaps that's too denunciatory. She crosses the junction again and doesn't speak until I've hurried after her. "It's too high to see," she says. "You'd have to jump. I thought you might have from the bus."

I feel as if I'm in a dream or threatened by one. "Jumped?"

"Seen. They aren't letting anyone up."

"I'd say there's been some kind of burst. A water main, it looks like. It's come up through the graves and smashed some coffins."

My words can't reduce the memory to themselves. I could imagine she's able to see what I'm unable to avoid recalling— the not quite lifeless twitches of the corpses in the water— until she makes the reason for her moment's silence clear. "It must be the tunnel they reopened this afternoon," she says. "The friends were right, it leads up there."

I can't tell how she feels about this—apprehensive or excited or both? I also wonder "Leads from where?"

"One of Williamson's houses down the hill. There was always a story that he and his wife had an underground way to the church. They used to appear there and nobody saw where they'd come from."

"Never mind that," I say, because it's yet another remnant of history to add to the chatter that's trying to invade my consciousness. "Where did all the water come from? How can it have come uphill?"

"It was underneath the section they were clearing. We heard it start to break through and got out just in time. The entire tunnel and all the ones connected with it must be flooded. Just think, Gavin, you could have had a drowned girlfriend."

Her mouth widens with a smile, but I'm not quite able to respond. We're opposite the churchyard, where a policeman has just clapped a hand over his mouth as he recoils from stooping to some object. The next moment drops spatter my forehead, and I have the thoroughly unwelcome notion that they're from the water that has burst through the grave. Or are my brows exuding them? I stop short of imagining they've welled up from my brain as Lucinda retreats beneath the bus shelter and I recognise the start of yet another downpour. It isn't only because we're too close to the graveyard and its exposed contents that I say "Aren't we going in your house?"

Lucinda looks away from the swarm of police in the churchyard. Wistfulness, if that's what it is, has resurfaced in her eyes. "Come on, then," she says. "You'll have to see."

Chapter Forty-four

A Literary Proposition

As I follow Lucinda up the garden path, which resembles a track through a marsh rather than between the halves of the small lawn, something starts to flap at my back. It puts me in mind of some undefined but vast shape that has awakened in a dark place. The sound gives way to pattering, an amplified version of the onset of the rain. The police are erecting a tent to conceal the remains in the graveyard. Lucinda glances towards it and hurries to unlock her front door.

The wide high-ceilinged hall is white as innocence. At least, the walls would be except for the afternoon darkness, which appears to have soaked into the turfy green carpet that extends along the hall and up the stairs. Pots of ferns are lined up along the skirting-board of the party wall. I've seen those before, but not the photographs that decorate the hall and climb beside the stairs as if they're striving towards the skylight. As I realise that all the photographs were taken underground, Lucinda says "I want to see."

When she runs upstairs I have a sense of her ascending towards the light. She's in the front bedroom by the time I realise that she means to look into the churchyard. I hurry after her, not only in case she finds she would rather not be alone with the view. Another sound besides her soft footsteps is audible in the room—a surreptitious lapping of water.

I'm halfway up the stairs when the skylight begins to vibrate. I could be gazing at the underside of an aquarium. As soon as I reach the landing I see what I heard in the bedroom. A water bed draped with a leafy quilt, from beneath which a pair of pillows peeks, occupies a good deal of the floor. The vibration of my footfalls sets it in motion again as I join Lucinda at the window.

Two policemen are struggling to raise the tent against the downpour, and I'm reminded of a giant umbrella. The pool around the tottering obelisk has grown turbulent with rain. Surely that's the only movement or at least the only source of any, however restless the glistening bones appear to be. That's just water surging over them; they can't really be putting on translucent flesh. I'm grateful when the tent hides them, even if I might have liked to be sure what was happening to them. The sight of the policemen stepping well back doesn't help. "Poor things," says Lucinda.

As I retreat from the window the water bed stirs again, and I could fancy that it's eager to be used. I don't need to be reminded that I'm in not just her house for the very first time but the bower of her bedroom, and being teased by a faint perfume from the army of cosmetics on the Victorian dressing-table. Their twins float low on the surface of the oval mirror, which shows me shambling across the room against a backdrop of ferny wallpaper. I wait beneath the inundated skylight until Lucinda emerges from the room, and then I say "So are you going to tell me?"

"What would you like to know, Gavin?"

This only makes me aware how little I'm sure I would like. I gesture at the subterranean photographs, which appear to be coming obscurely alive with shadows of rain. "Why are you doing this?"

"How about a book?"

"How about one? Which book?"

"Yours, I hope."

She's trying on a smile, but I feel as if she's referring to a development that has escaped my consciousness. "I've got nothing to do with any book."

"I was thinking you could write one. I hope it wasn't just my dream."

"Don't start talking about those." Even if Lucinda hasn't, I'm certain someone has kept putting dreams or rather the subject of them into my head. Somewhat less sharply I add "What kind of book?"

"About Liverpool. That's what you're all about, Gavin. If you aren't going to be able to do so many tours you should publish everything instead, the history and all your stories. You never know, it could help revive your tours."

We've been descending the stairs like the leaders of a stately ritual procession through animated adumbrations of water. I'm distracted by the photographs, which seem to form even more of a labyrinth than the tunnels they depict. Perhaps that's simply in my head. As Lucinda takes another step down and turns yet again to me I'm reduced to protesting "They aren't my stories."

"If they're the city's that's better still, isn't it? It made you and they're part of it just like you."

I've begun to find her eagerness unsettling, and I have to say "I'm not sure how I can use these pictures when I wasn't there."

"We'll get you down there, don't worry. I just thought I should take them while I could," she says and gazes up at me from the hall. "Do you think you might like my dream, sorry, my proposal a little bit?"

"More than a bit, and forget what I said about dreams." I take hold of her shoulders, murmuring "You understand if my mind's elsewhere at the moment. I only wish I knew where."

"You will, I'm certain." She puts more reassurance into resting her soft grasp on my hands, then glances past me at an almost shapeless noise—another onslaught of rain above the stairs. "What would you like to do now?" she says.

The sense of water revives my thirst. "I wouldn't mind a drink," I croak.

"Will it be all right from the tap?"

"I'm not my father."

I follow her past subterranean vistas to the kitchen. It's brimming with water or at least with liquid shadows, which crawl over items—cupboards, a table and chairs, kitchen equipment, a stone sink—so pale they might have forgotten what sunlight is like. Beyond the window a garden and the backs of houses are yielding most of their shape to the rain on the glass. Lucinda fills a pair of tankards inscribed LIVING LIVERPOOL from the tap, which delivers with such spirit that it wets her hand. While I gulp she sips and then refills my tankard as I ask "Did you get any pictures today?"

"A few before we had to run for it. I haven't had time to print them out." She fetches her handbag from the foot of the banisters and produces a small black Frugo Digital camera. "See what you make of them," she says and switches on the screen.

Her hand must still be wet from the tap. I wipe the camera on my shirt before examining the miniature images, which show yet more tunnels stretching into darkness. I assume they're in geographical sequence, unless Lucinda looked back to take some of the photographs, but they add to my sense of an indefinable labyrinth, whether Williamson's or in my skull or both. Most of the tunnels have arched brick roofs, but some passages are roughly triangular. A few of the photographs include explorers leading the way or glancing at the camera, their faces blanched by the flash. They're the only signs of life, although two successive images produce an illusion of some other movement in the dimness. I toggle between these and then zoom in, none of which clarifies the impression. "What were you taking there?" I have to ask.

Lucinda sips from Living Liverpool and tilts her head. "One of the side tunnels."

"Yes, but what were you trying to catch?"

"Just the focus. I wasn't sure I'd got it first time."

"Then what did you think you were seeing?"

"I couldn't tell you, Gavin. Someone thought they heard

water and that rather distracted me. They were all for getting out, and we did."

I zoom in closer—too close for clarity. Zooming out doesn't help either. In the first image, the long narrow triangular passage seems to end at a wall glistening with moisture and pallid with lichen that has never seen the sun, but in the second the passage leads only into darkness. Did the flash fall short of the depths on that try? I needn't imagine that the first image shows a body—even part of one—that shrank from the light like a snail into a shell before the flash could work again. I'm even less happy to wonder if it had already started shrinking—in which case, from what size and shape?—by the time the flash caught it in the act, and so I'm glad when the blackbird in my pocket twitches awake and starts to sing. The phone doesn't identify the caller, and I can only blurt "Hello?"

"Who's that?"

"I know who I am," I tell him with all the conviction I can summon. "Who are you?"

"You first."

I manage not to clench my fingers on the keypad. "Gavin Meadows. Satisfied? Your turn."

"Were you in here before?"

"In where, you—" Barely in time I control the explosion of language enough to say "Is that Frugone? Then I was."

"Gerry here." He pauses long enough for me to wonder if he's the salesman I approached, and then he says "I've got your information."

"Go ahead. Go ahead."

His hesitation makes me repeat the plea, which he uses as an excuse for another silence. At last he says with some pique "It was from Brookland Street near the docks."

"What's there?"

"How should I know? I'm just telling you what you asked. That's your fifty quid's worth."

"Well, thank—"

By now he has departed with an electronic bleep that sounds like censorship. Perhaps he's afraid of being over-heard. Lucinda holds out my tankard in case I need a drink. My voice has indeed grown hoarse. As I take a gulp she says "Was it good news?"

"It has to be. It's where my father sent his last text from."

"Oh, Gavin, where?"

"Brookland Street. It's somewhere by the docks. Have you got a street map?"

I'm at her back as she opens the door to the front room, where I glimpse leaves sprouting from far too many surfaces in the restless dimness. She switches on the light, revealing that the leaves are printed on the cushions of a suite as well as on the wallpaper. A table squatting in front of the settee is piled with volumes of old maps of Liverpool. As Lucinda stoops to them she says "These are for your book as well."

She selects a volume and turns to the index. She's leafing through the maps when I see from the cover that the latest is no more recent than James Maybrick. "Here it is," she says. "The site of, well, that may not still be there."

I don't know why this should make me nervous to ask "What?"

She rests a fingertip on the page as she holds up the book, then moves her hand away. Her finger hasn't left a mark on the page; the grey not quite oval stain beneath the short narrow street bridged by a railway is a dock. "Just a church," she says. "St Cuthbert's church."

Chapter Forty-five

A Distant Song

As Lucinda's car reaches the top of the hill, having emerged from the garage near the houses, a last sweep of the windscreen wipers shows me the churchyard. Just a few inches of the tent are visible above the wall. Two policemen flank the gateway to bar the inquisitive, specifically a woman with two hounds straining at their leashes as if they're eager to hunt the denizens of the graveyard. The policemen remind me so much of guards that I could imagine they're enacting some historical memory. I lose sight of them as the car starts downhill, and I try to leave the stirrings of history behind as well.

The rain has stopped, but clouds are lingering or reforming above the river. There's no reason I should fancy that they're waiting for us to arrive at the street near the dock. I'm already sufficiently troubled by wondering why we're bound there, but where else can we go? Brookland Street passes under a railway bridge, which sounds like the location of my father's last call. The church was mentioned on the phone-in after his appeal, but how significant is that? Like the request slip he filled in, it could be a clue that seems to lead only to another random dead end in the labyrinth of my search. The thought prompts me to grope in my pocket for the slip.

Suppose it has grown as illegible as the page of John Strong's notes? It isn't, but I have to wait while the car descends the hill to Pembroke Place. Traffic lights halt us outside an old infirmary that the university has taken over, and I flourish the slip. "That's why I was in the stacks."

Lucinda accords it barely a glance before concentrating on the road. "All right, Gavin, I believe you."

I wave it in front of her. "Does it look familiar?"

"Don't do that unless you want us to have an accident." She pushes the slip away, although the lights are staying red, and gives it another blink. "I deal with them every day," she says.

"You don't at the moment, and you know what I mean." When she accelerates as the lights drop to green I say "My father wrote it. It's his request for John Strong's papers. It proves they exist after all."

"How does it?"

We're passing the School of Tropical Medicine. My mouth has grown dry again, and my forehead prickles as if the school has released a fever. Once upon a time these symptoms of disease were feared by people who lived here, close to the upper reaches of the Pool. I swallow and croak "One of you took it in the stacks."

"That doesn't really prove anything either, does it? We don't assume people make requests up."

"He didn't. I saw it in the catalogue." I don't know whether I'm flapping the slip for emphasis or from frustration as I insist "And this was on the shelf where they brought the papers from."

"Was there a gap? There wasn't, Gavin, was there? I looked."

"You couldn't have looked too hard if you didn't find this. Why was it there if nobody brought him anything?"

"Maybe they left it to try and avoid an argument."

I feel as if not just the dark clouds but the shops on both sides of London Road are shutting off light from my mind. I could wish they would give way to the old mills and cottages and the view of fields beyond. For a moment, as a shaft of light between them finds the car, the landscape seems to have reverted, but the clouds have released a sunbeam along

a side street. As the library comes into view beyond the
Welly Market I say "More like they wanted to start one."

"Why on earth should anybody want to do that?"

"Maybe to get rid of him. He didn't make a row till he was
told the papers didn't exist, did he? So the question's back to
you. Why should somebody want him kept out of the library?"

"Do you want me to argue or drive?"

I'm tempted to ask why she can't do both, but perhaps I've
made her miss the direct route to the docks. We're speeding
down the concrete flyover that mocks the age of William
Brown Street behind its back. Just ahead of the slope to the
second Mersey Tunnel we veer left at Deadman's Lane. Addison Street, it's called Addison Street, the birthplace of
James William Carling, who used to say the dead sent him
dreams. Perhaps he meant the recently deceased Edgar Al-
lan Poe, whose work Carling illustrated while he lived in
Virginia at the same time as James and Florence Maybrick.
He died in the workhouse on Brownlow Hill, close to a lunatic asylum and far too much else, and I'm glad when Lucinda interrupts the monologue of history. "I did find
something to show you," she says. "I can't now."

I won't ask why. She drives along Leeds Street and turns
right at Pinfold Lane—Vauxhall Road, which takes us
deeper into High Rip territory. I stay quiet—even my mind
does, thank God—while she drives into a side street that
leads under a railway bridge towards the river. Graffiti glisten like bones dredged up in the dimness beneath the arch.
The large ungainly letters spell KEEP OUT, but we're back
in the open before I'm sure whether the last word is TROGS
or FROGS; there's not much difference between them, after
all. The little that remains of the narrow street takes us between a small industrial estate and a row of rudimentary
houses to Great Howard Street, where Lucinda turns left
towards the Pier Head. The vista is dominated by a glassy
greenish skyscraper like a challenge to the past, but it's still

distant when she steers left again. "See, you could trust me," she says.

We're in Brookland Street. The sign tells me so, and the double vowel eyes me with pupils that someone has added, spanning the width of each letter. The left-hand pavement is walled off by an edge of the industrial estate. To the right is a patch of waste ground inside a vandalised wire fence, which extends across the far end of the stub of a street in front of a bricked-up railway arch. Presumably the fence was intended to prevent trespassers from climbing onto the railway. "Thanks," I say as enthusiastically as I'm able and climb out of the car.

The sky seems to sink to meet me, so that I could fancy its darkness is seeping into my head. Certainly the view in front of me—the waste ground scattered with debris and bristling with gloomy weeds—is no more illuminating than illuminated. A few jagged sections of mosaic must have belonged to the floor of the bombed church. A diagonal stretch of mosaic has been prised up, revealing an elongated patch of clay. At first I think only the age of the clay is troubling me, whyever it should, and then I see that it has preserved a set of tracks.

They can't be footprints—not their actual shapes. They're too varied, both in their sizes and their grotesquely varied outlines, which appear to be trying vainly to resemble the prints of naked human feet. Weathering must have distorted them, but I can see why the caller to the phone-in said the ruins were supposed to feature a demon's tracks. Perhaps people thought the church was meant to hold down any lingering presence, but how does this help me find my parents? If my father came to examine the tracks, that was hours ago. I'm distracted by a blurred scrap of song, which at first I think is behind me on the docks, though it isn't a sea shanty. It's a feeble or faraway rendition of "You'll Never Walk Alone." I stare along the main road, where the only signs of life are speeding vehicles, and the side street opposite, which leads to the dock road and its massive fifteen-foot wall. "I don't know where to go from here," I complain. "What were you going to show me?"

Lucinda hesitates and then reaches in her handbag for the Frugo Digital. "I'm not sure if it's any use just now."

She searches backwards through the calendar before handing me the camera. The miniature screen displays a page of text from which long esses sprout like reeds in a marsh. I have to zoom in to identify the first page of Colquitt's *Description of Liverpool*. Given that the book is less than two centuries old, the antique esses suggest that he was trying to fish for the past.

> *"Me to describe in verse my muse alarms;*
> *Our native land attracts by secret charms;*
> *Oft when remote from these salubrious shores*
> *We wish to see our country and its stores.*
> *Behold the Pool, where Neptune's kin doth dream*
> *Of antic life in marsh and secret stream . . ."*

I have to scan back and forth to read all this. My efforts simply leave me more aware how wretched a poet he was. There's no trace of the second couplet that my father copied down, and I thrust the camera at Lucinda. "You're right, it's no—"

"Look at the next one, Gavin."

I toggle to it and peer closer. The afternoon twilight seems to intensify the lurid glare of the shrunken page, which is covered with handwriting—not my father's. There's virtually no space between the lines, and the letters bend so steeply to the right they're almost prone, like a forest in a great relentless storm. As I zoom in I could imagine that I'm being drawn into the past, because despite the absence of elongated esses this is the first draft of Colquitt's poem.

> "Shall the muse now relate of Liverpool,
> Seated near Mersey's banks serenely cool?"

So the unpublished version is even worse, but part of the next line catches my eye. As I scan across the couplets they begin, though not immediately, to grow familiar.

> "Subject to frequent rains though fit to trade,
> And to receive large ships which here are made.
> Behold the Pool, where Neptune's kin doth dream
> Of antic life in marsh and secret stream.
> Nay, though the Pool be buried furlongs deep,
> This stifles not the maggots of its sleep . . ."

I feel as though I'm close to one—as though the doggerel itself is one. The distant song drifts into my consciousness and prevents me from grasping my ill-formed thoughts. "You see, I've been trying to help," Lucinda says. "I found that in the stacks."

Her remarks and the photograph are distracting, but from what? She rests a soft hand on my wrist and murmurs "So do you see, if I've no problem saying that's real—"

"Quiet a moment. Can you hear that?"

"I can't. What—"

"Quiet. You're not giving it a chance."

She looks hurt as she takes her hand away to extend a finger across her lips. I don't know if the wistful mime of muteness is intended to placate me or amuse me, but it's simply another distraction from the sound of "You'll Never Walk Alone." As the dogged performance recedes into the distance I'm growing surer that I don't only recognise the song. I've also begun, however reluctantly, to suspect where it's coming from, but it has retreated farther by the time I squeeze through the gap in the fence.

"What are you doing?" Lucinda calls, but that can't delay me. Nor can the wire mesh that claws at my sleeve. I stride across the remains of the mosaic, which scrapes its stones together underfoot, to the railway arch. I'm yards short of it when the song recommences, having fallen silent as if the singer sensed my approach. I don't believe he can, because he's on the far side of the wall of bricks inside the arch. He isn't just beyond it; the hollowness of his voice betrays that he's in some kind of tunnel—a long one, by the sound of it. He's my father.

Chapter Forty-six

Under the Stone

For a moment I think the bridge is somehow deeper than the arch, as though it has achieved a dream of becoming a tunnel. Or could the entire landscape be something else's dream? I can't let my half-awake fancies distract me; they feel as if the premature gloom is summoning too many elements of sleep. "It's me," I shout. "It's Gavin. Don't go away again."

"What is it?" Lucinda cries through the fence. "What do you think you can hear?"

"I don't think." I mustn't imagine that she's trying to blot out my father's voice, which fell silent as soon as I raised mine. "Quiet till I say," I exhort her and stoop to the bricked-up arch.

Is the dimness hindering my vision, or are my eyes misbehaving somehow? I feel as if my senses are undergoing some adjustment by the time I distinguish a gap in the bricks at the bottom right-hand corner of the arch. Though it puts me in mind of a burrow, surely it's a vandal's work. I go down on my knees in the rubble and crouch to the gap. "Gavin . . ." Lucinda says more or less under her breath.

Perhaps I look as if I'm prostrating myself to a god I've rediscovered. My efforts don't show me much; it's far darker beyond the bricks. The ground within the arch appears to stir, and even if that's just an effect of straining my eyes, I find it unappealing. I still have the camera. Holding it close to the gap, I set off the flash.

Something pale and encrusted with earth rears up beneath the arch and then retreats into the blackness. Despite the illusion of movement, which almost makes me lose my balance, it isn't alive. If I'm not mistaken, it's a trapdoor. I poise the camera again and am waiting for the flash to recharge when Lucinda calls "Don't waste it. Wait, I've got a torch."

I needn't visualise her leading me into the depths below the trapdoor with a flambeau in her hand. She hurries to the car for a flashlight, which she uses to hold back the ragged edge of the fence while she slips through. She halts some feet away from me on a weedy section of mosaic. "Gavin, you've got to tell me what you think you're hearing."

"I'm not just now." When she only gazes at me I add "My father."

"In there."

"Yes, in there. There's more to it than it looks like. I'll show you. Take a look."

Her sole response is to hand me the flashlight. I switch it on and poke it through the jagged aperture. I have to go down on all fours and then, not without some one-armed wobbling, move the beam in an arc before I can put the space beyond the bricks together in my head. The wall and its twin on the far side of the arch have enclosed a section of the street, where pavements strewn with rubble flank an equally littered stub of roadway. The object I mistook for a trapdoor is a raised flagstone on the right-hand pavement. I have to hold the flashlight by the very end of its rubbery tube before I'm sure that the blackness exposed by the flagstone isn't just a square patch of earth. It's a hole deeper than the beam can reach. "I knew it," I blurt.

"What did you think you knew, Gavin?"

"See for yourself. You can't see from there."

As I rise to my feet, leaving the flashlight in the gap, Lucinda squats and crouches forward. I'm about to demand a reaction by the time she says "Children."

"Where? What do you mean?"

"Children must have broken in, mustn't they? Nobody else would do that."

"Maybe, but they aren't who's there now."

She waves the flashlight at the bricked-up darkness. "Nobody is, Gavin."

"Not in there, below it. There's a tunnel if you look."

The beam alights on the raised flagstone and sinks into the beginnings of the depths. "I wouldn't call that a tunnel," says Lucinda. "You aren't saying a grown person would try to get in it."

"Yes, I am. They have. There's room."

"But why would anybody want to?"

"I'll be finding out. Can I get through?"

As she stands up I see her eyes are moist. "I suppose you have to exhaust every avenue," she says.

However grotesque my behaviour appears, it has to be right. I'm returning to all fours when Lucinda says "You won't need the camera as well, will you?"

I hand it to her and go prone on the rubble, a position from which it feels unnatural to speak. "I'll shout if I need to," I tell her. "My phone isn't going to work."

I can think of nothing more to say, and so I crawl through the gap, hitching myself on knees and elbows over the rubble. Bricks scrape my shoulders until I crouch lower. My heel sends a piece of debris across the waste ground with a clatter and a clink, and then I'm through, shoving the flashlight ahead. Its beam slithers along the littered pavement and draws the walls out of the dark. As I wobble to my feet there's a prolonged rumble overhead, and the bridge shudders all around me. The disturbance isn't thunder or an earthquake, it's the reverberation of a train, and only the unsteadiness of the flashlight beam shifted the walls. The resonance gathers under the bridge and fills my ears until I feel as if it's undermining all my senses while I examine where I am.

It smells like a dungeon where the sunlight never enters— earthy and damp. The truncated sections of roadway and pavements resemble an exhibit in a museum, a sample of a street from some undetermined past. The museum itself would be derelict, given the patches of lichen glistening with moisture on the walls. The raised flagstone puts me in mind of a grave, perhaps because it's resting against a mound of earth. As I step forward the light pokes ever deeper into the square hole, which has roughly the same outline as the flagstone. I'm at the edge before I see exactly what's beneath. The hole penetrates several feet of clay, below which is a tunnel scattered with fragments of brick that must have formed part of the ceiling. Propped more than a foot beneath the hole in the pavement, a ladder irrelevantly reminiscent of a window-cleaner's stands on the floor of the tunnel.

As the rumble of the train continues to oppress my senses I wonder what the sequence of events may have been. Could vibrations from the railway have weakened the tunnel roof? Perhaps nobody knew the tunnel was there. If it wasn't Williamson's doing—there's no record that he dug so close to the river—he's rumoured to have had imitators. It isn't so far from the site of the castle, from which a tunnel led to the Pool, and it's nearer still to Exchange Flags, the stage James Maybrick trod while he conducted his business. That whole area is underlaid by passages and subterranean rooms, and how far may the burrows extend in this direction? Even the known tunnels under the city are said to be as numerous as the streets. I'm being distracted by the stream of consciousness that's the history of Liverpool and by the thunder penned beneath the bridge. Did someone dig the hole because they heard sounds in the tunnel? Whatever they found, is that why the bridge—this one and no other along the embankment—was closed off? Did they neglect to make the hole safe, or was it reopened after the arch was bricked up? All of this feels like yet another secret the city is trying to keep, and I've resolved none of it by the time the train draws its tail across the bridge. As the rumble fades into the distance I hear the sound it has been concealing. It's "You'll Never Walk Alone," farther off than previously but just as audible. My mother has joined in.

She sounds less convinced by the message of the song than my father seems determined to be. I'm lifting my free hand to help me send a shout to them when Lucinda says "I can hear something. Is that your father?"

"It's both of them. They're in here. They're somewhere down below."

"Shush, then." She plants her fists outside the gap, and her face appears between them. "Let me listen," she says.

She's making more noise than I was, and my parents have gone quiet. I'm on the verge of accusing her until they start another verse. Her intent face loses its expression, and she wriggles through the gap, so much more deftly than I managed that she makes me feel clumsy and bloated. Once she rises gracefully to her feet I say "Hold this for me till I'm down."

As I extend the flashlight to her the walls quiver. Shadows stream up her face, playing with its shape. Her features grow steadier, outlining her concern, as soon as she takes the flashlight. I give her a quick hug, which feels softer than I like, but I've no time to improve on it. Though the song is still audible, mostly in my father's voice, it's retreating into the depths.

I stand on the brink of the hole and reach with one foot for the ladder. I teeter on the edge, stretching my leg down, until Lucinda extends her free hand to grasp my right one. She keeps hold, leaning so far forward that it begins to look precarious, while I balance on the top rung and grope for the next and establish a slippery foothold. As I step down again she releases me and straightens up to her full height, training the flashlight on the hole. I rest my hands on the gritty pavement and stretch a leg downwards, wishing I weren't so bulky. My foot locates the next rung, and I close my fingers around the topmost. Apparently I'm less out of shape than I feared, because twisting my body a little allows me to descend without touching the clay on any side. Only a trickle of soil dislodged by the ladder makes me afraid that the hole may collapse.

In a few seconds I'm through it and clambering down the rest of the ladder. As my head clears the underside of the ceiling, so does the flashlight beam. It expands, becoming dimmer, to show me an arched brick tunnel about eight feet high, leading both ways into blackness. Is it one of the disused sewers? I can hear the faintest lapping to my right, from the direction of the river. The dogged song is off to my left, however far away. I clutch at the rungs, which feel moist enough for many years of condensation, and hasten down the ladder. Fragments of the roof crunch underneath, though most of the debris is piled against the walls. The instant I set foot on the floor the light is snatched away, and I have more than a moment of breathless panic. "Here it comes," Lucinda calls.

Kneeling at the edge of the hole, she lowers the flashlight towards me. She's holding it by the lens, muffling the glow, which blurs her face and her outstretched arm. As I start back up the ladder she opens her hand. She must expect me to catch the flashlight, but I barely do, clutching it with splayed fingers and thumping it against my chest. I'm reclaiming my breath from a gasp when the ladder begins to shiver as if it's magnifying the panic I experienced. "Hold it so I can see where I'm going," says Lucinda.

I've barely left the ladder and raised the flashlight beam when she descends into it with the swiftness of an acrobat performing a familiar routine. Of course she must have gained experience in the Williamson tunnels. Her progress drags the light down, stopping up the hole with blackness—that is, I lower the beam. It probes the empty dark that leads towards the river. Brick dust crunches beneath Lucinda's feet as she steps on the floor. "Which way are we going?" she says.

Her call from above silenced my parents. "If you didn't shout you could hear."

"I'm not shouting, Gavin."

"You need to keep quieter than that." The tunnel amplifies my whisper while rendering it thin and shrill. "His text said not to look for them," I resent having to admit.

"Why would he say that? Do you think they're—"

"I don't know. I don't care. I just care about saving them."

"I'll surprise you how quiet I can be, then. You won't even know I'm here unless you want to."

I see her mouth this more than I hear the words. It's less reassuring than she presumably intends, because it makes me wonder if anybody else is being stealthy in the dark. As I swing the beam past the ladder, the tunnel appears to dilate while the shadows of rungs scurry over the wall. Darkness floods up from the river when I turn the beam inland. At its farthest extent, which is as dim as the glow of a guttering candle, I'm just able to distinguish that the tunnel starts to curve to the right, in the general direction of the Castle and the mouth of the Pool. I'm pacing away from the ladder, putting on speed once the floor is clear of rubble, when the song is revived somewhere ahead.

At least my parents aren't troubled by the light, because they're too far off to see it. Surely they won't be able to hear my footsteps for a while, although I wish I could be as discreet as Lucinda; I have to keep glancing over my shoulder to confirm she's still following me. She must be staying back in case we bump into each other, though the tunnel is wide enough for us to walk abreast. Can I be quieter? Working on how fast I can stride without making any appreciable noise brings me no closer to my parents, but they don't seem to be receding either. By the time I reach the bend in the tunnel my footfalls aren't too far from noiseless. The hush is broken mostly by my parents' unequal duet until I hear voices at my back.

The lit section of tunnel reels around us as I twist to face Lucinda. A glistening shape swells up behind her on the wall that's blackened with patches of damp, but it's her shadow. The passage must have amplified the voices, unless my nerves did, because the speakers are out of range of the flashlight. They aren't even in the tunnel; they're above it. As I strain to understand them, my ears feel as if they're expanding. In a few moments I manage to hear "Sounds like somebody's having a singalong."

"Let's see what they've got to sing about," the answer comes, so muffled that the speakers must be outside the bridge. This isn't as reassuring as I would like, because they're Wrigley and Maddock.

Chapter Forty-seven

WHERE IT LED

Lucinda looks transfixed by the light I'm directing past her. Her face has grown blank, the eyes in particular. She must be concentrating on the sounds outside the tunnel, unless she's doing her best not to distract me or to make any inadvertent noise. At least the police can't reach my parents before we do. For a change I'm glad they've taken so long to discover where my father's message came from. They won't be able to follow until they clear more of a way, since I was barely able to fit through the gap. I put a finger to my lips and point around the bend with the flashlight. As I turn in that direction the first speaker says "They won't be singing when they see us."

"They'll be singing on the other side of their faces."

I want to believe the tunnel is playing another acoustic prank. How can they already sound closer? Surely I would have heard them enlarging the gap in the bricks. Then one of them says "Black as a Paki's arsehole down there" with a laugh I'd rather not understand—I feel as if the darkness is releasing his true self—and there's no question that he's inside the bridge, because his voice is directly above the hole in the roof of the tunnel. "Just like home," says his companion.

I would prefer not to interpret this either. Any inclination I might have had to confront the men has fled into the dark. I ought to be using the time it will take them to squeeze through the hole in the pavement—using it to ensure that we and the light are hidden by the bend. It curves as far as I can see, and I lengthen my strides, even when the light sways like a vessel in a storm. I've advanced just a few yards when a body drops into the tunnel, followed almost immediately by another.

They sound like large soft heavy sacks. I have the quite unnecessary notion that they expanded as they struck the floor. Mightn't they be bags of some kind of equipment? Apparently not, since one remarks "Didn't know I could still do that."

"We never lose it, us."

They've silenced my parents—indeed, the impacts did. I can't let the newcomers or any thoughts of them delay me, and I stride along the tunnel as its depths work like a parched throat. Stealth is still with me, though I hardly need it, since I hear heavy footfalls padding at my back. I can't help glancing over my shoulder, but only Lucinda is to be seen. She widens her eyes, asking a mute question or simply acknowledging me. I mustn't speak, though I'm disturbed by the sight behind her. The beam in front of me lends a tinge of visibility to a short stretch of the passage we've traversed, but beyond this there isn't a trace of light. Despite their speed, Wrigley and Maddock seem to be in total darkness.

Surely the bend is concealing whatever light they have. The tunnel curves for another hundred yards or so before straightening to release the unsteady beam into the depths. What's barring the way in the distance? It can't be a dead end, unless my parents have turned aside somewhere I've yet to locate. Suppose I didn't notice a side passage, and the police are now between me and my parents? What am I afraid the men will do to them? I would rather not dream of that, even in daylight—the daylight I suppose is still above us in the world. In a few seconds I'm able to distinguish the prospect ahead. Though it isn't a blockage, it's almost as unwelcome. It's a fork that splits the tunnel in half.

One narrow passage carries straight on, while the other bends sharply to the left, further inland. The bend is the nearest place to hide, but tracks lead along the second passage.

There are none in its neighbour. I go swiftly but as good as silently to the junction, where I turn to Lucinda. I finger my lips again and point ahead, then indicate the flashlight and wave my hand over it as though extinguishing a candle. I have to hope this is eloquent enough as I hurry into the tunnel.

How far can we go before the men are close enough to see our light? I would run if I could be sure of staying unheard. The soft footfalls behind me sound closer—they can hardly be growing larger. I glance back to find Lucinda wide-eyed with the dimness. I'm sure the men are nearly at the bend, and I repeat my gestures to conjure silence and darkness. The gestures won't work by themselves. I press my spine against the wall and take hold of Lucinda's arm to help me communicate or perhaps just for reassurance as I switch the flashlight off.

At once I might as well have no eyes. In one sense the absolute blackness is reassuring; my parents must be safely out of sight, since whatever light they're using is. I have time to wonder how irrationally I'm behaving, not to mention why, before the large flat footsteps reach the section of tunnel that splits in half. At once my anxiety makes far too much sense, because Wrigley and Maddock are finding their way with no light of any kind.

I feel as if I'm dreaming their approach, an impression the blackness exacerbates. Can't they be wearing equipment that lets them see in the dark? It seems unnecessary, and it would mean they can see us. I wish Lucinda wouldn't draw any attention by moving, even though she has only closed a hand over mine on her arm. She increases her grip as the loose heavy footfalls advance. They sound too soft for shoes, and I have the unpleasant fancy that the men have left their clothes elsewhere—under the bridge, perhaps. There's a slithery element to the footsteps, and a clumsiness that might suggest the searchers haven't quite decided how to walk. As they halt at the division of the tunnels Lucinda clenches her hand on mine, and I imagine eyes swelling huge to peer at us out of the dark. My mouth is parched with holding my breath by the time the footsteps veer into the adjacent tunnel.

They haven't reached the bend when I almost drop the flashlight. Either Wrigley or Maddock has begun to bellow "You'll Never Walk Alone," and his colleague is quick to join in, though not to find the same key. At least the disordered chorus should keep my parents away from them. As the song recedes around the bend, I have to assume that the performers are mocking the version they heard. Perhaps the tunnel is distorting the sounds, which are growing so parodic that I could imagine they're emerging from mouths without much of a shape or at least lacking a constant one. It isn't a notion I enjoy having in the dark. I wait until the voices seem muffled by distance, and then I force myself to wait for another few breaths before reviving the flashlight beam.

Lucinda clutches at my arm, and I turn to see her squeezing her eyes tight as if they've grown too used to the dark. Some seconds pass before she blinks. In a moment she does so more widely, and she speaks—her lips move, at any rate. "What is it?" she seems to be asking.

I shake my head and shrug and raise my brows to their fullest elevation and stretch my arms wide, thumping the wall with the flashlight. The rubber casing mutes the impact, but I'm yearning to take the noise back as Lucinda repeats her question loud enough for me to hear, unless it's a variation. "What are they—"

"Talk later," I just about murmur. When she looks dissatisfied I nod in the direction of the song, which is so malformed by now that it suggests the croaking mouths have grown even more uncertain of their shape. "Do you want them getting to my parents?"

"What do you think they—"

"I don't want to think." All this whispering is no good for my nerves. Lucinda's fingers stretch to cling to my arm, but I ease it free. "No time," I mutter as I set off along the tunnel.

Has hitting the wall damaged the flashlight? The beam appears to flicker, and my heartbeat flutters in response. Surely the light is wavering just with my haste. Wrigley and Maddock have fallen silent, even their ponderously purposeful tread. Either they're out of earshot or they've halted to listen. They can't hear Lucinda if I can't, and I'm finding more stealth myself. I do my best to steady the beam as it discovers an object as tall as the roof ahead. It must be another division of the tunnels. The blurred prints on the discoloured floor will show which way my parents have gone. The dim edge of the flashlight beam snatches at the obstruction as I make for it, until I'm forced to acknowledge that I've been seeing and then trying to see what I wanted to be there. It isn't a junction. The roof has collapsed.

There's a gap at the top of the mound of clay and bricks, but it's just a few inches wide and high, and almost eight feet above the floor. My parents could never have scaled the mound. Nobody has climbed it; the dents that suggest otherwise would belong to the hands and feet of someone far too large to fit through the gap. I swing around, lowering the flashlight as Lucinda's eyes wince. "They've gone the other way," I whisper.

"Quick, then."

I wonder why she isn't following her own advice until she holds out her hand. Perhaps she's had enough of being blinded. She takes the flashlight with both hands and turns it back the way we came. Her movements are defter than mine; although I have almost to run to keep up with her, the beam hardly wobbles. As it spills beyond the junction I manage to overtake her. "Let me have it now," I mouth.

"It was making me feel seasick."

Is there a glimmer of rebuke in her eyes? I could think she feels distrusted. I need to believe I have some control of the situation, that's all. She plants the flashlight in my hand, but I don't immediately send the beam into the left-hand passage. Why are Wrigley and Maddock so silent? Are they creeping after my parents, in which case they must be taking an inhuman amount of care, or waiting for them to betray where they are? As I dodge into the passage I aim the flashlight at the floor, causing a fall of darkness that looks not much less solid than earth.

I can't help thinking of the collapsed roof. How old is the tunnel—how weakened by its history? I could imagine that the unstable hovering dark is poised to seep into my head like someone else's dream. The bend in the tunnel resembles one, since it shows no sign of growing straight. Are we being led towards some part of the site of the Pool? Perhaps that's unavoidable, but trying to grasp which section of the city we're beneath feels too much like an invitation to a reverie that's waiting to be entertained. The subterranean dark can't suffocate my consciousness, but it's so much of a relief to see the tunnel straighten out at last that I risk lifting the flashlight beam.

The tunnel has begun to slope upwards. At the limit of the vista of glistening brick that the beam strains to illuminate there's unrelieved darkness. My parents have to be in or surely beyond this, and it must be concealing Wrigley and Maddock. I need to be quiet but equally quick. I'm taking some comfort from achieving both, while Lucinda keeps up her surreptitiousness at my back, when I falter, raising the beam that I'd lowered. To the left is a side tunnel.

I want it to be a dead end, and that's what I see when I reach the entrance, but only a bend is blocking my view. I hold the beam low and strain my ears until they feel waterlogged with silence. When Lucinda parts her lips I gesture so fiercely that she seems to think I'm waving her away. As I beckon to her, a movement that comes close to slapping my apologetic face, I hear a distant voice.

It's my mother. She seems to be protesting, and I'm afraid

Wrigley and Maddock may have found my parents. I swing the flashlight beam along the main tunnel towards her voice, revealing only emptiness, nothing like footprints. I've advanced just a few paces when my mother finishes speaking, and I hold my breath. She must be waiting for an answer, because in a moment she has one. "It's this way," her companion declares.

He's my father. They were simply arguing. I'm restraining a shout for fear of silencing them when a voice says "That's them."

If it isn't Wrigley it's Maddock, and it's behind me. As I spin around, the flashlight beam comes too. Lucinda's eyes look enlarged by dismay. We're alone in the tunnel. I don't want the beam to reach into the side passage, and I jerk the flashlight up. In a moment the tunnels are swamped by utter blackness.

I have the absurd and useless fancy that I've brought it upon us by wishing to stay inconspicuous. A rubbery thud is followed by two heavier metallic ones, and the flashlight gives up most of its weight. As I hear the batteries trundle away a second voice says "Them for sure."

Wrigley and Maddock must have been standing still to listen, because now I hear them start towards us. I can't tell how far away they are, but the sloppy footfalls are so ponderous that they might be deliberately lingering over the chase. Do they think their quarry can't escape? Trying to understand them only aggravates my panic. I don't know what Lucinda murmurs as she plants a hand on my arm, but I'm reminded not just of her presence. "Camera," I whisper drymouthed. "Flash."

Her hand leaves my arm, and I feel more alone in the dark than I ought to. As the footfalls advance, sounding somehow inconsistent, I urge "Flash, quick."

"I have to switch it on, Gavin."

Why hasn't she, or does she mean she's done so? Presumably she had to fumble in her handbag. In a moment there's a thin electronic whine, and then the glow of the sensor reddens the tunnel around us. It doesn't show me the batteries, and a glance behind me is no help. The flash goes off, displaying the route all the way back to the bend without a battery in sight. "Try again," I mutter desperately as the dark falls on us. "The other tunnel."

"It's recharging. It takes a few seconds."

How much of her calm is an effort or even a pretence? If it's meant to reassure me as well as herself, it doesn't work for me. The camera begins to whine about its task, but the ill-matched footsteps are louder. They sound close to the main tunnel, and I blurt "No time."

Lucinda closes her fingers around my arm. "Let me past, then."

She slips between me and the wall before I can ask "What are you doing?"

Since she has released my arm I'm not sure where she is, and I can't help starting as her moist breath enters my ear. "We don't need the torch," she whispers. "We can use the flash if we have to, but it's straight on for a long way now."

She means the route the flashlight showed, of course. She leaves me with a last whisper. "Stay close to me."

Is this advice or a plea? I'm just able to hear her striding ahead. If she's so confident despite the blackness, surely I can be. I seem to sense the walls as a solid chill on either side of me. There's no point in clutching the useless flashlight, and I drop it, hoping it may trip up a pursuer or two. I lurch blindly forward and am beginning to pick up speed when the sounds of pursuit emerge from the side tunnel. They're oddly imprecise, which makes me all the more anxious to keep up with Lucinda. I can, and silently too. They don't seem to be gaining on us. I'm wishing my parents would make some noise, to reassure me that we're catching up with them, when Lucinda murmurs "Careful. There's a bend."

Can I sense it? Her voice is moving to the right, and I think I'm distinguishing the presence of the walls, two looming blocks of stony damp and chill. I feel I'm keeping them more or less the same distance from me as I follow Lucinda. Certainly I'm aware when the curve ends, though perhaps that's because she's advancing straight ahead. We've left the undefined sounds of pursuit beyond it. I'm beginning to think I can ignore my sightless state when I bump into Lucinda, who has halted. "Wait," she whispers. "What are we going to do now?"

She hasn't finished speaking when the sensor reddens the darkness, revealing that the way ahead is less straightforward. In another moment the flash shows me that we've reached a second fork. As my eyes wince I make out that the right-hand passage carries on while its neighbour bends left. What's the point of that or indeed of the whole underground system? Blackness fills my aching eyes again and seems to flood my mind. I'm trying to think of an answer for Lucinda when she murmurs "You go ahead, Gavin."

"What are you saying?"

"I'll go the other way. One of us will find Deryck and Gillian."

I can't call to them. Any response would alert Wrigley and Maddock. I feel robbed of speech, and before I can answer Lucinda, she whispers "Take this."

She's pressing the camera into my hand. "What about you?" I protest.

"I'll find my way, don't worry. I'm used to it now. Go on, quick. No time."

"But couldn't we—" I blurt, a pathetic attempt to delay her, since I've no idea what to add. She closes my fingers around the camera and plants a swift kiss—hardly more than a touch of flesh and a hint of moisture—on my cheek.

The lingering sensation seems to elongate the moment, unless my yearning to prolong it does. As it leaves me I realise she has too. "Wait," I mouth, but I can't risk hindering her further when footfalls are padding or otherwise advancing to the bend behind us. They sound too close for me to dare to use the flash. Instead I thumb the button halfway down to trigger the sensor. The division of the tunnel glows like embers, and I glimpse Lucinda striding fast but soundlessly along the left-hand passage. Without hesitation she vanishes into it like a creature of the dark.

I can't hesitate either. I send the meagre glow along the other tunnel to remind me exactly where the walls are, and then I lift the strap of the camera over my head and set forth into the blackness. I was afraid that without Lucinda my instincts would fail me, but this doesn't seem to be the case; so long as I proceed straight ahead I'm able to avoid the walls. It isn't fear of a collision in the dark that halts me, it's my mother. "We're there again," she's saying in a tone that distance renders obscure. "It's so huge."

"We'll get through it, love."

I can't remember the last time my father addressed her so affectionately, or is it meant to reassure her? They're in the same tunnel as me, and I start forward before faltering. Have I time to fetch Lucinda? I'm shuffling around to stay clear of the walls when I hear Wrigley and Maddock reach the junction. Their disconcertingly assorted footfalls and their thick breaths, which apparently require some slobbering, aren't the only noises. Lucinda has started to run. "I hear something in its hole," says Wrigley or Maddock.

"Halt in the name of the law."

This sounds unsettlingly old-fashioned. Perhaps it's meant to be a joke. The policeman doesn't shout it, he pronounces it as a remark. It earns a slobbery laugh from his companion, who says "Let's show them what we're here for."

While this may not be ominous in itself, their burst of throaty mirth is. Their amusement trails off as it enters the other tunnel. I can't bear it or the thought that they're after Lucinda, even if she's trying to decoy them away from my parents. "Why don't you leave us all alone," I blurt.

I don't shout, but I don't restrain my voice either, and it brings a response. "There's another of them."

"All yours."

Stealth is pointless now, and I aim the camera at the junction. When the sensor doesn't reach I use the flash, calling out "It'll take more than one of you in your condition."

I hardly know what I'm saying. Besides revealing nobody, the flash has blinded me, stopping up my eyes with pallid after-images. The undefined shapes have begun to expand and grow as red as a sensor when in the distance my mother cries "Was that you, Gavin?"

"It's me. I'm coming," I shout but face the junction while I say "I've found my parents. Sorry to have troubled you. We don't need you any more."

Perhaps I'm trying to clutch at some remnant of normality as I wait for my eyes to recover. "Was that you, Gavin?" says a voice in the other tunnel.

He doesn't have to croak so much to sound mocking, but his companion does too. "You called us up. Can't just send us back."

As a soft heavy tread—at least, a series of noises that suggests leathery bags are being dropped and dragged along the floor—starts towards me I stumble around, thumbing the camera button. The redness of my vision solidifies, forming into dim bricks underfoot and to either side. The moment I'm sure where the walls are I release the button and stride ahead.

I can make as much noise as I like, which seems to give me the confidence to lengthen my strides. I might risk sprinting, although surely I should check no bend is imminent, or would the acoustic warn me? I'm growing convinced that I can sense the route somehow. In a way the problem is the absence of distractions: I can't hear Lucinda or my parents. Wrigley and Maddock are silent too, even whichever of them is following me. Surely he can't have fallen too far behind to be audible; is he managing to keep his sounds to himself, however close he is? I imagine a bloated shape gaining on me with huge but unnaturally soundless leaps, reaching out an elongated arm to seize me with lengthened fingers. What if this isn't only my imagination? I can't bear not seeing. As I take hold of the camera I realise that the flash needn't blind me. Better still, it should blind any pursuer.

I narrow my eyes as I spin around and press the button. For at least a second it produces only the glow of the sensor, and then the sight I was leaving behind rears up with the flash. It's an empty tunnel.

Although my slitted eyes wince, I can see that the passage is deserted all the way back to the junction. Did nobody follow me after all? As reddened darkness fills my vision I wonder if I could have passed another tunnel without noticing. Suppose not just the pursuer but my parents are in there? I thumb the button, to be rewarded by the electronic whine. I'm growing both dry-mouthed and clammy with frustration, a contrast that suggests my body no longer knows how to process the water that is its fundamental element, when my mother says "Never mind shushing me, Deryck. Where has he gone?"

I mustn't be dismayed by how she sounds—far away in the dark, her voice flattened and distorted by an acoustic I can't place. She's somewhere along the tunnel I've been following. "I'm here," I call and turn in that direction.

The camera has recharged enough to activate the sensor. I glimpse a stretch of floor and walls and even a hint of the ceiling. I have the impression—perhaps I owe it to the last time I used the flash—that they carry straight on for a considerable distance, which gives me the confidence to press on through the dark. I've heard no response to my call, and I'm wary of insisting; there's no need to remind any pursuer that my parents are ahead, although I seem to have left behind the sense of pursuit. It could almost have been some kind of dream.

My progress through the dark reminds me of one, especially since I've reverted to stealth. As long as I don't need to hear my own sounds or to oversee the working of my muscles, my consciousness is prepared to let them go. I'm happy to be unaware how drenched I recently was, a sensation my body has subsumed. I've begun to feel like a sleepwalker despite my strides and my wakefulness. How far have I come? Where am I beneath? I must be within the ancient boundaries of Liverpool. Has night fallen up there? I attempt to read my watch by the glow of the sensor and then, having narrowed my eyes that felt enlarged by the dark, with the aid of the flash. That's no use either. Moisture has rendered the face of the watch as featureless as a still pool.

The condensation is inside the glass. At least the flash confirmed that the tunnel leads straight ahead. I don't know when it finished sloping upwards. I wait for the residue of light to drain from my eyes, and then I let my body find the way. By now I'm convinced that the night is overhead, and my mind seems to reach up for it, only to be assailed by the impression that the landscape above me is showing too much of its age. I see a muddy lane made tortuous by haphazard ungainly houses in which lights flicker like will-o'-the-wisps that have strayed from the surrounding marsh. Black water crawls along the unpaved roadway towards the fitful glow of a lantern elevated beside a weather-beaten cross, behind which a cruciform shadow is prancing on the rutted mud. All this is oppressively real, and I can only fend it off by dredging my mind out of the past. That doesn't work, because now I seem to be underneath a Victorian street more squalid than its predecessor. Tenements on either side of the enclosed court swarm with families, more than one of them to some of the cramped barely furnished rooms. They huddle away from the windows, which are letting in wind and rain along with the stench of the open sewer that runs along the middle of the lane. Are they also anxious to keep away from the denizens of the cellars? Whoever lives down there is closer to the darkness and the mud; it's easy to believe that's where they came from. They're closer to me as well, and as my mind engages with them, theirs seem to reach for me.

My mind recoils, shrinking like my eyes when the flash dazzled them, but the images stay more vivid than a remembered dream. Though the darkness lends them conviction, I mustn't waste the power of the camera. They were the past, just remnants of the past, surely reshaped by waking dreams of it. Aren't the earlier versions of the city not just drafts that were later reworked but a kind of dream the landscape had? Certainly I feel as if I wasn't alone in dreaming what I just imagined. Perhaps the entire city and whatever it produces, human and otherwise, is a vast expansive recurring dream. If the dream I had in Frog's Lane—in Whitechapel—wasn't only mine, what does that imply or portend? I could fancy I'm an oracle who went unheard, not least by myself. My growing ease with the subterranean darkness has set my mind free to drift, but this doesn't help my search. The clamour of the past within my skull seems to have given way to the babbling of John Strong—of his incoherent dreaming onto the page. I need to concentrate on whatever lies ahead.

If the city is a dream or a series of dreams rendered solid, how much truer must this be of its buried secrets? They're closer to the dark, after all—the solidified dark that's the earth, which has done its best to engulf and diffuse and blacken the Pool. The proliferation of forgotten tunnels might have been trying to recapture the freedom of water, which brick and stone can't begin to approximate. My mind sounds more than ever like John Strong, so that fumbling for the button on the camera feels like a bid to return to the present as well as to illuminate the route.

The nearest section of the tunnel glows like embers someone's breathing on, and I'm just able to see that it comes to some kind of an end. Is it a sharp turn or a junction? The tunnel can't be blocked. The glow of the sensor wavers as I hurry forward, and it feels as if my consciousness is fluctuating. The tunnel does indeed end, but it isn't quite impassable.

Bricks have been dislodged from the wall across it, revealing utter blackness.

The gap is about seven feet high and not much wider than my body. When I slit my eyes and set off the flash, it illuminates a passage through the sandstone. It's too irregular to be artificial; it isn't even upright but slants a few inches leftwards, extending further than my wary vision can take in. I have to wonder why it was bricked up and why it has been reopened, not to say from which side. Far more important, can my parents have squeezed through? They would have had a struggle if not worse. I'm waiting for the camera to recharge when my mother says "He'll find us." She's too distant for me to judge her tone—I can barely distinguish her words—but she's somewhere ahead. I step into the passage at once.

I hadn't grasped how thoroughly it slants. I have to bend well to the left to avoid bumping into the walls. Before long I feel so alarmingly contorted that I keep resting my hand on that side of the passage. The stone is so moist and smooth that I'm in no doubt the channel was formed by water. It seems to take minutes to straighten up, and I've scarcely rediscovered how to walk erect when my head is forced down by the roof. I'm made to duck and then to stoop, pressing my chin against my chest until I might as well not have a neck. At last I emerge into a narrow lofty chamber and regain my breath, but the route has further trials to offer. The ceiling drops again, so relentlessly that I'm reduced to a crouch and then to a squat in which I have to shuffle along on my haunches. How can my parents have dealt with this stretch? I feel as if the passage is teaching me all the shapes I never realised my body could adopt. My parents must be ahead, if only because they couldn't have turned back; the passage is too constricted. I haven't been able to rise from my squat when I'm required to squirm around a protracted bend with both hands on the walls. The sensation is so disconcerting that I resort to the flash, which shows me that the roof stays

low until the bend cuts off the view. At least the walls are
bare stone, however much they had begun to feel like slippery flesh. I keep reminding myself how it looked—how it
must still look—until at last, having changed direction
more than once, the passage widens and grows straight and
high. I celebrate this with a glimpse of reddish dimness, but
the prospect the sensor displays isn't so appealing: while the
roof stays a few inches above my head, the walls close in so
that there's barely space for me to walk between them. Before long I have to sidle, pressing my hands against the walls
and eventually stretching out my arms on either side of me
in an attempt to feel less confined. They only revive the
sense that the substance of the walls is too close to my own,
an impression that seems especially concentrated in the
blackness in front of my face. It's a struggle to reach for the
camera, and when I succeed in triggering the sensor it shows
me a glistening patch of sandstone, as far as I can discern it
while being almost blinded by the nearness of the glow. The
sight lacks reassurance, because I feel as if my right hand,
which is groping ahead of the rest of me, is about to encounter an unwelcome presence in the dark. Something does indeed stir beneath my fingers, and I snatch my hand away. As
I clutch at the camera the sensor flares again, and I'm just
able to see that the chilly restless tendrils are trickles of water. They aren't enough to flood the passage, although my feet
grow wet as I sidle past. As my fingertips encounter more of
the thin streams on the sandstone I begin to have the unhelpful notion that the water is flowing up the wall. I mustn't
give in to the idea or waste the batteries of the camera. A
wet tendril seems to writhe away from my fingers, and another feels as though it's dodging them, and then my hand
and arm grope into space as far as they can reach.

I have a sense of teetering on the brink of an abyss. As I
recoil, the camera blunders against the wall. The echo of
the impact suggests that the unseen space is enormous. My
wary fingers grope along the streaming wall until it curves

out of reach. They fumble at the dark and eventually locate the opposite wall, which curves away too. I inch towards the point where the passage widens, and then I press my clammy palms against the clammy walls while I edge one foot forwards. The floor continues ahead and to either side, but I rest my left hand on the wall for safety as I try the sensor. It shows me only a short stretch of wet floor ribbed like part of an enormous buried skeleton, and so I use the flash.

It glares on the walls and the roof—at least, the nearest sections of them. The cave outside the passage rises to a height of twenty feet or more and grows at least as broad, but on the far side there's blackness that the flash failed to alleviate, suggesting that I'm in the antechamber to a vaster cavern. It seems advisable to stay close to a wall, and I follow the right-hand one, having reminded myself of its course with the sensor. I can't afford to be daunted by an impression that the cave is taking advantage of the darkness—that it's changing or about to change in some way while I'm unable to see. If the floor feels soft as well as wet, that has to be mud or moss, and I don't need to touch the wall. It isn't until my footsteps audibly change that I'm driven to employ the flash.

I've reached the far side of the cave. It does indeed give onto a larger space—so large that the flash leaves the depths ahead of me utterly dark. I barely glimpse the left-hand wall in the moment of illumination, but the other one is closer. As I make to follow it my mother says "That wasn't lightning."

While she sounds more distant than ever, she's somewhere ahead. My father mumbles incomprehensibly, and then they're silent. They can't be in the cavern, since there isn't even a glimmer of whatever they're using to find their way, unless the place is so gigantic that distance has rendered their light invisible to me. Are they close to an exit? Is that why one of them thought the flash could be lightning? I'm afraid that if I call to them they might flee into the city, where I'll have to start searching for them all over again. Perhaps my mother wouldn't let this happen, but I can't take the risk. "It was me," I only mouth, though vigorously enough to feel my lips take various shapes, as I set off along the wall.

An echo dogs my footsteps, such as they are. It seems bent on demonstrating how minute they are by comparison with the vast blackness. Otherwise there's silence so profound that it feels as if a crowd is holding its breath. Certainly I have a sense of being awaited. Has my mother succeeded in halting my father? I need to be quick. I lift the strap over my head and hold the camera in front of me at arm's length as I activate the sensor.

The reddish dimness glistens on a length of wall and a strip of smooth floor alongside it. The glimpse lends me the confidence for a few strides into the dark. Surely it can help me ward off the idea that more than my parents are awaiting me—that a multitude or something at least as considerable will be revealed next time I use the sensor. It's just an unwelcome dream born of the darkness, which I can also blame for my sense that some all-encompassing transformation is imminent. Or has it already taken place under cover of the blackness? Some change has definitely overtaken my footsteps. They're surrounded by more space, that's all, or is it a different kind of space? I advance a defiant pace, and another, before I can't bear the uncertainty. I stretch out my arm to its fullest extent—I feel as if the dark is adding to its span—and press the button halfway down.

The sensor exhibits another length of wall and the corresponding strip of floor. What's odd about the sight? It's somehow different from the last section of cave that I saw. The visible area of the floor is narrower. Surely the batteries aren't running out, but what's the alternative? When I direct the sensor away from the wall, it still displays just a length of floor less than a yard wide. I hold the camera out and set off the flash.

It doesn't just illuminate my route. It frames the darkness that's ahead and, worse, beside me. The lit section of the floor was so narrow because there's no more to it. I've been striding carelessly along a ledge not much wider than my body above a chasm too extensive and too deep for the flash to touch its limits.

I stagger back from the drop, too violently. My elbow collides with the wall. Although the impact feels softer than stone ought to be, it sends a jolt of pain along my arm, and the camera flies out of my hand. I hear it fall on the ledge and skitter over the brink. All I can do is wait in despair to hear it end up at the bottom of the chasm. It slithers down a wall and then, except for a momentary mocking echo, there's silence.

Could it have fallen so far that it's out of earshot? I'd rather think that than believe it was caught as it fell. Whatever did that would be able to see in the dark. Presumably the hand or other appendage that caught it would have to be soft enough to engulf the impact, which is one more idea I'd rather not have just now. I need to focus all my consciousness on reaching the end of the unseen ledge.

How far have I come along it? If I retreat, might I be able to find a safer way, particularly since I can't imagine my parents could have used this one? Perhaps I just don't want to think of them in such a plight. Suppose I go back only to discover there's no other route across the cavern? "Where are you?" I can't help pleading like a lost child. "How did you get where you are?"

My voice comes back flattened, somehow suffocated. I don't know if I want to learn why the echo sounds like that. Otherwise there's utter silence, and I have the sense again of a multitude holding its collective breath. Might this be the presence that deadened the echo? That's another notion I can live without—another distraction from finding my way along the ledge. I have to go on. I'm too dismayed by the prospect of retreating from my parents in the dark.

I rest my spine against the wall and plant my hands on either side of me and inch in the direction I was following. I'm no longer able to judge how soft the wall is or I am. My sensations are at the mercy of the dark that presses into my face to remind me how much of it is waiting beyond the ledge. I could imagine the entire subterranean place is holding its breath, anticipating the fatal step I'm about to take, and withholding its own nature as well. I have the irrational but obstinate fancy that the ledge is growing narrower. I can't recall seeing that, but have I sidled past the stretch the flash illuminated? I'm struggling with a compulsion to reach out a foot to find the edge when I realise that the darkness needn't have me wholly in its power.

I still have a source of light—the display screen of my mobile. No doubt I overlooked it because it doesn't work as a phone down here. My father must have used his to light the way, and of course Lucinda has hers. I feel as if history has lost its stultifying grip on me, and I'm entitled to let out a gasp of relief. I rest my left hand on the wall as I grope for the mobile. Perhaps I was the only one holding his breath. I suck in another, and so does the wall under my hand.

At least, it swells like part of the chest of an enormous denizen of the dark—a small part. The movement isn't enough to send me off the ledge, but by the time I've realised that, it's too late. Before I can think I've sprung away from the wall. I teeter on the edge, and my entire body tries to shrink back from the drop. It feels as if the core of my panic is striving to draw the whole of me into itself. In an attempt to hurl myself backwards I throw out my hands in front of me. If the blackness were as solid as my eyes suggest I could shove myself away from it. It isn't, and my hands plunge into it, taking the rest of me with them.

It snatches away all sense of myself as well as my breath. Aren't I supposed to have time to view edited highlights of my history? My mind is shrinking inwards, and I wish I could do that too. I squeeze my eyes tight as if this can bring

the fall or at least my awareness of it to an end. The floor of
the cavern does both, driving a last residue of breath out of
me with a thin cry that leaves words behind.

I'm sprawling on all fours. At first this is all I dare to feel.
As I push myself up on my uncontrollably shivering arms I
discover no broken bones or even much in the way of bruises
apart from the renewed throbbing of my forehead. How soft
is the floor? It seems to yield beneath my hands, so that I'm
afraid they're about to sink in. I push myself away from it
and stagger blindly to my feet. The elastic surface gives a
little but supports me, and I do my best not to fancy that the
cave is a gigantic shell on whose contents I'm standing. I
stumble away, but where am I floundering in the dark? I've
taken just a couple of inadvertent steps when I hear a sound.

It's a wordless murmur from any number of mouths. It
seems to come from every side. It robs me of movement, or
perhaps a desperate hope does—the hope that if I stay still,
whatever surrounds me may lose interest in me. Now it's silent again, but does this mean it's holding its breath while it
waits for me to be unable not to move? The sound made me
think of a hive, or at any rate a swarm of creatures with a
consciousness as single as their voice. Perhaps I could see
them by the light of my mobile, but I suspect I would find
that I'd have preferred to leave them unseen. They can't be
everywhere, or I would have felt their presence while I was
on my hands and knees. I have to risk a glimpse if I'm to find
my way through the subterranean multitude. I begin to inch
my hand towards the pocket that contains the mobile.
Though it's too stealthy for even me to hear, the movement
is greeted by another murmur.

They can see me. They're everywhere around me, close to
the floor. The voices have grown harsher, more like a chorus
of croaking. There's no point in trying to be surreptitious,
and I shove my hand into my breast pocket. Grabbing the
mobile feels like clutching at a last symbol of the world I
took for granted. The prospect of seeing by the glow of the

display screen becomes even less attractive as my action is hailed by another chorus. It's no longer in unison, and it doesn't seem to be entirely inarticulate. "Rip," the voices are croaking. "Rip."

I can't help recoiling, though I'm afraid I'll tread on members of the chorus. This doesn't happen, and for some moments I can't tell what has. I've managed to stumble to a halt, but that's because my feet are sinking into the medium I took to be the floor of the cavern. I didn't immediately recognise the process because the substance is too much like my own.

I struggle to drag myself free, both of the soft fleshy substance and of the insidious notion. My efforts only sink me deeper, and the voices rise to welcome me. Their utterances are growing more varied. "Brick," I seem to hear in the midst of the disorganised clamour, and perhaps also "Deryck" and "Strong."

I can't think of using the light now. I abandon the mobile in my pocket and fling out my hands as the eager medium closes over my waist. It feels like a mouth, but it has several. More than one gapes under my hands as I try to shove myself upwards. I'm desperate to finish touching the substance around me. It contains entire faces, though they're uncertain of their shapes and of how to keep separate and even of where their eyes and mouths are meant to be located. Do they feel extruded or half digested and recomposed? That and the sensation of frantic swarming are too much to bear, and I snatch my hands away, only to sink up to my armpits. Unstable faces mouth mine or croak in my ears. They and their kind seem to have just one message now—the first syllable of my name.

Perhaps they aren't a multitude. Perhaps there's just a solitary entity, since many limbs are working in unison, extending their fingers to capture my arms and pull me down. Certainly the chorus has become synchronised again, and the cavern echoes with the chanted syllable as the fleshy medium engulfs my face. My mind and my innards seem to clench on the thought of suffocation, and I feel close to losing my awareness of this burial in a substance that isn't quite flesh or mud. My mind stops short of closing down, because I'm still able to breathe. Perhaps whatever has caught me is breathing for me, which may be worst of all.

Chapter Forty-eight

Towards the Light

I'm lying on stone in the dark. I feel both reborn and released from a dream too vast for one of mine. Perhaps I was engulfed by a horde of dreams, unless that was the dreamer, if there's any difference. Perhaps the swarming mass was composed of a spawn of dreams that couldn't hatch—dreams too inchoate to reach the surface or survive there, instead staying mired in the dark. However substantial they were, they seemed too unsure of their nature to be more than first drafts or experiments. Perhaps that's why they were so desperately loquacious, overwhelming me with their clamour—words almost too short to be called words, fragments of language that the city must once have understood, utterances too ancient to have retained their meaning, unless they have yet to come into use. There were whole thoughts too, solitary or pieced together by several voices, but I want to have left them behind, along with the cavern and its contents. Above all I believe I would prefer not to dwell on whatever process has left me where I am. Recapturing my sense of myself will be enough.

I feel not much more solid than water. I'm afraid of finding out that I no longer have much use of my limbs. I raise my head on its not entirely stable neck and peer into the dark. It seems unwilling to reveal any perspective, let alone the faintest glimpse of my surroundings, but I can tell that I'm attempting to see downwards. My feet are lower than the rest of me. I'm lying faceup on a slope.

The darkness into which I'm peering feels like silence rendered visible. If it's holding its breath, what is it waiting for this time? I scramble away from it on my back. My limbs are rediscovering their strength, and I flounder off my back and start to crawl. Before long I'm able to rise onto all fours, and soon I risk wavering to my feet. Some instinct has kept me clear of any nearby walls, but how far can I safely go without seeing where I am?

As I grope in my pocket I'm afraid the mobile will have been mislaid when I was cast up on the stony shore. My fingers close on it, however. I fumble it out and poke at the keypad, to no visible effect. Was the battery damaged or drained of power in the midst of my struggles? I'm about to jab the keys more fiercely when they and the miniature screen light up.

I can't help hoping for some sign of a message, but there's none. Of course there's no signal down here. I turn the mobile away from me and do my best to blink the dazzle out of my eyes. In a few moments I manage to distinguish that I'm in a wide natural passage. It slopes steadily upwards, and the floor is slightly concave. So long as I follow the bottom of the curve I'll be sure of walking straight, even in the dark.

I haven't seen or heard what I most want to—my parents and Lucinda. I mustn't let the silence at my back deter me from looking for them. Suppose they're all nearby and somehow unable to make a sound or afraid to betray their whereabouts? Could following the ledge have misled them back into the cavern? The thought is enough to make me turn the way I must have come.

The glow of the mobile glides over the right-hand wall and emerges dimly from the passage. Beyond the rounded entrance I can see little except a great deal of darkness. I'm not certain if I glimpse a movement like a vast wave withdrawing sluggishly from the light—still less that the wave is composed of restless heads and limbs or parts of both. Any movement subsides out of reach of the light, and I'm preparing to venture closer in case I may have left my parents or Lucinda behind when I hear a sound.

It's somewhere up the passage. It's a distant song. For some reason I think of a fragment of the song about loving Jack—"The jolly days are done, and the last goodbyes are whispered"—but before it ends I recognise "You'll Never Walk Alone." There were more than two voices, however indistinct, and I'm so dizzy with relief that I feel in danger of losing my balance as I turn to the upward slope. I let the phone show me the route again, and then I slip the mobile into my pocket. My confidence increases as I begin to stride up the incline, but I wish the song would renew its promise. In a while it does—at least, it starts again from the first line. Though it doesn't sound closer, it's growing louder. There are more voices, but I don't recognise any of them.

They're in the open. I'm hearing football fans in the upper world. It makes me feel utterly unlike them, excluded by more than the song. If only I could hear a familiar voice! Wouldn't at least my father join in if my parents were ahead? Must I go back, however far towards the surface I've progressed? The prospect feels like more than one kind of reversion, and I can't help protesting aloud. "Where are you now? Why are you leaving me like this?"

"We're here."

It has to be the most welcome sound I've ever heard, yet it seems not much more likely than a dream. Lucinda and my parents spoke in chorus, adding to the sense of unreality. How did I manage to pass them in the dark? They must have made certain they weren't noticed—of course, because they couldn't know if I was Wrigley or Maddock. I take out my mobile and press a key, but as soon as the phone lights up my father says "Don't do that."

I can't see how he could be talking to me, and I'm turning to face them when he says "I'm telling you, switch it off."

"Why, what's the problem?"

"It gets in our eyes. We don't need it. We can find the way like you have."

I mustn't risk an argument that he might use as a reason

to separate us again. I relocate the way ahead with the glow
of the keypad before consigning the mobile to my pocket,
where it glimmers like a luminous insect and then fades. I'm
not entirely unhappy to have relinquished it, since it dazzled
me as well. Though I hadn't time to distinguish my companions, hearing them behind me is enough. I wait until the
scraps of lingering pallor have sunk into my eyes, and then I
say "Everyone all right, then?"

"Never better," says my father.

Lucinda and my mother murmur in agreement. There's so
much I want to ask, but it can wait for us to reach the open,
where I'll be able to see that my father doesn't make another
bid to disappear. Besides, I need to concentrate on the route,
and I can best do that by putting out of my mind whatever
happened in the cavern. I take a pace towards the distant
song that echoes down the passage, but at once I'm afraid
my father may slip away again in the dark. "Can you let me
hear you?" I say. "Let me know you're there."

"Will this do you?" my father says and begins to sing.
"When you walk . . ."

My mother joins in, and so does Lucinda by the end of
the second line. "Don't be afraid," my mother exhorts and
then stops singing, but only to say "You as well, Gavin."

I pick up the song at the end of the fourth line. We aren't
singing along with the football crowd; we're half a verse behind, and I feel as if we're trying to compete or to resemble
them and failing at both. Eventually we let the final line go,
and as the echo of the last word makes its way into the dark
I announce "I'll start this time."

I don't until the football crowd recommences the song.
Will that help us stay unnoticed? Surely there's no need to,
but it may be best if we don't sound as if we're mocking the
crowd. Joining in with them feels like being potentially able
to lose ourselves among them, but why should any of us do
that? The last thing I want is to lose anyone again. Singing
along with the crowd lets me feel a little closer to the surface,

but I don't dare to put the impression into words until another one grows more definite. Unless my eyes have adjusted so miraculously that I can see in the dark, there's the faintest trace of light ahead.

I may have taken twice as many strides as there are lines in the song before I'm any surer. A faint pale glow is seeping around a bend in the passage. I grow dry-mouthed with restraining my hopes until I reach the bend. Beyond it the floor grows level, all the way to a heap of earth and rubble that blocks the passage.

I'm seeing this by the whitish glare that streams through a gap in the roof. Is it moonlight? No, it's coming from a lamp in the street along which the football crowd is marching. "Wait," I say, because I don't want my party to make for the light only to discover there's no way out. "Let me see."

I feel as if I'm conducting a final tour, first ensuring that the route is safe. Where am I leading my party? Not to any resolution of the enigmas that have been troubling me, I'm sure. Maybrick and Williamson and the rest of them will live because they're unexplained—because that's how the city wants its legends to remain. As I approach the gap I have to reduce my eyes to mere slits to cope with the glare. I can see what I need to see. Chunks of sandstone offer a way to climb up the heap of earth, and the foot of a ladder is buried in the ground above the gap in the roof.

"Don't come yet," I call and glance back. Lucinda and my parents have turned the bend. The streetlight paints everything monochrome and blurs my revived vision, so that they're just indefinite discoloured shapes. I couldn't even count them at the moment, and I'm relieved when one of them says "Careful."

That's my mother, and Lucinda echoes her. "Watch out for yourself, Gav," says my father.

"Just let me check," I say and clamber up the incline. The rocks embedded in the earth stay firm beneath my weight. Above the jagged gap is sandstone at least two feet thick.

I grasp a rung of the ladder and heave myself through. The ladder sinks into the ground, but not much. I take hold of the next rung, and the next, and then my head is in the open.

A swelling chorus of "You'll Never Walk Alone" seems to greet my appearance. Ordinarily I would stay clear until the streets are clear of incorrigible revellers and broken glass, but not when I need to bring my parents and Lucinda to the surface. The crowd can't see me, I gather once my slitted eyes begin to adjust to the direct glare, any more than I can see them. I'm in a hole like the grave of a giant. It's alive with dark shapes—shadows of the crowd marching past the barrier around the roadworks. I'm several yards beneath the edge of the street, to which the ladder extends. I venture up two rungs, and then I'm able to see a street sign. It's Richmond Street, which leads to Williamson Square. I'm beneath Frog's Lane—beneath Whitechapel.

It seems more appropriate than I can grasp that my haphazard tour should end here. Perhaps at last the chattering of history will let me rest, though I feel pregnant with undefined dreams. More of the crowd tramps past, recommencing the song. It's beginning to resemble a ritual—the march and the red banners some of the singers are waving. How surprised are they going to be at the sight of my companions and me? I haven't time to imagine how they will react. Emerging from underground feels like a dream come true, and perhaps soon I'll remember which one. "All right," I call into the passage and wait until Lucinda and the others move into view. My eyes are still growing used to the unaccustomed light, so that I can scarcely distinguish the cluster of shapes in the passage. "Hop up," I say hoarsely. "It's safe."

NATE KENYON

"A voice reminiscent of Stephen King in the days of *'Salem's Lot.*" —*Cemetery Dance*

They were just a group of high school kids looking for a place to party. They didn't know the end of the world was comingt. Now, alone and trapped belowground in a state-of-the-art bomb shelter, they are being stalked—and the creatures that come for them through the dirt and ash are like nothing anyone has ever seen before.

There is a new ruling life-form on earth, and these six humans are the only remaining prey.

"Superb! Readers [will be] left breathless."
—*Publishers Weekly* on *The Reach* (Starred Review)

SPARROW ROCK

ISBN 13: 978-0-8439-6377-9

INTERACT WITH DORCHESTER ONLINE!

Want to learn more about your favorite books and authors?

Want to talk with other readers that like to read the same books as you?

Want to see up-to-the-minute Dorchester news?

VISIT DORCHESTER AT:

DorchesterPub.com
Twitter.com/DorchesterPub
Facebook.com (Search Pages)

DISCUSS DORCHESTER'S NOVELS AT:

Dorchester Forums at DorchesterPub.com
GoodReads.com
LibraryThing.com
Myspace.com/books
Shelfari.com
WeRead.com

☐ YES!

Sign me up for the Leisure Horror Book Club and send my FREE BOOKS! If I choose to stay in the club, I will pay only $8.50* each month, a savings of $7.48!

E: _____

RESS: _____

PHONE: _____

IL: _____

☐ I want to pay by credit card.

☐  VISA   ☐ MasterCard.   ☐ DISCOVER

ACCOUNT #: _____

IRATION DATE: _____

ATURE: _____

ail this page along with $2.00 shipping and handling to:
Leisure Horror Book Club
PO Box 6640
Wayne, PA 19087
Or fax (must include credit card information) to:
610-995-9274
You can also sign up online at **www.dorchesterpub.com**.

lus $2.00 for shipping. Offer open to residents of the U.S. and Canada only.
Canadian residents please call 1-800-481-9191 for pricing information.
If under 18, a parent or guardian must sign. Terms, prices and conditions subject to
change. Subscription subject to acceptance. Dorchester Publishing reserves the right